DEAD EVER AFTER

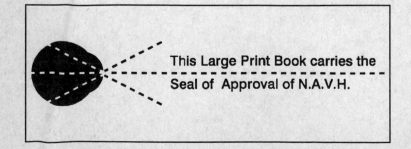
This Large Print Book carries the
Seal of Approval of N.A.V.H.

DEAD EVER AFTER

CHARLAINE HARRIS

WHEELER PUBLISHING

A part of Gale, Cengage Learning

GALE
CENGAGE Learning

Detroit • New York • San Francisco • New Haven, Conn • Waterville, Maine • London

GALE
CENGAGE Learning·

LIBRARY OF CONGRESS CATALOGING-IN-PUBLICATION DATA

Harris, Charlaine.
    Dead ever after / by Charlaine Harris.
        pages ; cm. — (A Sookie Stackhouse novel series) (Wheeler publishing large print hardcover)
    ISBN 978-1-4104-5707-3 (hardcover) — ISBN 1-4104-5707-9 (hardcover) 1. Stackhouse, Sookie (Fictitious character)—Fiction. 2. Vampires—Fiction. 3. Werewolves—Fiction. 4. Louisiana—Fiction. 5. Large type books. I. Title.
    PS3558.A6427D4255 2013b
    813'.54—dc23   2013008229

Published in 2013 by arrangement with The Berkley Publishing Group, a member of Penguin Group (USA) Inc.

Printed in the United States of America
1 2 3 4 5 6 7 17 16 15 14 13

This book is dedicated to the loyal readers who have followed this series from beginning to end. Some of you were reading the books before True Blood, *and some came after, but you were all amazingly generous with your ideas, speculations, and votes on Sookie's future. There isn't a way I could make all of you happy with the ending of the series, so I've followed my own plan, the one I've had all along, and I hope you agree that it's fitting.*

ACKNOWLEDGMENTS

For the past fourteen years, I've lived with a young woman named Sookie Stackhouse. She has become as familiar to me as the back of my own hand. It feels almost incredible to remember that after I wrote the first chapter of her story in 1999, my agent, Joshua Bilmes, had a hard time finding a home for Sookie. After two years, John Morgan at Ace thought publishing *Dead Until Dark* might be a good idea. So there are two *very* important thank-yous. Joshua has been my agent my entire writing career, and John is still my friend.

After John Morgan left Penguin (temporarily), I became the charge of renowned editor Ginjer Buchanan. She's had assistants come and go, but Kat Sherbo facilitated the incredibly difficult project of *The Sookie Stackhouse Companion*. And did it with grace.

A huge shout-out must go to the cover

artist who has made my books so distinctive. Lisa Desimini, bless you forever.

There are too many people to thank, and I'm afraid I'll miss someone, but here goes. For *Dead Ever After,* attorney Mike Epley gave me invaluable advice, as he has on previous books. Mike, thanks for taking the time to answer long e-mails about women who get in legal trouble because they date vampires. Any mistakes I've made with this material are my own and don't reflect on Mike's excellence as a lawyer.

I can't neglect two friends who've become my readers and advisers, friends who've given me feedback and reassurance and encouragement in the past few years. Without them, this would have been much, much harder. Dana Cameron and Toni L. P. Kelner . . . I love ya. FPC forever!

On my website, www.charlaineharris.com, many thanks for the dedication of Dawn Fratini, who had no idea what she was getting into or how the site would explode. While I'm thinking of the website, let me thank my moderators, past and present, who not only have helped me in extremely trying situations but have also become my friends. Mods emeriti include Katie Phalen, Debi Murray, Beverly Battillo, and Kerri Sauer. Mods still manning the board include Victoria Koski, Michele Schubert, MariCarmen Eroles, and Lindsay Barnett. Rebecca Melson has been a tremendous help, in so many ways.

Finally, a huge hug of gratitude must go to Paula Woldan, also known as bffpaula, my assistant, my close friend, and my rock of a companion in journeys into the unknown. We have had a great time with great people on our travels, and I was able to relax and enjoy it because Paula always knew what was happening.

Victoria Koski, wearing a completely different hat from her moderator's Stetson, came on board to save me from drowning in the sea of detail that had become the Sookie Stackhouse series. Victoria assumed control of the ship just in time to keep it from foundering, and she's kept me pretty much on course since then. Thanks, continuity editor extraordinaire.

Alan Ball, who loved my books, gave them an incredible boost when he decided they might make a good television show. Thanks, Alan, for hours of entertainment and for some extraordinary experiences I would never have had if you and Christina and Gianna hadn't become part of my lifescape.

When I began the Sookie books, my daughter was eight years old. Now she's graduating from college. That fact, more than any other time marker, shocks me into the realization that I've been detailing Sookie's adventures for a very long time. So thanks to my family, particularly my husband, for putting up with all the absences, the distractions, the surprise visitors, and the embarrassing attention from strangers. Hal, Patrick, Timothy, Julia . . . I love you more than life. And our newer family members are just as dear.

My most profound gratitude must go to you, the readers, for your devotion to and investment in these characters I dreamed up. Thanks for sticking with me through the books that succeeded and the books that fell a bit short of my aspirations. I have always tried to give you my best; to me, that's part of the unwritten contract between writer and reader. I appreciate the incredible emotional response you have given me in return.

— CHARLAINE HARRIS

PROLOGUE

JANUARY

The New Orleans businessman, whose gray hair put him in his fifties, was accompanied by his much younger and taller bodyguard/ chauffeur on the night he met the devil in the French Quarter. The meeting was by prearrangement.

"This is really the Devil we're going to see?" asked the bodyguard. He was tense — but then, that wasn't too surprising.

"Not *the* Devil, but *a* devil." The business-man was cool and collected on the outside, but maybe not so much on the inside. "Since he came up to me at the Chamber of Commerce banquet, I've learned a lot of things I didn't know before." He looked around him, trying to spot the creature he'd agreed to meet. He told his bodyguard, "He convinced me that he was what he said he was. I always thought my daughter was simply deluded. I thought she imagined she had power because she wanted to have something . . . of her own. Now I'm willing to admit she has a certain talent, though nowhere near what she thinks."

It was cold and damp in the January night, even in New Orleans. The businessman shifted from foot to foot to keep warm. He told the bodyguard, "Evidently, meeting at a crossroads is traditional." The street was not as busy as it would be in the summer, but there were still drinkers and tourists and natives going about their night's entertainment. He wasn't afraid, he told himself. "Ah, here he comes," the businessman said.

The devil was a well-dressed man, much like the businessman. His tie was by Hermes. His suit was Italian. His shoes were custom-made. His eyes were abnormally clear, the whites gleaming, the irises a purplish brown; they looked almost red from certain angles.

"What have you got for me?" the devil asked, in a voice that indicated he was only faintly interested.

"Two souls," said the businessman. "Tyrese has agreed to go in with me."

The devil shifted his gaze to the bodyguard. After a moment, the bodyguard nodded. He was a big man, a light-skinned African American with bright hazel eyes.

"Your own free will?" the devil asked neutrally. "Both of you?"

"My own free will," said the businessman.

"My own free will," affirmed the bodyguard.

The devil said, "Then let's get down to business."

"Business" was a word that made the older man comfortable. He smiled. "Wonderful. I've got the documents right here, and they're signed." Tyrese opened a thin leather folder and withdrew two pieces of paper: not parchment or human skin, nothing that dramatic or exotic — computer paper that the businessman's office secretary had bought at OfficeMax. Tyrese offered the papers to the devil, who gave them a quick glance.

"You have to sign them again," the devil said. "For this signature, ink is not satisfactory."

"I thought you were joking about that." The businessman frowned.

"I never joke," the devil said. "I do have a sense of humor, oh, believe me, I do. But not about contracts."

"We actually have to . . . ?"

"Sign in blood? Yes, absolutely. It's traditional. And you'll do it now." He read the businessman's sideways glance correctly. "I promise you no one will see what you are doing," he said. As the devil spoke, a sudden hush enveloped the three men, and a thick film fell between them and the rest of the street scene.

The businessman sighed elaborately, to show how melodramatic he thought this tradition was. "Tyrese, your knife?" he said, looking up to the chauffeur.

Tyrese's knife appeared with shocking suddenness, probably from his coat sleeve; the blade was obviously sharp, and it gleamed in the streetlight. The businessman shucked off his coat and handed it to his companion. He unbuttoned his cuff and rolled up his sleeve. Perhaps to let the devil know how tough he was, he jabbed himself in the left arm with the knife. A sluggish trickle of blood rewarded his effort, and he looked the devil directly in the face as he accepted the quill that the devil had somehow supplied . . . even more smoothly than Tyrese had produced the knife. Dipping the quill into the trail of blood, the businessman signed his name to the top document, which the chauffeur held pressed against the leather folder.

After he'd signed, the businessman returned the knife to the chauffeur and donned his coat. The chauffeur followed the same procedure as his employer. When he'd signed his own contract, he blew on it to dry the blood as if he'd signed with a Sharpie and the ink might smear.

The devil smiled when the signatures were complete. The moment he did, he didn't look quite so much like a prosperous man of affairs.

He looked too damn happy.

"You get a signing bonus," he told the businessman. "Since you brought me another soul. By the way, how do you feel?"

"Just like I always did," said the businessman. He buttoned up his coat. "Maybe a little angry." He smiled suddenly, his teeth looking as sharp and gleaming as the knife had. "How are you, Tyrese?" he asked his employee.

"A little antsy," Tyrese admitted. "But I'll be okay."

"You were both bad people to begin with," the devil said, without any judgment in his voice. "The souls of the innocent are sweeter. But I delight in having you. I suppose you're sticking with the usual wish list? Prosperity? The defeat of your enemies?"

"Yes, I want those things," the businessman said with passionate sincerity. "And I have a few more requests, since I get a signing bonus. Or could I take that in cash?"

"Oh," the devil said, smiling gently, "I don't deal in cash. I deal in favors."

"Can I get back to you on that?" the businessman asked after some thought. "Take a rain check?"

The devil looked faintly interested. "You don't want an Alfa Romeo or a night with Nicole Kidman or the biggest house in the French Quarter?"

The businessman shook his head decisively. "I'm sure something will come up that I do want, and then I'd like to have a very good chance of getting it. I was a successful man until Katrina. And after Katrina I thought I would be rich, because I own a lumber business. Everyone needed lumber." He took a deep breath. He kept on telling his story, despite the fact that the devil looked bored. "But getting a supply line reestablished was hard. So many people didn't have money to spend because they were ruined, and there was the wait for the insurance money, for the rest. I made some mistakes, believing the fly-by-night builders would pay me on time. . . . It all ended up with my business too extended, everyone owing me, my credit stretched as thin as a condom on an elephant. Knowledge of this is getting around." He looked down. "I'm losing the influence I had in this city."

Possibly the devil had known all those things, and that was why he'd approached the businessman. Clearly he was not interested in the businessman's litany of woes. "Prosperity it is, then," he said briskly. "And I look forward to your special request. Tyrese, what do you want? I have your soul, too."

"I don't believe in souls," Tyrese said flatly. "I don't think my boss does, either. We don't mind giving you what we don't believe we have." He grinned at the devil, man-to-man, which was a mistake. The devil was no man.

The devil smiled back. Tyrese's grin vanished at the sight. "What do you want?" the devil repeated. "I won't ask again."

"I want Gypsy Kidd. Her real name is Katy Sherboni, if you need that. She work at Bourbon Street Babes. I want her to love me the way I love her."

The businessman looked disappointed in his employee. "Tyrese, I wish you'd asked for something more lasting. Sex is everywhere you look in New Orleans, and girls like Gypsy are a dime a dozen."

"You wrong," Tyrese said. "I don't think I have a soul, but I know love is once in a lifetime. I love Gypsy. If she loves me back, I'll be a happy man. And if you make money, boss, I'll make money. I'll have enough. I'm not greedy."

"I'm all about the greed," said the devil, almost gently. "You may end up wishing you'd asked for some government bonds, Tyrese."

The chauffeur shook his head. "I'm happy with my bargain. You give me Gypsy, the rest will be all right. I know it."

The devil looked at him with what seemed very much like pity, if that emotion was possible for a devil.

"Enjoy yourselves, you hear?" he said to both of the newly soulless men. They could not tell if he was mocking them or if he was sincere. "Tyrese, you will not see me again until our final meeting." He faced the businessman. "Sir, you and I will meet at some date in the future. Just give me a call when you're ready for your signing bonus. Here's my card."

The businessman took the plain white card. The only writing on it was a phone number. It was not the same number he'd called to set up the first rendezvous. "But what if it's years from now?" he said.

"It won't be," said the devil, but his voice was farther away. The businessman looked up to see that the devil was half a block away. After seven more steps he seemed to

18

melt into the dirty sidewalk, leaving only an impression in the cold damp air.

The businessman and the chauffeur turned and walked hastily in the opposite direction. The chauffeur never saw this version of the devil again. The businessman didn't see him until June.

JUNE

Far away — thousands of miles away — a tall, thin man lay on a beach in Baja. He was not in one of the tourist spots where he might encounter lots of other gringos, who might recognize him. He was patronizing a dilapidated bar, really more of a hut. For a small cash payment, the proprietor would rent patrons a large towel and a beach umbrella, and send his son out to refresh your drink from time to time. As long as you kept drinking.

Though the tall man was only sipping Coca-Cola, he was paying through the nose for it — though he didn't seem to realize that, or perhaps he didn't care. He sat on the towel, crouched in the umbrella's shade, wearing a hat and sunglasses and swim trunks. Close to him was an ancient backpack, and his flip-flops were set on the sand beside it, casting off a faint smell of hot rubber. The tall man was listening to an iPod, and his smile indicated he was very pleased with what he heard. He lifted his hat to run his fingers through his hair. It was golden blond, but there was a bit of root showing that hinted his natural color was nearly gray. Judging by his body, he was in his forties. He had a small head in relation to his broad shoulders, and he did not look like a man who was used to manual labor. He didn't look rich, either; his entire ensemble, the flip-flops and the swim trunks, the hat and the cast-aside shirt, had come from a Wal-Mart or some even cheaper dollar store.

It didn't pay to look affluent in Baja, not with the way things were these days. It wasn't safe, gringos weren't exempt from the violence, and most tourists stayed in the established resorts, flying in and out without driving through the countryside. There were a few other expats around, mostly unattached men with an air of desperation . . . or secrecy. Their reasons for choosing such a hazardous place to live were better not discovered. Asking questions could be unhealthy.

One of these expats, a recent arrival, came to sit close to the tall man, too close for such proximity to be an accident on a thinly populated beach. The tall man gave the unwelcome newcomer a sideways look from behind his dark glasses, which were obviously prescription. The newcomer was a man in his thirties, not tall or short, not handsome or ugly, not reedy or muscular. He was medium in all aspects, physically. This medium man had been watching the tall man for a few days, and the tall man had been sure he'd approach him sooner or later.

The medium man had carefully selected the optimum moment. The two were sitting in a place on the beach where no one else could hear them or approach them unseen, and even with satellites in the atmosphere it was probable that no one could see them without being spotted, either. The taller man was mostly hidden under the beach umbrella. He noticed that his visitor was sitting in its shadow.

"What are you listening to?" asked the medium man, pointing to the earbuds inserted in the tall man's ears.

He had a faint accent; maybe a German one? From one of those European countries, anyway, thought the tall man, who was not well traveled. And the newcomer also had a remarkably unpleasant smile. It *looked* okay, with the upturned lips and the bared teeth, but somehow the effect was more as if an animal were exposing its teeth preparatory to biting you.

"You a homo? I'm not interested," the tall man said. "In fact, you'll be judged with hellfire."

The medium man said, "I like women. Very much. Sometimes more than they want." His smile became quite feral. And he asked again, "What are you listening to?"

The tall man debated, staring angrily at his companion. But it had been days since he'd talked to anyone. At last, he opted for the truth. "I'm listening to a sermon," he said.

The medium man exhibited only mild surprise. "Really? A sermon? I wouldn't have pegged you for a man of the cloth." But his smile said otherwise. The tall man began to feel uneasy. He began to think of the gun in his backpack, less than an arm's length away. At least he'd opened the buckles when he'd put it down.

"You're wrong, but God won't punish you for it," the tall man said calmly, his own smile genial. "I'm listening to one of my own old sermons. I spoke God's truth to the multitudes."

"Did no one believe you?" The medium man cocked his head curiously.

"Many believed me. Many. I was attracting quite a following. But a girl named . . .

A girl brought about my downfall. And put my wife in jail, too, in a way."

"Would that girl's name have been Sookie Stackhouse?" asked the medium man, removing his sunglasses to reveal remarkably pale eyes.

The taller man's head snapped in his direction. "How'd you know?" he said.

JUNE

The devil was eating beignets, fastidiously, when the businessman walked up to the outside table. The devil noticed the spring in Copley Carmichael's step. He looked even more prosperous than he had when he was broke. Carmichael was in the business section of the newspaper frequently these days. An infusion of capital had reestablished him very quickly as an economic force in New Orleans, and his political clout had expanded along with the money he pumped into New Orleans's sputtering economy, which had been dealt a crippling blow by Katrina. Which, the devil pointed out quickly to anyone who asked, he'd had simply nothing to do with.

Today Carmichael looked healthy and vigorous, ten years younger than he actually was. He sat at the devil's table without any greeting.

23

"Where's your man, Mr. Carmichael?" asked the devil, after a sip of his coffee.

Carmichael was busy placing a drink order with the waiter, but when the young man was gone, he said, "Tyrese has trouble these days, and I gave him some time off."

"The young woman? Gypsy?"

"Of course," said Carmichael, not quite sneering. "I knew if he asked for her, he wouldn't be pleased with the results, but he was so sure that true love would win in the end."

"And it hasn't?"

"Oh, yes, she's crazy about him. She loves him so much she has sex with him all the time. She couldn't stop herself, even though she knew she was HIV positive . . . a fact she didn't share with Tyrese."

"Ah," the devil said. "Not my work, that virus. So how is Tyrese faring?"

"He's HIV positive, too," Carmichael said, shrugging. "He's getting treatment, and it's not the instant death sentence it used to be. But he's very emotional about it." Carmichael shook his head. "I always thought he had better sense."

"I understand you wish to ask for your signing bonus," the devil said. Carmichael saw no connection between the two ideas.

"Yes," Copley Carmichael said. He

24

grinned at the devil and leaned forward confidentially. In a barely audible whisper he said, "I know exactly what I want. I want you to find me a cluviel dor."

The devil looked genuinely surprised. "How did you learn of the existence of such a rare item?"

"My daughter brought it up in conversation," Carmichael said, without a hint of shame. "It sounded interesting, but she stopped talking before she told me the name of the person who supposedly has one. So I had a man I know hack into her e-mail. I should have done that earlier. It's been illuminating. She's living with a fellow I don't trust. After our last conversation, she got so angry with me that she's refused to see me. Now I can keep tabs on her without her knowing, so I can protect her from her own bad judgment."

He was absolutely sincere when he made this statement. The devil saw that Carmichael believed that he loved his daughter, that he knew what was best for her under any circumstance.

"So Amelia had been talking to someone about a cluviel dor," the devil said. "That led her to bring it up with you. How interesting. No one's had one for . . . well, in my memory. A cluviel dor would have been made by the fae . . . and you understand, they are not tiny, cute creatures with wings."

Carmichael nodded. "I'm astounded to discover what exists out there," he said. "I have to believe in fairies now. And I have to consider that maybe my daughter isn't such a screwball after all. Though I think she's deluded about her own power."

The devil raised his perfect eyebrows. There seemed to be more than one deluded person in the Carmichael family. "About the cluviel dor . . . the fae used them all. I don't believe there are any left on earth, and I can't go into Faery since the upheaval. A thing or two has been expelled *out* of Faery . . . but nothing goes in." He looked mildly regretful.

"There is one cluviel dor available, and from what I can tell, it's being concealed by a friend of my daughter's," Copley Carmichael said. "I know you can find it."

"Fascinating," the devil said, quite sincerely. "And what do you want it for? After I find it?"

"I want my daughter back," Carmichael said. His intensity was almost palpable. "I want the power to change her life. So I know what I'll wish for when you track it down for me. The woman who knows where it is . . . she's not likely to give it up. It was

26

a legacy from her grandmother, and she's not a big fan of mine."

The devil turned his face to the morning sun, and his eyes glowed red briefly. "Imagine that. I'll set things in motion. The name of your daughter's friend, the one who may know the whereabouts of the cluviel dor?"

"She's in Bon Temps. It's up north, not too far from Shreveport. Sookie Stackhouse."

The devil nodded slowly. "I've heard the name."

JULY

The next time the devil met with Copley Carmichael, three days after their conversation at Café du Monde, he dropped by Carmichael's table at Commander's Palace. Carmichael was waiting for his dinner and busy on his cell phone with a contractor who wanted to extend his credit line. Carmichael was unwilling, and he explained why in no uncertain terms. When he looked up, the devil was standing there in the same suit he'd worn when they'd met the first time. He looked cool and impeccable.

As Carmichael put the phone down, the devil slid into the chair across from his.

Carmichael had jumped when he recognized the devil. And since he hated being surprised, he was unwise. He snarled, "What the hell do you mean coming here? I didn't ask you to visit!"

"What the hell, indeed," said the devil, who didn't seem to take offense. He ordered a single malt whiskey from the waiter who'd materialized at his elbow. "I assumed you'd want to hear the news of your cluviel dor."

Carmichael's expression changed instantly. "You found it! You have it!"

"Sadly, Mr. Carmichael, I do not," said the devil. (He did not sound sad.) "Something rather unexpected has thwarted our plans." The waiter deposited the whiskey with some ceremony, and the devil took a sip and nodded.

"What?" Carmichael said, almost unable to speak for anger.

"Miss Stackhouse used the cluviel dor, and its magic has been expended."

There was a moment of silence fraught with all the emotions the devil enjoyed.

"I'll see her *ruined,*" said Copley Carmichael venomously, keeping his voice down with a supreme effort. "You'll help me. That's what I'll take instead of the cluviel dor."

"Oh my goodness. You've used your signing bonus, Mr. Carmichael. Mustn't get greedy."

"But you didn't get me the cluviel dor!" Even though he was an experienced businessman, Carmichael was astonished and outraged.

"I found it and was ready to take it from her pocket," said the devil. "I entered the body of someone standing behind her. But she used it before I could extract it. *Finding it* was the favor you requested. You used those words twice, and 'track it down' once. Our dealings are concluded." He tossed back his drink.

"At least help me get back at her," Carmichael said, his face red with rage. "She crossed us both."

"Not me," said the devil. "I've seen Miss Stackhouse up close and talked to many people who know her. She seems like an interesting woman. I have no cause to do her harm." He stood up. "In fact, if I may advise you, walk away from this. She has some powerful friends, among them your daughter."

"My daughter is a woman who runs around with witches," Carmichael said. "She's never been able to make her own living, not completely. I've been researching her 'friends,' very discreetly." He sighed, sounding both angry and exasperated. "I understand their powers exist. I believe that now. Reluctantly. But what have they done with those powers? The strongest among them lives in a *shack.*" Carmichael's knuckles rapped against the table. "My daughter could be a force in society in this town. She could work for me and do all kinds of charity stuff, but instead she lives in her own little world with her loser boyfriend. Like her friend Sookie. But I'll even the score there. How many powerful friends could a waitress have?"

The devil glanced over to his left. Two tables away sat a very round man with dark hair, who was by himself at a table laden with food. The very round man met the devil's eyes without blinking or looking away, which few men could do. After a long moment, the two nodded at each other.

Carmichael was glaring at the devil.

"I owe you nothing for Tyrese any longer," said the devil. "And you are mine forever. Given your present course, I may have you sooner than I'd expected." He smiled, a chilling expression on his smooth face, and he rose from the table and left.

Carmichael was even angrier when he had to pay for the devil's whiskey. He never even noticed the very round man. But the very round man noticed him.

CHAPTER 1

The morning after I raised my boss from the dead, I got up to find him sitting half-dressed in my backyard on my chaise lounge. It was about ten a.m. on a July day, and the sun was bathing the backyard in brilliant heat. Sam's hair was turned into a bright tangle of red and gold. He opened his eyes as I came down the back steps and crossed the yard. I was still in my nightshirt, and I didn't even want to think about my own hair. It was pretty much one big snarl.

"How are you feeling?" I asked very quietly. My throat was sore from the screaming I'd done the night before when I'd seen Sam bleeding out on the ground in the backyard of the country farmhouse Alcide Herveaux had inherited from his father. Sam drew up his legs to give me room to sit on the chaise. His jeans were spattered with his dried blood. His chest was bare; his shirt must have been too nasty to touch.

31

Sam didn't answer for a long time. Though he'd given his tacit permission for me to sit with him, he didn't seem to embrace my presence. Finally, he said, "I don't know how I feel. I don't feel like myself. It's like something inside me changed."

I cringed. I'd feared this. "I know . . . that is, I was told . . . that there's always a price for magic," I said. "I thought I'd be the one paying it, though. I'm sorry."

"You brought me back," he said, without emotion. "I think that's worth a little adjustment period." He didn't smile.

I shifted uneasily. "How long have you been out here?" I asked. "Can I get you some orange juice or coffee? Breakfast?"

"I came out here a few hours ago," he said. "I lay on the ground. I needed to get back in touch."

"With what?" I may not have been as awake as I thought I was.

"With my natural side," he said, very slowly and deliberately. "Shapeshifters are nature's children. Since we can turn into so many things. That's our mythology. Back before we blended into the human race, we used to say that when we were created, the mother of all the earth wanted a creature so versatile it could replace any race that died out. And that creature was a shapeshifter. I

could look at a picture of a saber-toothed tiger and be one. Did you know that?"

"No," I said.

"I think I'll go home. I'll go to my trailer and . . ." His voice trailed off.

"And what?"

"Find a shirt," he said, finally. "I do feel strange. Your yard is amazing."

I was confused and not a little worried. Part of me could see that Sam would need some alone time to recover from the trauma of dying and coming back. But the other part of me, the one that had known Sam for years, was upset that he sounded so un-Sam. I'd been Sam's friend, employee, occasional date, and business partner — all those things and more — for the past few years. I would have sworn he couldn't surprise me.

I watched him, narrow-eyed, as he worked his keys out of his jeans pocket. I got up to give him room to slide off the chaise and walk to his truck. He climbed into the cab and looked at me through the windshield for a long moment. Then he turned the key in the ignition. He raised his hand, and I felt a surge of pleasure. He'd lower his window. He'd call me over to say good-bye. But then Sam backed out, turned around, and went slowly down the driveway to

Hummingbird Road. He left without a word. Not "See you later," "Thanks a lot," or "Kiss my foot."

And what had he meant about my yard being amazing? He'd been in my yard dozens of times.

At least I solved that puzzlement quickly. As I turned to trudge inside — through some extraordinarily green grass — I noticed that my three tomato plants, which I'd put in weeks ago, were heavily laden with ripe red fruit. The sight stopped me in my tracks. When had that happened? The last time I'd noticed them, maybe a week ago, they'd looked scraggly and in dire need of water and fertilizer. The one on the left had seemed on its last legs (if a plant can have legs). Now all three plants were lush and green-leafed, sagging against their frames with the sheer weight of the fruit. It was like someone had dosed them with an elevated version of Miracle-Gro.

With my mouth hanging open, I rotated to check out all the other flowers and bushes in the yard, and there were plenty of them. Many of the Stackhouse women had been ardent gardeners, and they'd planted roses, daisies, hydrangeas, pear trees . . . so many blooming and green things, planted by generations of Stackhouse women. And I'd

been doing a poor job of keeping them in good trim.

But . . . what the hell? While I'd been sunk in gloom the past few days, the whole yard had taken steroids. Or maybe the Jolly Green Giant had paid a visit. Everything that was supposed to be blooming was laden with brilliant flowers, and everything that was supposed to bear fruit was heavy with it. Everything else was green and glossy and thick. How had this come about?

I plucked a couple of especially ripe and round tomatoes to take in the house. I could see that a bacon-and-tomato sandwich would be my lunch choice, but before that I had a few things to accomplish.

I found my cell phone and checked my list of contacts. Yes, I had Bernadette Merlotte's number. Bernadette, called Bernie, was Sam's shapeshifter mom. Though my own mother had passed when I was seven (so maybe I wasn't the best judge), Sam seemed to have a good relationship with Bernie. If there ever was a time to call in a mom, this was it.

I won't say we had a comfortable conversation, and it was shorter than it should have been, but by the time I hung up, Bernie Merlotte was packing a bag to come to

Bon Temps. She'd arrive in the late afternoon.

Had I done the right thing? After I'd hashed the issue over with myself, I decided I had, and I further decided I had to have a day off. Maybe more than one. I called Merlotte's and told Kennedy that I had the flu. She agreed they'd call me in a crisis, but otherwise they'd leave me alone to recover.

"I didn't think anyone got the flu in July. But Sam called in to say the same thing," Kennedy said with a smile in her voice.

I thought, *Dammit.*

"Maybe y'all gave it to each other?" she suggested archly.

I didn't say a word.

"Okay, okay, I'll only call if the place is on fire," she said. "You have a good time getting over the flu."

I refused to worry about the rumors that would undoubtedly start making the rounds. I slept a lot and wept a lot. I cleaned out all the drawers in my bedroom: night table, dressing table, chest of drawers. I pitched useless things and grouped other items together in a way that seemed sensible. And I waited to hear . . . from anyone.

But the phone didn't ring. I heard a lot of nothing. I had a lot of nothing, except tomatoes. I had them on sandwiches, and the minute the red ones were gone, the plants were hung with green ones. I fried a few of the green ones, and when the rest were red, I made my own salsa for the first time ever. The flowers bloomed and bloomed and bloomed, until I had a vase full in almost every room in the house. I even walked through the cemetery to leave some on Gran's grave, and I put a bouquet on Bill's porch. If I could have eaten them, I'd have had a full plate at every meal.

ELSEWHERE

The red-haired woman came out of the prison door slowly and suspiciously, as if she suspected a practical joke. She blinked in the brilliant sun and began walking toward the road. There was a car parked there, but she didn't pay it any attention. It never occurred to the red-haired woman that its occupants were waiting for her.

A medium man got out of the front passenger seat. That was how she thought of him: medium. His hair was medium brown, he was medium tall, he was medium built, and he had a medium smile. His teeth, however, were gleaming white and perfect. Dark glasses hid his eyes. "Miss Fowler," he called. "We've come to pick you up."

She turned toward him, hesitating. The

sun was in her eyes, and she squinted. She'd survived so much — broken marriages, broken relationships, single motherhood, betrayals, a bullet wound. She was not of a mind to be an easy target now.

"Who are you?" she asked, standing her ground, though she knew the sun was mercilessly showing every line in her face and every deficiency in the cheap hair dye she'd applied in the jail bathroom.

"Don't you recognize me? We met at the hearing." The medium man's voice was almost gentle. He took off his dark glasses, and a chime of recognition sounded in her brain.

"You're the lawyer, the one that got me out," she said, smiling. "I don't know why you did that, but I owe you. I sure didn't need to be in jail. I want to see my children."

"And you will," he said. "Please, please." He opened the rear door of the car and gestured for her to get in. "I'm sorry. I should have addressed you as Mrs. Fowler."

She was glad to climb inside, grateful to sink back onto the cushioned seat, delighted to revel in the cold air. This was the most physical comfort she'd had in many months. You didn't appreciate soft seats and courtesy (or good mattresses and thick towels) until you didn't have them.

"I been Mrs. a few times. And I been Miss, too," she said. "I don't care what you call me. This is a great car."

"I'm glad you like it," said the driver, a tall man with graying hair clipped very short. He turned to look over the seat at the red-haired woman, and he smiled at her. He took off his own dark glasses.

"Oh my God," she said, in an entirely different tone. "It's you! Really! In the flesh. I thought you was in jail. But you're here." She was both awed and confused.

"Yes, Sister," he said. "I understand what a devoted follower you were and how you proved your worth. And now I've said thank you by getting you out of jail, where you in no way deserved to be."

She looked away. In her heart, she knew her sins and crimes. But it was balm to her self-regard to hear that such an esteemed man — someone she'd seen on television! — thought she was a good woman. "So that's why you put up all that money for my bail? That was a hell of a lot of cash, mister. More money than I'd ever earn in my life."

"I want to be as staunch an advocate for you as you were for me," the tall man said smoothly. "Besides, we know you're not going to run." He smiled at her, and Arlene thought about how fortunate she was. That

39

someone would put up over a hundred thousand dollars for her bail seemed incredible. In fact, suspicious. *But,* Arlene figured, *so far so good.*

"We're taking you home to Bon Temps," said the medium man. "You can see your children, little Lisa and little Coby."

The way he said her kids' names made her feel uneasy. "They ain't so little anymore," she said, to drown out that flicker of doubt. "But I sure as he . . . sure want to lay eyes on them. I missed them every day I was inside."

"In return, there are a few little things we want you to do for us, if you will," the medium man said. There was definitely a slight foreign cadence to his English.

Arlene Fowler knew instinctively that those few things would not really be little, and definitely not optional. Looking at the two men, she didn't sense they were interested in something she might not have minded giving up, like her body. They didn't want her to iron their sheets or polish their silver, either. She felt more comfortable now that the cards were spread out on the table and about to be flipped over. "Uh-huh," she said. "Like what?"

"I really don't think you'll mind when you hear," said the driver. "I truly don't."

"All you have to do," said the medium man, "is have a conversation with Sookie Stackhouse."

There was a long silence. Arlene Fowler looked back and forth at the two men, measuring and calculating. "You going to get me put back in jail if I won't?" she said.

"Since we got you out on bail pending your trial, I guess we could make that happen," said the tall driver mildly. "But I would certainly hate to do that. Wouldn't you?" he asked his companion.

The medium man shook his head from side to side. "That would be a great pity. The little children would be so sad. Are you afraid of Miss Stackhouse?"

There was silence while Arlene Fowler wrestled with the truth. "I'm the last person in the world Sookie'd want to see," she hedged. "She blames me for that whole day, the day . . ." Her voice trailed off.

"The day all those people got shot," the medium man said pleasantly. "Including you. But I know her slightly, and I think she'll let you have a conversation. We will tell you what to say. Don't worry about her talent. I think all will be well in that regard."

"Her talent? You mean her mind-reading? Some talent!" Arlene, surprisingly, laughed. "That's been the curse of her life."

41

The two men smiled, and the effect was not pleasant at all. "Yes," agreed the driver. "That has been a curse for her, and I imagine that feeling will get worse."

"What do you want with Sookie, anyway?" Arlene asked. "She ain't got nothing but that old house."

"She's caused us, and a few other people, a great deal of trouble," said the driver. "Let's just say she's got some trouble coming."

CHAPTER 2

The night of my second day of solitude, I faced the fact that I had to go to see Eric. Sure, he really should have visited me. He'd been the one to skedaddle when I'd raised Sam from the dead, because (I figured) he was sure it meant I loved Sam more than I loved him. But I would go to Shreveport, and we would talk, because Eric's silence was painful to me. I watched some of the fireworks go up in the city park — today was the Fourth of July — but then I went inside to dress. I was giving in to my impulse. I was going to Fangtasia.

I wanted to look as good as I could, but I didn't want to overdo it. I didn't know who I'd be seeing, though I wanted to talk to Eric by himself.

I hadn't heard from any of the vampires I knew who frequented Fangtasia. I didn't know if Felipe de Castro, King of Arkansas, Louisiana, and Nevada, was still in Shreveport, meddling in Eric's affairs, making Eric's life difficult. Felipe had brought his girlfriend, Angie, and his second-in-command, Horst, with him, just to compound Eric's vexation. Felipe was treacherous and wily, and his little entourage was much of a kind with their leader.

I also didn't know if Freyda, Queen of Oklahoma, was still in town. Eric's maker, Appius Livius Ocella, had signed a contract with Freyda that (to my mind) basically sold Eric into slavery with Freyda, but in a really cushy way: as her consort, with all the benefits you might imagine would pertain to such a job. Only thing was, Appius hadn't checked with Eric first. Eric was torn, to put it mildly. Leaving his job as sheriff was not something he'd ever planned to do. If ever there was a vampire who enjoyed being a big fish in a small pond, that vampire was Eric. He'd always been a hard worker, and he'd made plenty of money for the ruler of Louisiana, whoever that happened to be. Since the vampires had come out of the coffin, he'd done much more than make money. Tall, handsome, articulate, dynamic, Eric was a great poster boy for mainstreaming vampires. And he'd even married a human: me. Though not in a human ritual.

Of course, he had his darker side. He was

a vampire, after all.

All the way to Shreveport from Bon Temps, I wondered for the fiftieth time if I was making a huge mistake. By the time I'd pulled up to the back door of Fangtasia, I was so tense I was shaking. I'd put on my favorite pink dotted sundress, and I yanked the halter into place and took a few deep breaths before I knocked. The door swung open. Pam was leaning against the wall in the hallway, her arms crossed on her chest, looking broody.

"Pam," I said, by way of greeting.

"You shouldn't be here," she said.

Granted, I knew that her first allegiance was to Eric, and it always would be. Nonetheless, I'd thought Pam liked me a bit, as much as she ever would a human, and her words smarted like a slap in the face. I didn't need to hurt any worse than I already did, but I'd come here to see if I could smooth things over with Eric a little, tell him that he was wrong about Sam and me, find out what he'd decided about Freyda.

"I need to talk to Eric," I said. I didn't try to enter. I knew better.

At that moment, the door to Eric's office flew open. He stood framed in the doorway. Eric was big and golden and all male, and normally when he saw me, he started smiling.

Not tonight.

"Sookie, I can't talk to you now," he said. "Horst will be here any second, and he doesn't need to be reminded you exist. They've called in a lawyer to go over the contract."

It was like he was talking to a stranger, and furthermore, a stranger who had very little business appearing on his doorstep. In fact, Eric seemed both angry and wounded.

I had a mouthful — and heart full — of things I wanted to say. More than almost anything else in the world, I wanted to put my arms around him and tell him how much he meant to me. But as I took a half step in his direction, Eric moved back and shut the office door.

I froze for a moment, trying to absorb the shock and hurt, and keep my face from crumpling. Pam glided toward me and put one hand on my shoulder to spin me around and guide me away from the door. After it clanged shut behind us, she said into my ear, "Don't come here again. It's too dangerous. There's too much going on, too many visitors." And then she raised her voice and said, "And don't come back until he calls you!" She gave me a little shove that

46

propelled me into the side of my car. And then she zipped back inside and closed the door with that quick vampiric movement that always seemed like magic, or a really good video game.

So I went home, brooding over Pam's warning and Eric's words and demeanor. I thought about crying but didn't have the energy. I was too tired of being sad to make myself even sadder. Obviously, there was a lot of upheaval at Fangtasia and a lot of things hanging in the balance. There was nothing I could do about it except stay out of the way in the hope that I'd live through the change in regime, whatever that turned out to be. It was like waiting for the *Titanic* to sink.

Another morning went by, another day I passed holding my emotional breath, waiting for something to happen . . . something conclusive, or terrible.

I didn't feel as though I were waiting for the other shoe to drop; I felt as though I were waiting for an anvil to fall on my head. If I hadn't met with such a crushing reception when I went to Fangtasia, I might have tried to shake things up on my own, but I was discouraged, to put it in the mildest possible way. I took a very long, hot walk through the woods to put a basket of tomatoes on the Prescotts' back porch. I mowed my meadowlike lawn. I found I always felt better when I was outside: more whole, somehow. (And that was good, because there was a shitload of yard work to do.) But I brought my cell phone with me every step I took.

I waited for Sam to call me. But he didn't. Neither did Bernie.

I thought Bill might come over to let me know what was going on. He didn't.

And so ended another day of noncommunication.

The next day, when I got up, I had a message of sorts from Eric. He had texted me — *texted me*! — and not even personally, but through Pam. She relayed a stiff message, informing me that he'd talk to me later in the week. I had cherished a hope that perhaps Pam herself would show up to bawl me out or to enlighten me about how Eric was faring . . . but no.

As I sat on the front porch with a glass of iced tea, I examined myself to see if my heart was broken. I was so emotionally exhausted, I couldn't tell. As I saw it, maybe melodramatically, Eric and I were struggling with the chains of the love that had bound us together, and it didn't seem we could

48

either break free of those chains or resume them.

I had a dozen questions and conjectures, and I dreaded the answers to all of them. Finally, I got out the weed whacker, my least favorite yard tool.

My gran used to say, "You pays your money, and you takes your choice." I didn't know where the saying had originated, but now I understood what it meant.

"Of course," I said out loud, because the radio was playing and I couldn't hear myself think over it, "if you make a decision, you have to abide by the consequences." I hadn't even made a conscious decision to use the cluviel dor to save Sam; I'd acted instinctively when I saw him die.

Finally, I'd reached my saturation limit on this retroactive second-guessing. I threw down the weed whacker and screamed out loud. *Screw* all this brooding.

I was sick of thinking about it.

So I was delighted, after I'd put away all the yard tools and showered, to hear a car crunching up my gravel driveway. I recognized Tara's minivan. As she drove past the kitchen window, I peered out to see if the twins were strapped into their car seats, but the windows were tinted too dark. (Seeing Tara in a minivan was still a shock, but during Tara's pregnancy she and JB had vowed to be model parents, and part of that picture was a minivan.) Tara's shoulders were rigid as she walked to the door, but at least she was coming to the back door as friends should. She didn't fool with knocking. She opened the back door onto the laundry room/porch and yelled, "Sookie! You better be here! Are you decent?"

"I'm here," I said, turning to face her as she came into the kitchen. Tara was wearing some stretchy brown pants and a loose white blouse, her dark hair in a braid down her back. Her makeup was minimal. She was lovely as always, yet I couldn't help but notice she'd let her eyebrows stray all over. Motherhood could sure wreak havoc on a woman's grooming. Of course, having two at one time would make "me time" extra hard to come by. "Where are the babies?" I asked.

"JB's mom's got 'em," she said. "She was drooling at the chance to keep 'em for a few hours."

"So . . . ?"

"How come you're not going to work? How come you're not answering your e-mail or picking up your mail at the end of the driveway?" She tossed a bundle of envelopes of all sizes and a magazine or two onto the kitchen table. She glared at me as she continued, "You know how nervous that makes people? People like me?"

I was a little embarrassed at the chunk of truth in her accusation that I'd been selfish in staying out of touch while I'd been *trying to understand myself and figure out my life and my future.* "Excuse *me,*" I said sharply. "I did call in sick to work, and I'm surprised you want to risk taking my germs back to the babies!"

"You look fine to me," she said, without a speck of sympathy. "What happened to you and Sam?"

"He's all right, isn't he?" My anger faltered and disappeared.

"He's had Kennedy working in his place for days. He talks to her by phone. He doesn't come over to the bar." She was still glaring at me, but her stance was softening. I could tell from her thoughts that she was genuinely concerned. "Kennedy's real happy to do extra bartending, since she and Danny are saving up to rent a house together. But that business can't run itself, Sookie, and Sam hasn't missed four days at the bar, if he was in Bon Temps, since he bought the place."

That last part was mostly a muted blah-blahblah. Sam was all right.

I sat in one of the kitchen chairs a little too hastily.

"Okay, tell me what happened," Tara said, and sat opposite me. "I wasn't sure I wanted to know. But I guess now you better tell me."

I did want to talk to someone about what had happened at Alcide Herveaux's country place. But I couldn't tell Tara the whole story: the captive rogue Weres, Jannalynn's betrayal of her pack and her leader, the horrible things she'd done. I couldn't imagine how Sam was feeling. Not only had he learned the true nature of his girlfriend — though evidence suggested that he'd always suspected Jannalynn was playing a deeper game — but he had to absorb her death, which had been truly gruesome. Jannalynn had been trying to kill Alcide, her pack-leader, but she'd given Sam a mortal wound instead. Then Mustapha Khan had executed her.

I opened my mouth to try to begin the story, and found I didn't know where to start. I looked at my friends-since-childhood buddy helplessly. She waited, with a look that said she intended to sit right there in my kitchen until I answered her. Finally, I said, "The gist of it is that Jannalynn is now completely and permanently out of the picture, and I saved Sam's life. Eric feels that I should have done something for him, instead. Something significant, that I was aware of." I left off the punch line.

"So Jannalynn *hasn't* gone to Alaska to visit her cousin." Tara was compressing her lips to keep from looking as freaked as she felt. But there was a hint of triumph, too. She was thinking she had known something was fishy about that story.

"Not unless Alaska has gotten a lot hotter."

Tara giggled; but then, she hadn't been there. "She did something that bad? I read in the paper that someone had confessed over the telephone to the officer in charge of Kym Rowe's murder and then vanished. Would that be Jannalynn, by any chance?"

I nodded. Tara didn't seem shocked. Tara knew all about people who did bad things. Two of them had been her parents.

"So you haven't talked to Sam since then," she said.

"Not since the next morning." I hoped Tara would say she'd seen him, talked to him, but instead she moved on to a topic she considered more interesting.

"What about the Viking? Why is *he* pissed? His life didn't need saving. He's already dead."

I held my hands palms up and open, trying to think how to phrase it. Well, I might as well be honest, if not graphic. "It's like . . . I had a magic wish. I could have used it for Eric's benefit, to get him out of a bad situation. And it would have changed his future. But instead, I used it to save Sam." And then I'd waited for the repercussions. Because using strong magic always had consequences.

Tara, who had had bad experiences with vampires, smiled broadly. Though Eric had saved her life once upon a time, she included him in her generic dislike of the undead. "Did a genie grant you three wishes or something?" she said, trying to keep the pleasure out of her voice.

Actually, though she was joking, that was almost the truth. Substitute "fairy" for "genie" and "one wish" for "three wishes," and you'd have the story in a nutshell. Or in a cluviel dor.

"Kind of like that," I said. "Eric does have a lot on his plate right now. Stuff that will completely transform his life." Though what I said was absolutely true, it came out sounding like a weak excuse. Tara tried not to sneer.

"Has anyone from his posse called you? What about Pam?" Tara was thinking I had reason to worry if the area vampires had decided I was nothing to them. And she was right to be concerned. "Just because you break up with the big guy doesn't mean they hate you, right?" She was thinking they probably did.

"I don't think we've exactly broken up," I said. "But he's pissed off. Pam passed along a message from him. A *text message.*"

"Better than a Post-it note. Who *have* you heard from?" Tara asked impatiently. "All this weird shit has happened, and no one's calling you to talk about it? Sam's not over here scrubbing your floors and kissing your feet? This house should be full of flowers, candy, and male strippers."

"Ah," I said intelligently. "Well, the yard's strangely full of flowers. And tomatoes."

"I spit on the supes who've let you down," Tara said, fortunately not suiting action to words. "Listen, Sook, stick with your human buds and leave the others by the side of the road." She meant it all the way down to her bones.

"Too late for that," I said. I smiled, but it didn't feel as though it fit my face right.

"Then come shopping. I need some new bras, since I'm Elsie the Cow these days. I don't know how much longer I can keep this up."

Tara, breastfeeding twins, was notably more bosomy. Maybe more than a bit curvier, too. But I was hardly one to point fingers, and I welcomed the change of focus in our conversation. "How are the kids doing?" I said, smiling more genuinely. "I'm gonna have to babysit them some night so you and JB can go to the movies. How long has it been since you went out together?"

"Since six weeks before I was due," she said. "Mama du Rone has kept them twice during the day so I could go to the store, but she doesn't want to keep 'em at night when Papa du Rone is home. If I can pump enough milk to get ahead of the little monsters, JB would take me to the Outback. We could eat steak." There was an avid look to her mouth. Tara had been craving red meat ever since she'd started nursing. "Besides, since Hooligans closed, JB doesn't have to work at night anymore."

JB had been employed at Hooligans as well as at a health club, where he was a trainer. At Hooligans, he'd been doing the (nearly) full monty on ladies' night to raise extra money for the twins' birth. I hadn't spared a moment to think about the fate of the building and business since the owner, my cousin Claude, had vanished from the human world. That was definitely something

56

to worry about when I ran out of other, more important stuff.

"Just let me know next time you're in a steak mood," I assured Tara, pleased at the prospect of doing her a good turn. "Where were you thinking of shopping today?" Suddenly, I was anxious to get out of the house.

"Let's go to Shreveport. I like the maternity and baby shop there, and I want to drop by that consignment shop on Youree, too."

"Sure. Let me put on some makeup." In fifteen minutes I was dressed in clean white shorts and a sky blue T-shirt, my hair in a neat ponytail and my skin thoroughly moisturized. I felt more like myself than I had in several days.

Tara and I talked all the way over to Shreveport. Mostly about the babies, of course, because what's more important than babies? But included in the conversation were Tara's mother-in-law (a great woman); Tara's shop (not faring too well this summer); Tara's assistant, McKenna (whom Tara was trying to fix up with a friend of JB's); and other items of interest in the Taraverse.

On this very hot summer day in July, it felt comfortingly normal to be having this gossip session while we took a gal-pal road trip.

Though Tara owned and operated an upscale boutique, it didn't carry specialty clothes like maternity and new-mom wear. She said, "I want me some breastfeeding bras and a breastfeeding nightgown from Moms 'N More, and at the consignment place I want to pick up a couple of pairs of shorts, since I can't get my fat baby ass into my pre-baby shorts. You need anything, Sookie?"

"I do have to get a dress for Jason and Michele's wedding," I said.

"Are you in it? They set a date yet?"

"I'm the only attendant as of now. They narrowed it to a couple of dates, but they're waiting to pick one after they hear from Michele's sister. She's in the army, and she may or may not be able to get leave on those dates." I laughed. "I'm sure Michele will ask her, too, but I'm a sure thing."

"What color you need to wear?"

"Any color I like. She says she doesn't look good in white, and besides, she went that route for her first wedding. Jason's wearing a tan suit, and Michele's wearing chocolate brown. It's a cocktail dress, and she says it looks great on her."

Tara looked skeptical. "Chocolate brown?"

she said. (Tara did not think that was suitable for a wedding.) "You should look today," she continued more cheerfully. "Of course, you're welcome to look at my shop, but if you see something today at the consignment shop, that would be perfect. You're only going to wear it once, right?"

Tara carried pretty clothes, but they were expensive, and her selection was limited by the size of the shop. Her suggestion was really practical.

We stopped at Moms 'N More first. The maternity and new-mom shop held little interest for me. I'd been dating vampires for so long that pregnancy was not something I thought about, at least not very often. While Tara talked lactation with the saleswomen, I looked at the diaper bags and the adorable baby items. New mothers were certainly beasts of burden. Hard to believe that once upon a time, babies had been raised without diaper bags, breast pumps, special trash cans for disposable diapers, plastic keys, walkers, premade baby food, plastic pads for changing, special detergent to wash baby clothes . . . and on and on and on. I touched a tiny green-and-white-striped sleeper with a lamb on the chest. Something deep inside me shivered with longing.

I was glad when Tara completed her purchase and we left the store.

The consignment shop was only a mile away. Since "fancy used clothes" didn't sound very enticing, the owners had gone for Second Time's the Charm. Tara seemed slightly embarrassed at visiting a used-clothing store, no matter how upscale it looked.

"I have to look nice since I've got a clothing store," she told me. "But I don't want to spend a lot on bigger pants, since I hope I won't be wearing a size up for long." Tara was actually two sizes up, her head told me.

This is one of the things I hate about being telepathic.

"Only makes sense," I said soothingly. "And maybe I'll see something for the wedding." It seemed highly unlikely that the original owner of the dress would turn up at Jason's wedding, and that was my only qualm about purchasing a garment someone else had worn a time or two.

Tara knew the owner, a bony redhead, whose name appeared to be Allison. After a hug of greeting, Tara hauled out pictures of the twins . . . maybe a hundred pictures. I was completely unsurprised.

I'd seen the real thing, so I wandered away to check out the "better" dresses. I found my size and began to slide the hangers along the rack one by one, taking my time about it. I was more relaxed than I had been in a week.

I was glad Tara had winkled me out of the house. There was something wonderfully normal and reassuring about our shopping expedition. The air-conditioned shop was peaceful, since the music was turned down very, very low. The prices were higher than I'd expected, but when I read the labels, I understood why. Everything here was good quality.

I scooted aside a hanger holding a terrible purple-and-green garment, and I came to a complete stop, enraptured. The next dress was a rich yellow. It was sleeveless, lined, and scoop-necked, with a large, flat bow curving around the middle of the back. It was beautiful.

"I love this dress," I said out loud, feeling profoundly happy. This was shallow, all right? I knew that. But I'll take joy where I find it.

"I'm going to try this on," I called, holding it up. The owner, deep in Tara's delivery story, didn't even turn around. She raised her hand and waved it in acknowledgment. "Rosanne will be right with you," she called.

The dress and I went past the curtain into

the changing area. There were four cubicles, and since no one else had entered the store, I wasn't surprised to find them all empty. I wriggled out of my shorts and my T-shirt in record time. Holding my breath with suspense, I slid the dress off its hanger and over my head. It settled on my hips like it was happy to be there. I reached behind me to zip it up. I got the zipper halfway to its destination, but my arms can only bend so far. I stepped out to see if I could detach Tara from her fascinating conversation. A young woman, presumably Rosanne, was standing right outside, waiting for me to emerge. When I saw her, I felt a faint buzz of familiarity. Rosanne was in her late teens, a sturdy kid with her brown hair braided and rolled in a bun. She was wearing a neat pants outfit in French blue and cream. Surely I'd seen her before?

"I'm so sorry I wasn't on the floor to help you!" she said. "What can I do for you? You need help with that zipper?" She'd started speaking almost as soon as I'd emerged from the curtain, and it wasn't until she finished that she took a good look at my face.

"Oh, shit!" Rosanne said, so sharply that the shop owner turned around to look.

I gave the elegant Allison an "everything's

all right here" smile, hoping I wasn't lying.

"What's the matter with you?" I whispered to Rosanne. I looked down at myself, searching for something that would explain her alarm. Had I started my period? What? When I didn't see anything alarming, I looked up at her anxiously, waiting for her to tell me why she was so agitated.

"It's you," she breathed. "You're the one."

"I'm the one *what*?"

"The one who has such big magic. The one who raised that twoey from the dead."

"Oh." Revelation. "You're in the Long Tooth pack, I guess? I thought I'd seen you somewhere before."

"I was there," she said, with an unblinking, unnerving intensity. "At Alcide's farm."

"That was kind of awful, huh?" I said. And it was the last thing I wanted to talk about. Back to the matter at hand. I smiled at Rosanne the werewolf. "Hey, can you zip me up?" I turned my back to her, not without trepidation. In the full-length mirror, I saw her looking at me. It didn't take a telepath to interpret that expression. She was afraid to touch me.

The remnants of my good mood crashed and burned.

When I'd been a child, some people had regarded me with a blend of unease and disgust. Telepathic children can say the worst things at the worst times, and no one likes them for it or forgets that they blurted out something private and secret. Telepathy in a child is nothing short of terrible. Even I, the actual telepath, had felt that way. Some people had been absolutely frightened by my ability, which I hadn't had the skill to conceal. After I'd gained some control over what I said when I "overheard" something startling or awful from the thoughts of a neighbor, I'd seldom seen that expression. I'd forgotten how painful it could be.

"You're scared of me," I said, stating the obvious because I simply couldn't think of what else to do. "But you have nothing to fear from me. You're the one with claws and fangs."

"Hush, Allison'll hear you," she whispered.

"You're still in the closet?"

"Here at work I am," she said, her voice deeper and rougher. At least she didn't look frightened any longer, which had been my goal. "You know how hard it is for two-natured girls, when they start changing? Harder than it is for the boys. One in twenty of us ends up a permanent psycho bitch. But if you can get through your teens, you're pretty nearly home free, and I'm almost there. Allison is nice, and this is a low-stress place. I've worked here every summer. I want to keep this job." She looked at me pleadingly.

"Then zip me up, okay? I have no intention of talking about you. I just need a frickin' dress," I told her, really exasperated. I wasn't unsympathetic, but I truly felt I had enough problems at the moment.

She hesitantly reached up with her left hand to grip the top of the dress, held the zipper with her right, and in a second I was enclosed properly. The bow covered the zipper and was held in place by snaps. Since summer is prime tanning time, I was a lovely brown, and the deep yellow looked . . . wonderful. The dress wasn't cut too low at the top, and it was just high enough at the hem. A little dab of my previous good mood returned.

While I hadn't enjoyed Rosanne's assumption that I'd "out" her simply for my own pleasure, I could understand her worries. Sort of. I'd met two or three women who hadn't made it through their supe adolescence with their personality intact; this condition was something to fear, all right. With an effort, I shoved the whole exchange away. When I could focus on my image in the mirror, I felt a flutter of sheer gratification. "Wow, it's so pretty," I said. I smiled at her reflection, inviting her to lighten up with me.

But Rosanne was silent, her face still unhappy. She was not going along with my "we're all happy girls" program. "You did do that, right?" she said. "Bring the shifter back from the dead."

I could see I wasn't going to get to enjoy the thrill of shopping victory. "It was a one-time-only event," I said, my smile vanishing. "I can't do it again. I don't even want to do it again." I realized I might not have used the cluviel dor if I'd had time to think about it. I might have doubted it would work, and that doubt would have weakened my will. My witch friend Amelia had told me once that magic was all about will.

I'd had plenty of will when I'd felt Sam's heart quit beating.

"Is Alcide doing all right?" I asked, making another effort to shift the topic.

"The packmaster is well," she said formally. Though she was a Were, I could see into her mind clearly enough to tell that though she'd overcome her initial fear, she had deep reservations about me. I wondered if the whole pack now shared that distrust. Did Alcide believe I was some kind of super witch?

Nothing could be further from the truth.

I'd never been super anything.

"Glad to hear he's okay. I'll take the dress," I said. *At least,* I figured, *I can salvage something from this encounter.* When I went to the checkout counter, I saw that while Rosanne and I had had our uncomfortable heart-to-heart, Tara had found a couple of pairs of shorts and a pair of jeans, very good labels. She seemed pleased, and Allison did, too — because she wouldn't have to look at any more baby pictures.

As I left the shop, the dress in a bag over my arm, I looked back to see the young Were watching me through the front window, a mixture of respect and fear on her face.

I'd been so absorbed in my own reaction to what I'd done to Sam — for Sam — that I'd never worried about how other witnesses might react.

"So what was with you and that girl?" Tara said abruptly.

"What? Nothing."

Tara gave me a massively skeptical look. I was going to have to explain. "She's a Were from Alcide's pack, but she's keeping her second nature a secret from her employer," I said. "You don't feel obliged to tell Allison, I hope?"

"No, who Allison hires is up to her." Tara

shrugged. "Rosanne's been there since she was a kid, coming in after school. As long as she does the work, what difference does it make?"

"Good. We'll keep it under our hats, then."

"Rosanne didn't look happy with you," Tara said, after a long moment.

"No . . . no, she wasn't. She thinks . . . I'm a witch, a really terrible witch. Terrible in the sense of being very powerful and scary."

Tara snorted. "I can tell she doesn't know you worth a damn."

I smiled, but it was a weak effort. "I hope it's not a widespread opinion."

"I would have thought they could *smell* if you were bad or not."

I tried to look indifferent. "They should know better, but since they don't, I'm just going to have to weather it out."

"Sook, don't you worry. If you need us, you call JB and me. We'll strap those babies into their car seats, and we'll be right over. I know I've failed you some . . . disappointed you some . . . in the past couple of years. But I swear I'll help you, no matter what."

I was taken aback by her vehemence. I looked sharply at my friend. There were tears in her eyes, even while she pulled out into traffic and turned the car back toward

Bon Temps.

"Tara? What're you talking about?"

"I did fail you," she said, her face grim. "In so many ways. And I failed myself. I made some really dumb decisions. I was trying so hard to escape the way I was brought up. For a couple of years, I would have done *anything* to make sure I never had to live like I had at my folks' house again. So I looked for protection, and you know how that turned out. When that was over, I hated vampires so much I couldn't listen to your problems. I've grown up now, though." She gave a sharp and decisive nod, as though in her opinion she'd taken the final step in spiritual growth.

This was the last thing in the world I'd expected: a declaration of reconciliation by my oldest friend. I started to deny every negative thing she'd said about herself. But she'd been so honest that I had to be honest in return — at least, in a tactful kind of way. "Tara, we've always been friends. We'll always be friends," I said. "If you've made mistakes, I have, too. We just got to do the best we can. We're coming out the other side of a lot of trouble, both of us." Maybe.

She pulled a Kleenex out of her purse and blotted her face with one hand. "I know we'll be okay," she said. "I know it."

I wasn't convinced of that, at least about my own future, but I wasn't going to ruin Tara's moment. "Sure we will," I said. I patted her hand on the steering wheel.

For a few miles we drove in silence. I looked out the window at the fields and ditches, choked with growth, the heat hovering over them like a giant blanket. If weeds could flourish with such vigor, maybe I could, too.

CHAPTER 3

Our shopping trip jolted me out of my rut of worry. When Tara went home, I sat down to make some resolutions.

I promised myself I would go in to work the next day, whether or not I heard from Sam. I had a part interest in the bar, and I didn't have to get Sam's permission to show up. I gave myself a rousing speech before I realized I was being ridiculous. Sam wasn't denying me entrance to the bar. Sam hadn't told me he didn't want to see me. I had stayed at home of my own volition. Sam's noncommunication might mean many things. I needed to get off my butt and find out.

I heated up a DiGiorno's that night, since no one would deliver out on Hummingbird Road. Actually, the Prescotts, my neighbors closer to town, got their pizza delivered, but no one wanted to venture onto the long, narrow driveway to my house after dark. I'd learned lately (from the thoughts of patrons at Merlotte's) that the woods around my house and along Hummingbird Road had a reputation of being haunted by creatures *frightening beyond belief.*

Actually, that was absolutely true — but the creatures that had sparked the rumor were now departed to a country I couldn't visit. However, there was a dead man strolling through my yard as I tried to fold the cardboard disk that had been under the pizza. Those things are hell to get into kitchen garbage bags, aren't they? I'd finally managed it by the time he reached the back door and knocked.

"Hey, Bill," I called. "Come on in."

In a second he was standing in the doorway, inhaling deeply to better catch the scent he was scouting for. It was strange to see Bill breathe. "Much better," he said, in a voice that was almost disappointed. "Though I think your dinner had a little garlic on it."

"But no fairy smell?"

"Very little."

The smell of a fairy is to vampires what catnip is to cats. When Dermot and Claude had been in residence, their scent had pervaded the house, lingering even when they were not actually there. But my fae kin were gone now. They'd never come back. I'd left the upstairs windows open for one whole night to dispel the lingering eau de fae, and that was no small step in this heat.

"Good," I said briskly. "Any gossip? Any news? Anything interesting happening at your place?" Bill was my nearest neighbor. His house lay right across the cemetery. In that cemetery was his headstone, erected by his family. They'd known Bill's body wasn't there (they thought he'd been eaten by a panther), but they'd given him a place of rest. It hadn't been a panther that had attacked Bill, but something much worse.

"Thanks for the beautiful roses," he said. "By the way, I've had a visitor."

I raised my eyebrows. "Good one? Bad one?"

He raised an eyebrow. "Depends," he said.

"Well, let's go sit in the living room while you tell me about it," I said. "Do you want a bottle of blood?"

He shook his head. "I have an appointment with a donor later." The Federal Bureau of Vampire Affairs had left that issue up to the individual states. Louisiana had permitted private registries first, but the state donor program was much safer for the donor *and* the vampire. Bill could get human blood under supervised conditions.

"How is that? Is it creepy?" I'd wondered if it might be like making a sperm donation: necessary and even admirable, but somewhat awkward.

"It's a little . . . peculiar," Bill admitted. "The element of the hunt, the seduction . . . all gone. But it's human blood, and that's still better than the synthetic."

"So you have to go to the facility, and then what?"

"In some states they can come to you, but not in Louisiana. We make an appointment and go in and register. It's a storefront clinic. In the back there's a room with a couch. A big couch. And they show in the donor."

"You get to pick the donor?"

"No, Louisiana BVA wants to take the personal element out of it."

"So why the couch?"

"I know, mixed messages. But you know how good a bite can be, and there was going to be more than biting going on, no matter what."

"You ever get the same person twice?"

"Not yet. I'm sure they keep a list, trying to keep the vampires and the humans apart after they've met at the bureau."

While we talked, Bill had taken a seat on my own couch, and I tucked my legs under

74

me in the big old armchair that had been Gran's favorite. It was curiously comfortable to have my first real boyfriend as a casual visitor. We'd both been through a few relationships since we'd broken up. Though Bill had told me (often) that he would be very glad to resume our intimacy, tonight that topic was not on his mind. Not that I could read Bill's thoughts; since vampires are dead, their brains just don't spark like human brains. But a man's body language usually lets me know when he's considering my womanly attributes. It was really great, really comforting, to have a friendship with Bill.

I had switched on the overhead light, and Bill looked white as a sheet beneath its glare. His glossy dark brown hair looked even darker, his eyes almost black. He was hesitating over his next topic, and I was not as relaxed and comfortable all of a sudden.

"Karin is in town," he said, and looked at me solemnly.

I could tell I was supposed to be smacked in the face with this information, but I was utterly at sea. "Who would that be?"

"Karin is Eric's other child," he said, shocked. "You hadn't ever heard her name?"

"Why would I? And why should I be excited that she's in town?"

"Karin is called the Slaughterer."

"Well, that's silly. 'The Slaughterer' is just . . . cumbersome. 'Karin the Killer' would be way better."

If Bill had been prone to such gestures, he would have rolled his eyes. "Sookie . . ."

"Look at what a great fighter Pam is," I said, diverted. "Eric must really like strong women who can defend themselves."

Bill looked at me pointedly. "Yes, he does."

Okay, I was going to take that as a compliment . . . maybe kind of a sad one. I hadn't set out to kill people (or vampires or werewolves or fairies) or to conspire to kill them or even to feel like killing them . . . but I had done all those things in the course of the past two years. Since Bill had walked into Merlotte's and I had seen him — my first vampire — I had learned more about myself and the world around me than I'd ever wanted to know. And now here we were, Bill and me, sitting in my living room like old buddies, talking about a killer vamp.

"You think Karin might be here to hurt me?" I said. I gripped my ankle with my hand and squeezed. Just what I needed, another psycho bitch after me. Hadn't the Weres pretty much cornered that market?

"That's not the feeling I get," Bill said.

"She's *not* out to get me?" Your life was

not right when you were actually surprised that someone didn't want to kill you.

"No. She asked me many, many questions about you, about Bon Temps, about the strong people and the weak people in your circle. She would have told me if her intent had been to harm you. Karin is not as complex as Pam . . . or Eric, for that matter."

I had about four instant responses to Bill's information, but I wisely shut my mouth on all of them. "I wonder why she didn't come right to my door to ask, if she wanted to know all that," I contented myself with saying.

"I believe she was gathering information for some purpose of her own."

Sometimes I just didn't get vampires.

"There are a few things you need to understand about Karin," Bill said briskly, when I didn't respond out loud. "She takes . . . umbrage . . . at any perceived slight to Eric, any disparagement. She was with him for many years. She was his guard dog."

I was glad I always had a Word of the Day calendar on the kitchen counter. Otherwise, I'd have had to whip out a dictionary to get through that sentence. I started to ask Bill, if Karin was so hung up on Eric, why hadn't

I met her before? But I skipped that in favor of telling him, "I don't go around disparaging Eric. I love Eric. It's not my fault he's upset with me. Or that his asshole of a maker engaged him to a vampire he hardly knows." I sounded just as bitter as I felt. "She should take umbrage with *that.*"

Bill looked thoughtful, which made me very nervous. He was about to say something he knew I wouldn't like. I squeezed my ankle a little harder.

"All the Area Five vampires know what happened at the Long Tooth pack meeting," he said.

That wasn't exactly a shocker. "Eric told you." I cast around for something else to say. "It was a horrible night," I said honestly.

"He returned to Fangtasia in a towering rage, but he wasn't specific about what had made him that way. He said, 'Damn wolves,' a few times." Here Bill was careful to stop. I figured Eric had added "Damn Sookie" a few times, too. Bill continued, "Palomino is still dating that Were, Roy, the one who works for Alcide." He shrugged, as if to say there was no accounting for taste. "Since we were all naturally curious, she called Roy to discover the details. She relayed the story to us. It seemed important for us to know." After a moment Bill added, "We'd asked

Mustapha, since we could tell he'd been fighting, but he would not comment. He is very closemouthed about what's going on in the Were world."

There was a long silence. I simply didn't know how to respond, and Bill's face at this moment didn't give me any clues. Mostly, I was feeling a rush of appreciation for Mustapha, the Were who was Eric's daytime guy. Mustapha was that rare thing, a person who could keep his mouth shut.

"So," I made myself say, "you're thinking . . . what?"

"Does it make any difference?" Bill asked.

"You're being very mysterious."

"You're the one who kept a huge secret," he pointed out. "You're the one who had the fairy equivalent of a wishing well in your possession."

"Eric knew."

"What?" Bill was genuinely startled.

"Eric knew I had it. Though I didn't tell him."

"How did he know this?"

"My great-grandfather," I said. "Niall told him."

"Why would Niall do such a thing?" he said, after an appreciable pause.

"Here's Niall's logic," I said. "Niall thought that I needed to find out if Eric

79

would pressure me to use the cluviel dor for Eric's own benefit. Niall wanted it himself, but he didn't take it because it was intended for me to use." I shivered when I remembered how Niall's impossibly blue eyes had blazed with desire for the enchanted object, how sharply he'd had to rein himself in.

"So in Niall's view, giving Eric this piece of knowledge was a test of Eric's love for you."

I nodded.

Bill contemplated the floor for a minute or two. "Far be it from me to speak in Eric's defense," he said at last, with a hint of a smile, "but in this instance, I will. I don't know if Eric actually intended you to, say, wish Freyda had never been born or to wish that his maker had never met her . . . or some other wish that would have gotten him out of Freyda's line of sight. Knowing the Viking, I'm certain he hoped you would be *willing* to use it on his behalf."

This was a conversation of significant pauses. I had to think over his words for a minute to be sure I understood what Bill was telling me. "So the cluviel dor was a test of Eric's sincerity, in Niall's eyes. And the cluviel dor was a test of my love for Eric, in Eric's eyes," I said. "And we both failed the test."

Bill nodded, one sharp jerk of his head.

"He would rather I had let Sam die."

Bill let me see how startled he was. "Of course," he said simply.

"How could he think that?" I muttered, which was a stupidly obvious (and obviously stupid) question to ask myself. A much more pertinent question was, *How could two people in love so misjudge each other?*

"How could Eric think that? Don't ask *me*. It's not my emotional reaction that matters," Bill said.

"I'd be glad to ask Eric, if he'd just sit down and talk to me," I said. "But he turned me away from Fangtasia two nights ago."

Bill had known that, I could tell. "Has he gotten in touch with you since that happened?"

"Oh, yes indeedy. He got Pam to text me to say he'd see me later."

Bill did a great impression of a blank wall.

"What do you think I should do?" I asked out of sheer curiosity. "I can't bear this halfway state. I need resolution."

Bill sat forward on the couch, his dark brows raised. "Ask yourself this," he said. "Would you have used the cluviel dor if it had been — say, Terry or Calvin — who was mortally wounded?"

I was stunned by the question. I groped for words.

After a moment, Bill got up to leave. "I didn't think so," he said. I scrambled to my feet to follow him to the door.

"It's not that I think Terry's life, anyone's life, isn't worth a sacrifice," I said. "It's that it might not ever have occurred to me."

"And I'm not saying you're a bad woman for that hesitation, Sookie," Bill told me, reading my face accurately. He put a cold hand to my cheek. "You're one of the best women I've ever met. However, sometimes you don't know yourself very well."

After he had drifted back into the woods and I had locked the house up tight, I sat in front of my computer. I had planned to check my e-mail, but instead I found myself trying to unravel Bill's meaning. I couldn't concentrate. Finally, without clicking on the e-mail icon, I gave up and went to bed.

I guess it's not too surprising that I didn't sleep well. But I was up and out of bed by eight, utterly tired of hiding out in my house. I showered and put on my makeup and my summer work uniform — Merlotte's T-shirt, black shorts, and New Balance walking shoes — and got in the car to drive to work. I felt much better now that I was following my normal routine. I was also very nervous as I parked on the graveled area behind the bar.

I didn't want to stand staring at Sam's trailer, centered in its little yard at right angles to the bar. Sam might have been standing at a window, looking out. I averted my eyes and hurried in the employees' entrance. Though I had my keys in my hand, I didn't need them. Someone had gotten there before me. I went directly to my locker and opened it, wondering if I'd see Sam behind the bar, how he'd be, what he'd say. I stowed my purse and put on one of the aprons hanging from a hook. I was early. If Sam wanted to talk to me, there was time.

But when I walked up front, the person behind the bar was Kennedy Keyes. I felt distinctly flattened. Not that there was anything wrong with Kennedy; I'd always liked her. Today she was as bright and shiny as a new penny. Her rich brown hair was glossy and hanging in loose curls across her shoulders, she was made up with great care, and her sleeveless pink tank fit very snugly, tucked into her linen slacks. (She had always insisted bartenders shouldn't have to wear a uniform.)

"Looking good, Kennedy," I said, and she spun around, her phone to her ear.

"I was talking to my honey. I didn't hear you come in," she said chidingly. "What have you been up to? You over 'the flu'? I started to bring you a can of Campbell's Chicken Noodle." Kennedy couldn't cook and was proud of it, which would have shocked my grandmother, I can tell you. And she hadn't believed I was sick for a moment.

"I felt awful. But I'm a lot better now." In fact, I was. I felt surprisingly glad to be back in Merlotte's. I'd worked here a lot longer than I'd held any other job. And now I was Sam's partner. The bar felt like home to me. I felt as though I'd been away a month. Everything looked just the same. Terry Bellefleur had come in real early to get everything sparkling clean, as usual. I began to take the chairs off the tables where he'd put them while he mopped. Moving swiftly, with the efficiency of long practice, I got the tables squared away and began rolling silverware into napkins.

After a few minutes, I heard the employee entrance opening. I knew the cook had arrived because I heard him singing. Antoine had worked at Merlotte's for months now, longer than many other short-order cooks had lasted. When things were slow (or simply when the spirit moved him), he sang.

Since he had a wonderful deep voice, no one minded, least of all me. I couldn't carry a tune in a bucket if it were raining, so I thoroughly enjoyed his serenades.

"Hey, Antoine," I called.

"Sookie!" he said, appearing in the service hatch. "Glad you back. You feeling better?"

"Right as rain. How are your supplies holding out? Anything we need to talk about?"

"If Sam don't come back to work soon, we got to make a trip to Shreveport to the warehouse," Antoine said. "I've got a list started. Sam still sick?"

I borrowed a leaf from Bill's book. I shrugged. "We've both had a bug," I said. "Everything'll be back to normal in three shakes of a lamb's tail."

"That'll be good." He smiled and turned to get his kitchen ready. "Oh, a friend of yours come by yesterday."

"Yeah, I forgot," Kennedy said. "She used to be a waitress here?"

There were so many ex-waitresses that I'd take half an hour if I started trying to guess her name. I wasn't interested enough to do that, at least not right then, when there was work to be done.

Keeping the bar staffed was a constant issue. My brother's best bud, Hoyt Fortenberry, was soon to marry a longtime Merlotte's barmaid, Holly Cleary. Now that the wedding was close, Holly had cut back on her work hours. The week before, we'd hired tiny, bone-thin Andrea Norr. She liked to be called "An" (pronounced *Ahn*). An was curiously prim but attracted men like soda cans attract wasps. Though her skirts were longer and her T-shirts were looser and her boobs were smaller than all the other barmaids, men's eyes followed the new hire every step she took. An seemed to take it for granted; we'd have known it if she hadn't, because of all the things she liked (and by now we knew most of them), most of all she liked to talk.

The minute An came in the back door, I could hear her, and I found myself smiling. I hardly knew the woman, but she was a hoot.

"Sookie, I seen your car outside, so I know you're back at work, and I'm real glad you came in," she called from somewhere back by the lockers. "I don't know what bug you had, but I hope you're over it, 'cause I sure don't want to get sick. If I can't work, I don't get paid." Her voice was getting progressively closer, and then she was standing face-to-face with me, her apron strapped on, looking spic-and-span in a Merlotte's T-shirt and calf-length yoga tights. An had told me during her job interview that she never wore shorts outside the home because her father was a preacher, that her mother was the best cook in An's hometown, and that she herself had not been allowed to cut her hair until she'd left home at eighteen.

"Hi, An," I said. "How's it been going?"

"It's been going great, though I missed seeing you and I hope you're all better."

"I do feel much better. I have to run over and talk to Sam for a minute. I noticed that the salt and pepper shakers need topping up. You mind?"

"Let me get right on that! Just show me where the salt and pepper are stored. I'll fill those up in a jiffy." I'd say this for An: She was a hard worker.

Everyone was doing what they should be doing. I had to, myself. I took a deep breath. Before I could chicken out, I marched out the back door of the bar and over to Sam's trailer, following the path of stepping-stones. For the first time, I registered that a strange car was parked beside Sam's pickup, a little economy car with dents and dust as its main motif. It had Texas plates.

I wasn't completely surprised to find a dog

curled up on the welcome mat on the little porch Sam had added outside the front door of his trailer. My approach was no surprise to the dog, either. It was on its feet at the sound of my footsteps, watching intently as I passed through the gate and crossed the green grass on the neat stepping-stones.

I stopped a respectful distance from the steps and eyed the dog. Sam could transform himself into almost anything warm-blooded, so it was possible this dog was Sam . . . but I didn't think so. He usually picked a collie form. This sleek Labrador just didn't have the right feel.

"Bernie?" I asked.

The Lab gave a neutral sort of bark, and her tail started wagging.

"Are you going to let me knock on the door?" I asked.

She seemed to think about it for a minute. Then she trotted down the steps and out onto the grass. She watched me go up to the door.

I turned away from her (with a little misgiving) and knocked. After a long, long minute, Sam opened it.

He looked haggard.

"Are you okay?" I blurted. It was clear he was not.

Without speaking, he backed up to let me in. He was wearing a short-sleeved summer shirt and his oldest blue jeans, worn so thin in spots that there were little splits in the fabric. The interior of the trailer was surprisingly gloomy. Sam had tried hard, but he couldn't make the trailer completely dark — not on a bright, hot day like today. Between the drawn curtains, the light came in in sharp shards, like brilliant glass slivers.

"Sookie," Sam said, sounding somehow remote. That scared me more than anything else. I eyed him. Though it was hard to see the details, I could tell Sam was unshaven, and though he was naturally wiry, he looked as though he'd lost ten pounds. He'd showered, at least; maybe Bernie had insisted. When I'd evaluated Sam, I looked around at the living room, as best I could. The sharp contrasts of light hurt my eyes.

"Can I open the curtains?" I asked.

"No," he said, his voice sharp. Then he seemed to reconsider. "Well, okay, one."

Moving slowly and carefully, I pulled back a curtain over the window mostly shaded by an oak tree. Even so, as light brightened the trailer, Sam winced.

"Why does the sunshine bother you?" I asked, trying to sound absolutely calm about it.

"Because I died, Sookie. I died and came back." He didn't sound bitter, but he sure didn't sound happy.

Okayyyyy. Well, since I hadn't heard a word from Sam, I'd figured he wasn't dancing in the streets over his experience, but I guess I'd thought he'd at least be, I dunno, *pleased* about it. That he would say something along the lines of, *Gosh, you wonderful woman, now that I've had time to rest and reflect, I thank you for altering your life forever by bringing back mine. What an amazing gift.*

That's what I'd figured.

So. Wrong again.

CHAPTER 4

Sam's mom scratched at the door. Since Sam was still standing in his "tense and tortured" pose, I obliged. Bernie walked in on four paws, nosed at Sam's leg for a second, and went into the little corridor leading to the bedrooms.

"Sam," I said, to get his attention. He looked at me, but I wasn't getting a lot of expression from him. "You got a bar to run," I said. "You got people depending on you. After all the stuff you've been through, don't flake out now."

His eyes seemed to focus on me. "Sookie," he said, "you don't understand. I *died.*"

"*You* don't understand," I retorted with some heat. "I was there. I had my hand on you when your heart quit beating. And I brought you back. Maybe that's what you should be thinking about, huh? The 'brought back' part?"

If he said "I died" one more time, I was

going to slap him silly.

Bernie, in woman form, entered into the living room dressed in khaki shorts and a blouse. Sam and I were too locked in our conversation to speak to her, though I sort of waved my hand in her direction.

"You had a cluviel dor," Sam said. "You really had one."

"I did," I said. "Now it's only a pretty thing that looks like a compact."

"Why did you have it with you? Did you expect what was going to happen?"

I shifted uneasily. "Sam, who could expect that? I just figured there wasn't any point in having something like that if you didn't have it on you to use. Maybe Gran wouldn't have died if she'd kept it on her."

"Like a fairy Life Alert," Sam said.

"Yeah. Like that."

"But you must have had a plan for it, a use. I mean, it was a gift . . . to keep. Maybe to save your own life."

I looked away, getting more and more uncomfortable. I'd come over here to find out what was happening in Sam's head, not to raise questions (or answer questions) that might lay a burden on him he shouldn't have to assume.

"It *was* a gift, which means I could use it as I chose," I said, trying to sound brisk and matter-of-fact. "And I chose to start your heart again."

Sam sat down in his dilapidated armchair, the only item in the trailer that looked as though it needed to be kicked to the curb.

Bernie said, "Have a seat, Sookie." She came farther into the room and stared down at her oldest son, the only family member who had received the shifter gene. "I see you looking at the old chair," she said conversationally, when Sam didn't speak. "That was my husband's. It was the only thing of his I gave away when he died, because it just reminded me of him too much. Maybe I should have kept it, and maybe if I'd looked at it every day, I wouldn't have married Don."

Maybe Bernie's problem wasn't so much marrying Don as not telling him before the wedding that she could turn into an animal. But Don shouldn't have shot her when he found out, either. You don't just haul off and shoot the one you love.

" 'Maybe' is such a bad word," I said. "You can 'maybe' yourself back to Adam and Eve and the serpent."

Bernie laughed, and Sam looked up. I could see a glimmer of his former self in that look. The bitter truth welled up in my throat like bile. The price of bringing back

93

Sam from death was that he wasn't quite the same man anymore. The experience of death had changed him, maybe forever. And maybe resurrecting him had changed me.

"How are you feeling physically?" I said. "You seem a little shook up."

"That's one way to put it," he said. "The first day Mom was here, she had to help me walk. It's weird. I was okay riding back with you that night, and I drove home okay next morning. But after that it was like my body had to relearn things. Sort of like . . . after a long sickness. I've felt so bad, and I can't figure out why."

"I guess part of it is that process of grief."

"Grief?"

"Well, it would only be natural," I said. "You know. Jannalynn?"

Sam looked at me. His expression was not what I expected; it was compounded of confusion and embarrassment. "What about her?" he asked, and I could swear his puzzlement was genuine.

I cut my eyes toward Bernie, who was every bit (and more understandably) as unenlightened as Sam. Of course, she hadn't been at the pack meeting, and she hadn't talked to anyone else who'd been there until now. She'd met Jannalynn, though I wasn't sure she'd known how involved Sam had been with the werewolf. There'd been sides of Jannalynn that few men would want their moms to see.

"That Were that showed up at the house?" Bernie said. "The one Sam didn't want me to know he'd been seeing?"

I felt horribly awkward. "Yes, that Jannalynn," I said.

"I have been wondering why I hadn't heard from her," Sam said readily. "But considering all the bad things she was accused of — and the fact that I believed she'd done them — I hadn't planned on seeing her again. Someone told me she'd gone to Alaska."

There wasn't a psychologist hotline at hand. I didn't know how to handle this.

"Sam, do you remember what happened to you that night? You remember why we were there?" Begin at the beginning.

"Not exactly," he admitted. "It's pretty hazy. Jannalynn was accused of doing something to Alcide, right? I remember feeling mad and pretty miserable, because I'd liked her so much when we started dating. But I wasn't exactly surprised, so I guess I'd figured out that she wasn't basically . . . a good person. I remember driving to Alcide's farm with you, and I remember seeing Eric and Alcide and the pack, and I think I

95

remember — there was a swimming pool? And some sand?"

I nodded. "Yeah, a swimming pool and a sand volleyball area. Remember anything else?"

Sam began to look uneasy. "I remember the pain," he said. He sounded hoarse. "And something about the sand. It was all . . . I remember riding back in the truck, with you driving."

Well, shit. I hated to be the designated revelator. "You've forgotten a few things, Sam," I said, as gently as I could. I'd heard of people forgetting traumatic stuff, especially when they'd been badly injured: people in car wrecks, people who'd gotten attacked. I figured Sam was entitled to blank out on a thing or two since he'd actually passed over.

"What did I forget?" He was looking at me with the sidelong wide eyes of a nervous horse, and his back was stiff as a board. Somewhere in his head, he knew what had happened.

I held out my hands to him, palms up. *Do you really want to do this now?*

"Yeah, I guess I should know," he said. Bernie crouched by her son's chair in a distinctly nonhuman way. She was looking at me with a level gaze. She knew I wasn't going to say anything that would make Sam feel better. I could understand her unhappiness with me, but Bernie or no Bernie, I had to go through with it.

"Since Jannalynn turned traitor and almost killed Warren with neglect while she held him hostage, she and Mustapha Khan fought," I said, paring down the story to the essentials that affected Sam. "You remember Mustapha?"

Sam nodded.

"She got a trial by combat, though I don't know the hows and whys of that. I was surprised they'd give her the privilege. But she and Mustapha were fighting with swords."

Suddenly Sam's face went white. I paused, but he didn't say anything, so I went on.

"Jannalynn was doing real well, but instead of focusing on beating Mustapha, she decided to make one last attempt to control the pack — at least, I guess that was her goal." I exhaled deeply. I'd thought about that night over and over, and I still didn't understand. "Or maybe she just had an impulse, to get the better of Alcide, to have the last word, sort of. Anyway, Jannalynn maneuvered the fight until she was close to where you and Alcide were standing." I paused again, hoping that he would tell me to stop, that he remembered what came next.

He didn't, though by now he looked almost as pale as a vampire. I bit my lip and braced myself to continue.

"She leaped for Alcide and swiped down with her sword, but Alcide saw her coming in time and jumped to the side. Instead, you got cut. She never intended to hurt you."

Sam didn't respond to my lame attempt at consolation. *Sure, your lover killed you, but she didn't really mean to. 'Kay?*

"So . . . the blow was bad, as you know. You fell down, and there was . . . It was pretty awful." I'd thrown away the clothes I'd been wearing. And Sam's shirt, the one he'd left at my house. "You got cut," I said. "You got cut so bad you died."

"It hurt," he said, hunching over as if a strong wind were blowing at him. Bernie put her hand over her son's.

"I can't even imagine," I said quietly, though I was certainly no stranger to pain. "Your heart stopped beating. I used my cluviel dor to heal you and bring you back."

"You were calling me. You told me to live." Now he was finally looking at me directly, meeting my eyes.

"Yes," I said.

"I remember opening my eyes again to see your face."

"Your heart started beating again," I said, as the enormity of it swept over me. My skin tingled all over.

"Eric was standing behind you, looking down at us as though he hated us," Sam said. "And then he was gone, vamp quick."

"Do you remember us talking on the way home?"

He ignored that question. "But what happened to Jannalynn?" he said. "Isn't that what you were going to tell me?"

He'd walked right by her body — and her head — as I'd helped him get to his truck. He'd looked at the corpse. I could see why he didn't want to recall that. I didn't, either, and I hadn't even liked Jannalynn.

"Mustapha executed her," I said. I didn't elaborate.

Sam's gaze was fixed on me, but there wasn't anyone home. I had no idea what he was thinking. Maybe he was trying to recall what he'd seen. Maybe he remembered very clearly and didn't want to.

Bernie was shaking her head at me from behind Sam's shoulder. She thought Sam had had enough, and she was ready for me to go; that was easy to read even if you weren't a telepath. I'm not so sure I would have walked out otherwise — I figured I needed to offer a little more debriefing — but this was Sam's mother. I heaved myself to my feet, feeling about ten years older than when I'd knocked on the trailer door.

"See you later, Sam," I said. "Please come back to work soon." He didn't answer. He was still staring at the spot where I'd been sitting.

"Good-bye, Sookie," Bernie said. "You and me need to have a talk later."

I would rather walk on nails. "Sure," I said, and left.

Back in the bar, the working day proceeded in a strangely normal rhythm. It can be hard to recall that not everyone knows all the big events that occur in the supe world, even when those events take place right under the noses of the general human populace. And even if every human soul in the bar knew, they might not care very much.

The big topic of bar gossip was Halleigh Bellefleur fainting at the Rotary Club when she'd stood up to go to the bathroom. Since she was seven months pregnant, everyone was concerned. Terry, her husband's cousin, came in to get some fried pickles, and he was able to reassure us that Halleigh was fine, that Andy had taken her right in to her doctor. According to Terry, the doctor had told Andy and Halleigh that the baby had been pressing against something, and when the baby shifted, Halleigh's blood pressure had, too. Or something like that.

The lunch rush was moderate, which made sense since the Rotary was meeting at the Sizzler Steak House. When we were down to a light sprinkle of customers, I turned my tables over to An while I ran to the post office to pick up the bar mail. I was horrified to see how much had accumulated in the Merlotte's box. Sam's recovery took on a new urgency.

I brought the mail back to the bar and settled in Sam's office to go through it. Sure, I'd been working at Merlotte's for five years. I'd paid attention, and I knew a lot about how the business was run. Now I could write checks and sign them, but there were decisions that had to be made. Our cable contract for the bar was up for renewal, and Sam had talked about switching providers. Two charity fund-raisers had asked for expensive liquor to auction off. Five local charities just flat-out asked for money.

Most startling of all, we'd gotten a letter from a Clarice lawyer, a guy new to the area. He wanted to know if we were going to pay for the emergency room visit of Jane Clementine Bodehouse. The lawyer gently threatened to sue Merlotte's for Jane's mental and physical suffering if we didn't cough up. I looked at the figure at the bottom of a copy of Jane's bill. Damn. Jane had ridden in the ambulance and had an X-ray. She'd also required some stitches, which might as well have been of spun gold thread.

"Shepherd of Judea," I muttered. I reread the letter.

When Merlotte's had been firebombed the previous May, Jane, one of our alcoholic customers, had been cut by flying glass. She'd been treated by the ambulance drivers, who'd taken her to the emergency room to be checked over. She'd had a few stitches. She'd been fine . . . drunk, but fine. All her injuries had been minor. Jane had been reminiscing about that night in the past week or two, recalling her own bravery and how good that had made her feel. Now she was sending us a huge bill and threatening to sue?

I scowled. This was way beyond Jane's thinking capacity. I was willing to bet this new lawyer was trying to drum up some business. I figured he'd called Marvin, told him that his mom was due some money to compensate for all her suffering. Marvin, who was sick to death of hauling Jane away from Merlotte's, must have been very open to the notion of getting some money back from Merlotte's, after his mom had poured so much into it.

A knock at the door put an end to my speculations. I swung around in Sam's swivel chair to see someone I'd never expected to see again. For a second, I thought I'd pass out, like Halleigh Bellefleur at the Rotary Club.

"Arlene," I said, and got stuck. That was all I could manage. My former coworker — my former good friend — seemed to be waiting for me to say something more. Finally, I thought of adding, "When did you get out?"

This moment was not only awkward in the extreme but completely unnerving. The last time I'd seen Arlene Fowler (aside from in a courtroom), she had been part of a conspiracy to murder me in a particularly horrible way. People had gotten shot that day. Some had died. Some had been wounded. Some of those had recovered in jail.

Oddly enough, considering I was facing a conspirator in my murder, I was not afraid of her.

All I could think about was how much Arlene had changed. She'd been a curvy woman a few months ago. Now she was thin. Her hair was still defiantly red, but it was shorter and drier, lank and lifeless. The wrinkles around her eyes and mouth were cruelly evident in the overhead light. Arlene's time in jail hadn't been that long, but it seemed to have aged her in dog years.

"I got out four days ago," she said. She'd been giving me the same kind of scrutiny I'd given her. "You're looking good, Sookie. How's Sam?"

"He's sick today, Arlene," I said. I felt a little light-headed. "How are Lisa and Coby?"

"They're confused," she said. "They asked me why Aunt Sookie hasn't come by to see them."

"I thought it would be real weird if I visited them, all things considered." I held her eyes with my own until she nodded reluctantly and looked away. "Specially since I was sure you must have said some awful things about me. You know, when you decided to lure me to your place so your buddies could nail me to a cross."

Arlene flushed and looked down at her hands.

"Did they stay with Helen when you were

away?" I asked, not knowing what else to talk about.

Arlene's new best bigot buddy had promised to take care of the kids when she'd taken them from Arlene's trailer before the shooting started.

"No. She got tired of 'em after a week. She took 'em to Chessie."

"Chessie Johnson?"

"She was Chessie Fowler before she married Brock," Arlene explained. "Chessie is — was — first cousin to my ex." (The ex whose name Arlene had kept, though she'd been married several times. Rick Fowler had perished in a motorcycle accident in Lawton, Oklahoma.) "When Jan Fowler died out at the lake in that fire, she left Chessie some money. Chessie ain't hurting. She loves those kids. It could have been worse." Arlene didn't sound angry with Helen, just resigned.

Frankly (and call me punitive), what I wanted to see was Arlene feeling angry with herself. Yet I didn't detect anything like that, and I could see Arlene inside and outside. What I heard from her thoughts was a bright streak of malice, a lack of hope or enterprise, and a dull loathing of the world that had treated her so ill . . . in her estimation.

"Then I hope the kids are doing well with the Johnsons," I said. "I'm sure they've missed their mama." I'd found two true things to say. I wondered where Sam's gun was. I wondered how fast I could get to it if it was in the right-hand drawer of his desk, as I suspected it was.

She looked as if she were about to cry, just for a second. "I think they have. I've got a lot of explaining to do to those two."

Gosh, I'd be glad when this conversation was over. At least there was one emotion I could recognize, and it was regret for what she'd done to her family. "You got out awful early, Arlene," I said, suddenly realizing what was most surprising about her presence in Sam's office.

"I got me a new lawyer. He bonded me out on appeal," she said. "And my behavior in jail was good, naturally, since I had a lot of motivation. You know, Sookie, I never would have let them hurt you."

"Arlene, you can't lie to me," I reminded my former friend. The pain of Arlene's betrayal was a red, sore scar on my spirit.

"I can tell you don't trust me," Arlene said.

No shit, Sherlock. I waited for the words I saw coming next. She was going to play the reformation card.

"And I don't blame you," Arlene said. "I don't know where my head was at, but it sure wasn't on my shoulders. I was full of unhappiness and rage, and I was looking for a way to blame it on someone else. Hating the vampires and werewolves was the easiest thing to do." She nodded solemnly, righteously.

Someone had had a little therapy.

I'm not mocking therapy; I've seen it do people a lot of good. But Arlene was aping the ideas of the counselor just as she'd aped the ideas of the anti-supernatural Fellowship of the Sun. When was she going to come up with some convictions of her own? It seemed incredible to me now that I'd admired Arlene so sincerely for years. But she had a great zest for life, she had an easy chemistry with men, she had two cute children, and she made her own living. These were enviable things to lonely me.

Now I saw her differently. She could attract men but not keep them. She could love her children but not enough to stay out of jail and take care of them. She could work and raise her kids but not without a constant stream of men through her bedroom.

I'd loved her for her willingness to be my friend when I had so few real ones, but I understood now that she'd used me as a babysitter for Coby and Lisa, an unpaid house cleaner, and a cheering section and admirer. When I came into my own life, she'd tried to have me murdered.

"Do you still want me dead?" I said.

She winced. "No, Sookie. You were a good friend to me and I turned on you. I believed everything the Fellowship was preaching."

Her thoughts matched her words, at least as far as they went. I was still not much of a person in Arlene's estimation. "And that's why you came by today? To mend fences with me?"

Though I saw the truth in her thoughts, I couldn't really believe it until she said, "I came to see if Sam would think of hiring me again."

I could not think of a response, I was so astonished. She began to shift around as I stared at her. Finally, I felt able to answer. "Arlene, I feel sorry for your kids, and I know you want to get them back and take care of them," I said. "But I can't work with you here at Merlotte's. You must know that would be impossible."

She stiffened and raised her chin. "I'll talk to Sam," she said, "and we'll just see what he has to say." The old Arlene surfaced. She was sure if she could appeal to a man, she'd get her way.

"I do the hiring here now. I'm part owner," I said, poking myself in the chest with my forefinger. Arlene stared, definitely shocked. "It wouldn't work in a million years. You must know that. You betrayed me in the worst possible way." I felt a pang of grief, but I wasn't sure what element of this encounter grieved me most: the fate of Arlene's kids or the fact that people could hand out hate like candy and find takers.

The struggle in Arlene's face made for uncomfortable viewing. She wanted to lay into me, but she'd just told me she had changed and that she understood her former ways were wrong, so she couldn't really defend herself. She'd been the dominant one in our "friendship," and she was grappling with the fact that she had no sway over me any longer.

Arlene took a deep breath and held it for a moment. She was thinking about how angry she was, thinking about protesting, thinking about telling me how disappointed Coby and Lisa would be — when she realized none of that would make any difference because *she'd been willing to see me hung on a cross.*

"That's right," I said. "I don't hate you, Arlene." I was surprised to realize that was true. "But I can't be around you. Ever."

Arlene spun on her heel and left. She was going to find her new friends and pour all her bitterness into their ears. I could tell that right from her head. Not surprisingly, they were guys. Trust Arlene. Or rather, don't.

Sam's mother slipped into the doorway in Arlene's wake. Bernie remained standing half in, half out, watching Arlene's progress until my former friend was out Merlotte's front door. Then she took the chair Arlene had vacated.

This was going to be my day for really uncomfortable conversations.

"I heard all that," Bernie said. "And someday you'll have to tell me the backstory. Sam's asleep. Explain what happened to him." Bernie looked a lot more human. She was about my height, and slim, and I noticed that she'd restored her hair to the same color as Sam's, a red-gold. Bernie's hair minded better than Sam's ever had. I wondered briefly if she was dating someone. But at the moment, she was all business and all mother.

She already knew the gist of the story, but I filled in the blanks.

"So Sam was involved with this Jannalynn, the one who showed up at our house in Wright, but he was beginning to have doubts about her." Bernie was scowling, but she wasn't angry with me. She was angry that life wasn't being good to Sam, because she loved him dearly.

"I think so. He was nuts about her for a while, but that faded." I wasn't going to attempt to explain his relationship, and it wasn't my responsibility. "He'd come to a few realizations about her, and it was — well, not exactly breaking his heart; at least, I don't think so — but it was painful."

"What are you to him?" Bernie looked me right in the eyes.

"I'm his friend, his good friend, and I'm his business partner now."

"Uh-huh." She eyed me in a way I could only describe as skeptical. "And you sacrificed an irreplaceable artifact to save his life."

"I wish you'd quit bringing that up," I said, and winced. I'd sounded like a ten-year-old. "I was glad to do it," I added in a more adult tone.

"Your boyfriend, this Eric, left the werewolf land right after."

She was drawing some incorrect conclusions. "Yeah . . . it's a long story. He didn't expect me to use the cluviel dor like that. He thought I should use it to . . ."

"Use it to benefit him." She ended my

111

sentence for me, which is one of my least favorite things.

But she was right.

She dusted her hands together briskly. "So Sam's alive, you're out a boyfriend, and Jannalynn's dead."

"That sums it up," I agreed. "Though the boyfriend thing is kind of hanging fire." I suspected I was clinging to ashes rather than fire, but I wasn't going to say that to Bernie.

Bernie looked down at her own hands, her face inscrutable while she thought. Then she looked up. "I may as well go back to Texas," she said abruptly. "I'll stay tonight to make sure he wakes up stronger tomorrow before I take off."

I was surprised at her decision. Sam appeared far from recovered. "He seems pretty unhappy," I said, trying to sound nonjudgmental.

"I can't make him happy," Bernie said. "He's got all the raw material. He just has to work with it. He's going to be all right." She gave a little nod, as if once she said the words, he had to be so.

Bernie had always seemed like a down-to-earth woman; however, I thought she was a little too dismissive of Sam's emotional recovery. I could hardly insist she stay. After all, Sam was in his thirties.

"Okay," I said uncertainly. "Well, you have a good night, and call me if you need me."

Bernie got out of the chair and knelt before me. "I owe you a life," she said. She got to her feet more easily than I would have, though she was almost twice my age. And then she was gone.

ELSEWHERE
in Bon Temps

"She said no," Arlene Fowler told the tall man and the medium man. The old trailer was hot and the door was open. It was musty and cluttered inside. No one had lived in it for a while. The sun flowed through the bullet holes, creating odd patterns of light on the opposite wall. Arlene was sitting in an old chrome-and-vinyl dinette chair while her two guests sat forward on the battered couch.

"You knew she would have to," said the medium man, a bit impatiently. "We expected that."

Arlene blinked. She said, "Then why'd I have to go through it? It just made me feel terrible. And it took time off from what I had to spend going over to see my kids."

"I am sure they were glad to see you?" the medium man said, his pale eyes fixed on

Arlene's worn face.

"Yes," she said, with a small smile. "They were real glad. Chessie, not so much. She loves them kids. They looked like they'd settled in there. They're doing real well in school, both of them."

Neither of the men was at all interested in the children's progress or welfare, but they made approving noises.

"You made sure to go through the bar's front entrance?" the tall man asked.

Arlene nodded. "Yeah, I spoke to three people. Just like you said. Am I through now?"

"We need you to do one more thing," the tall man said, his voice smooth as oil and twice as soothing. "And it won't be hard."

Arlene sighed. "What's that?" she said. "I need to be looking for a place to live. I can't bring my kids here." She glanced around her.

"If it weren't for our intervention, you wouldn't be at liberty to see your children," the medium man said gently, but his expression wasn't gentle at all.

Arlene felt a prickle of misgiving. "You're threatening me," she said, but hardly as if that surprised her. "What do you want me to do?"

"You and Sookie were good friends," the

tall man said.

She nodded. "Real good friends," she said.

"So you know where she keeps an extra key outside her house," the medium man said.

"Yes, I do," she said. "You planning on breaking in?"

"It's not really breaking in if you have a key, is it?" The medium man smiled, and Arlene tried to smile back.

"I guess not," she said.

"Then what we need is for you to use that key and go inside. Open the drawer in her bedroom where she keeps her scarves. Bring us a scarf you've seen her wear before."

"A scarf," Arlene said. "What you going to do with it?"

"Nothing to worry about," the tall man said. He smiled, too. "You can be sure she won't enjoy the result. And since she turned you down for a job, and since you wouldn't be here in this place if it weren't for her, that shouldn't bother you at all."

Arlene mulled that over for a moment. "I guess it doesn't," she said.

"Well, you know she's at work now," said the medium man. "So I think right now would be a good time to go there. And in case her house is warded, carry this." He handed her a strange old coin. At least, it looked old, and it was surprisingly heavy for its size. "Keep it in your pocket at all times," he said.

Arlene was startled. She looked down at the small object dubiously before she put it in her pocket. "Well, okay. I'll go to Sookie's now. Then I got to go look at rental places. When will that money be in my account?"

"Tomorrow," the tall man assured her. "And you'll find your own place, and your kids will be able to move back in with you."

"And this is all you want me to do? I asked her for a job, and in a little bit I go get a scarf from her drawer? With this thing in my pocket?"

"Well, you'll have to meet us and give us the scarf and coin," the tall man said, shrugging. "That's no big deal."

"Okay," said Arlene. "If my old car will make it there. It isn't doing too good after being parked in Chessie's backyard since I been in jail."

"Here's some gas money," the tall man said, pulling out his wallet and handing Arlene some cash. "We wouldn't want you running out of gas."

"No," said the medium man. "We wouldn't want that."

"I'll call you on that cell phone you gave me, when I got the scarf," Arlene said. "We can meet tonight."

The two men looked at each other silently. "Tonight will be great," the tall man said after a second or two. "Just great."

CHAPTER 5

I saw Terry Bellefleur for the second time that day while I was putting gas in my car at the Grabbit Kwik. He was filling up his pickup. Terry's Catahoula, Annie, was in the back of the truck. She was interested in everything that was going on at the gas station, though she was panting heavily in the heat.

I knew just how she felt. I was glad I'd waited until evening to take care of this task. At least the pavement didn't look like it was rippling, and I didn't have to let my tongue hang out.

After Terry pulled his charge slip from the pump, I called to him. He turned and brightened. "Hey, Sook. How's Sam doing? I was glad to see you today. I wish I'd sat at your tables instead of that An's. She talks the hind leg off a donkey."

He was the only guy I knew who didn't want to howl at the moon when he saw An

Norr. "Sam may be back on the job tomorrow," I said.

"Crazy, you both getting sick at the same time."

He was also the only person in Bon Temps who would say that without leering. I'd "overheard" several comments in the bar today about Sam and me both being AWOL for four days. "So, how's Jimmie?" I asked. Jimmie was his girlfriend; at least I thought that was their relationship. I was pleased to see that Terry's hair had been cut and combed, and that he'd shaved in the past couple of days. Jimmie was a good influence.

"She's real good," he said. "I asked her dad if I could marry her." Terry looked down a little nervously as he told me this important fact. Terry had had a rough time as a POW in Vietnam. He'd come away with a multitude of physical and mental problems. I was so happy he'd found someone, and proud of his determination to do the right thing.

"What did her dad say?" I was genuinely curious. Though Jimmie was a little younger than Terry, I was a little surprised to hear she still had her father.

"He said if Jimmie's kids didn't mind, it was okay with him."

"Kids," I said, scrambling to get a foothold on the slippery slope of the conversation.

"She got two sons and a daughter, nineteen, twenty, and twenty-two," Terry said, and to give him credit, he seemed happy about that. "They all got children. I now have me some grandkids."

"So her children were happy about the idea of a stepfather?" I smiled broadly.

"Yeah," he said, turning red. "They were real pleased. Their dad passed away ten years ago, and he was a mean bastard, anyway. Things ain't been easy for Jimmie."

I gave him a hug. "I'm so happy for you," I said. "When's the wedding?"

"Well." He turned even redder. "It was yesterday. We went across the state line to Magnolia and got married."

I had to exclaim a little and pat him on the back a few times, but people were waiting for us to move so they could pull up to the pumps. I couldn't leave without patting Annie, too, and congratulating her also on gaining a spouse. (Her last litter had been sired by Jimmie's Catahoula, and surely her next one would be, too.) Annie seemed as pleased as Terry.

I was still smiling to myself as I stopped at the end of my driveway to check my mailbox. I told myself this was the last time I'd be out in the heat until tomorrow. I almost dreaded getting out of the air-conditioned car again. In July, at seven o'clock, the sun was still up and would be for more than an hour. Though the temperature was no longer approaching one hundred, it was plenty hot. I still had sweat trickling down my back from pumping my gas. All I could think about was getting in my shower.

I didn't even look through my little pile of mail. I tossed it on the kitchen counter and made a beeline for my bathroom, stripping off my sweaty clothes as I walked. A few seconds later, I was under a stream of water and blissfully happy. My cell phone rang while I was rinsing off, but I decided not to hurry. I was enjoying the shower too much. I toweled off and turned on my hair dryer. The whir of the warm air seemed to echo through the rooms.

I cast the chest of drawers a proud glance when I went in the bedroom. I knew everything in it was organized, as was everything in the night table and everything in the vanity. I didn't have control over much in my life, but by golly, my drawers were tidy. I noticed one was pulled out, just a little. I frowned. I habitually pushed drawers all the way in. That was one of my mom's rules, and though I'd lost her when I was only seven, it had stuck with me. Even Jason was careful to close drawers all the way.

I pulled it open and looked inside. My odds-and-ends drawer (stockings, scarves, evening purses, and belts) was still orderly, though the scarves didn't seem to be lined up quite like I'd left them, and one of the brown belts was mixed in with the black belts. Huh. After staring at the drawer's contents for a long moment, wishing I could get the items to talk, I pushed the drawer shut, this time making sure it closed properly. The sound of wood meeting wood was loud in the quiet house.

The big old place, which had sheltered Stackhouses for more than a hundred and fifty years, had never seemed particularly empty until I'd had long-term houseguests. After Amelia had left to go back to New Orleans to pay her debt to the coven, I'd felt like my home was a lonely place. But I'd readjusted. Then Claude and Dermot had moved in . . . and left for good. Now I felt like a small bee bumbling around inside an empty hive.

Just at this moment, I found it was actually comforting to think that across the cemetery, Bill would rise; but he was dead until dark.

I felt a touch of melancholy when I

thought of Bill's dark eyes, and slapped myself on the cheek. Okay, now I was just being silly. I wasn't going to let sheer loneliness drive me back to my ex. I reminded myself I was still Eric Northman's wife under vampire custom, though he wasn't talking to me right now.

Though I was reluctant to attempt to approach Eric again for several reasons (I have my pride and it was hurt), I was sick of waiting and wondering what was happening in the closed society of the vampires.

Oh, sure, I reflected, *they're glad to see me when I have a good plan for killing someone, but when I want a relationship update, I'm not hearing from a single soul.*

Not that I was bitter or anything. Or mad, or hurt. Or knew if vampires had souls.

I could feel myself shake all over like a dog coming out of a pond. Regret, impatience, flying off me. Was it my place to worry about souls? No. That was up to a higher power than me.

I glanced outside to see that it was just full dark. Before I could have another thought, I picked up my cell phone and speed-dialed Eric. I had to do this before I lost my nerve.

"Sookie," he said, after the second ring, and I let myself feel surprised. I'd truly

123

doubted he'd answer.

"We need to talk," I said, making a huge effort to sound calm. "After my visit to Fangtasia, I understand that you're dodging me. You made it clear that you don't want me visiting the club. I assume you don't want me dropping by your place, either. But you know we have to have a conversation."

"Then talk."

Okay, this was going pretty damn badly. I didn't have to look in a mirror to know I was wearing my mad face. "Face-to-face," I said, and it sounded like I was biting out the words. Too late, I had second thoughts. This was going to be painful in the extreme. Wouldn't it be better to just let our relationship drift away — avoid having the conversation I was almost certain I could script ahead of time?

"I can't come tonight," Eric said. He sounded as if he were on the moon, he was so distant. "There are people in line to see me, much to be done."

And still his voice was empty. I let my anger rip, in that sudden way I have when I'm tense. "So we take second place. You could at least sound sorry," I said, each word distinct and bitter.

"You have no idea how I feel," he said. "Tomorrow night." And he hung up.

"Well, fuck him and the horse he rode in on," I said.

After gearing up for a marathon conversation, Eric's quick cutoff left me overflowing with restless energy.

"This is no good," I told the silent house. I turned on the radio and I started dancing. That is something I *can* do, though at the moment my skill was not important. It was the activity that counted. I threw myself into it. I thought, *Maybe Tara and I can do a dance exercise program together.* She and I had done routines together all through high school, and it would be easy for Tara to get back in shape that way (not that I needed to bring that up when I asked her). To my dismay, I was huffing and puffing after less than ten minutes, a not-so-subtle reminder that I myself could use a regular exercise program. I drove myself to continue for fifteen more minutes.

When I collapsed onto the couch, I felt relaxed, exhausted, and just about in need of another shower. As I sprawled there, taking deep breaths, I noticed my answering machine was blinking. In fact, it was blinking frequently. I had more than one message. I hadn't checked my e-mail in days, either. Plus, I'd gotten that call on my cell phone while I'd been in the shower. I had to reconnect with the world.

First, the answering machine. After the first beep, I heard a hang-up. I didn't recognize the number. Then a call from Tara to tell me she thought baby Sara had allergies. Then a request to take an important survey. It wasn't too surprising that amid all this exciting communication, I began to think about the lawsuit again.

Jane Bodehouse loved wrestling. Maybe if I called the only wrestler I knew, a guy named T-Rex, I could get her some ringside tickets. She'd be so happy she'd drop her lawsuit against Merlotte's . . . if she was even aware of it.

And there I was, back to worrying.

After my phone messages, I checked my e-mails. Most of them suggested I enlarge my nonexistent penis or help desperate lawyers get huge sums of money out of Africa, but one was from my godfather, Desmond Cataliades, the mostly demon lawyer who had (in my view) given me the bane of my existence when he "gifted" me with telepathy. In his view, he'd endowed me with a priceless advantage over other humans. I'd received this birth present because I was the granddaughter of Mr. Cataliades's great friend Fintan and Fintan's, well, his girlfriend — my grandmother, Adele Stack-

126

house. Not only was I a descendant of a fairy, I possessed the "essential spark." Whatever that was. And that was why I'd been lucky enough to manifest the telepathy. Mr. Cataliades wrote:

Dearest Sookie, I am back in New Orleans, having settled my issues with the local supernatural community and done some essential detective work. I hope to visit you very soon to verify your well-being and to give you some information. I hear rumors of what is happening in your life, and those rumors disturb me.

Me, too, Mr. C. Me, too. I responded by telling him that I was doing okay and that I'd be glad to see him. I wasn't sure if any of that was true, but it sounded good.

Michele, Jason's fiancée, had e-mailed me two days ago from her job at the car dealership.

Hi Sookie! Let's get a pedicure together tomorrow! I have the morning off. What about nine o'clock at Rumpty?

I'd had only one pedicure before, but I'd enjoyed it, and I liked Michele fine; but we didn't necessarily have the same idea about what constituted a good time. However, she was going to be my sister-in-law soon, and I sent back an abject apology for not checking my e-mail sooner.

Tara had sent me a message.

Hey girlfriend, I really enjoyed our road trip. I'm wearing the shorts right now, lol. We have to do something about the babies' room, I can hardly get my fat ass in there. I thought it was big enuf before I had twins! I'm hiring a babysitter so I can get back to work part time. Here are some more pictures of the babies.

They didn't look much different from the way they had in the pictures she had yesterday. Nonetheless, I sent her an admiring message. I know what a friend should do. I wondered how Tara and JB could increase the size of the babies' little room. Sam was pretty handy with carpentry. Maybe they'd rope him in, too.

I'd gotten a text from Jason. "U working 2morrow?" I assured him I was. He probably needed to drop in to talk about some detail of the wedding, which was going to be about as casual as a wedding could be.

I thought of turning on the television, but it was summer, so there wasn't much point. I'd read instead. I got the top book off the library stack on my bedside table and was pleased to discover it was the latest Dana Stabenow. It's really a treat to read about Alaska when it's a summer day that peaked at 104 degrees. I hoped that maybe someday I'd get up there. I wanted to see a grizzly bear, and I wanted to see a glacier, and I wanted to eat fresh salmon.

I found I was holding the book in both hands and imagining. Since I couldn't concentrate on the page, I might as well throw supper together. It was getting late. While I made a salad with cherry tomatoes and dried cranberries and chopped chicken, I tried to picture how big a grizzly might be. I'd never seen any kind of bear in the wild, though twice I'd found prints in the woods I was pretty sure were a black bear's.

I was in a better mood altogether as I ate and read, two of my favorite activities.

It had been a long day, what with one thing and another, and by the time I crawled into my bed, I was ready to sleep. A peaceful night with no dreams; that was what I wanted. And for a while, I got it.

"Sookie."

"Mmmh?"

"Wake up, Sookie. I need to talk to you."

My bedroom was quite dark. Even the little night-light I left on in the bathroom was out. But I knew, even before I caught his familiar scent, that Eric was in my room.

"I'm awake," I said, still struggling to clear the sleep out of my head. The jolt of fear I'd gotten had gone far toward that end. "Why are you sneaking in like this? I gave you a key for emergencies, not for surprise night visits."

"Sookie, listen to me."

"I'm listening." Not happy about this approach to conversation, though.

"I had to be curt on the phone. There are ears all around me. No matter what happens in public — no matter what — don't doubt that I love you and care about your welfare . . . as much as I am able."

Not good.

"And you're telling me this because you're going to do something bad to me in public," I said, sadly unsurprised.

"I hope it won't come to that," he said, and he put his arms around me. In happier times, I'd found that being close to Eric in the summer was very pleasant because his body temp was so low, but I wasn't in the mood to enjoy the sensation just at the moment. "I have to go," he said. "I had only an hour when I wouldn't be missed. I was angry when you saved Sam. But I can't just dismiss you as if I didn't care. And I can't leave you unprotected tonight. My guard will be here if you consent."

"What guard? Okay," I said dazedly. He was leaving someone in the yard?

I felt him get off the bed, and after a second I heard the back door open.

What the *hell*?

I collapsed back onto the bed, and I spent a few minutes wondering if it was even possible I'd get some more sleep. I looked at the clock. Eleven forty-five p.m.

"Sure, wander in and get in bed with me. I don't mind," I said. "Please, wake me up and scare me to death. I *love* it!"

"Is that an invitation?" said a voice from the dark.

I did scream then.

CHAPTER 6

"Who the hell are you?" I asked, fighting the paralysis in my throat.

"Sorry!" said an accented voice. "I'm Karin."

I couldn't place the accent — not Cajun or Spanish or English. . . . "How'd you get in?"

"Eric let me in. You said you consented to be guarded."

"I thought he meant someone would be outside."

"He said, 'here.' "

I thought back over the conversation I'd just had, which I didn't remember any too well. "If you say so," I said doubtfully.

"I do," said the calm voice.

"Karin, why are you here?"

"To guard you," she said, with obvious patience.

"To keep me here? Or to keep other people out?"

"Other people out," Karin said. She didn't sound irritated, just matter-of-fact.

"I'm going to turn on the light," I said. I reached over to my bedside lamp and switched it on. Karin the Slaughterer crouched by the door to my room.

We regarded each other. Weirdly, after a moment, I could see Eric's progression. If I was a golden blonde and Pam was a paler true blonde, Karin's hair was at the ash blond end of the spectrum. It fell in heavy waves down her back. Her face was utterly bare of makeup and utterly lovely. Her lips were narrower than mine, as was her nose, but her eyes were wide and blue. Karin was shorter than me or Pam, but just as curvy. Karin was Me 101.

Eric ran true to type.

The biggest difference was not in our features but in our expressions. When I looked into Karin's eyes, I knew she was a stone-cold killer. All vampires are, but some have more aptitude for it than others. And some take more pleasure in it than others. When Eric had turned Pam and Karin, he'd gotten blond warriors.

If I became a vampire, I'd be like them. I thought of things I'd already done. I shivered.

Then I saw what she was wearing.

"Yoga pants?" I said. "A dread vampire wears *yoga pants?*"

"Why should I not? They are comfortable," she said. "Freedom of movement. And very washable."

I was on the verge of asking her what detergent she used and if she washed them on the cold cycle when I stopped myself. Her sudden appearance had really thrown me for a loop.

"Okay, I'm betting you heard everything Eric said to me. Would you care to expand on his very unsatisfactory conversation?" I asked, moderating my voice to a calm-and-casual level.

"You know as well as I what he was telling you, Sookie," Karin said. "You don't need me to interpret, even assuming my father Eric wanted me to do that."

We kept silent for a moment, me still in the bed and her crouching a few feet away. I could hear the bugs outside when they resumed droning in unison. *How'd they do that?* I wondered, and realized I was still stunned with sleep and shock.

"Well," I said. "It's been fun, but I need to get some rest."

"How is this Sam doing? The one you returned from the dead?" Karin asked unexpectedly.

134

"Ahhh . . . well, he's having a little trouble adjusting."

"To what?"

"To being alive."

"He was hardly dead any time," Karin scoffed. "I'm sure he is singing your praises? I'm sure his gratitude is heartfelt?" She wasn't sure at all, but she was interested in hearing my answer.

"Not so's you'd notice," I admitted.

"That's very strange." I could not begin to imagine why she was curious.

"I thought so, too. Good night, Karin. Can you watch me from outside my room?" I switched off my light.

"Yes, I can do that. Eric didn't say I had to stay by your bed and watch you sleep." And there was a little ripple in the darkness to indicate she'd gone. I didn't know where she'd stationed herself, and I didn't know what she'd do when day came, but frankly, that belonged in the big pile of things that weren't my problem. I lay back and considered my immediate future. Tomorrow, work. Tomorrow night, apparently I was scheduled to have some kind of painful public confrontation with Eric. I couldn't get out of it, since I simply didn't see not showing up as an option. I wondered where Arlene had found to lay her head tonight. I hoped it wasn't nearby.

The upcoming schedule of events didn't seem very attractive.

Do you sometimes wish you could fast-forward a week? You know something bad's coming up, and you know you'll get through it, but the prospect just makes you feel sick. I worried for about thirty minutes, and though I knew there was no point in doing so, I could feel my anxiety twisting me up in a knot.

"Bullshit," I told myself stoutly. "This is utter bullshit." And because I was tired, and because there was nothing I could do to make tomorrow any better than it was going to be, and because I had to live through it somehow, eventually I fell back asleep.

I'd missed the weather report the day before. I was pleasantly surprised to wake up to the sound of heavy rainfall. The temperature would drop a little, and the bushes and grass would lose their coating of dust. I sighed. Everything in my yard would grow even faster.

By the time I'd gone through my morning routine, the downpour had slacked off a bit, from torrential to light, but the Weather Channel told me heavy rain would resume in the late afternoon and might continue intermittently through the next few days.

That was good news for all the farmers and, therefore, for Bon Temps. I practiced a happy smile in the mirror, but it didn't sit right on my face.

I dashed out to my car through the drizzle without bothering to open my umbrella. Maybe a little adrenaline would help me get going. I had very little enthusiasm for anything today held. Since I wasn't sure if Sam would be able or willing to walk across the parking lot to work, I might have to stay until closing. I couldn't keep dumping so much responsibility on employees unless I gave them a bump in pay, and we simply couldn't afford that right now.

As I pulled up behind the bar, I noticed that Bernie's car was gone. She'd meant it when she said she was leaving. Should I go in the bar first or try to catch Sam in his trailer?

While I was still debating, I caught a glimpse of yellow through the rain on my windshield. Sam was standing by the Dumpster, which was conveniently placed between the kitchen door and the employee entrance. He was wearing a yellow plastic rain poncho, one he kept hanging in his office for such occasions. At first, I was so relieved to see him I didn't absorb the message in his body language. He was standing, frozen and stiff, with a bag of garbage in his left hand. He'd shoved the sliding Dumpster lid aside with his right. He was looking into the Dumpster, all his attention focused on something inside.

I had that sinking feeling. You know, the one you get when you realize your whole day has just turned south. "Sam?" I opened my umbrella and hurried over to him. "What's wrong?"

I put my hand on his shoulder. He didn't twitch; it's hard to surprise a shapeshifter. He also didn't speak.

There was more odor than usual coming from the Dumpster.

I choked, but made myself look into the hot metal confines, half-full with bagged garbage.

Arlene wasn't in a bag. She was lying on top. The bugs and the heat had already started to work on her, and now the rain was falling on her swollen, discolored face.

Sam dropped the garbage bag to the ground. With obvious reluctance, he bent forward to touch his fingers to Arlene's neck. He knew as well as I that she was dead. There was nothing in her brain for me to register, and any shifter could smell death.

I said a very bad word. Then I repeated it

a few times.

After a moment Sam said, "I never heard you say that out loud."

"I don't even think it that often." I hated to enlarge on this particular piece of bad news, but I had to. "She was just here yesterday, Sam. In your office. Talking to me."

By silent mutual consent, we moved over to the shelter of the oak tree in Sam's yard. He'd left the Dumpster open, but the raindrops would not hurt Arlene. Sam didn't say anything for a long moment. "I guess lots of people saw her?" he asked.

"I wouldn't call it *lots* of people. We didn't have that many customers. But whoever was in the bar had to have seen her, because she must have come through the front door." I thought for a second. "Yeah, I didn't hear the back door open. She came back to your office while I was working on the mail, and she talked to me for maybe five or ten minutes. It seemed like forever."

"Why would she come to Merlotte's?" Sam looked at me, baffled.

"She said she wanted her job back."

Sam closed his eyes for a long moment. "Like that was going to happen." And he opened them, looking right into mine. "I am so tempted to take her body out of here and dump it somewhere else." He was asking me a question; though I was shocked for a split second, I understood his feelings very well.

"We could do that," I said quietly. "It would sure . . ." *Save us a lot of trouble. Be a terrible thing to do. Take the focus of any investigation away from Merlotte's.* "Be messy," I concluded. "But doable."

Sam put an arm around my shoulders and tried to smile. "They say your best friend will help you move a body," he said. "You must be my best friend."

"I am," I said. "I'll help you move Arlene in a New York minute — if we really decide that's the right thing to do."

"Oh, it isn't," Sam said heavily. "I know it's not. And you know it's not. But I hate the thought of the bar being involved in another police investigation . . . not only the bar, but us personally. We have enough to heal from already. I know you didn't kill Arlene, and you know I didn't. But I don't know if the police will believe that."

"We could put her in the trunk of my car," I said, but I didn't even convince myself that we were going to act on that. I could feel the impulse dying away. To my surprise, Sam hugged me, and we stood in the shade of the tree for a long moment, water dripping down on us as the rain died away to a light drizzle. I'm not sure what Sam was thinking exactly, and I was glad of that; but I could read enough from his head to know that we were sharing a reluctance to start the next phase of today.

After a while, we released each other. Sam said, "Hell. Okay, call the cops."

With no enthusiasm, I called 911.

While we waited, we sat on the steps of Sam's porch. The sun popped out as though it had been cued, and the moisture in the air turned to steam. This was as much fun as sitting in a sauna with clothes on. I felt sweat trickle down my back.

"Do you have any idea what happened to her, what killed her?" I asked. "I didn't look that close."

"I think she was strangled," Sam said. "I'm not sure, she was so bloated, but I believe something is still around her neck. Maybe if I'd watched more episodes of *CSI* . . ."

I snorted. "Poor Arlene," I said, but I didn't sound too grieved.

Sam shrugged. "I don't get to pick who lives and who dies, but Arlene wouldn't have topped my list of people I'd ask mercy for."

"Since she tried to have me killed."

"And not just killed quick," Sam said. "Killed slow and awful. Taking all that into consideration, if there had to be a body in my garbage, I'm not too sorry it's hers."

"Too bad for the kids, though," I said, suddenly realizing there were two people who would miss Arlene for the rest of their lives.

Sam shook his head silently. He was sympathetic to the kids' plight, but Arlene had been transforming into a less-than-stellar mom, and she would have warped them right along with herself. Arlene's adopted brand of extreme intolerance was as bad for children as radiation.

I heard a siren, and as it got louder, my eyes met Sam's in resignation.

What a mess the next two hours were.

Both Andy Bellefleur and Alcee Beck arrived. I tried to stifle a groan. I was friends with Andy's wife, Halleigh, which made this situation doubly awkward . . . though at the moment, social awkwardness was not on the top of my list of worries, and it was preferable to dealing with Alcee Beck, who simply didn't like me. At least the two patrol officers doing the actual evidence gathering were familiar to us; Kevin and Kenya had both graduated from the training course for collecting and processing evidence.

That must have been some course, because the Ks sure seemed to know what they were doing. Despite the smothering heat (the rain didn't seem to have worked in the cooling-down department), the two went about their jobs with careful efficiency. Andy and Alcee took turns helping them and asking us questions, most of which we couldn't answer.

When the coroner came to pick up the body, I heard him remark to Kenya that he figured Arlene had been strangled. I wondered if the pathologist who did the autopsy would reach the same conclusion.

We should have gone inside Sam's trailer, where it was cool, but when I suggested it, Sam said he wanted to keep an eye on what the police were doing. With a long sigh, I pulled my knees up to my chin to get my legs in the shade. I propped my back against the door of the trailer, and after a moment Sam propped his against the rails around the little porch. He'd long since discarded the plastic poncho, and I'd pulled up my hair on top of my head. Sam went in the trailer and came out with two glasses of iced tea. I drank mine in three big gulps and held the cold glass to my forehead.

I was sweaty and gloomy and scared, but at least I wasn't alone.

After Arlene's body had been tagged and bagged and started its pathetic journey to the nearest state medical examiner, Andy came over to talk to us. Kenya and Kevin were now searching the Dumpster, which had to be one of the world's worst tasks — definitely worthy of *Dirty Jobs.* They were both sweating like pigs, and from time to time they'd vent their feelings verbally. Andy was moving slowly and wearily, and I could tell the heat was getting him down.

"Arlene just got out less than a week ago, and she's dead," Andy said heavily. "Halleigh's feeling poorly, and I'd rather be home with her than out here, for God's sake." He glared at us as if we'd planned this encounter. "Dammit, what was she doing here? Did you see her?"

"I did. She came to ask for a job," I said. "Yesterday afternoon. Of course, I told her no. She walked out. I didn't see her after that, and I left for home about . . . seven, or a little later, I guess."

"She say where she was staying?"

"Nope. Maybe in her trailer?" Arlene's trailer was still parked in the little clearing where she'd been (a) shot and (b) arrested.

Andy looked skeptical. "Would it even be still hooked up to electricity? And there must be twenty bullet holes in that thing."

"If you've got somewhere to go to, that's where you go," I said. "Most people have to do that, Andy. They don't have a choice."

Andy was sure I was accusing him of being an elitist since he was a Bellefleur, but I wasn't. I was just stating a fact.

He eyed me resentfully and turned even redder. "Maybe she was staying with friends," he plowed on.

"I just wouldn't know." I privately doubted if Arlene had that many friends anymore, especially ones who would have wanted to host her. Even people who didn't like vampires and didn't think much of women who consorted with the undead might think twice about buddying up to a woman who'd been willing to lure her best friend to a crucifixion. "She did say when she was leaving the bar that she was going to go talk to her two new friends," I added helpfully. I'd heard that in her thoughts, but I'd heard it. I didn't have to spell it out. Andy got all freaked-out when he had to think about what I could do. "But I don't know who she meant."

"You know where her kids are?" Andy asked.

"I do know that." I was pleased to be able to contribute more. "Arlene said they'd been staying with Chessie and Brock John-

145

son. You know them? They live next to where Tray Dawson had his repair shop."

Andy nodded. "Sure. Why the Johnsons, though?"

"Chessie was a Fowler. She's related to the kids' dad, Rick Fowler. That's why Arlene's buddy Helen dumped the kids there."

"And Arlene didn't pick 'em up when she got out?"

"Again, I don't know. She didn't talk like they were with her. But we didn't exactly have a cozy chitchat. I wasn't happy to see her. She wasn't happy to see me. She thought she'd be talking to Sam, I reckon."

"How many times was she married?" Andy finally plopped down in one of Sam's folding aluminum chairs. He pulled out a handkerchief and mopped his forehead.

"Well. Hmm," I said. "She was with John Morgan for about ten minutes, but she never counted that. Then Rene Lenier. Then Rick Fowler, then Doak Oakley, then back to Rick. Now you know everything I do, Andy."

Andy wasn't satisfied with that, as I'd known he wouldn't be. We went over the conversation I'd had with the dead woman, from soup to nuts.

I gave Sam a despairing glance while Andy was looking down at his notes. My patience was wearing thin. Sam interjected, "Why was Arlene out, anyway, Andy? I thought she'd be in a cell for years!"

Embarrassment turned Andy's face even redder than the heat. "She got a good lawyer from somewhere. He filed an appeal and asked she be out on bail before the formal sentencing. He pointed out to the judge that she was a mother, practically a saint, who needed to be with her kids. He said, 'Oh, no, she didn't plan to take part in the killing, she didn't even know it was going to happen.' He practically cried. *Of course* Arlene didn't realize her asshole buddies were planning on killing Sookie. Right."

"*My* killing," I said, straightening up. "The killing of *me*. Just because she didn't plan on personally hammering in a nail . . ." I stopped and took a deep breath. "Okay, she's dead. I hope that judge enjoys being all sympathetic now."

"You sound pretty angry, Sookie," Andy said.

"Of course I am angry," I snapped. "You would be, too. But I didn't come over here in the middle of the night and kill her."

"How do you know it was the middle of the night?"

"I sure can't slip anything by you, Andy," I said. "You got me there." I took a deep

147

breath and told myself to be patient. "I know it had to have happened in the middle of the night because the bar was open until midnight . . . and I don't think anyone would have murdered Arlene and put her in the trash while the bar was full and the cooks were working in the kitchen, Andy. By the time the bar closed, I was asleep in my bed, and I stayed that way."

"Oh, you got a witness to that?" Andy smirked. There were days I liked Andy more than others. Today was not one of those days.

"Yes," I said. "I do."

Andy looked a little shocked, and Sam's face was carefully blank. But I myself was pretty glad that I'd had a nocturnal visitor or two. I'd known this moment would come while I sat sweating and waiting for Arlene's body to be removed. I'd thought it through. Eric had said he wanted his visit to be kept secret, but he hadn't said anything about Karin's.

"Who's your witness?" Andy said.

"A — woman named Karin. Karin Slaughter."

"You switching teams, Sookie? Did she stay all night?"

"None of your business what we were doing, Andy. Last night before the bar closed,

Karin saw me at my house, and she knows I stayed there."

"Sam, what about you? Anyone at your house?" Now Andy was sounding heavily sarcastic, as if we were covering up something.

"Yes," Sam said. Again, Andy looked surprised, and not happy.

"All right, who? Your little girlfriend from Shreveport? She come back from Alaska?"

Sam said steadily, "My mom was here. She left early this morning to get back to Texas, but you can sure call her. I can give you her phone number."

Andy copied it down in his notebook.

"I guess the bar has to be closed today," Sam said. "But I'd appreciate being able to open as soon as I can, Andy. These days, I need all the business I can get."

"You should be able to open at three this afternoon," Andy said.

Sam and I exchanged glances. That was good news, but I knew the bad news was not over, and I tried to convey that to Sam with my eyes. Andy was about to try to shock us with something. I wasn't sure what it was, but I could tell he was baiting his trap.

Andy turned away with an air of unconcern. Abruptly, he turned back to us with the sudden pounce of someone springing an ambush. Since I could read his mind, I knew what was coming. I kept my face blank only because I've had years of practice.

"You recognize this, Sookie?" he asked, showing me a picture. It was a gruesome close-up of Arlene's neck. There was something tied around it. It was a scarf, a green and peacock blue scarf.

I felt remarkably sick.

"That looks kind of like a scarf I used to have," I said. In fact, it was exactly like a scarf I'd gotten by default: the one the werebat Luna had tied around my eyes in Dallas when the shifters had been rescuing me.

That seemed like a decade ago.

Feverishly, I tried to remember what had happened to the scarf. I'd gone back to my hotel with it. After that, I'd left it in my belongings in a Dallas hotel room and returned to Shreveport on my own. Bill had deposited my little suitcase on my porch when he'd returned, and the scarf had been tucked inside. I'd hand-washed it, and it had come out real pretty. Also, it was a memento of an extraordinary night. So I'd kept it. I'd worn it tucked into my coat in winter, tied it around my ponytail the last time I wore my green sundress . . . but that had been a year ago. I was sure I hadn't used it this summer. Since I'd just cleaned out my bedroom drawers, I'd have seen it when I was refolding my scarves, but I had no specific memory of that, which didn't mean a thing. "I sure don't remember the last time I saw it," I said, shaking my head.

"Hmmm," said Andy. He didn't like to think I'd strangled Arlene, and he didn't believe I could have gotten her in the Dumpster by myself. *But,* he thought, *don't people who drink vampire blood get real strong, for a while?* This was one reason vamp blood was the hottest illegal drug around.

I started to tell him out loud that I hadn't had any vampire blood in a long time. But luckily, I thought twice.

There was no point in reminding Andy that I could read his thoughts. And there was no point in telling him that I *had* been very strong from vamp blood . . . but in the past.

I sagged against the wall of the trailer. If Sam's mother could provide Sam an alibi, and if Andy believed Bernie . . . that would leave me as prime suspect. Karin would back up my story, I was certain, but in the eyes of the local law, her testimony would be almost worthless. Andy would be less likely to believe Karin simply because she was a vampire. Other officers who were familiar with the vampire world would believe Karin would have helped me dump Arlene's body if I'd asked her, because she was Eric's child and Eric was my boyfriend, as far as everyone knew.

Hell, I was pretty sure Karin would have killed Arlene for me, if I'd asked. It might take Andy and Alcee a while to figure that out, but they would.

"Andy," I said, "I couldn't get Arlene in that Dumpster if I tried for a month, not without a hoist. You want to test me for vampire blood, you go right ahead. You won't find any in my system. If I'd choked Arlene to death, I hope I wouldn't leave my scarf around her neck. You may not think much of me, but I'm not dumb."

Andy said, "Sookie, I never have known what to think of you." And he walked away.

"That could have gone better," Sam said, in a huge understatement. "I remember you wearing that scarf last winter. You wore it to church, tied around your ponytail, with a black dress."

Well. You never know what men will remember. I started to feel a little touched and tender. Sam said, "You were sitting right in front of me, and I was looking at

152

the back of your head the whole service."

I nodded. That was more like it. "I wish I knew what had happened to it since then. I'd like to know who got it out of my house and used it on Arlene. I know I wore it to the bar once. I don't know if it got lifted out of my purse or stolen from my drawer in my bedroom. That's gross and sneaky." At that moment I remembered my drawer being ajar. I wrinkled my nose, thinking of someone pawing through my scarves and panties. And one or two things had seemed to be out of place. I told Sam about the little incident. "It doesn't sound like much when I say it out loud, though," I concluded ruefully.

He smiled, just a little upturn of his lips, but I was glad to see it. His hair was wilder than usual, which was saying something. The sun caught the reddish bristles on his chin. "You need to shave," I said.

"Yeah," he agreed, but absently. "We'll check it out. I was wondering . . . Andy knows you can read minds. But it seems like he can't keep that in his head when he's talking to you. Does that happen a lot?"

"He knows, but he doesn't know. He's not the only one who acts that way. The people who do get that I'm different — not just a little crazy — they still don't seem to get it

153

completely. Andy's a true believer. He really understands that I can see what's in his head. But he just can't adapt to that."

"You can't hear me that way," Sam said, just to reaffirm what he already knew.

"General mood and intent, I pick up. But not specific thoughts. That's always the way with supernaturals."

"Like?"

It took me a minute to interpret that. "Like, right now I can tell you're worried, you're glad I'm here, you're wishing we'd cut the scarf off her neck before the police got here. It's easy to get that, because I'm wishing the same damn thing."

Sam grimaced. "That's what I get for being squeamish. I knew there was something around her throat, but I didn't want to look any closer. And I definitely didn't want to touch her again."

"Who would?" We fell silent. We sweated. We watched. Since we were sitting on Sam's own steps, looking over his own hedge, they could hardly tell us to go away. After a while, I got so bored that I called or texted the people due to work today to tell them to come in at three. I thought of all the lawyers I knew, and debated which one to call if I had to. Beth Osiecki had prepared my will, and I'd liked her real well. Her

154

partner, Jarrell Hilburn, had prepared the document that formalized my loan to Sam to keep the business afloat, and he'd also prepared the paperwork giving me part interest in the bar.

On the other hand, Desmond Cataliades was very effective and personally interested in me, since he'd been best buds with my biological grandfather. But he was based in New Orleans and had a brisk trade, since he was knowledgeable about both the supernatural world and American law. I didn't know if the part-demon would be able or willing to come to my aid. His e-mail had been friendly, and he'd talked about coming to see me. It would cost me an arm and a leg (not literally), but as soon as the bank released the check from Claudine's estate, I'd be good for his fee.

In the meantime, maybe the police would find another suspect and make an arrest. Maybe I wouldn't need a lawyer. I thought about the last statement I'd received for my savings account. After the ten thousand I'd put into Merlotte's, I had around three thousand remaining from the money I'd earned from the vampires. I'd just inherited a lot of money — $150,000 — from my fairy godmother, Claudine, and you'd think I'd be sitting pretty. But the bank issuing the check had come under sudden and vigorous scrutiny by the Louisiana government, and all its checks had been frozen. I'd called my bank to find out what was up. My money was there . . . but I couldn't use it. I found this utterly suspicious.

I texted Eric's daytime man, Mustapha. "Hope Karin will be available to tell police she saw me last night and I was home the whole time," I typed, and sent it before something happened to stop me. That was a huge hint, and I hoped Karin got it.

"Sookie," Alcee Beck said, and his deep voice was like the voice of doom. "You don't need to be telling anyone what's happening here." I hadn't even seen him approach, I was so lost in calculation and concern.

"I wasn't," I said honestly. That was what I called a fairy truth. The fae didn't out-and-out lie, but they could give a convoluted version of the truth to leave a completely false impression. I met his dark eyes and I didn't flinch. I'd faced scarier beings than Alcee.

"Right," he said disbelievingly, and moved away. He went out to the edge of the parking lot to his car, which was pulled into the shade of a tree, and bent to reach in the open window. As he walked back to the bar, putting on his sunglasses, I thought I saw a quick motion in the woods by his car. Weird. I shook my head to clear it, looked again. I saw nothing, not a flicker of movement.

Sam got us two bottles of water from the trailer refrigerator. I opened mine gratefully and drank, then held the chilly bottle to my neck. It felt wonderful.

"Eric visited me last night," I said, without any premeditation. I saw Sam's hands go still. I very carefully wasn't looking at his face. "I'd gone to see him at Fangtasia, and he wouldn't even talk to me while I was there. It was beyond humiliating. Last night he stayed about five minutes, tops. He said he wasn't supposed to be there. Here's the thing. I've got to keep it secret."

"What the hell . . . ? Why?"

"Some vampire reason. I'll find out soon enough. The point is, he left Karin there. She's his other child, his oldest. She was supposed to protect me, but I don't think Eric ever thought of something like this happening. I think he thought someone was going to try to sneak in the house. But assuming Karin will tell Alcee and Andy that I didn't leave my house last night, he did me a great good deed."

"If the police will accept the word of a vampire."

"There's that. And they can't question her

until tonight. And I have no idea how to get in touch with her, so I left a message with Mustapha. Here's Part Two of the bad Eric stuff. He told me I would be seeing him tonight, but he warned me I wouldn't like it. It sounded pretty official. I kind of have to go, if I'm not in jail, that is." I tried to smile. "It's not going to be fun."

"You want me to come with you?"

That was an amazing offer. I appreciated it, and I said so. But I had to add, "I think I have to get through this by myself, Sam. Just now, the sight of you might make Eric more . . . upset."

Sam nodded in acknowledgment. But he looked worried. After some hesitation, he said, "What do you *think* is going to happen, Sook? If you have to go, you have the right to have someone with you. It's not like you are going to a movie with Eric or something."

"I don't think I'm in physical danger. I'm just . . . I don't know." I believed — I anticipated — that Eric was going to repudiate me publicly. I just couldn't push the words out of my throat. "Some vampire bullshit," I muttered dismally.

Sam put his hand on my shoulder. It was almost too hot for even that slight contact, but I could tell he was trying to let me know

158

he was ready to back me up. "Where are you two meeting?"

"Fangtasia or Eric's house, I suppose. He'll let me know."

"The offer stands."

"Thanks." I smiled at him, but it was a weak attempt. "But I don't want anyone more agitated than they're gonna be." Meaning Eric.

"Then call me when you get home?"

"I can do that. Might be pretty late."

"That doesn't matter."

Sam had always been my friend, though we'd had our ups and our downs and our arguments. It would be insulting to tell him that he didn't owe me anything for bringing him back to life. He knew that.

"I woke up different," Sam said suddenly. He'd been thinking during the little pause, too.

"How?"

"I'm not sure, yet. But I'm tired of . . ." His voice trailed off.

"Of what?"

"Of living my life like there'll be plenty of tomorrows so what I do today doesn't matter."

"You think something's going to happen to you?"

"No, not exactly," he said. "I'm afraid

nothing will happen to me. When I work it out, I'll let you know." He smiled at me; it was a rueful smile, but it had warmth.

"Okay," I said. I made myself smile back. "You do that."

And we returned to watching the police do their thing, each sunk in our own thoughts. I hope Sam's were happier than mine. I didn't see how the day could get much crappier. But it could.

ELSEWHERE
that night

"I think we can call him now," the medium man said, and took out his cell phone. "You take care of the throwaway."

The tall man extracted a cheap cell phone from his pocket. He stomped on it a few times, enjoying the crushing of the glass and metal. He picked up the carcass of the telephone and dropped it into a deep puddle. The short driveway from the road to the front of the trailer was dimpled with such puddles. Anyone driving in would be sure to press the phone into the mud.

The medium man would have preferred some method of disposal that completely obliterated the little collection of circuitry and metal, but that would do. He was frowning when the call he placed went through.

"Yes?" said a silky voice.

"It's done. The body's found, the scarf was on it, I retrieved the magic coin, and I've planted the charm in the detective's car."

"Call me again when it happens," said the voice. "I want to enjoy it."

"Then we're through with this project," the medium man said, and he might have been a little hopeful that was so. "And the money will be in our accounts. It's been a pleasure working with you." His voice was quite empty of sincerity.

"No," said the voice on the other end. It held such promise; you just knew that whoever could speak that way must be beautiful. The medium man, who'd actually met the owner of the voice, shuddered. "No," the voice repeated. "Not quite through."

CHAPTER 7

By the time I was able to leave work, I felt like I'd been steamed and left out on the counter.

We had gotten to open at three on the dot, to my surprise. By then rumors and facts had spread all over Bon Temps. A big crowd showed up at Merlotte's just pining to get the lowdown on what had actually happened. What with questions from every customer and the endless speculations of Andrea Norr, I was fixing to start screaming.

"So who could have put her in the Dumpster, and how'd they get her in there?" An said for the fiftieth time. "Antoine puts the kitchen trash in there. That's disgusting."

"It sure is," I said, just managing not to bite her head off. "That's why we're not going to talk about it."

"Okay! Okay! I get your drift, Sookie. Mum's the word. At least I'm telling everyone that you didn't do it, sweetie." And she went right back to talking. There was no doubt that gossipy An had the mysterious "it." Following her movements around the bar was like watching an all-male rendition of the wave.

It was nice to know that An was telling everyone I wasn't guilty, but it was depressing to think that anyone would have assumed I was. An's reasoning echoed that of the detectives. It seemed impossible that a lone woman could lift Arlene, literally a dead weight, up into the mouth of the Dumpster.

In fact, when I tried to picture the insertion, the only way such a maneuver would work for one person would be if the killer already had Arlene over his shoulder (and I was using *his* because it would take a strong person to lift Arlene that way). She had gotten skinny, but she was still no featherweight.

Two people could do it easily enough — or one supernatural of any gender.

I glanced over at Sam, working behind the bar. Since he was a shifter, he was incredibly strong. He could easily have tossed Arlene's corpse into the trash.

He could have, but he hadn't.

The most obvious reason was that he

would never put Arlene's corpse in the Dumpster right behind his business in the first place. Second, Sam would never have staged himself finding the body with me as witness. And third, I simply didn't believe he would have killed Arlene, not without some compelling reason or in the heat of some terrible struggle. Fourth, he would already have told me if either of those circumstances applied.

If Andy understood that I couldn't get Arlene in there by myself, he must be trying to figure out who would help me do such a thing. When I considered that, I *did* have a lot of friends and acquaintances who were not strangers to body disposal. They would help me with few questions asked. But what did that say about my life?

Okay, screw the brooding introspection. My life was what it was. If it had been tougher and bloodier than I'd ever imagined . . . that was a done deal.

Suspect Number One for "helping Sookie dispose of a body" came in right after that. My brother, Jason, was a werepanther, and though he hadn't ever changed publicly, word had gotten around. Jason had never been able to keep his mouth shut when he was excited about something. If I'd called him to help me put a woman in a Dumpster, he would have jumped in his pickup and been there as fast as he could drive.

I waved at my brother as he walked in the door holding hands with his Michele. Jason was still stained and sweaty after a long, hot day's work as a boss of one of the parish road crews. Michele looked perky in contrast, in her red polo shirt all the employees wore at the Schubert Ford dealership. They were both in the throes of marriage fever. But like everyone else in Bon Temps, they were fascinated by the death of a former Merlotte's server.

I didn't want to talk about Arlene, so I headed them off by telling Michele I'd found a dress to wear in the wedding. Their forthcoming ceremony took precedence over everything else, even a lurid death in the parking lot. As I'd hoped, Michele asked me a million questions and said she was going to come by to look at it, and she told me Greater Love Baptist (Michele's dad's church) was willing to lend their folding tables and chairs for the potluck reception at Jason's house. A friend of Michele's had volunteered to make the cake as her wedding present to the happy couple, and the mother of another friend was going to do the flowers at cost. By the time they'd finished their meals and paid their tab, the word "strangled" hadn't entered the conversation.

That was the only respite I had the whole evening. Though I'd noticed the bar crowd was thin the previous day, an amazing number of people now told me they'd seen Arlene enter Merlotte's. They'd all spoken to her personally before watching her go to the office. And they'd all watched her leave (either five or fifteen or fifty minutes afterward) with steam coming out of her ears. No matter how their stories varied on other points of interest, to me that was the important memory: that she'd left, alive and unharmed. And angry.

"Did she come to ask your forgiveness?" Maxine Fortenberry asked. Maxine had come in to have supper with two of her cronies, buddies of my grandmother's.

"No, she wanted a job," I said, with as much frank and open honesty as I could plaster on my face.

All three women looked delightfully shocked. "Not really," Maxine breathed. "She had the gall to ask if she could have her job back?"

"She couldn't see why not," I said, lifting a shoulder as I gathered up their dirty plates. "You all want a refill on your tea?"

"Sure, bring the pitcher around," Maxine

said. "My Lord, Sookie. That just takes the cake."

She was absolutely right.

The next moment I had to spare was spent cudgeling my brain to try to remember when I'd last seen that blue and green scarf. Sam had said he remembered me wearing it to church with a black dress. That would have been to a funeral, because I didn't like to wear black and reserved it for the most serious occasions. Whose funeral? Maybe Sid Matt Lancaster's? Or Caroline Bellefleur's? I'd been to several funerals in the past couple of years, since most of Gran's friends were aging, but Sam wouldn't have gone to those.

Jane Bodehouse drifted into Merlotte's close to suppertime. She clambered onto her usual stool at the bar. I could feel my face get tight and angry when I looked at her. "You've got some nerve, Jane," I said baldly. "Why do you want to drink here, when you're so damaged by the firebomb incident? I can't believe you can endure coming in here, you suffered so much."

She was surprised for a second until the cogs in her brain turned enough to give up the memory that she'd hired a lawyer. She looked away, ostentatiously, trying to brazen it out.

The next time I passed her, she'd asked Sam to give her some more pretzels. He was reaching for the bowl. "Better hurry," I said bitchily. "We don't want Jane to get upset and call her lawyer." Sam looked at me in surprise. He hadn't seen the mail yet. "Jane's suing us, Sam," I said, and marched to the hatch to give the next order to Antoine. "For her hospital expenses and maybe for her mental distress," I threw over my shoulder.

"Jane," Sam said behind me, genuinely amazed. "Jane Bodehouse! Where are you gonna drink if you sue us? We're the only bar in the area that lets you in these days!" Sam was telling her no more than the truth. Over the years, most of the bars in the area had come to refuse to serve Jane, who was prone to make sloppy passes at any man in her immediate vicinity. Only the drunkest men responded, because Jane wasn't as careful with her personal hygiene as she had been even a year before.

"You can't stop serving me," she said indignantly. "Marvin says so. And that lawyer."

"I think we can," Sam said. "Starting now. You even know what that lawsuit says?" That was a shrewd bet.

As if he'd heard us, here came Marvin

through the door, and he was mighty mad. "Mama!" he called. "What are you doing here? I told you, you can't come here no more." He caught my eye and glanced away, abashed. Everyone in Merlotte's stopped what they were doing to listen. It was almost as good as reality television.

"Marvin," I said, "I'm just hurt down to my toes that you would treat us like this. All these times I've called you instead of letting your mama drive home. All these times we've cleaned her up when she got sick, to say nothing of the night I stopped her from taking a guy into the ladies' room. Are you going to keep your mama at home every night? How are you going to cope?"

I wasn't saying anything that wasn't the truth. And Marvin Bodehouse knew it.

"Just half the emergency room bill, then?" he said, pathetically.

"I'll pay her bill," Sam said handsomely. Of course, he hadn't seen it. "But only after we get a letter from your lawyer saying you're not going to seek anything else."

Marvin glared down at his shoes for a second. Then he said, "I guess you can stay, Mama. Try not to drink too much, you hear?"

"Sure, honey," Jane said, tapping the bar in front of her. "A chaser for that beer," she told Sam, in a lady-of-the-manor voice.

"Putting that on your tab," Sam said. And suddenly the life of the bar was back to normal. Marvin shuffled out, and Jane drank. I felt sorry for both of them, but I was not in charge of their lives, and all I could do was try to keep Jane off the roads when she was drunk.

An and I worked hard. Since everyone who came in proved to be hungry (maybe they needed fuel to produce their gossip), Antoine was so busy he lost his temper a couple of times, an unusual occurrence. Sam tried to find time to smile and greet people, but he was hustling to keep up with bar orders. My feet hurt, and my hair needed to be released from its ponytail, brushed, and put back up. I was looking forward to a shower with a craving almost sexual in its intensity. I actually managed to forget my appointment — I wasn't going to call it a date — with Eric for later that night, but when it crossed my mind I realized I hadn't gotten a definite time or place from him.

"Screw it," I said to the plate of curly fries I was carrying to a table of auto-shop mechanics. "Here you go, fellas. And here's some hot sauce, if you want to live dangerously. Eat and enjoy."

Right on the heels of that thought, Karin glided through the front door. She looked around her as if she were in the monkey house at the zoo. Her eyebrows elevated slightly. Then she locked in on me, and she made her way toward me with a smoothness and economy of movement I envied.

"Sookie," she said quietly, "Eric needs you to come to him now." We were attracting no small amount of attention. Karin's beauty, her pallor, and her creepy glide were a combo that added up to *Watch me, I'm beautiful and lethal.*

"Karin, I'm working," I said, in that sort of hiss that comes out when you're pissed off but trying to keep your voice down. "See? Earning a living?"

She looked around her. "Here? Truly?" Her tiny white nose wrinkled.

I took hold of my temper with both hands. "Yes, here. This is my business."

Sam came up, trying hard to act casual. "Sookie, who's your friend?"

"Sam, this is Karin the — this is Karin Slaughter, my alibi for last night. She's here to tell me Eric needs me in Shreveport. Now."

Sam was trying to look genial, but it didn't reach his eyes. "Karin, nice to meet you.

We're pretty busy. Can't Eric wait for an hour?"

"No." Karin didn't look stubborn or angry or impatient. She looked matter-of-fact.

We stood silently regarding each other for a long moment.

"All right, Sook, I'll take your tables," Sam said. "Don't worry about it. We'll manage."

"You're the boss, Sam." Karin's arctic eyes gave my boss — my partner — a laserlike examination.

"I'm the boss, Sam," he said agreeably. "Sook, I'll come if you need me . . ."

"I'll be fine," I said, though I knew that wasn't true. "Really, don't worry."

Sam looked torn. A group of thirtyish women who were celebrating a divorce began hollering for a refill on their pitcher of beer. They were the deciding factor. "Will you be responsible for her safety?" Sam said to Karin.

"With my existence," Karin said calmly.

"Let me get my purse," I told Karin, and hurried to the lockers at the back of the storeroom. I whipped off my apron, dropped it in the "dirty" barrel, and changed into a clean T-shirt from my locker. I brushed my hair in the ladies' room, though since it had a dent all around from the elastic band, I had to put it back up in its ponytail. At least it looked neater.

No shower, no fresh dress, no nice shoes. At least I had lipstick.

I stuck my tongue out at the mirror and slung my purse over my shoulder. Time to face the music, though I didn't know what tune would be playing.

I didn't know how Karin had arrived at Merlotte's; maybe she could fly, like Eric. She rode with me in my car to Shreveport. Eric's oldest child wasn't much of a talker. Her only question was, "How long did it take you to learn to drive a car?" She seemed mildly interested when I told her I'd taken driver's education in high school. After that, she stared ahead of her. She might be thinking deep thoughts about the world economy, or she might be totally miffed that she'd gotten escort detail. I had no way of knowing.

Finally, I said, "Karin, I guess you just got to Louisiana recently. How long had it been since you'd seen Eric?"

"I arrived two days ago. It had been two hundred and fifty-three years since I saw my maker."

"I guess he hadn't changed much," I said, perhaps a bit sarcastically. Vampires never changed.

"No," she said, and fell silent again.

She wasn't going to give me a way to ease into the topic I had to broach. I simply had to take the plunge. "Karin, as I asked Mustapha to tell you, the police in Bon Temps may want to talk to you about when you saw me last night."

Karin did turn to look at me then. Though I was watching the road, I could see the movement of her head out of the corner of my eye.

"Mustapha gave me your message, yes. What shall I say?" she asked.

"That you saw me in my house about eleven thirty or midnight, whichever it was, and that you watched the house until daybreak, so you know I didn't leave," I said. "Isn't that the truth?"

Karin said, "It might be." And then she didn't say one more word.

Karin was pretty fucking irritating. Excuse me.

I was actually glad to get to Fangtasia. I was used to parking in the back with the staff. Just as I was about to drive around the row of stores, Karin said, "It is blocked off. You must leave your car out here."

Since the first time I'd been here with Bill, I'd seldom parked in front with the customers. I'd been a privileged visitor for months. I'd fought and bled with the Fangtasia staff, and I'd counted some of them as my friends, or at least my allies. Now, apparently, I was one of the crowd of casual human thrill-seekers. It hurt a little bit.

I was sure that would prove to be the least of my hurts.

While I was giving myself a pep talk, I was cruising through the rows of cars looking for a space. The search took a few minutes. I could hear a faint strain of music when we got out of the car, so I knew there must be a live band tonight ("live" in the sense that they were actually onstage).

Every now and then a vampire group would play a few sets at Shreveport's only vamp bar, and this seemed to be one of those nights. Newly turned vampires played covers of music they had loved in life, recent human music, but the old vampires would play things that living people had never heard, mixed in with some human songs they found appealing. I'd never met a vampire who didn't love "Thriller."

At least Karin and I were able to bypass the line waiting at the cover charge booth, which was occupied by a snarling Thalia. I was glad to see her arm had reattached, and I tapped my own right forearm and gave her a thumbs-up. Her face relaxed for a moment, which was as close as Thalia got to a smile unless flowing blood was involved.

Inside the club, the noise level was tolerable. The sensitivity of vamp hearing kept the volume at a level I could endure. Crowded together on the little music platform was a cluster of very hairy men and women. I was willing to bet they'd been turned in the sixties. The nineteen sixties. On the West Coast. It was a big clue when they ended "Honky Tonk Women" to flow into "San Francisco." I peeked at their tattered jeans. Yep, bell-bottoms. Headbands. Flowered shirts. Flowing locks. A slice of history here in Shreveport.

And then Eric was standing beside me, and my heart gave a little leap. I didn't know if it was happiness at his proximity, or apprehension that this might be the last time I'd see him, or simple fear. His hand touched my face as his head bent toward mine. He said into my ear, just loud enough for me to hear, "This is what has to be done, but never doubt my affection."

He bent even closer. I thought he was going to kiss me, but he was just getting my scent. Vampires only inhale when they really want to savor a smell, and that was what he was doing.

He took my hand to lead me to the management part of the bar, to his office. He looked back at me once, and I could tell he was reminding me without words that he wanted me to remember that whatever was coming was all a show.

Every muscle in my body tensed.

Eric's office wasn't big, and it wasn't grand, but it sure was crowded. Pam was leaning against a wall, looking amazingly suburban-chic in pink capris and a flowered tank, but any relief I might have experienced on seeing a familiar face was simply swamped by more apprehension when I recognized Felipe de Castro — King of Nevada, Louisiana, and Arkansas — and Freyda, Queen of Oklahoma. I'd been sure they'd be there, one or the other, but to see both . . . my heart sank.

The presence of royalty never meant anything good.

Felipe was behind the desk, sitting in Eric's chair, naturally. He was flanked by his right hand, Horst Friedman, and his consort, Angie Weatherspoon. Angie was a leggy redhead I'd hardly exchanged two words with. I'd hate her forever because she'd danced on Eric's favorite table while wearing spike-heeled shoes.

Maybe I would write a rap song called "Flanked by His Flunkies."

177

Maybe Eric's table wasn't my problem any longer.

Maybe I should crawl back into my right mind instead of freaking out.

There was a throw rug in front of the desk. Eric and I had been literally called on the carpet.

"Looking real, Sookie," Pam said. Of course she would comment on my waitress outfit. I probably smelled like French fries.

"I didn't have a choice," I said.

"Meees Stekhuss," Felipe said pleasantly. "How nice to see you again."

"Hmmm," Freyda said, from her chair against the wall facing the door. It seemed she disagreed.

I glanced behind me to see that an expressionless Karin was blocking the doorway. Pam was Emo Emma compared to Karin. "I'll be right outside," Eric's oldest announced. She took a step back, and then she shut the door very firmly.

"So here we are, a big extended family," I said. Kind of shows you how nervous I was.

Pam rolled her eyes. She didn't seem to feel that now was the time for humor.

"Sookie," Felipe de Castro said, and I saw we'd dispensed with honorifics. "Eric has called you here to release you from your marriage to him."

It was like being smacked in the face with a large dead fish.

I made myself hold still, made my face freeze. There's halfway wanting, or suspecting, or even expecting — and there's knowing. Knowing at least has some certainty about it, but also a sharper, deeper pain.

Of course, I'd had conflicted feelings about my relationship with Eric. Of course, I'd more or less seen the handwriting on the wall. But no matter Eric's little midnight visit and his previous hurried heads-up, this bald pronouncement was a shock — one I wasn't going to bow down to, not in front of these creatures. I began sealing off little compartments inside myself — just like the ones that had theoretically ensured that the *Titanic* was unsinkable.

I did not even glance at Freyda. If I saw pity in her face, I would jump her and try to smack her down, whether that meant suicide or not. I hoped she was sneering in triumph, because that would be more tolerable.

Looking at Eric's face was out of the question.

All this rage and misery swept through me like a windstorm. When I was certain my voice wouldn't quaver, I said, "Is there some paper to sign, some ceremony? Or shall I just walk out?"

"There is a ceremony."

Of course there was. Vampires had a ritual for everything.

Pam came to my side with a familiar black velvet bundle in her hands. To my vague surprise, though I wasn't really feeling much of anything, she leaned over to give me a cold kiss on the cheek. She said, "You just nick yourself on the arm and you say, 'This is yours no longer,' to Eric. You hand the knife to Eric." She unfolded the velvet to expose the knife.

The ceremonial blade was gleaming and ornate and sharp, just as I remembered it. I had a momentary impulse to sink it into one of the silent hearts around me. I didn't know which one I'd aim for first: Felipe's, Freyda's, or even Eric's. Before I could think of this too much, I took the knife in my right hand and poked my left forearm. A tiny trickle of blood coursed down my arm, and I felt every vampire in the room react.

Felipe actually shut his eyes to savor the bouquet. "You are giving up more than I ever imagined," he murmured to Eric. (Felipe moved to the top of my stab-in-the-heart list instantly.)

I turned to face Eric, but I kept my eyes

on his chest. To look up at his face would be to risk cracking. "This is yours no longer," I said clearly, with a certain amount of satisfaction. I held the knife out in his general direction, and I felt him remove it from my grasp. Eric bared his own forearm and stabbed himself — not the jab I'd given my arm, but a real slice. The dark blood flowed sluggishly down his arm to his hand and dripped on the worn carpet.

"This is yours no longer," Eric said quietly.

"You may go now, Sookie," Felipe said. "You will not come to Fangtasia again."

There was nothing left to say.

I turned and walked out of Eric's office. The door opened magically in front of me. Karin's pale eyes met mine briefly. There was no expression on her lovely face. No one said a word. Not "Good-bye," or "It's been swell," or "Kiss my foot."

I made my way through the dancing crowd.

And back to my car.

And I drove home.

CHAPTER 8

Bill was sitting in a lawn chair in my back-yard. I got out of my car and stared across the hood at him. I had two conflicting impulses.

The first was to invite him into my house for some vengeance sex.

The second, smarter one was to pretend I hadn't seen him.

Apparently, he wasn't going to speak until I did, which proved how smart Bill could be on occasion. I was sure, simply because of his presence and the intensity with which he regarded me, that he was fully aware of what had happened tonight. My smarter self prevailed after a brief internal struggle, and I spun around and went into the house.

The necessity of focusing on my driving was gone. The pressure of the presence of the vampires was gone. I was so glad to be alone with no one to watch my face crumple.

I couldn't totally blame Eric. But I did, mostly. He'd had a choice, whether he'd admitted it to himself or not. Though his culture demanded he honor his dead sire's agreement and marry the Queen of Oklahoma, I believed that Eric could have finagled his way out of that agreement. I didn't accept his contention that he was helpless in the face of Appius's wish. Sure, Appius had already set the machinery in motion with Freyda before he'd consulted Eric. Maybe he'd even collected a finder's fee from the Queen of Oklahoma. But Eric could have bullshitted his way free somehow. He could have discovered another candidate for the position of Freyda's consort. He could have offered financial compensation. He could have . . . done *something*.

Faced with the choice between loving me for my short lifetime and beginning an upward climb with the rich and beautiful Freyda, he had made the practical decision.

I'd always known that Eric was a pragmatist.

There was a quiet knock at the back door. Bill, checking on my well-being. I went out onto the porch and flung the door open, saying, "I just can't talk . . ."

Eric stood on the steps. The moonlight

was kind to him, of course, gilding the blond mane and the handsome face.

"What the fuck are you doing here?" I looked over his shoulder. Bill was nowhere in sight. "Now that I'm not your wife, I thought you and Freyda would be . . . consummating your new relationship."

"I told you not to pay attention to what happened," he said. He took a small step forward. "I told you it meant nothing to me."

I didn't invite him in. "Pretty hard to believe it meant nothing to your king. And Freyda."

"I can keep you," he said, with absolute confidence. "I can work out a way. You may not be my wife in name, but you are in my heart."

I felt like a pancake that had just been flipped over on the griddle. I had to go through this *again*? I snapped.

"Not just no, but *hell* no. Don't you hear yourself? You're lying to me and to yourself." I wanted to smack his face so badly my hand hurt.

"Sookie, you're mine." He was beginning to be angry.

"I am not. You said that in front of everyone."

"But I told you, I came to you in the night

and told you I would —"

"You told me that you loved me as much as you were able," I said, almost bouncing on the balls of my feet in agitation. "It seems pretty clear that you're not able."

"Sookie, I would never have dismissed you like that, so publicly, if I hadn't been sure you understood that the ceremony was for the benefit of the others."

"Wait, wait, wait," I said, holding up a hand. "You're telling me that as far as you're concerned, you plan to find a way to keep me somewhere secret from Freyda, so you can sneak off and be with me from time to time? And to be your piece on the side, I'd have to move to Oklahoma and lose my house and friends and business?"

I knew from the expression on his face that that was exactly what he'd planned. But I was also sure he could never have really believed I would say yes to such an arrangement. If he had, he truly didn't know me.

Eric lost *his* temper. "You never gave our marriage honor! You always thought I would leave you! I should have turned you without asking, as I did Karin and Pam! Or better yet, gotten Pam to turn you! We need not have parted, ever again."

And then we were staring at each other —

him furious, me horrified. We'd talked about my becoming a vampire one night in bed, after fireworks sex, and the idea had surfaced at other times. I'd always said clearly that I didn't want that.

"You considered doing that. Without my consent."

"Of course," he said, emphatically, impatiently, as if my not understanding his intent was ridiculous. "Naturally, I did. I knew if you were turned . . . you would be so glad. There is nothing better than being a vampire. But you seemed repulsed by the idea. At first I thought, 'She loves the sun — but she loves me, too.' But I began to wonder if in your heart you really despised what I am." His brows drew together; he was not only angry, he was hurt.

That made two of us.

I said, "And yet you were thinking of turning me into something you thought I despised." I felt incredibly depressed. My energy left me and I slumped in my shoes. I said wearily, "No, I do not despise what you are. I just want to live my human life."

"Even if it means without me."

"I didn't know I had to make a choice."

"Sookie, common sense — you have plenty of that — must have told you so. I am sure of it."

186

I threw up my hands in despair. "Eric, you tricked me into a marriage. I worked around that in my head because I could see you did it to protect me, and maybe you also did it out of your own sense of . . . mischief. I loved you. And I felt flattered that you wanted us to be united in your world's eyes. But you're right when you say I never regarded our marriage as equal to a human church marriage — which, the only time I brought it up, you mocked."

He flung his arm out as if he were struggling to make a point by gesture, a point that he couldn't make verbally.

I held up my hand again. "I'm being completely honest with you. Let me finish, then you can say whatever you need to. I have loved you for months, with . . . with ardor and devotion. But I don't think there's any way we can resolve this. Because you *must know* that saying you 'thought there would still be a way for us to be together' is just plain bullshit. You know that I would never leave home to live some kind of half life as your girl on the side, sneaking sex from time to time until Freyda found out I was there and killed me. Going through the same humiliation that I did tonight. Over and over."

"I should have known you would never

leave Sam," Eric said, with heavy bitterness.

"Leave Sam out of this. This is about you and me."

"You never believed we would be lovers forever. You were sure someday I would leave you, when you grew old."

I thought that over. "Since I'm trying to be honest here, you should try that, too. You would never have even considered staying with me when I grew old. You *always* assumed you would turn me, even though I told you I never wanted to be a vampire." We'd come full circle in this awful conversation. I stepped back and closed the porch door. To put an end to the pain, I said, "I rescind your invitation."

I went back into the house, and I did not look out the windows. The love we'd had for each other lay broken irreparably. It bled out somewhere on my back doorstep.

If the day had been rough, with Arlene's murder and the subsequent furor, and the trip to Fangtasia had been rougher, this conversation with Eric was the roughest thing of all. I sat in my living room in Gran's favorite chair, staring into space, my hands on my knees. I didn't know if I wanted to cry or scream or throw something or throw up. I sat there like a sphinx, thoughts and images tumbling through my head.

I was sure I had done the right thing, though I regretted bitterly some of the things I'd said. But they'd all been true. The hour after Eric left was like the second after I'd persuaded myself to rip off a bandage so I could tend to the wound.

Who could not love Eric? He was bigger than life, literally. Even dead, he was more vital than almost all the men I knew. Clever and practical, protective of his own, a renowned fighter, he was nonetheless full of joie de vivre — or maybe I should call it joie de mort. And he had a sense of humor and adventure, qualities I'd always found incredibly attractive. Plus, jeez, *sexy*. Eric's wonderful body matched his great skill in using it.

But still . . . I would not be a vampire for him. I loved being human. I loved the sunshine; I loved the daytime; I loved to stretch out on a chaise lounge in the backyard with the light surrounding me. And though I was not a good Christian, I was a Christian. I didn't know what would happen to my soul if I was turned into a vampire, and I didn't want to risk it — especially since I'd done some pretty bad things in my time. I wanted some years to atone.

I wasn't blaming Eric for those bad things

I'd done. Those transgressions were on me. But I didn't want the rest of my life to be like that. I wanted a chance to come to terms with the lives I'd taken, the violence I'd seen and I'd dealt out, and I wanted to be a better person . . . though at the moment, I wasn't sure how to accomplish that.

I was sure that being Eric's secret mistress was not the path to that goal.

I pictured myself in some little apartment in Oklahoma, without any family or friends, spending long days and longer nights waiting for Eric to steal an hour or two to come by. I'd be waiting every night for the queen to find me and kill me . . . or worse. If Eric turned me, or got Pam to do the deed, I'd at least have my days taken care of; I'd be dead in a small, dark space. Maybe I'd spend my nights hanging around with Pam and Karin, we three blondes, waiting at Eric's beck and call — for eternity. I shuddered. The mental image of me hanging around with Karin and Pam — like Dracula's females, waiting for an unwary passerby in some Gothic castle — was simply disgusting. I'd want to stake myself. (After a year or two, probably Pam would be glad to oblige me with that.) And what if Eric ordered me to kill someone, someone I cared about? I'd have to obey him.

And that was if I survived the change, which was by no means certain. I read every week about bodies that had been found in hastily dug graves, bodies that had never reanimated, never clawed their way to the surface. People who'd thought it would be cool to be undead and persuaded or paid some vampire to turn them. But they hadn't risen.

I shuddered again.

There was more to think about and more ground to retread, but suddenly I was dazed with exhaustion. I wouldn't have imagined I could get into bed and close my eyes ever again, after a day like today . . . but my body thought otherwise, and I let it rule.

I might rue what I'd said this night when I woke up in the daytime. I might call myself a fool and pack my bags for Oklahoma. Right now, I had to let my regrets and conjectures go. As I scrubbed my face at the bathroom sink, I remembered I'd made a promise. Instead of calling Sam and having to answer questions, I texted him. "Home okay, bad but over."

I slept without dreams and woke to another day of rain.

The police were at my door, and they arrested me for murder.

The tall man was lying back on the double bed, his big hands clasped over his belly, his expression totally satisfied. "God be praised," he said to the ceiling. "Sometimes the evildoers get punished as they deserve."

His roommate ignored him. He was on the telephone again. "Yes," the medium man was saying. "It's confirmed. She's been arrested. Are we through here now? If we stay any longer, we run the risk of being noticed, and in my companion's case . . ." He glanced over at the other bed. The tall man had left his bed to go to the bathroom, and he'd shut the door. The medium man continued in a hushed voice. "In his case, recognized. We couldn't use the trailer because the police were sure to search it, and we couldn't risk leaving trace, even with the Bon Temps police department. We've been changing motels every night."

The rich male voice said, "I'll be there tomorrow. We'll talk."

"Face-to-face?" The medium man sounded neutral, but since he was alone, he let his expression show his apprehension.

He heard the man on the other end laughing, but it was more like a series of coughs.

"Yes, face-to-face," the man said.

After he'd ended the conversation, the medium man stared at the wall for a few minutes. He didn't like this turn of events. He wondered if he was worried enough to forgo the remainder of his pay for this job.

He hadn't lasted this long without being wily and without knowing when to cut his losses. Would his employer really track him down if he left?

Gloomily, Johan Glassport concluded that he would.

By the time Steve Newlin came out of the bathroom zipping up his pants, Glassport was able to relate the conversation without revealing by any blink of an eyelash how repugnant he found the idea of meeting their employer again. Glassport was ready to turn out the lights and crawl into his bed, but Newlin wouldn't shut up.

Steve Newlin was in an exceptionally good mood, because he was imagining several things that might happen to the Stackhouse woman while she was in jail. None of these things was pleasant, and some of them were pornographic, but all of them were couched in terms of what Steve Newlin's personal Bible interpreted as hellfire and damnation.

CHAPTER 9

I never would have imagined I could be glad my grandmother was dead, but that morning I was. It would have killed Gran to see me arrested and put into a police car.

I never had experimented with bondage, and now I surely never would. I hate handcuffs.

I had a trite-but-true moment when Alcee Beck told me he was arresting me for murder. I thought, *Any minute now I'll wake up. I didn't really wake up when I heard the doorbell. I just dreamed it. This isn't real, because it can't be.* What convinced me that I was awake? The expression on Andy Bellefleur's face. He was standing behind Alcee, and he looked stricken. And I could hear right in his brain, he didn't think I deserved to be arrested. Not on the evidence they had. Alcee Beck had had to talk long and hard to convince the sheriff that I should be arrested.

194

Alcee Beck's brain was strange; it was black. I'd never seen anything like it, and I couldn't get a handle on it. That couldn't mean anything good. I could feel his determination to put me in jail. In Alcee Beck's mind, I might as well have "GUILTY" tattooed on my forehead.

When Andy put the cuffs on me, I said, "I assume I'm uninvited to Halleigh's baby shower."

"Aw, Sookie," he said, which was hardly adequate.

To do Andy justice, he was embarrassed, but I wasn't exactly in the mood to do *him* any justice when he was doing me none. "I think you know I never hurt Arlene," I said to Andy, and I said it very evenly. I was proud of myself for keeping a sealed and stern façade, because inside I was dying of humiliation and horror.

He looked as if he wanted to say something (he wanted to say, *I hope you didn't but there's a little evidence says you did but not enough I don't know how Alcee got a warrant*), but he shook his head and said, "I got to do this."

My sense of unreality lasted all through the booking process. My brother, God bless him, was standing at the jail door when they brought me in, having heard through the instant messaging circuit what had happened. His mouth was open, but before he could vocalize all the angry words I could see crowding his brain, I started talking. "Jason, call Beth Osiecki, and tell her to get down here soon as she can. Go in the house and get the phone number for Desmond Cataliades, and call him, too. And call Sam and tell him I can't come to work tomorrow," I added hastily, as I was marched into the jail and they shut the door on my brother's anxious face. Bless his heart.

If this had happened even a week, two weeks ago, I could have been confident that Eric, or even perhaps my great-grandfather Niall (prince of the fairies), would have me out in the wink of an eye. But I'd burned my bridges with Eric, and Niall had sealed himself into Faery for complicated reasons.

Now I had Jason.

I knew every single person I saw during the process of being booked. It was the most humiliating experience of my life, and that was saying something. I discovered I was being charged with second-degree murder. I knew from Kennedy Keyes's discussion of her time in jail that the penalty for second-degree murder would be life in prison.

I do not look good in orange.

There are worse things than humiliation

and worse things than wearing a jail outfit (baggy tunic and drawstring pants). That's for sure. But I have to say, my cup was full and overflowing, and I was ready for some goodness and mercy. I was so agitated that I was glad to see the cell door. I thought I'd be alone. But I wasn't. Jane Bodehouse, of all people, was passed out and snoring on the bottom bunk. She must have had a few adventures after Merlotte's closed the night before.

At least she was out of it, so I had plenty of time to adjust to my new circumstances. After ten minutes of processing, I was bored out of my mind. If you'd asked me how it would be to sit without work to do, without a book, without a television, without even a telephone, I would have laughed because I couldn't have imagined such a situation.

The boredom — and my inability to get away from my own fearful conjectures — was awful. Maybe it hadn't been so bad for Jason when he'd been in jail? My brother didn't like to read, and he wasn't much on reflection, either. I would ask him how he'd managed, the next time I saw him.

Now Jason and I had more in common than we'd ever had in our lives. We were both jailbirds.

He'd been arrested for murder, too, in the

past, and like me, he was innocent, though evidence had pointed in his direction. Oh, poor Gran! This would have been so awful for her. I hoped she couldn't see me from heaven.

Jane was snoring, but seeing her familiar face was somehow homey. I used the toilet while she was out of it. There would be plenty of awfulness in my future, but I was trying to forestall a little bit of it.

I'd never been in a jail cell before. It was pretty disgusting. Tiny, battered, scarred, concrete floor, bunk beds. After a while, I got tired of squatting on the floor. Since Jane was sprawled across the bottom bunk, with some difficulty I hauled myself to the top level. I thought of all the faces I'd seen through the bars as I'd gone to my cell: startled, curious, bored, hard. If I'd known all the people on the free side of the bars, I'd also recognized almost all those men and women on the other side, too. Some were just fuckups, like Jane. Some of them were very bad people.

I could hardly breathe, I was so scared.

And the worst part — well, not the worst part, but a real bad part — was that I was guilty. Oh, not of Arlene's death. But I had killed other people, and I'd watched many more die at the hands of others. I couldn't even be sure I remembered them all.

In a kind of panic, I scrambled to recall their names, how they'd died. The harder I tried, the more the memories became jumbled. I saw the faces of people I'd watched perish, people whose deaths I hadn't caused. But also I saw the faces of people (or creatures) I'd killed; the fairy Murry, for example, and the vampire Bruno. The werefox Debbie Pelt. Not that I'd gone out hunting them because I had a beef with them; they'd all been intent on killing me. I kept telling myself that it had been okay to defend my life, but the reiteration of their death scenes was my conscience letting me know that (though I was not guilty of the crime that had put me here) jail was not a totally inappropriate place for me to be.

This was the rock-bottom moment of my life. I had a lot of clarity about my own character; I had more time than I wanted to think about how I'd landed where I was. As unpleasant as the first hours in the cell were, they got worse when Jane woke up.

First, she was sick from both ends, and since the toilet was sitting completely exposed, that was just . . . disgusting. After Jane weathered that phase, she was so miserable and hungover that her thoughts were dull throbs of pain and remorse. She

199

promised herself over and over that she would do better, that she would not drink so much again, that her son would not have to fetch her again, that she would start that very evening to cut way back on the beers and shots. Or since she felt so horrible today, maybe tomorrow would be soon enough. That would be much more practical.

I endured a few more mental and verbal cycles like this before Jane realized she had a companion in the cell and that her new buddy wasn't one of her usual cell mates.

"Sookie, what are you doing here?" Jane said. She still sounded pretty puny, though God knew her body should be empty of toxins.

"I'm as surprised as you are," I said. "They think I killed Arlene."

"So she did get out of jail. I really did see her, not last night but the night before," Jane said, brightening a little. "I thought it was a dream or something, since I was sure she was behind bars."

"You saw her? Somewhere besides Merlotte's?" I didn't think Jane had been in Merlotte's when Arlene had come to speak to me.

"Yeah, I was gonna tell you yesterday, but I got sidetracked by that lawyer talk."

"Where did you see her, Jane?"

"Oh, where'd I see her? She was . . ." This was clearly a big effort for Jane. She ran her fingers through her snarled hair. "She was with two guys."

Presumably these were the friends Arlene had mentioned. "When was this?" I tried to ask this very gently, because I didn't want to risk knocking Jane off course. She wasn't the only one who was having a hard time staying on track. I had to concentrate hard to both breathe and ask coherent questions. After Jane's episodes of illness, it smelled pretty awful in our little bunkhouse.

Jane tried to recall the time and place of her Arlene encounter, but it was such a struggle and there were so many less taxing things to think about that it took her a while. However, Jane was at heart a kind person, so she fumbled through her memories till she arrived at success. "I seen her out back of . . . you remember that real big guy who repaired motorcycles?"

I had to clamp down on myself to keep my voice casual. "Tray Dawson. Had a shop and a house out where Court Street turns into Clarice Road." Tray's large shop/garage stood between Tray's house and Brock and Chessie Johnson's, where Coby and Lisa were living. There were only woods behind

201

those houses, and since Tray's was the last one on the street, it was a secluded spot.

"Yeah. She was out there, in back of his house. It's been closed for a while now, so I got no idea what she was doing."

"You know the guys she was with?" I was trying so hard to sound casual, trying so hard not to inhale the terrible miasma, that my voice came out in a squeak like a mouse that was being strangled.

"No, I ain't seen them before. One of 'em was kind of tall and skinny and bony, and the other one was just plain looking."

"How'd you come to see them?"

If Jane had had enough energy to look uncomfortable, she would have. As it was, she looked a tad woeful. She said, "Well, that night I thought about going by the nursing home to see Aunt Martha, but I stopped off at the house to have a little drink, so by the time I got to the nursing home, they said the place was closing to visitors, it being pretty late and all. But I run into Hank Clearwater there, you know, the handyman? He was leaving after visiting his dad. Well, me and Hank have known each other forever, and he said we could have a drink in his car, and before you know it one thing led to another, but we thought he better move the car somewhere a little

202

more private, so he pulled into the woods across the street from the nursing home, there's a little track through the woods where kids run four-wheelers. We could see the backs of the houses on Clarice Road. They all got those big security lights. Helped us see what we were doing!" She giggled.

"So that's how you were able to see Arlene," I said, since I didn't even want to think about Hank and Jane.

"Yeah, that's how come I saw her. I thought, 'Damn, that's Arlene, and she's out, and she tried to kill Sookie. What's up with that?' Those men were real close to her. She was handing them something, and then Hank and I . . . got to . . . talking, and I never saw them again. Next time I looked up, they were gone."

Jane's piece of information was very important to me in a dubious kind of way. On the one hand, it might help clear me or at least give the law grounds for doubting that I'd had any part in killing Arlene. On the other hand, Jane was not what you would call a reliable witness, and her story could be shaken up with one arm tied behind a policeman's back.

I sighed. As Jane began a monologue about her long "friendship" with Hank

Clearwater (I'd never be able to have him in to work on my plumbing after this), I had some random thoughts of my own.

My witness, Karin the Slaughterer, would not rise until full dark, which would not be achieved until quite late. (Not for the first time, I told myself how much I hated daylight saving time.) Karin was a better witness than Jane because she was obviously sharp, alert, and in her right mind. Of course, she was dead. Having a vampire as a witness to your whereabouts was not a glowing testimonial. Though they were now citizens of the United States, they were not treated or regarded like humans, not by a long shot. I wondered if the police would get around to interviewing Karin tonight. Maybe they'd already sent someone to Fangtasia before she'd turned in today.

I considered what Jane had told me. A tall, thin guy and a plain guy, not locals or Jane would have recognized them. With Arlene. In the area behind the house next door to where her children were staying with Brock and Chessie Johnson. Late, on the night Arlene was murdered. That was a big development.

Kevin, in a clean, crisp uniform, brought us lunch an hour later. Fried bologna, mashed potatoes, sliced tomatoes. He looked at me with as much distaste as I'd looked at the food.

"You can just cut that out, Kevin Pryor," I said. "I no more killed Arlene than you can tell your mama who you're living with."

Kevin turned bright red, and I knew my tongue had gotten the better of me. Kevin and Kenya had been living together for a year now, and most people in town knew about it. But Kevin's mom could pretend she didn't know because Kevin didn't tell her face-to-face. There wasn't a thing wrong with Kenya, except for Kevin's mom she was the wrong color to be a girlfriend to Kevin.

"You just shut up, Sookie," he said. Kevin Pryor had never said a rude thing to me in his life. I suddenly realized that I didn't look the same to Kevin now that I was wearing orange. From being someone he should treat with respect, I'd become someone he could tell to shut up.

I stood and looked into his face through the bars separating us. I looked at him for a long moment. He turned even redder. There was no point in telling him Jane's story. He wasn't going to listen.

Alcee Beck came back to the cells that afternoon. Thank God he didn't have the key to our cell. He loomed outside it, silent and glowering. I saw his big fists clench and unclench in a very unnerving way. Not only did he want to see me go to jail for murder, he would love to beat me up. He was spoiling for it. Only the thinnest thread kept him anchored to self-restraint.

The black cloud was still in his head, but it didn't seem as dense. His thoughts were leaking through.

"Alcee," I said, "you know I didn't do this, right? I think you do know that. Jane has evidence that two men saw Arlene that night." Even though I knew Alcee didn't like me, for reasons both personal and professional, I didn't think he would persecute (or prosecute) me for his own reasons. Though he was certainly capable of some corruption, some graft, Alcee had never been suspected of being any kind of vigilante. I knew he hadn't had any personal relationship with Arlene, for two reasons: Alcee loved his wife, Barbara, the librarian here in Bon Temps, and Arlene had been a racist.

The detective didn't respond to my words, but I could tell there was a question or two going on in his thoughts about the righteousness of his actions. He departed, his face still full of anger.

Something was so wrong inside Alcee

Beck. Then it came to me: Alcee was acting like someone who'd been possessed. That was a key thought. I finally had something new to think about; I could spend infinite time picking the thought apart.

The rest of the day passed with excruciating slowness. It's bad when the most interesting thing that happens to you all day is getting arrested. The women's jailer, Jessie Schneider, sauntered down the hall to tell Jane that her son couldn't pick her up until tomorrow morning. Jessie didn't speak to me, but she didn't have to. She gave me a good long look, shook her head, and walked back to her office. She'd never heard anything bad about me, and it made her sad that someone who'd had such a good grandma had ended up in jail. It made me sad, too.

A trustee brought us our supper, which was pretty much lunch revisited. At least the tomatoes were fresh, since there was a garden at the jail. I'd never thought I'd get tired of fresh tomatoes, but between my own burgeoning plants and the jail produce, I would be glad when they were out of season.

There wasn't a window in our cell, but there was one across the corridor, high up on the wall. When the window got dark, all I could think of was Karin. I prayed very earnestly that (if she hadn't been already) she would be contacted by the police, that she would tell the truth, that the truth would literally set me free. I didn't get a lot of sleep that night after the lights went out. Jane snored, and someone over in the men's section was screaming from about midnight to one a.m.

I was so grateful when morning came and the sun broke through the window across the corridor. The weather report two days ago had forecast Monday as sunny, which meant a return to very high temperatures. The jail was air-conditioned, which was a good thing, since it meant I wasn't quite exasperated enough to kill Jane, though I came mighty close a couple of times.

I sat cross-legged on my top bunk, trying hard to think about nothing, until Jessie Schneider came to get us.

"You got to go in front of the judge now," she said. "Come on." She unlocked the cell and gestured us out. I'd been afraid we'd be shackled, but we weren't. We were hand-cuffed, though.

"When am I getting to go home, Jessie?" Jane asked. "Hey, you know Sookie didn't do nothing to Arlene. I saw Arlene with some men."

"Yeah, when did you remember that?

When Sookie reminded you?" Jessie, a big, heavy woman in her forties, didn't seem to bear either of us any ill will. She was so accustomed to being lied to that she simply didn't believe anything an inmate said, and very little anyone else told her, either.

"Awww, Jessie, don't be mean. I did see her. I didn't know the men. You ought to let Sookie go. Me, too."

Jessie said, "I'll tell Andy you remembered something." But I could tell she didn't hang any weight on Jane's words.

We went out a side door and directly into the parish van. Jessie had two other prisoners in tow by that time: Ginjer Hart (Mel Hart's ex-wife), a werepanther who had a habit of passing bad checks, and Diane Porchia, an insurance agent. Of course, I knew Diane had been picked up (which sounded better than "arrested") for filing false insurance claims, but I'd kind of lost track of her case. Women were transported separately from men, and Jessie, accompanied by Kenya, drove us over to the courthouse. I didn't look out the window, I was so ashamed that people could see me in this van.

There was a hush when we filed into the courtroom. I didn't look at the spectator section, but when attorney Beth Osiecki waved her hand to catch my attention, I almost wept from relief. She was sitting in the front row. Once I'd noticed her, I caught a glimpse of a familiar face over her shoulder.

Tara was sitting behind the places saved for lawyers. JB was with her. The babies sat in two infant seats between them.

In the row behind sat Alcide Herveaux, leader of the Shreveport werewolf pack and owner of AAA Accurate Surveys. Next to him was my brother, Jason, and his packleader, Calvin Norris. Jason's friend and best man, Hoyt Fortenberry, was nearby. Chessie Johnson, who was keeping Arlene's kids, was having a low-voiced conversation with Kennedy Keyes and her boyfriend, Danny Prideaux, who not only worked at the home builders' supply but was also Bill Compton's daytime guy. And right by Danny glowered Mustapha Khan, Eric's daytime guy, and Mustapha's buddy Warren, who gave me a wispy smile. Terry Bellefleur stood at the back, shifting from foot to foot uneasily, his wife, Jimmie, at his side. Maxine Fortenberry came in, her walk ponderous and her face as angry as a thunderstorm. She'd brought another friend of Gran's with her, Everlee Mason. Maxine was wearing her righteous face. It was clear that coming into the courtroom was something she'd never had to do in her life, but by golly she was going to do it today.

I had a moment of sheer amazement. Why were all these people here? What had brought them to the courtroom on the same day I had a hearing? It seemed like the most incredible coincidence.

Then I caught the thoughts in their brains, and I understood that there was no coincidence. They were all here on my behalf.

My vision suddenly blurry from tears, I followed Ginjer Hart as she entered the defendants' pew. If the jail orange looked awful on me, it wasn't doing Ginjer any favors, either. Ginjer's bright red hair was a direct slap in the face to the Day-Glo shade of the ensemble. Diane Porchia, with her neutral coloring, had fared better.

I didn't really care about how we looked in our jail clothes. I was trying not to think about the moment. I was so touched that my friends had come, so horrified they'd seen me handcuffed, so hopeful I'd get out . . . so terrified I wouldn't.

Ginjer Hart was bound over for trial since no one stepped forward to bail her out. I wondered if Calvin Norris, leader of the werepanthers, hadn't shown up to stand bail for his clanswoman, but I learned later that this was Ginjer's third offense and that he'd warned her the first and second times that his patience had a limit. Diane Porchia made bail; her husband was sitting in the last row, looking sad and worn-down.

Then, finally, it was my turn to step forward. I looked up at the judge, a kindly but shrewd-looking woman. Her nameplate read "Judge Rosoff." She was in her fifties, I thought. Her hair was in a bun, and her oversized glasses made her eyes look like a Chihuahua's.

"Miss Stackhouse," she said, after looking at the papers in front of her. "This is your arraignment for the murder of Arlene Daisy Fowler. You're charged with second-degree murder, which carries a penalty of life in prison. You have counsel present, I see. Miss Osiecki?"

Beth Osiecki took a deep breath. I suddenly understood that she'd never represented someone charged with murder. I was so frightened I could hardly listen to the back-and-forth between the judge and the attorney, but I heard it when the judge said she'd never seen so many friends turn out for a defendant. Beth Osiecki told the judge I should be released on bail, especially in view of the very slim evidence that connected me to Arlene Fowler's murder.

The judge turned to the district attorney, Eddie Cammack, who never came to Merlotte's, went to church at Tabernacle Baptist, and raised Maine coon cats. Eddie looked as horrified as if Judge Rosoff were being asked to release Charles Manson.

"Your honor, Miss Stackhouse is accused of killing a woman who was a friend to her for many years, a woman who was a mother and . . ." Eddie ran out of good things to say about Arlene. "Detective Beck says Miss Stackhouse had solid reasons to want Arlene Fowler dead, and Fowler was found with Miss Stackhouse's scarf around her neck, behind Miss Stackhouse's workplace. We don't believe she should be freed on bail." I wondered where Alcee Beck was. Then I spotted him. He was glowering at the judge like someone had suggested whipping Barbara Beck on the courthouse lawn. The judge glanced at Alcee's angry face and then dismissed him from her mind.

"Has this scarf been proved to be Miss Stackhouse's?" Judge Rosoff asked.

"She admits the scarf looks like one she had."

"No one saw Miss Stackhouse wearing the scarf recently?"

"We haven't found anyone, but . . ."

"No one saw Miss Stackhouse with the

victim around the time of the murder. There's no compelling physical evidence. I understand Miss Stackhouse has a witness to her whereabouts the night of the murder?"

"Yes, but . . ."

"Then bail is granted. In the amount of thirty thousand dollars."

Oh, yay! I had that much money, thanks to Claudine's legacy. But there was that suspicious freeze on the check. Shit. As quickly as my mind ran through these ups and downs, the judge said, "Mr. Khan, you stand surety for this woman?"

Mustapha Khan rose. Maybe because he resented having to be in a courtroom (he'd had some serious brushes with the law), Mustapha was in full "Blade" mode today: black leather vest and pants (how'd he stand that in the heat?), black T-shirt, dark glasses, shaved head. All he needed was a sword and multiple guns and blades, and since I knew him, I knew those would be somewhere near.

"My boss does. I'm here to represent his interests, since he's a vampire and can't appear in the day." Mustapha sounded bored.

"My goodness," Judge Rosoff said, sounding mildly entertained. "That's a first. All right, your bail has been set at thirty thousand dollars, Miss Stackhouse. Since your family, home, and business are here and you've never lived anywhere else in your life, I think you're a low flight risk. You seem to have plenty of community ties." She glanced over the papers in front of her and nodded. All was right and tight with Judge Rosoff. "You are released on bail pending your trial. Jessie, return Miss Stackhouse to the jail and process her out."

Of course, I had to wait for everyone else, including the male prisoners, to have their moment in court. I wanted to leap up and run away from that bench where I sat with the other defendants. It was all I could do to refrain from sticking out my tongue at Alcee Beck, who looked like he was going to have a heart attack.

Andy Bellefleur had come in to stand beside his cousin Terry. Terry whispered in his ear, and I knew he was telling Andy I'd made bail. Andy looked relieved. Terry punched Andy in the arm, and not in a "hey, buddy" kind of way. "I told you so, asshole," he said audibly.

"Not *my* doing," Andy said, a little too loudly. Judge Rosoff looked pained.

"Bellefleurs, please remember where you are," she said, and they both stood at attention, absurdly. The judge had a twitch at the corners of her mouth.

When all the prisoners had been arraigned, Judge Rosoff nodded and Jessie Schneider and Kenya herded us out into the van. A second later, the parish bus began loading the male prisoners. Finally, we were on our way back to the jail.

An hour later I was dressed in my own clothes again, walking out into the sun, a free woman. My brother was waiting. "I didn't think I'd ever get to pay you back when you stood by me when I was in jail," he said, and I winced. I hadn't ever pictured that happening myself. "But here I am, picking you up at the hoosegow. How'd you like those toilets?"

"Oh, I'm thinking of having them put in at the house, to remind me of good times." Since he was my brother, he ground it in for a couple more minutes. My nickname was now "Jailbird," and my picture on Facebook had bars drawn over it. And on and on.

"Michele?" I asked, when Jason ran out of funny comments. Since we'd been together all our lives, Jason understood what I meant without the whole sentence.

"She couldn't get off work," he said, meeting my eyes so I'd know he wasn't lying. As if I couldn't have told by seeing directly into his brain. "She woulda come, but her boss wouldn't let her off."

I nodded, ready to believe Michele didn't think I was guilty.

"The last time we talked about Eric, you and him were on the outs," Jason said. "But he must be carrying a torch to have bailed you out like that. That's a shitload of money."

"I'm surprised myself," I said. And that was a huge understatement. Based on past experience, when Eric got angry at me, he let me know about it. When he'd decided I was being prissy about killing a few enemies in a bloodbath, he'd bitten me without bothering to take away the pain. I'd let that incident go by without having a showdown over it — a mistake on my part — but I hadn't forgotten it. After our terrible confrontation the night before my arrest, I had never expected this magnanimity from Eric. Even attributing it to a sentimental gesture on his part didn't match what I knew of Eric. I definitely wanted to ask Mustapha a few questions, but he was nowhere to be seen. Neither was Sam, which was somewhat more of a surprise.

"Where do you want to go, Sis?" Jason was trying not to act like he was in a hurry, but he was. He had to get back to work;

he'd taken an extended lunch hour to come to court.

"Take me to the house," I said, after a second's thought. "I have to shower and put on clean clothes and, I guess . . . go in to work. If Sam wants me there. I might not be such an advertisement for the place now."

"Are you kidding? He went nuts when he heard they arrested you," Jason said, as if I should have known what had happened while I was in jail. Sometimes Jason got what I was kind of jumbled up with "psychic" or even "omniscient."

"He did?"

"Yeah, he went to the station to yell at Andy and Alcee Beck on Sunday. Then he called the jail about a million times to ask how you were doing. And he asked the judge who the best criminal lawyer in the area was. By the way, Holly's been working in your place while you were out sick and this morning, just to pick up a little extra cash for the wedding. She says don't worry! She don't want to come back regular."

When we got to Hummingbird Road, I thought, *I'm really free.* I didn't know if I'd ever recover from the overwhelming humiliation of being arrested and going to jail, but I assumed that when I'd gotten over the oppressive weight of the experience, I'd have learned some lesson God wanted me to learn.

I had a moment of thinking of our Lord being dragged through the streets and pelted with offal and then having his court hearing in a public place. Then being crucified.

Well, *not that I was comparing myself to Jesus,* I told myself hastily, but I'd done that kind of backward, right? Almost been crucified, *then* been arrested. We had something in common, Jesus and me! I threw that thought out of my mind as not only a gross exaggeration, but maybe even blasphemy, and focused instead on what to do with my new freedom.

Shower first, for sure. I wanted to wash off the jail smell, plus I hadn't showered since Saturday morning. If I'd gone back to my cell after the courtroom, I could have showered with the other female inmates. Woo-hoo!

Jason had been silent during our drive to my house, but that didn't mean his brain hadn't been busy. He was glad Michele was cool with my arrest, because it sure would have been uncomfortable if she'd thought his sister was guilty, and that might have delayed the wedding. Jason really wanted to get married.

"Tell Michele to come see the dress I bought for my bridesmaid dress, anytime," I said, as Jason pulled up behind the house. I'd retrieved my purse when I'd been released, so I had my keys.

Jason gave me a blank look.

"The one I bought to wear to your wedding. I'll call her later."

Jason was used to me chiming in on his thoughts. He said, "Okay, Sook. You take it easy today. I never believed you done it. Not that she didn't have it coming."

"Thanks, Jason." I was genuinely touched, and of course I knew he was completely sincere.

"Call me if you need me," he said, and then he took off for work. I was so glad to unlock the door and be back in my own home, I almost started crying. And after being jammed into a jail cell with a hungover Jane Bodehouse, it was exquisitely sweet to be alone. I glanced at the telephone answering machine, which was blinking furiously, and I was certain there were some e-mails waiting for me. But a shower came first.

While I dried my hair with a towel, I looked out the window at the shimmering landscape. Everything looked dusty again, but it would be a couple of days before I needed to water, thanks to the recent rain. I actually looked forward to getting out in the yard, because after jail it looked incredibly beautiful. The extravagant growth and lushness had only increased while I was gone.

I put on makeup, because I needed to feel attractive. I put a ton of moisturizer on my newly shaved legs and sprayed on a little spritz of perfume. This was more like it. Every second I felt more like myself, Sookie Stackhouse, bar owner and telepath, and less like Sookie the Jailbird.

I pushed down the Play button on the answering machine.

Here are the people who didn't believe I should have been arrested: Maxine; India; JB du Rone's mom; Pastor Jimmy Fullenwilder; Calvin; Bethany Zanelli, coach of the high school softball team; and at least seven others. I had to feel touched that they'd bothered to call to express their feelings, even though I'd been in jail and it had been possible I'd never get to hear their encouraging messages. I wondered if I should write a thank-you note to each caller. My grandmother would have.

As I listened to Kennedy Keyes's voice telling me Sam had said I shouldn't come in today and I should rest, I could see by the counter that I had only one more message. A man's voice came on. I didn't recognize it. He said, "You had no right to take away my last chance. I'm going to make sure you pay for it." I looked at the number. I didn't recognize it, either. Was I shocked at the determination in his voice? Yes. But I wasn't surprised. I know how people really are. I can hear their thoughts. I couldn't read the brain of someone who'd left a phone message, but I know intent when I hear it. My anonymous caller had meant every word he'd said.

Now it was my turn to make a phone call. "Andy, I need you to come out here and listen to something," I said when he picked up his cell. "You may not want to, but if I'm in danger, you gotta protect me, right? I didn't lose that when I got arrested?"

"Sookie," Andy said. He sounded massively tired. "I'm on my way."

"And do me a favor, okay? This is weird, and I know you won't want to do it, but you tell Alcee Beck to clean out his car. I'm pretty sure there's something in his car that shouldn't be there." I'd had so much time to think in jail that I'd remembered a little flash of memory: Alcee's car parked by the woods. The odd flicker of movement I'd seen from the corner of my eye. The fact that Alcee was so insanely determined I be arrested and charged that I'd thought, *It's*

222

almost like he's under a spell.

That seemed like such a good fit, I was sure it was true.

CHAPTER 10

Though Sam hadn't wanted me to come in the day I was released from jail, I went in to work the next morning. On one level, it was such a normal thing to do that my preparations felt quite ordinary. On another level, since I'd spent part of my jail time thinking I might never get to walk back into Merlotte's again, I was nervous about making a public appearance after facing such an ugly allegation.

Andy Bellefleur had listened to the threat on my answering machine and taken the little tape with him. I'd wished I'd been smart enough to make a copy before he drove off. I hadn't needed to ask him if he'd conveyed my request to Alcee Beck. I heard from his thoughts that he hadn't, that he was already in bad with Alcee because Andy'd maintained they shouldn't arrest me, while Alcee had bulled ahead with the charges. So there was something I'd have to take care of myself.

After Jason's account of Sam's agitation at my arrest, I'd expected a big welcome back to the bar. In fact, I'd expected Sam would call me the night before, but he hadn't. Now, seeing him behind the bar, I smiled and started over to give him a hug.

Sam looked at me for a long moment, and I felt the conflict rolling off him. If fireworks had been exploding out of his brain, he couldn't have been more lit up. But then his whole face shut down, and he turned his back to me. He began polishing a glass furiously. I was surprised it didn't shatter in his fingers.

To say I was hurt and bewildered would be understating by about a ton. I didn't think Sam was exactly angry with me for being arrested, but he was angry about something. Though I got hugs from all the bar staff and at least six customers, Sam avoided me like I was Typhoid Mary.

"Jail isn't catching," I said tartly, the third time I had to pass him to pick up plates from the serving hatch. He had turned away to examine the list of emergency phone numbers as if there were some new information on it that had to be memorized in the next five minutes.

"I . . . I know that," he said, biting off

whatever he'd been about to say. "Good you're back." An Norr came up to get a pitcher of beer, and that cut our conversation off at the knees . . . if you could call our exchange a conversation. I went about my business, but I was fuming. Not for the first time, I wanted to know what Sam was thinking, but since he was a shapeshifter, I could only feel that his thoughts were dark and frustrated.

That made two of us.

On the plus side, if any bar patrons were scared of being served by a woman who'd been arrested for murder, they didn't act like it. Of course, they were used to Kennedy, who not only had been arrested for killing her abusive ex-boyfriend but had actually done both the killing and the time to pay for it.

Sam was practically running a work-release program.

Somehow, thinking about Kennedy made me feel better, especially since she'd been one of the kind people who'd come to court the previous morning. Speaking of Kennedy (if only to myself), a couple of hours later she came in with her honey, Danny Prideaux, in tow. As always, Kennedy looked as if she'd just arrived at a hotel to check in for a pageant weekend: groomed from head to toe, wearing a turquoise and brown tank top and brown shorts. Her turquoise sandals boosted her up another two inches. How did she do it? I marveled at her.

After pausing for a moment so her entrance would register (something she did quite by habit), Kennedy crossed the floor to wrap her arms around me in a ferocious hug, which was a first. Apparently, we were now sisters under the skin. Though the comparison made me uncomfortable, I could hardly be holier-than-thou — so I reciprocated the hug and thanked her for her concern.

Kennedy and Danny were there for a drink before Danny went to his second job as daytime guy for Bill Compton. Danny met with Bill every other night, he told me, to get his orders and report on the results of his previous days. Today, he'd be over at the house to let in some workmen.

"So Bill keeps you busy?" I said, trying to think what Bill would need Danny to do.

"Oh, it's not bad," Danny said, his eyes fixed on Kennedy. "I wasn't working at the builders' supply today, so I'm meeting the security guys at the house to show them where Bill wants the sensors put. Then I'll wait while they do the installing."

It struck me as funny that Bill was getting

a security system. Surely humans needed intruder alerts more than vampires did? Actually, I might look into that when Claudine's bank was cleared to resume business. Getting a security system wasn't a bad idea.

Kennedy started talking about the bikini wax she'd gotten in Shreveport, and Danny's new employer was banished in favor of this more interesting topic, but the next idle moment I had I caught myself wondering if Bill's security system meant that he'd had some trigger event to suggest he really needed one. Since he was my nearest neighbor, I ought to know if someone had tried to break into his house. It would be all too easy to get so wrapped up in my own multilevel troubles that I forgot other folks had troubles, too.

Also, I was curious as hell. And it was a relief to think about something besides being an accused murderer and breaking up with my boyfriend.

Kennedy said, "What's your vampire got to say about this murder charge, Sookie?"

Her timing couldn't have been more perfect.

"Apparently, he put up my bail, but I think that was just for old times' sake," I said. I looked at her directly, so she'd get the message.

"Sorry," she said, after a moment's absorption of my message and the depth of my pit o' breakup misery. "Oh, wow."

I shrugged. And I could hear Kennedy wondering if I'd go back to Bill Compton now that I'd lost my second vampire lover.

Bless her heart. Kennedy just thought like that. I patted her hand and moved on to another customer.

I grew tired, really tired, by about seven o'clock. I'd outstayed the first shift and was well into the second, and on this Tuesday night the crowd was thin. I went behind the bar to talk to Sam, who was fidgeting around in a very un-Sam way.

"I'm gonna go, Sam, because I'm dead on my feet," I said. "That okay?"

I could see the tension in his body language. But he wasn't angry with me.

"I don't know who pissed you off, Sam, but you can tell me," I said. I met his eyes.

"Sook, I . . ." And he stopped dead. "You know I'm here if you need me. I've got your back, Sook."

"I got a real nasty message on my answering machine, Sam. It kind of scared me." I made a wry face to show him I hated being such a chicken. "I didn't recognize the number it came from. Andy Bellefleur said he'd look into it. I'm just saying that what

229

with one thing and another, I'm grateful that you said that. It means a lot. You've always been there for me."

"No," he said. "Not always. But I am, now."

"Okay," I said doubtfully. Something was really eating at my friend, and I had no way to pry it out of him, which normally wouldn't be a problem for me.

"You go home and get some rest," he said, and he put his hand on my shoulder.

I scraped up a smile and offered it to him. "Thanks, Sam."

It was still broiling hot when I left Merlotte's, and I had to stand by my car for a good five minutes with both the front doors open before I could bear to get inside. I had that icky sensation of sweat trickling down between my butt cheeks. My feet could hardly wait to be out of the socks and sneakers I wore to work. While I waited for the car to cool — well, to become less hot — I caught a flash of movement from the trees around the employee lot.

At first I thought it was a trick of the sunlight bouncing off the chrome trim on my car, but then I was sure I'd seen a person in the woods.

There was no good reason for anyone to be out there. To the rear of Merlotte's and facing onto another street lay the little Catholic church and three businesses: a gift shop, a credit union, and Liberty South Insurance. None of them were likely to have customers who would opt to wander in the fringe of woods, especially on a hot weekday evening. I wondered what to do. I could retreat to Merlotte's, or I could get in the car and pretend I hadn't seen anything, or I could dash into the woods and beat up whoever was watching me. I considered for maybe fifteen seconds. I didn't think I had enough energy to dash, though I had plenty of anger to fuel a beating. I didn't want to ask Sam for anything; I'd asked him for so much, and he was acting so odd today.

So, option two. But just to make sure someone knew what was happening . . . and I didn't get any more specific than that . . . I called Kenya. She answered on the first ring, and since she knew it was me calling, I saw that as a good thing.

"Kenya, I'm leaving work now, and there's someone out back skulking in the trees," I said. "I got no idea what anyone would want to do back there — there's nothing besides Sam's trailer — but I'm not going to try to handle that on my own."

"Good idea, Sookie, since you ain't armed and you ain't a cop," Kenya said tartly.

"Oh . . . you *aren't* armed, are you?"

Lots of people had personal handguns in our neck of the woods, and just about everyone had a "critter rifle." (You never knew when a rabid skunk would come up in your yard.) I myself had a shotgun *and* my dad's old critter rifle at home. So Kenya's question wasn't out of left field.

"I don't carry a gun with me," I said.

"We'll come check it out," she said. "You were smart to call."

That was nice to hear. A police officer thought I'd done something smart. I was glad to reach the turnoff into my driveway without any occurrence.

I picked up my mail, then went to the house. I wasn't thinking about anything in particular. I was still excited about the prospect of eating my very own food, after the indescribable slop we'd gotten in jail. (I knew the parish didn't have a big budget to feed prisoners, but damn.)

Despite my eagerness, I looked around me carefully before I got out of my car, and I had my keys in my hand. Experience had taught me it's better to be wary and feel ridiculous than to get conked on the head or abducted or whatever the enemy plan of the day might be.

I flew up the steps, crossed the porch, and

unlocked the back door quicker than you can say "Jack Robinson."

A little fearfully, I went to the answering machine in the living room and pressed the button to listen. Andy Bellefleur said, "Sookie, we traced the call. It came from a house in New Orleans owned by a Leslie Gelbman. That mean anything to you?"

I caught Andy at work. "I know several people in New Orleans," I said. "But that name means nothing to me." I didn't think any of them would be placing a hate call to me, either.

"The Gelbman house is up for sale. Someone had broken into it through the back door. The phone was still hooked up, and that's what the caller used to leave that message. Sorry we didn't find out who said that stuff. Did you recall any incident that would make that message mean something to you?"

He actually sounded sorry, which was nice. My opinion of Andy wavered back and forth. I think his opinion of me did, too. "Thanks, Andy. No, I haven't thought of anything I've ever done that could be construed as taking away someone's last chance." I paused. "Did you give Alcee my message?"

"Ahhhh . . . no, Sookie. Alcee and I aren't

on the best of terms right now. He still . . ." Andy's voice died away. Alcee Beck still thought I was guilty and was in a snit because I'd been released on bail. I wondered if it was Alcee I'd seen out in the woods around Merlotte's. I wondered how violently he felt about me being free.

"Okay, Andy, I understand," I said. "And thanks for checking on the phone call. Give Halleigh my best."

After I'd hung up, I thought of someone I should call about my present predicament. Jason had told me he hadn't gotten an answer when he'd called the part-demon lawyer Desmond Cataliades. I got out my address book, found the number Mr. Cataliades had given me, and punched it in.

"Yes?" said a small voice.

"Diantha, it's Sookie."

"Oh! Whathappenedtoyou?" This was said in Diantha's rapid-fire delivery, the words blurring together in her haste. "YournumberwasonUncle'scallerID."

"How'd you know something happened? Can you slow down a little?"

Diantha made an effort to enunciate. "Uncle's packing to come to see you. He's learned a couple of things that have him all worried. He had a twinge of fear. Uncle's usually right on the money when he has a twinge. And he has solid business reasons to talk to you, he says. He would have gotten there sooner, but he had to consult with some people that are pretty hard to catch." She exhaled. "Thatwhatyouwanted?"

I was tempted to laugh but decided I would not. I couldn't see her facial expression, and I didn't want my amusement to be misconstrued. "His twinge was right on the money," I said. "I got arrested for murder."

"Ofaredheadedwoman?"

"Yeah. How'd you know? Another twinge?"

"Thatwitchfriendofyourscalled."

After I chopped up that sentence into sound bites until I was sure I understood it, I said, "Amelia Broadway."

"Shehadavision."

Dang. Amelia was getting stronger and stronger.

"Is Mr. Cataliades there?" I asked, taking care to say it correctly. Ca-TAHL-e-ah-des.

There was empty air, and then a pleasant voice said, "Ms. Stackhouse. How nice to hear from you, even under the circumstances. I am setting off your way, shortly. Do you need my services as an attorney?"

"I'm out on bail now," I said. "I was kind of in a hurry to be represented, so I called

Beth Osiecki, a local lawyer." I sounded as apologetic as I could manage. "I did think of you, and if I'd had more time . . . I'm hoping you'll join in with her?" I was pretty damn sure Mr. Cataliades had had more experience defending accused murderers than Beth Osiecki.

"I'll consult with her while I'm in Bon Temps," said Mr. Cataliades. "If you'd like treats from New Orleans — beignets or the like — I can bring them with me."

"You were coming up to see me, anyway, Diantha says?" My voice faltered as I tried to imagine why. "Of course, I'm real glad you're coming to see me, and you're welcome to stay here at the house, but I may have to be at work some of the time." I could hardly beg off any more shifts at Merlotte's, management or no management. Besides, working was better than thinking. I'd had my days of thinking after I'd resurrected Sam, and a fat lot of good it had done me.

"I completely understand," the lawyer said. "I think perhaps you will need us to stay in the house."

"Us? Diantha's coming with you?"

"Almost certainly, and also your friend Amelia and perhaps her young man," he said. "According to Amelia, you need all the help you can get. Her father called her concerning you. He told her he'd seen an article in the papers about you."

That was heartwarming, since I'd only met Copley Carmichael once, and he and Amelia had anything but a smooth relationship. "Wonderful," I said, trying hard to sound sincere. "By the way, Mr. Cataliades, do you know someone named Leslie Gelbman?"

"No," he said instantly. "Why do you ask?"

I described the phone call and told him what Andy had discovered.

"Interesting and disturbing," he said succinctly. "I'll drive by that house before we leave."

"When do you think you'll get here?"

"Tomorrow morning," he said. "Until we arrive, be extremely careful."

"I'll try," I said, and he hung up.

The sun had just gone down by the time I'd eaten a salad and had my shower. I had a towel wrapped around my head (and nothing else on) when the phone rang. I answered it in my bedroom.

"Sookie," Bill said, his voice cool and smooth and soothing. "How are you tonight?"

"Just fine, thanks," I said. "Really tired." Hint, hint.

"Would you mind very much if I come over to your house for just a few moments? I have a visitor, a man you've met before. He's a writer."

"Oh, he came here with Kym Rowe's parents, right? Harp something?" His previous visit was not a pleasant memory.

"Harp Powell," Bill said. "He's writing a book about Kym's life."

Biography of a Dead Half-Breed: The Short Life of a Young Stripper. I really couldn't imagine how Harp Powell could spin the depressing tale of Kym Rowe into literary gold. But Bill thought writers were great, even small-time writers like Harp Powell.

"If we could just take a few minutes of your time?" Bill said gently. "I know the past few days have been very bad ones for you."

Sounded like he'd gotten the message, probably via Danny Prideaux, about my sojourn in jail.

I said, "Okay, give me ten minutes, and then you can come over for a short visit." When my great-grandfather Niall had left this land, he'd put a lot of magic in the ground. Though it was delightful to see the yard blooming and bearing fruit and being green, I found myself thinking I would have traded all the plants in the yard for one really good protection spell. Too late now!

Niall had taken my dog of a cousin, Claude, back into Faery to punish him for his rebellion and his attempt to steal from me, and left me with a lot of tomatoes in return. The last person to lay wards around my house had been Bellenos, the elf, and though he'd scorned other people's protective circles, I didn't exactly trust Bellenos's. I'd rather have a gun than magic any day, but maybe that was just American of me. I had the shotgun in the coat closet by the front door and Daddy's rediscovered critter rifle in the kitchen. When Michele and Jason had turned out all of Jason's closets and storage areas in preparation for Michele moving in, they'd found all kinds of stuff, items I'd vaguely wondered about for years, including my mom's wedding dress. (While I'd gotten Gran's house when she passed, Jason had inherited my parents' place.)

I glimpsed the wedding dress in the back of my closet when I opened it to pull out something to wear for my fairly unwelcome guests. Every time I saw the flounced skirt, I was reminded just how different I was from my mother; but every time, I wished I'd gotten to know her as an adult.

I shook myself and pulled out a T-shirt and jeans. I didn't fool with makeup, and my hair was still damp when the two men knocked at my back door. Bill had seen me in every stage of being dressed or undressed that was possible, and I didn't care what Harp Powell thought.

The reporter practically bolted into my kitchen. He looked agitated.

"Did you see that?" he asked me.

"What? Hello, by the way. 'Thanks, Ms. Stackhouse, for inviting me into your home at the end of a long, traumatic day.' " But he didn't get my sarcasm, though it was as wide as the river Jordan.

"We got stopped in the woods by a woman vampire," he said excitedly. "She was beautiful! And she wanted to know what we were doing going to your house and if we were armed. It was like going through security at the airport."

Wow. That was *great*. Karin was on duty in my woods! I did have security, and not only the magical kind. I had a real nighttime-patrol vampire.

"She's a friend of a friend," I said, smiling. Bill smiled back. He was looking spiffy tonight in dress slacks and a long-sleeved plaid cotton shirt, crisply ironed. Had he done the ironing? More likely, he'd gotten Danny to take all his shirts and slacks to a laundry. In sad contrast, Harp Powell was wearing khaki shorts and an ancient button-down shirt.

I had to offer my visitors a drink. Harp admitted he'd like a glass of water, and Bill accepted a bottle of TrueBlood. I stifled yet another sigh and brought them their beverages, Harp's glass tinkling with ice and Bill's bottle warm.

I should have also offered some small talk to cover the moment, but I was all out of chitchat. I sat with my hands folded on my knee, my legs crossed, and waited while they took their first sips and shifted into comfortable positions on the sofa.

"I called you Sunday night," Bill said, opening the conversational envelope, "but you must have been out."

He meant it as a transition remark, but I had a grim little frisson.

"Ah, *no,*" I said, giving him a significant look.

He stared at me. Bill can really stare.

"You know where I was Sunday night," I said, trying to be discreet.

"No, I don't."

Dammit. Why didn't Danny gossip more? "I was in jail," I said. "For killing Arlene."

You would have thought I'd dropped my drawers and bent over, their expressions were so shocked. In an unworthy way, it was pretty funny. "I didn't do it," I said, seeing they'd misunderstood me. "I'm just accused of it."

Harp used his napkin to pat his mustache, which was kind of wet now, after the drink of water. He needed a trim. "I'd love to know more about that, frankly," he said. And he meant that down to his bones.

"You're not teaching anymore?" I said. After the last time I'd met Harp, I'd Googled him. Bill had told me that Harp had been teaching at a community college and had had a few books published by a university press, historical novels of regional interest. More recently, Harp had been editing vampire reminiscences, with emphasis on their historical value.

"No, I'm writing full-time now." He smiled at me. "I cast my fate to the wind."

"You got fired," I said.

He looked taken aback, but not as taken aback as Bill. Yeah, I didn't think Bill had known that.

Harp said, "Yes, they said it was my interest in writing the books about vampires' personal histories that was taking too much of my time and my concentration, but I suspect it was because I became friends with a vampire or two." Trying to appeal to my love of vampires, I guess. "Last semester, I was teaching a night class in journalism at the Clarice Community College, and I got my undead friends to visit. The faculty complained to my boss, but the students were fascinated."

"Which would pertain to writing newspaper articles — how?"

"Which would give my students a richer background to draw from when they write. To give them a broader knowledge of the world, color their emotional palette."

"You're hooked on vamps." I rolled my eyes at Bill. "You're a literary fangbanger." It was all in Harp's head for me to see: the craving, the fascination, the sheer pleasure he took in being with Bill tonight. Even I was interesting to him, simply because he'd figured from my history that I'd had sex with vampires. He'd also gotten the impression that I was some kind of supernatural oddity in my own right. He wasn't sure how I was different from other people, but he knew I was. I cocked my head, examining his thoughts. He was a little different himself. Maybe a tiny drop of fae blood? Or demon?

I reached over and took his hand, and he looked at me with eyes as big as saucers while I rummaged around in his head. I didn't find anything in there that was morally gross or salacious. I would do this as a

243

favor to Bill.

"All right," I said, dropping his hand. "What are you here for, Mr. Writer?"

"What did you just do?" he asked, both excited and suspicious.

"I just decided to talk to you about whatever," I said. "So talk. What do you want to know?"

"What happened to Kym Rowe? What's your perspective?"

I knew the truth about what had happened to Kym Rowe, and I'd seen Kym's murderer beheaded.

"My perspective is that Kym Rowe was a desperate young woman without many morals. She was also hard up financially. From what I understand," I said cautiously, "someone hired her to seduce Eric Northman, and the same person killed her in Eric's front yard. I understand that the murderer confessed to the police and then left the country. Kym Rowe's death seems sad and meaningless to me."

I couldn't understand what Bill was getting out of hanging around with this guy. I suspected Bill's reverence for the written word had blinded him to Harp's inquisitive and intrusive habits. When Bill had grown up, books were fairly rare and precious. Or did Bill just need a friend so badly he was willing to make one of Harp Powell? I would have liked to check out Harp's neck for fang marks, but with his collar that was impossible. Dammit.

"That's the official story," Harp said, knocking back another swallow of water. "But I understand that you know more."

"Who might have told you that?" I looked at Bill. He gave a tiny shake of the head to indicate his innocence. I said, "If you think you will get another story, a different one, from me . . . you're absolutely wrong."

The former reporter backpedaled. "No, no, I just want some color to enhance my picture of her life. That's all. What it was like to actually be there that night, at that party, and to see Kym alive in her last minutes."

"It was disgusting," I said without thinking.

"Because your boyfriend, Eric Northman, drank blood from Kym Rowe?"

Duh! That was public record, too. But that didn't mean I enjoyed being reminded. "The party just wasn't my cup of tea," I said evenly. "I got there late, and I didn't like what I found when I walked in."

"Why not you, Ms. Stackhouse? That is, why didn't he drink from you?"

"That's really not any of your business,

Mr. Powell."

He leaned across the coffee table, all confidential and intense. "Sookie, I'm trying to write the story of this sad girl's life. To do her justice, I'd like all the details I can gather."

"Mr. Powell — Harp — she's dead. She won't ever know what you write about her. She's beyond worrying about justice."

"You're saying it's the living who count, not the dead."

"In this instance, yes. That's what I'm saying."

"So there are secrets to know about her death," he said, righteously.

If I'd had the energy, I'd have thrown up my hands. "I don't know what you're trying to get me to say. She came to the party, Eric drank from her, she left the party, and the police tell me a woman whose name they won't release called them to confess she'd strangled Kym."

I took a second to check my memory. "She was wearing a green and pink dress, real bright, kind of low-cut, with spaghetti straps. And high-heeled sandals. I can't remember what color they were." No underwear, but I wasn't going to mention that.

"And did you talk to her?"

"No." I didn't *think* I'd addressed her directly.

"But this bad behavior, this blood drinking, was offensive to you. You didn't like Eric Northman drinking from Kym."

Screw trying to be polite. By now, Bill had put down his bottle and moved to the edge of the couch as if he were ready to rocket to his feet.

"I did very thorough interviews with the police. I don't want to talk about Kym Rowe again, ever."

"And it's true," he said, as if I hadn't spoken, "that though the cops say Kym's killer confessed over the phone, she's never been caught, and she may be dead somewhere just like Kym Rowe is? You hated Kym Rowe and she died, and you hated Arlene Fowler and she died. What about Jannalynn Hopper?"

Bill's eyes lit up from within like brown torches. He hauled Harp up by his collar and marched him out of the house in a way that would have been pretty funny if I hadn't been so angry and so scared.

"I hope this is the end of Bill's fascination with writers," I said out loud. I would have loved to go to bed, but I figured Bill would be back. Sure enough, he knocked on the back door in ten minutes. He was alone.

I let him in, and I'm sure I looked as exasperated as I felt.

"I'm so sorry, Sookie," he said. "I didn't know any of this: that Harp had been fired, that he'd developed this fixation on vampires, that you had been arrested. I'm going to have a talk with Danny about keeping me better informed on local matters. What can I do to help you?"

"If you could find out who killed Arlene, it would really help." I may have sounded a little sarcastic. "It was my scarf around her neck, Bill."

"How did you get out, accused of such a crime?"

"Not only was there no absolutely damning evidence tying me to the murder, Eric sent Mustapha to bail me out, which I can't figure. We're not married anymore and he's leaving with Freyda. Why does he care? I mean, I don't think he hates me, but putting up bail money . . ."

Bill said, "Of course he doesn't hate you," but he said it a little abstractedly, as if he'd had a sudden thought. "Though I'm in communication with others at Fangtasia, I'm surprised he hasn't summoned me. It seems I should pay my sheriff a visit . . . and find out when he's leaving us." Bill sat sunk in thought for a long moment. "Who will be the next sheriff?" he said, and his whole body was tense.

Understandably, I hadn't gotten that far in my thinking. What with the losing-my-boyfriend heartache and the murder charge.

"That's a good question," I said, without much interest. "Be sure and let me know when you find out. I guess Felipe will bring in one of his people." I'd worry about that later, when I had the energy. A henchperson of Felipe's could sure make my life more difficult, but I couldn't think about it now.

"Good night, sweetheart," Bill said, to my surprise. "I'm glad to see Karin is earning her keep, though I didn't expect Eric would put her outside your house perpetually."

"Neither did I, but I think it's wonderful."

"I thought Harp was a gentleman. I was wrong."

"Think nothing of it." My eyelids were sagging shut.

He kissed me on the lips. My eyelids were suddenly wide apart. He stepped back, and I caught my breath. Bill had always kissed like a champion. If there'd been a kissing Olympics, he'd have advanced to the finals. But I wasn't starting anything up. I stepped back, too, and let the screen door close between us.

"Sleep well." And Bill was gone, across

the yard and into the woods, moving so swiftly and silently that I expected to see "zoom" marks behind him.

But he stopped dead just inside the tree line.

Someone had stepped out in front of him.

I caught the flowing movement of long pale hair. Karin and Bill were in conversation. I hoped Harp Powell didn't try to return to my woods and "interview" Karin. The last human male I'd known who'd been hooked on a vampire female had had a sad end.

And then I yawned and forgot all about the reporter. I locked every lock on every door and window, and crawled into bed.

CHAPTER 11

When I got up the next morning, it was pouring rain again — yay, no watering! — and I was still tired. I discovered that I didn't know when I'd scheduled myself to work, I didn't have any clean uniforms, and I was almost out of coffee. Also, I stubbed my toe on the kitchen table. All of it was annoying, for sure, but still better than being arrested for murder or waking up in jail.

I decided to pluck my eyebrows while the uniforms were tumbling in the dryer. One of the hairs was suspiciously light. I yanked it out and examined it. Was it *gray*?

I put on extra makeup, and when I thought I could sound calm, I called my co-boss.

"Sam," I said, when he answered the phone. "I can't remember when I need to be there."

"Sookie," he said, sounding simply weird. "Listen, you stay home today. You were a real trooper yesterday, but give yourself a break."

"But I want to work," I said, speaking very slowly, while I scrambled to figure out what was happening with my friend.

"Sook . . . today, no, don't come in." And he hung up.

Had the whole world gone crazy? Or was it just me? While I stood there holding my phone, doubtless looking like an idiot (which was okay, since there was no one to see me), the phone vibrated in my hand. I shrieked and almost threw it across the room, then gathered myself together and held it to my ear.

"Sookie," said Amelia Broadway, "we'll be there in a little over an hour. Mr. C said I should call you. Don't worry about breakfast, we've already eaten."

It was a measure of how busy my head was that I'd completely forgotten that my New Orleans company was arriving this morning. "Who all's with you?"

"It's me, Bob, Diantha, Mr. C, and an old buddy of yours. You'll be so surprised!" And Amelia hung up.

I hate surprises. But at least I had something to do. Upstairs, the bed in Claude's former room was made up with clean sheets, and I hauled an air mattress I'd gotten for

Dermot into the former attic, now a large, empty room with a very large closet. The cot Dermot had used until I'd gotten the air mattress was easy to set up in the second-floor sitting room. After everything was ready upstairs, I made sure the down-stairs hall bathroom was still clean, the bedroom across the hall from mine was ready, and the kitchen was orderly. Since I wasn't going to work, I put on some civilian shorts, black with white polka dots, and a white shirt.

Clean enough. Oh, food! I tried to figure out a menu, but I didn't know how long they'd be staying. And Mr. Cataliades was quite an eater.

By the time I heard a car on the gravel driveway, I was more or less ready for company, though I have to admit I wasn't too excited about having more visitors. Amelia and I hadn't parted on good terms in our last face-to-face discussion, though we'd been extending hands to each other across the Internet. Mr. Cataliades always had something interesting to say, but it was seldom news I wanted to hear. Diantha was a mother lode of unexpected talents and very handy to have around. And then there was the mystery guest.

Amelia dashed in first, rain spots all over

her blouse, and her boyfriend, Bob, was right on her heels. Bob particularly hated getting wet. I didn't know if that was because he'd spent time as a cat, or if it was because he simply liked dryness. Diantha danced inside, her small bony figure outlined with tight clothes in bright colors. Mr. Cataliades, in his usual black suit, pounded up the steps after her, moving swiftly despite his bulk.

The last person into the house was Barry Bellboy, formerly known as Barry Horowitz.

Years younger than me, Barry was the first telepath I met. Mr. Cataliades was Barry's great-great-grandfather, though I didn't know if Barry had been made aware of that or not.

Like Amelia and me, Barry and I hadn't parted on perfect terms. But we'd gone through a great ordeal together, and that made a bond between us that nothing could break, especially considering the fact that we shared the same disability. The last I'd heard, he'd been working for Stan, the King of Texas . . . though since Stan had been badly injured in the explosion in Rhodes, I had figured Barry'd really been working for Stan's lieutenant, Joseph Velasquez, since then.

Since I'd last seen Barry at a hotel in

Rhodes, he had aged and his body had matured. He'd completely lost his endearing gawkiness. Now he seemed more . . . intense and spidery. I handed him a towel to dry his face, which he did with vigor.

How are you? I asked him.

It's a long story, he said. *Later.*

"Okay," I said out loud. I turned away to greet my other guests. Amelia and I hugged rather awkwardly, inevitably reminded of our final quarrel the last time she'd been here, when she'd totally crossed the line into my personal life. Amelia had rounded out.

"Okay," she began. "Listen, just getting this out of the way. I've said this before, but I want to say it again. I'm sorry. Being such a good witch gave me inflated ideas of running your life, and I'm aware I overshot my boundaries. I won't do it again. I've been trying to mend my fences everywhere. I've been trying to create a relationship with my father, though he turned out to be nothing like I thought he was, and I'm learning some impulse control."

I looked at her carefully, a little confused about the reading I was getting. Amelia had always been an exceptional broadcaster, and she still was. She was sending off waves of sincerity and fear that I'd reject her apology. (However, she still thought very highly

255

of herself, with some justification.) But there was an extra vibe from her. "We'll give starting over a shot," I said, and we smiled at each other in a tentative way. "Bob, how you doing?" I turned to her companion. Bob was not a big man. If I had to pick two adjectives for Bob, they would be "dark" and "nerdy." But I could see that Bob, like Barry, had changed. He was carrying more weight, which looked good. Gauntness had not become him. And Amelia had been smartening up his wardrobe, including his glasses, which now looked sort of European and sophisticated.

"Dang, Bob, you clean up good," I told him, and his thin lips parted in a surprisingly charming smile.

"Thanks, Sookie, you're looking good yourself." He glanced down at his clothes. "Amelia thought I ought to update."

I still couldn't imagine how Bob had forgiven Amelia for turning him into a cat when she didn't know how to turn him back, but after his initial spasm of loathing sent him running to find his remaining family when he'd been returned to human form, he'd come back to her.

"Dear Sookie," said the nearly-all-demon Desmond Cataliades, and I embraced him. It was an effort, but that was what you did with friends. He didn't feel human to the touch, though he looked human enough, with his circular body and scanty dark hair, his dark eyes and jowly face. But there was a certain rubbery feel to his flesh that was not standard. He inhaled deeply while his arms were around me, and I had to fight to keep myself from flinching. Of course, he knew that. He was very skilled at keeping it secret that he could read minds like I could — but he was the one who'd made me what I was, and Barry, too.

"HeySookie," Diantha said. "Igottapee. Bathroom?"

"Of course, down the hall," I said, and off she sped, her hair and clothes dark with rain.

I made sure everyone had a towel, and there was a lot of milling around as I assigned rooms: Bob and Amelia downstairs across from me, Mr. C and Diantha in Claude's bedroom and sitting room upstairs, and Barry got the air mattress in the former attic/unfinished bedroom. My house was full of voices and activity. Feet went up and down the stairs, the bathroom door opened and shut repeatedly, and there was life around me. It felt good. Though Claude and Dermot had been less-than-stellar houseguests (especially the traitorous Claude), I'd missed the sound of them in the house, and most of all I'd missed Dermot's smile and willingness to help. I hadn't admitted that to myself until now.

"You could have put us upstairs, put the lawyer down here," Amelia protested.

"Yeah, but you need to save all of your energy for the baby."

"What?"

"The baby," I said impatiently. "I thought you might not like to hike up and down those stairs several times a day, plus you need to be close to a bathroom at night. At least, that's the way Tara was."

When she didn't reply, I turned away from the coffeepot to see that Amelia was staring at me very oddly. Bob, too.

"Are you telling me," Amelia said very quietly, "that I'm pregnant?"

I'd stepped right in it and gotten stuck. "Yeah," I said weakly. "I can feel the brain waves. You got a little one on board. I've never sensed a baby before. Maybe I was wrong? Barry?" He'd come in to hear the last part of our exchange.

"Sure. I thought you knew," he told Bob, who looked pretty much as if someone had socked him in the stomach. "I mean . . ." He looked from Bob to Amelia. "I thought you both knew. You're witches, right? I figured that was why we could sense the baby early. I thought you just didn't want to talk about it yet. Not publicly. I was trying to be tactful."

"Come on, Barry," I said. "I think we need to give them the room." I'd always wanted to say that. I took his hand and pulled him out to the living room, giving the parents-to-be the kitchen. I could hear the rumble of my godfather talking to his niece upstairs. For the moment, it was just me and Barry.

"What have you been doing?" I asked my fellow telepath. "Last time I saw you, you were pretty unhappy with me. But now you're here."

He looked unhappy and a little embarrassed. "I went back to Texas," he said. "Stan was pretty slow recovering, so I was under Joseph Velasquez. Joseph was struggling to keep control, threatening everyone with what would happen when Stan was back at full strength. Like a mom threatening her kids that their dad's going to come home and whip their butts. Finally, a vamp named Brady Burke sneaked into the recovery crypt — don't ask — and staked Stan. Brady's people came after Joseph, too, but Joseph beat them down and put Brady and his vamps out in the sun, and then killed Brady's human buddies."

"Joseph thought you should have warned him."

Barry nodded. "Of course, and he was right. I knew something was up, but I didn't know what. I was friends with a gal named Erica, one of Brady's donors."

"Friends with?"

"Okay, I was sleeping with Erica. So Joseph felt I should have known."

"And?"

He sighed and didn't look at me. "And yes, I knew they were planning something, but since I didn't know what it was, I didn't tell Joseph. I knew he'd come down on Erica like a ton of bricks to get it out of her, and I just couldn't — wouldn't — believe it was anything as drastic as a change of regimes."

"And what happened to Erica?"

"She was dead before I even knew about the coup."

There was a depth of self-loathing in his voice.

"We have limitations," I said. "We can't get accurate readings of every thought in every brain every minute. You know people don't think in whole sentences, like, 'I'm going to the First National Bank today at ten o'clock, and when I get there, I'm getting in line at Judy Murello's window. Then

260

I'm pulling out my .357 Magnum and rob-
bing the bank.' "

"I know that." The storm in his head
subsided a little bit. "But Joseph decided I
didn't tell him because of my relationship
with Erica. Mr. Cataliades showed up out
of nowhere. I don't know why. Next thing I
knew, I was leaving with him. I don't know
why he rescued me. Joseph made it pretty
clear I would never work for vampires again;
he was putting the word out."

Yep, Mr. C had definitely not told Barry
about their blood relationship. "You think
Erica knew about Brady's plan?"

"Yeah," Barry said, sounding tired and
sad. "I'm sure she knew enough to warn
me, and she didn't. I just never picked up
the plan from her. I'm sure she was sorry
she hadn't told me, before she died. But she
died, anyway."

"Tough," I said. Inadequate, but sincere.

"Speaking of tough, I hear your vamp's
going to get hitched to someone else." Barry
was all too quick to change the subject.

"It's all over vampireland, I guess," I said.

"Sure. Freyda is outstanding. Plenty of
guys have been trying to get in line to get a
piece of Freyda since it went around that
she was looking for a consort. Power plus
looks plus money, and plenty of room for

expansion in Oklahoma. Casinos and oil wells. With an ass-kicker like Eric behind her, she'll build an empire."

"That'll be just lovely," I said, sounding as tired and sad as he had. Barry seemed much more plugged into the gossip in the vampire world than I'd ever been. Maybe I'd been "among but not of" more than I'd needed to be. Maybe there was more truth to Eric's accusations about my prejudice against vampire culture than I'd believed. But vampires were users of humans, so I was mostly simply glad I'd never told Eric about my cousin Hadley's son, Hunter.

"So, there's another one of us?" Barry asked, and the question hit me hard. I was so damn used to being the only mind-reader around. In a second I was about an inch from his face, and my hand was gripping the front of his T-shirt.

"You say anything about Hunter to anyone, and I'll bet you have a really bad visitor some night," I said, meaning it with every atom in my body. My cousin Hunter was going to stay safe if I had to be the bad visitor myself. Hunter was only five, and I wasn't having him kidnapped and trained to serve some vampire king or queen. It was hard enough to reach adulthood if you were telepathic. Having people wanting to snatch you for the advantage you could give them? That would be a million times worse.

"Hey, back off!" Barry said angrily. "I came here to help you, not to make things worse. Cataliades must know."

"Just keep your mouth shut about Hunter," I said, and stepped away. "You know what a difference that will make. I'm not worried about Mr. Cataliades telling anyone."

"All right," Barry said, relaxing a fraction. "You can be sure I'll keep my mouth shut. I know how hard it is when you're a kid. I swear I won't tell." He expelled a deep breath to let out all the agitation. I did, too.

"You know who I saw ten days ago in New Orleans?" Barry said, his voice so hushed I had to lean forward to hear. I raised my eyebrows to let him know to get on with it. *Johan Glassport,* he said silently, and I felt a shiver run down my spine.

Johan Glassport was a lawyer. I've known many nice people who were lawyers, so I'm not going to make a lawyer joke out of this; Johan Glassport was also a sadist and a murderer. Evidently, when you're a brilliant lawyer, you can get away with a lot of stuff. He had. I'd last seen Glassport in Rhodes. I'd understood he'd gone to Mexico to hide out after the terrible explosion at the hotel.

He'd been on television then, part of the bedraggled and injured cluster of survivors, and I had always thought he feared he might be recognized by someone. There had to be plenty of people who dreaded the sight of him. *Did he see you?* I asked.

"I don't think so." *He was on a streetcar, and I was on the sidewalk.*

"It's never good to see Johan," I muttered. "Why is he back in the States?"

"I hope we never find out. And I'll tell you something strange. Glassport's brain was opaque."

"Did you tell Mr. Cataliades?" I said.

Yes. He didn't say anything, though. But he looked grim. Grimmer than usual.

"I did see him," Desmond Cataliades said, making one of his sudden appearances. "In fact, New Orleans has been full of unexpected creatures lately. But more about that later. Glassport told me he'd got business in Louisiana. He'd been hired by someone who had a great store of wealth. Someone who didn't want to be seen by anyone. Glassport said he had been out of the country recruiting at this someone's behest."

"I wonder who?"

"Ordinarily, I could have told you," the part-demon said. "But as Barry has said,

264

Glassport has acquired some kind of protection charm, perhaps fae in origin. I can't hear his thoughts."

"I didn't know you could buy such an item!" I was surprised. "Surely that's a hard thing to create?"

"Humans aren't capable of it. Only a few supernaturals."

That was why we were all looking anxious and concerned when Amelia came out of the kitchen, hand in hand with Bob.

"Aw, that's so sweet! But don't worry about us," she said, smiling. "Bob and I are happy as clams about the baby, now that we've gotten over the shock of it." I was glad to see her happiness, and Bob's, but I was also sorry I couldn't pursue the conversation about Johan Glassport to its conclusion. It was bad news that he was anywhere in Louisiana.

Amelia's smile began to falter when she didn't get the reaction she'd expected.

"Amelia and Bob are having a baby!" I said, making myself beam at Mr. Cataliades. Of course, he already knew it.

"Yeah, I'm pregnant, Mr. C!" She recovered her excitement in telling the part-demon lawyer. Obligingly, he did his best to look startled and delighted.

"We're going to raise the baby together.

Wait until I tell my father! He's gonna be so ticked because we're not married," Amelia said. She seemed a bit pleased at vexing her father, who ordered other people around all day, every day.

"Amelia," I said, "Bob doesn't have a real father left to share with this baby. This baby might enjoy having a grandfather."

Amelia was totally taken aback. I hadn't known I was going to say that until it popped out of my mouth. I waited to see if she'd be angry. I saw the flash of offense cross her mind, then a more mature thoughtfulness. "I'll think about that," she said, and that was certainly more than enough. "My dad's changed a lot lately, for sure." I could hear her thinking, *And kind of inexplicably.* I didn't know what to make of that.

"Interesting that you said that, Amelia," the demon lawyer said. "Let's talk about why we're here. There's much I wanted to say on the drive up here, but not only was I busy trying to check to see if we were being followed, I didn't want to have to repeat everything for Sookie."

Everyone settled in the living room. Diantha helped me carry out drinks and cookies and little napkins. I had definitely over-bought for that baby shower. No one seemed to mind the green and yellow rattles motif, though. I hadn't seen any napkins at Hallmark themed for a supernatural summit.

Mr. Cataliades acted as the chairman of this meeting. "Before we plan our course of action about the main topic — the accusation that Sookie murdered Arlene Fowler — there are others we need to discuss. Miss Amelia, I have to ask you to keep the news of your pregnancy confined to this group, just for the moment. Please don't make it the subject of any telephone calls or text messages to your nearest and dearest, though I know you're excited." He smiled at her in a way clearly meant to be reassuring.

Amelia was startled and concerned, expressions that sat oddly on someone as fresh and bright-eyed as she was. Bob dropped his gaze to the floor. He knew what Mr. Cataliades was saying, while Amelia did not.

"For how long?" she said.

"For only a day or two. Surely the news will wait that long?" He smiled again.

"All right," she agreed, after a glance at Bob, who nodded.

"Now to talk about the murder of Arlene Fowler," Mr. Cataliades said, as heartily as if he'd just announced that earnings for the last quarter were way up.

Clearly, the lawyer knew a lot of things I didn't know and was choosing not to share those items, which bothered me. But after he said the word "murder," he had my complete attention.

"Please tell us everything you know about the late Arlene, and tell us how you came to see her again after her release from prison," Mr. Cataliades said.

So I began talking.

CHAPTER 12

It took a surprisingly long time to relate everything I knew about Arlene and her activities, including my concerns about Alcee Beck. Bob, Amelia, Barry, Diantha, and Mr. Cataliades offered a lot of opinions and ideas, and asked a lot of questions.

Amelia focused on the two men Arlene had mentioned, presumably the same two men Jane had witnessed her meeting behind Tray Dawson's empty house. Amelia proposed to lay a truth spell on them to find out what Arlene had handed them. She was a little hazy about how she intended to track them down, but she told us that she had a few ideas. She made an effort to sound nonchalant, but she was quivering with eagerness.

Bob wanted to call a touch psychic he knew in New Orleans, and he wondered if we could persuade the police to let the psychic hold the scarf to get a reading. I said that was a definite no.

Barry thought we should talk to Arlene's kids and Brock and Chessie Johnson, to see if Arlene had said anything about her plans to them.

Diantha thought we should steal the scarf, and then they'd have no evidence on me at all. I have to admit, that option really resonated with me. I knew I hadn't done it. I knew the police weren't looking in the right direction. And, frankly, even more than I wanted Arlene's murderer to be found, I knew I didn't want to go to jail. At all. Ever again.

Diantha also wanted to search Alcee Beck's car. "I'll know a magic object when I see it," she said, and that was a truth no one could argue. The problem was, a skinny, strangely dressed white girl was going to look a little conspicuous searching anyone's car, much less the car of an African-American police detective.

Desmond Cataliades told us that in his opinion, the case against me was weak, especially since I had a witness who could place me in bed at my home at the probable time of the murder. "It's a pity your witness is a vampire — not only a vampire, but one new to the area and bound to your ex-lover," he said in his ponderous way.

"However, Karin is certainly better than no witness at all. I must talk to her soon."

"She'll be out in the woods tonight," I said, "if she follows her pattern."

"You truly believe that Detective Beck was spelled with something?"

"I do," I said. "Though I didn't understand what I was seeing at the time. I tried to get Andy Bellefleur to tell Alcee to search his car. I hoped Alcee would find the hex, or whatever you call it, and understand that he'd been supernaturally influenced against me. Obviously, that's not going to work. So if we can think of a way to get the magic object out of Alcee's vehicle, we need to move on that plan. When it's removed, I hope things will get a lot better for me." And God knew, I wanted things to get better. I glanced at the clock. It was one p.m.

"Amelia, we have some things we need to talk about," Mr. Cataliades said, and Amelia looked apprehensive. "But first, let's go into town and get lunch. Even passive deliberations call for energy."

We packed into Mr. Cataliades's rental van for the short drive into town. As we were seated at Lucky Bar-B-Q, we garnered more attention than I wanted. Of course, people recognized me, and there were a few glances and a few mutters — but I was pretty much prepared for that. The real eye-catcher was Diantha, who'd never dressed like an average human being because she wasn't. Diantha's clothes were bright and random. Green yoga tights, a cerise tutu, an orange leotard, cowboy boots . . . well, it was a bold ensemble.

At least she smiled a lot; that was something.

Even aside from Diantha's exceptional wardrobe choices (and that was a big "even aside"), we simply didn't look like we belonged together.

Luckily, our waiter was a high school kid named Joshua Bee, a distant cousin of Calvin Norris's. Joshua wasn't a werepanther, but as a connection of the Norris clan, he knew a lot about the world most humans didn't see. He was polite and quick, and he wasn't a bit frightened. That was a relief.

After we'd ordered, Desmond Cataliades was telling us about the progress of post-Katrina reconstruction in New Orleans. "Amelia's father has played a large part," he said. "Copley Carmichael's name is on a lot of rebuilding contracts. Especially in the last few months."

"He had some difficulties," Bob said quietly. "There was an article in the paper. We don't see Copley a lot, since he and

Amelia have issues. But we were kind of worried about him. Since the New Year came in . . . well, everything's turned around for him."

"Yes, we'll talk about that when we're in a more private place," Mr. Cataliades said.

Amelia looked worried, but she accepted that well.

I knew she didn't really want to know that her father was up to no good. She suspected it already, and she was frightened. Amelia and her father had an adversarial relationship on many fronts, but she loved him . . . most of the time.

Diantha was making cat's cradles with a piece of string she'd pulled from her pocket, Barry and Mr. Cataliades were having an awkward conversation about the true meaning of the word "barbecue," and I was trying to think of another conversational topic when an old friend of mine walked into Lucky's.

There was a moment's silence. You couldn't ignore John Quinn. Sure, Quinn was a weretiger. But even when people didn't know that (and most didn't), Quinn stood out. He was a big bald man, with olive skin and purple eyes. He looked spectacular in a purple tank top and khaki shorts. He was a man people noticed, and he was my only lover who looked his true age.

I jumped up to give him a hug and urged him to sit down. He pulled up a chair between me and Mr. Cataliades.

"I think I remember who's met Quinn and who hasn't," I addressed the table in general. "Barry, you met Quinn in Rhodes, I think, and Amelia, you and Bob know him from New Orleans. Quinn, you've met Desmond Cataliades and his niece, Diantha, I think."

Quinn nodded all around. Diantha abandoned her piece of string to look at Quinn full-time. Mr. Cataliades, who also knew Quinn was a large predator, was cordial but very much on the alert. "I went to your house first," Quinn told me. "I've never seen flowers bloom in the middle of the summer like that. And those tomatoes! Damn, those things are huge." It was like we'd seen each other yesterday, and I felt that warm and comfortable feeling I got around Quinn.

"My great-grandfather soaked the ground around my house with magic before he left," I said. "I think it was probably some kind of spell to make the land flourish. Whatever it was, it's working. How's Tij doing, Quinn?"

"Everything's going great," he said. He grinned, and it was like seeing a whole different person. "The baby's growing like crazy. You want to see a picture?"

"Sure," I said, and Quinn extracted his wallet and drew out one of those shadowy ultrasounds. There were two markers on the picture, showing where the baby began and ended, Quinn explained.

I'd seen a lot of Tara's ultrasounds — this baby seemed pretty big for a couple of months. "So, will Tijgerin have a baby sooner than a regular human?" I asked.

"Yeah. Weretigers are unique in that. And it's another reason traditional tiger moms spend their pregnancy and birth times away from people. Including the dad," Quinn said grimly. "At least she e-mails me every few days."

Time to change the subject. "I'm glad to see you, Quinn," I said, looking pointedly at Mr. Cataliades, who hadn't yet relaxed. And Diantha's wide-eyed stare didn't mean she was thinking of jumping Quinn's bones, but exposing them with her knife if the occasion arose. Diantha didn't like predators. "What brings you to Bon Temps?" I asked. I put my hand on his arm. *This man is my friend,* I said silently, and Mr. Cataliades nodded slightly but didn't look away.

"I came to help," Quinn said. "Sam put it on the board that someone had it in for you. You're a friend to the Shreveport wolf pack, you're a friend of Sam's, and you're a friend of mine. Plus, the scarf used to kill the lady was a Were gift to you."

Sam had definitely put a good spin on the scarf's history. The Weres had "gifted" it to me by using it as a blindfold so I wouldn't know where they'd taken me . . . the night I'd first met a werewolf. That night seemed so long ago! I had a fleeting second of incredulity that there'd ever been a time I hadn't known the extent of the supernatural world. And here I sat in Lucky Bar-B-Q with two witches, two part-demons, a telepath, and a weretiger.

"Sam has always been a good friend to me," I said, wondering again what the hell was going on with my good friend. (He'd put forth all this effort on my behalf, trying to drum up help for me in my time of need, but he could barely manage to look me in the face. Something was definitely rotten in the state of Bon Temps.) "That two-natured board must be hopping with news."

Quinn nodded. "Alcide had posted, too, so I stopped in at his office on my way here. He wants to know if one of his pack can scent in your house. I told him I was capable of any tracking that needed to be done, but he insisted the Weres help you out. You assume that the scarf was stolen from your house?"

Everyone at the table was listening intently, even Mr. C and Diantha. They'd finally accepted Quinn as a friend of mine. "Yes, that's what I believe. Sam remembers me wearing it to church, and that must have been to a funeral months ago. And I'm pretty confident I saw it when I cleaned out my scarf drawer last week. I think maybe I would have noticed if it *hadn't* been there."

Amelia said, "I can help there. I know a spell that might help you remember, especially if we have a picture of the scarf."

"I don't think I've got one, but I can draw a picture," I said. "It's got a feather pattern." The first couple of times I'd worn it, I hadn't realized that the subtle sweeps of color represented feathers. With the bright peacock colors, you'd think I'd have noticed earlier, but hell, it was just a scarf. A free scarf. And now it might cost me my life or my freedom.

"That might work," Amelia said.

"Then I'm willing to try it," I told Amelia. I turned to Quinn. "And the Weres can come sniff my house anytime they like. I keep it pretty clean, so I'm not sure what they'll pick up."

"I'm going to search your woods," Quinn

said. He wasn't asking.

"It's awful hot, Quinn," I said. "And snakes . . ." But my voice died away when I met his eyes. Quinn wasn't afraid of heat or snakes or much of anything.

We had a good time eating together, and Quinn ordered a sandwich because our food smelled so good. I couldn't even begin to tell everyone how grateful I was that they'd come, that they were helping me. When I'd thought three days before that I had only Jason on my side, how wrong I'd been. I was immensely, deeply grateful.

After lunch, we went by Wal-Mart to get some groceries for supper. To my relief, Mr. Cataliades and Diantha went to fill up their van at the gas station while the rest of us shopped. I simply couldn't imagine those two in Wal-Mart. I divided the list and handed it out, so we were done in no time.

As we filled up our cart, Quinn, a supernatural event planner, was telling me about a werewolf coming-of-age party that had turned into a free-for-all. I was laughing when we turned a corner and met Sam.

After his weirdness yesterday at the bar and on the phone today, I hardly knew what to say to Sam, but I was glad to see him. Sam looked pretty grim, and he looked even grimmer when I reintroduced him to Quinn.

"Yeah, man, I remember you," Sam said, trying to smile. "You come to give Sookie moral support?"

"Any kind of support she needs," Quinn said, not the happiest choice of words.

"Sam, I've talked about Mr. Cataliades, I know. He's brought Diantha and Barry and Amelia and Bob," I said hastily. "You remember Amelia and Bob, though maybe Bob was a cat last time you saw him. Come visit!"

"I remember them," Sam said between clenched teeth. "But I can't come by."

"What's stopping you? I guess Kennedy is working the bar."

"Yeah, she's got this afternoon."

"Then come on out."

He closed his eyes, and I could sense the words beating at his head, wanting to come out. "I can't," he repeated, and he rolled his cart away and left the store.

"What's up with him?" Quinn asked. "I don't know Sam well, but he's always been standing right behind you, Sookie, always in your corner. There's something compelling him to step aside."

I was so confused I couldn't speak. While we checked out and loaded the groceries into the back of the van, I chewed at the problem of Sam and what was happening with him. He wanted to come out to the house, but he wouldn't come out to the house. Because? Well, why would you *not* do something you wanted to do? Because you were being prevented.

"He's promised someone he won't," I muttered. "That's gotta be it." Could it be Bernie? I thought she liked me, but maybe I was reading her wrong. Maybe she thought all I was was trouble for her son. Well, if Sam had made her — or someone else — such a promise, there didn't seem to be anything I could do about it, but I would put the situation on the back burner of things that worried me. When there was room on the front burner, I'd move it forward. Because it sure made me hurt inside.

When the groceries were put away, we assembled again in the living room. I wasn't used to sitting around all day, and I felt a little restless as we all took the chairs we'd been in earlier. Quinn took the only one left, a kind of dumpy armchair I'd always planned on exchanging for something better . . . but I'd never gotten around to it. I tossed him a cushion, and he gamely tried stuffing it in the small of his back to make the chair a bit more comfortable.

"I have some things to tell all of you," Mr. Cataliades said. "And later, some things to tell Sookie individually . . . but now I have to tell you what I've witnessed and suspected."

This sounded so ominous that we all turned our attention to the part-demon.

"I'd heard that there was a devil in New Orleans," he said.

"*The* Devil? Or *a* devil?" Amelia asked.

"What an excellent question," Mr. Cataliades said. "In fact, *a* devil. The Devil himself seldom makes a personal appearance. You can imagine the crowds."

None of us knew quite what to say, so perhaps we couldn't.

Diantha laughed as if she were remembering something very funny. I, for one, didn't want to know what it was.

"Here's the most interesting fact," he said precisely. "The devil was dining with your father, Miss Amelia."

"Not dining on my dad, but dining with him?" She laughed for a second, but suddenly Mr. Cataliades's meaning sank in. Amelia's face drained of color. "Are you shitting me?" she asked quietly.

"I assure you I'd never do such a thing," he replied, with some distaste. He gave her a moment to absorb the bad news before continuing, "Though I know you aren't close to your father, I must tell you that he and his bodyguard have struck a deal with the devil."

Again, I kept my mouth closed. This was Amelia's thing to react to, I figured. Her dad.

"I wish I could say that I was sure he wouldn't do anything so dumb," she said. "But I don't even feel the impulse to say, 'He'd never do anything like that.' He would if he felt he was losing his business and his power . . . oh. So the reports in the papers were true a few months ago. His business didn't make a miraculous recovery. Not miraculous. Miracles are something holy. What's a miracle a devil would do?"

Bob took her hand, but he didn't speak.

"At least he didn't know I was pregnant, so he couldn't promise the devil our child," she said to Bob, and there was something feral about Amelia as she said that. She'd known she was pregnant for a few hours and already she'd switched into mom mode. "You were so right, Mr. Cataliades, to tell me not to telephone or text anyone to let them know about the baby."

Mr. Cataliades nodded gravely. "I am giving you this distressing news because you need to know it before you see him. Once you make a bargain with a devil, any devil, you begin to change, because your soul is forfeit. There's no redemption, so there's no incentive to try to be better. Even if you don't believe in an afterlife, the downward path is permanent."

Though I was sure the part-demon knew more than I did about the subject, I didn't believe redemption was ever beyond the power of God. But I knew this was not the moment to air my religious beliefs. This was the time to gather information.

I said, "So . . . I'm not trying to make this all about me, because obviously it's not, but . . . are you saying Mr. Carmichael is the one trying to get me put in jail?"

"No," said the lawyer. I breathed a sigh of relief. "I think someone else is doing that," he continued, and my relief vanished. How many enemies could I have? "However, I know for a fact that Copley Carmichael asked the devil for a cluviel dor."

I gasped. "But how would he even know about such a thing?" I asked. And then I glared at Amelia. I literally bit the inside of my mouth to keep from ripping into her. She looked stricken, and I forced myself to remember that Amelia was having a very rough day.

"I told him . . . Sookie had asked me to

look it up . . . and we never have anything to talk about, seems like . . . He's never believed I was a real witch, never given any sign he thought I was anything but ridiculous. I didn't imagine. How could I? That he would . . ." She faltered to a stop.

Bob put his arm around her. "Of course you didn't imagine that, Amelia," he said. "How could you? That this one time he'd decide to take you seriously?"

There was another uncomfortable pause. I was still exercising all my self-control, and everyone in the room realized it and gave me some slack.

Gradually, as Amelia wept, I let go of the arms of my chair (I was surprised not to see any dents). I wasn't going to rush over to hug her, because I wasn't that comfortable with Amelia's loose lips yet, but I could understand. Amelia had never been what you'd call discreet, and she'd always had a love/hate relationship with her father. If they were having one of their rare tête-a-têtes, she'd try to keep him interested in her conversation. And what was more interesting than a cluviel dor?

I knew one thing for sure: If my friendship with Amelia continued, I'd never, never tell her anything more important than a recipe or a prediction about the weather.

She'd stepped over the line *again.*

"So, he knew I had a cluviel dor and he wanted it," I said, impatient with Amelia's tearful repentance. "What happened then?"

"I don't know why the devil owed Copley a debt," said Mr. Cataliades. "But apparently, the cluviel dor was the payment Copley requested, and he steered the devil to you, Sookie. But you used the cluviel dor before the devil could wrest it from you . . . very fortunately for all of us. Now Copley is feeling thwarted, and he's not used to that, at least he's not since the New Year. He feels you owe him, somehow."

"But you don't think he'd kill Arlene and try to pin it on me?"

"He would have if he'd thought of it," Mr. Cataliades said. "But I think that's too devious, even for him. That is the work of a more subtle mind, a mind that wants you to suffer in jail for many years. Copley Carmichael is enraged and intends to harm you in the more direct way."

"Sookie, I'm sorry," Amelia said. She was composed now, and she held her head up with some dignity despite the tears on her cheeks. "I just mentioned the cluviel dor that once in a conversation I had with my dad. I don't know where he got all his other information. I don't seem to be a very good friend to you, no matter how much I love you and how hard I try."

I couldn't think of any response that wouldn't sound lame. Bob glared at me over Amelia's head. He wanted me to say something to make this all right. There simply wasn't any way to do that.

"I'm going to do everything I can to help you out," Amelia said. "That's why I came up here in the first place. But I'll try even harder now."

I took a deep breath. "I know you will, Amelia," I said. "You're truly a great witch, and I'm sure we're going to get through this." And that was the best I could do, just at this moment.

Amelia gave me a watery smile, and Quinn gave her a pat on the arm, and Diantha looked totally bored. (Not big with the emotional dialogue, Diantha.) Mr. Cataliades may have felt the same way, because he said, "We seem to have gotten over that bump in the road, so let me move on to something else of interest."

We all tried to look attentive.

"There's much more to talk about, but as I look around me, I see people who are tired and need recovery time," he said unexpectedly. "Let's resume tomorrow. A couple of us have little tasks to perform this evening or tonight."

Amelia and Bob went into their bedroom and shut the door, which was a relief to everyone. Barry asked if he could use my computer since he'd come away without his laptop, and I said yes, providing he didn't give anyone his location. I was feeling double paranoid, and I thought I had good reason. Mr. Cataliades and Diantha retreated upstairs to make phone calls about Mr. Cataliades's law practice.

Quinn and I took a walk, just so we could have some time by ourselves. He said he'd thought of resuming his dating life, after Tijgerin had given him the word that she wouldn't see him for a long time, but he just couldn't do it. He was going to have a child with Tij, and that gave him the feeling he was bound to her, even if she told him to stay away. It was galling that she wouldn't let him share in the upbringing of the baby, that she clung to the old ways with such determination and ferocity.

"You heard from your sister, Frannie?" I asked, hoping I wasn't bringing up another doleful subject. My heart lightened when he smiled.

"She's married," he said. "Can you believe it? I thought I'd lost her forever when she ran off. I thought she'd take drugs and

287

whore around. But once she got away from us, from me and Mom, she got a job as a waitress in a café in New Mexico. She met a guy at the café who does something in the tourist industry. Next thing you know, they went to a wedding chapel. So far, so good. How's your brother?"

"He's getting married to a woman who's not a supe," I said. "But she seems to love him for what he is, and she doesn't expect more than he can give." My brother's emotional and intellectual ranges were limited, though they were expanding bit by bit. Like Frannie, Jason had grown up a lot recently. After being bitten and becoming a werepanther, Jason's life had gotten chaotic, but now he was getting it together.

Besides our families, Quinn and I didn't really talk about anything in particular. It was a relaxing walk, even in the steamy heat that had followed the end of the rain.

He didn't ask me any questions about my situation with Eric, and that was a relief.

"After I do a tour through your woods, what else can I do for you, Sookie?" Quinn asked. "I want to do something besides sit around and hear stuff that's just embarrassing."

"Yeah, that was pretty awful. No matter how hard Amelia and I try to be friends, something always happens."

"It happens because she can't keep her mouth shut," Quinn said, and I shrugged. That was the way Amelia was. To my surprise, Quinn put his arm around me and pulled me close, and I wondered if I'd sent out the wrong signal.

"Listen, Sookie," he murmured, smiling down at me in a fond way, "I don't want to scare you or anything, but someone's in the woods and they're walking along the driveway parallel to us. You got any ideas who it might be? If they're armed?" His voice was not agitated, and I did my best to match his ease. It was incredibly hard not to turn to stare into the woods.

I made myself smile up at Quinn. "I sure don't. Not a human, or I'd get the brain signature. Can't be a vamp, it's daylight."

Quinn expelled all the breath in his lungs and drew in a chestful of air. "Ask me, it might be a fairy," he whispered. "I'm just getting a touch of fae. There are so many scents in the air after the rain."

"But the fae are all gone," I said, reminding myself to let my expression change. After all, I wouldn't be beaming at Quinn for five minutes while we strolled down the road. "That's what my great-grandfather told me."

"I think he was wrong," Quinn said. "Let's casually turn to head back to the house."

I took Quinn's hand and swung it enthusiastically. I felt like an idiot, but I needed something physical to do while I sent out my other sense. I finally found the brain signature of whatever creature lurked in the woods, which provided easy concealment due to the natural effects of summer (rain and light) and the benefits of Niall's blessing on the land. The closer to my house we got, the thicker the vegetation became. The area right at the edge of the yard might almost be a jungle.

"You think he's going to shoot?" I said with a smile. I swung Quinn's hand like I was a child walking with her grandpa.

"I don't smell a gun," he said. "Enough with the hand swinging. I need to be able to move quick."

I let go, somewhat embarrassed. "Let's try to get into the house. Without getting killed."

But whoever was stalking us didn't make a move. It was almost an anticlimax to walk across the enclosed back porch, wondering every second if something terrible would happen, and then to make it in the door and shut it behind us . . . and nothing happened. Nothing at all.

Barry had decided to make hamburgers to cook on the grill in the backyard. He was putting chopped onion and seasoned salt and green peppers in the meat and forming the patties, and he was mighty startled when we bolted into the kitchen and ducked.

"What the hell?" he said.

"Someone was out there," I said.

He crouched, too. He closed his eyes and concentrated. "I have no idea," he said, after a moment. "Whoever it was, he's left, Sookie."

"Smelled like a fairy," Quinn told Barry.

"They're all gone," Barry said. "That's what the Texas vampires told me. Said they'd cleaned out lock, stock, and barrel."

"They are all gone," I said. "I know that for a fact. So either Quinn's nose is wrong or we have a rogue."

"Or a reject," Barry said quietly.

"Or an escapee. Whatever he is, why is he skulking in the woods?" Quinn asked.

But I didn't have any answer. And when nothing else happened, we three began to think nothing would. Quinn decided to delay his search of the woods until the evening. There wasn't any point going out there now.

Though it felt anticlimactic, I began slicing tomatoes for the hamburgers, and then

I cut up a watermelon. Quinn volunteered to make some home fries. Since he'd put a ten-pound bag of potatoes in the cart today, I was glad he had a plan to use them up.

With all three of us working in the kitchen, supper came together. I pretended not to see when Quinn ate one burger before it was cooked, and Barry hastily volunteered to take the others out to the grill. I put together a baked bean casserole, and Quinn began frying the potatoes. I set the table and washed the preparation dishes.

It was almost like running a boarding-house, I thought, when I called everyone down for dinner.

CHAPTER 13

Amazingly, the meal went well. There was just enough room for us at the kitchen table when I opened two folding chairs my gran had kept in the living room closet.

Amelia had obviously been crying, but she was calm now. Bob touched her every chance he got. Mr. Cataliades explained that he and Diantha had recalled an errand in town, and after we'd shared hamburgers and French fries and beans and watermelon, they took off.

We all helped clear away the kitchen. After dinner, Barry sat in a living room armchair with his feet propped up, focusing on his e-reader. Bob and Amelia cuddled on the couch watching a rebroadcast of *The Terminator.* Cheerful. After consuming three cooked hamburgers and a quart of French fries, Quinn loped outside to conduct a fruitless search of the woods. After an hour, discouraged and filthy, he returned to the house to tell me that he had smelled two vampires (presumably Bill and Karin) and a faint trace of fairy in the place we'd been when we were followed. But there was nothing else to find. He was leaving for a motel by the interstate.

I felt hostess guilt over not having a bed to offer him. I did tell him I'd be glad to pay for his hotel room, and he gave me a look that would've made paint peel.

The two part-demons returned after dark, while I was reading, and they didn't look happy. They said good night very politely and clattered up the stairs to their room. With everyone in for the night, I decided my day could officially come to a close. It had been a pretty damn long one.

It's always possible for human beings to spoil their own peace of mind, and I did a good job of it that night. Despite the friends who had shown up with no expectation of reward, the friends who'd come a long way to help me, I worried about the friend who hadn't tried. I just couldn't figure Sam out any more than I could figure out why Eric had posted my bail when I was no longer his wife, or even his girlfriend.

I was sure he'd had some reason for doing me that large good turn.

Does it sound like I was labeling Eric as

ungenerous, uncaring? In some respects, and to some people, he was never those things. But he was a practical vampire, and he was a vampire about to become the consort of a true queen. Since dismissing me as his wife apparently was one of Freyda's conditions for marrying Eric (and frankly, I could sure understand that), I couldn't *imagine* her accepting Eric's decision to put up an awfully large amount of money to secure my freedom. Maybe that had been part of some negotiation? "If you'll let me bail out my former wife, I'll take a decreased allowance for a year," or something like that. (For all I knew, they negotiated how many times they would have sex.) And I had the most depressing mental image of the beautiful Freyda and my Eric . . . my former Eric.

Somewhere in the midst of wandering through a mental maze, I fell asleep.

I slept twenty minutes too late the next day and woke up to the awareness that my house was full of guests. I threw myself out of bed, aware of other brains firing into thought all over the house. I was showered and out in the kitchen quicker than greased lightning, and I fixed pancakes and bacon, put the coffeepot on, and got out the juice glasses. I listened to Amelia being sick in

the hall bathroom and sent a groggy Diantha into mine to speed up the shower process.

As the pancakes came off the griddle, I
slid them right onto plates so my guests
could eat them while they were hot. I put
out all the fruit I had, for the healthy
minded.

Mr. Cataliades *loved* pancakes, and Diantha was not far behind him in pancake
consumption. I had to make up some more
batter in a hurry. Then there were dishes to
wash (Bob helped) and my bed to make. So
I had plenty to do, but throughout the busy-
ness of my hands and thoughts, I was
unhappily aware that I hadn't heard from
Sam.

I e-mailed him.

I chose that format so I could say exactly
what I wanted to say without having to
restate it several times. I worked on my
composition for a while.

Sam, I don't know why you don't want
to talk to me, but I wanted you to know
that I'm ready to come to work any day
you need me. Please let me know how
you're feeling.

I read this message over several times and

decided it put the ball in Sam's court pretty firmly. It was perfect until I impulsively typed, "I miss you." And then I clicked Send.

After years of having what I considered a happy relationship with Sam — for the most part — with no effort at all, now that I'd actually made a sacrifice for him, we were down to e-mails and mysterious silences.

It was hard to understand.

I was trying to explain this to Amelia a few minutes later. She'd come upon me staring at the computer as if I were trying to will the screen to talk to me.

"What did you sacrifice?" she asked, her clear blue eyes intent on my face. When Amelia was in the right mood, she could be a good listener. I knew that Bob was shaving in the hall bathroom, Barry was out in the yard doing yoga stuff, and Mr. C and Diantha were having an earnest conversation at the edge of the woods. So it was safe to be frank.

"I sacrificed my chance to keep Eric," I said. "I gave it up to save Sam's life."

She bypassed the big important part of that to go straight to the painful questions. "If you have to use big magic to keep someone with you, was it really meant to be?"

297

"I never thought about it as an either/or," I said. "But Eric did. He's a proud guy, and his maker began the process of hitching him to Freyda without consulting Eric at all."

"And you know this how?"

"When he finally told me about it, he seemed . . . genuinely desperate."

Amelia looked at me like I was the world's biggest idiot. "Right, 'cause it's nobody's dream to go from managing a backwater area of Louisiana to being consort of a beautiful queen who's hot for you. And why did he end up telling you?"

"Well, Pam insisted," I admitted, feeling doubts overwhelm me. "But he hadn't told me because he was trying to think of a way to stay with me."

"I'm not saying anything different," she said. Amelia has never been tactful, and I could tell she was making a huge effort. "You're pretty great. But you know, honey . . . Eric is all about Eric. That's why I was so willing to encourage Alcide. I figured Eric would break your heart." She shrugged. "Or turn you," she added as an afterthought.

I jerked, involuntarily.

"He *did* mean to turn you! That asshole! He would have taken you away from us. I guess we're lucky all he did is break your heart!" She was absolutely furious.

"In all honesty, I don't know that my heart is broken," I said. "I'm depressed and sad. But I don't feel as bad as I did when I found out about Bill's big secret."

Amelia said, "With Bill — that was the first time, right? The first time you'd found out someone important to you had been deceiving you?"

"It was the first chance anyone had ever had to deceive me," I said, a new way to look at Bill's betrayal. "With humans I've always been able to tell, at least enough to be wary or mistrustful . . . not to buy into whatever line of bullshit they're handing out. Bill was the first sexual adventure for me, and he was the first man I ever said 'I love you' to."

"Maybe you're just getting used to being lied to," Amelia said bracingly, and that was so much like Amelia that I had to smile. She was self-aware enough to look a bit abashed, "Okay, that was awful. I'm sorry."

I mimed amazement, my eyes wide and my hands held open by my face.

"Bob told me that I needed to work on my people skills," Amelia said. "He said I was pretty blunt."

I tried not to smile too broadly. "Bob might be handy to have around after all."

"Now that I'm pregnant, especially." Amelia looked at me anxiously. "You sure we're having a baby? I mean, when I thought about it, I could kind of see that my body hadn't been working the way it was supposed to for a little while. And I feel thicker. But I'd never thought of having a baby. I just thought I was hormonal. I'm all weepy."

"Even witches sing the blues," I said, and she grinned at me.

"This is going to be one awesome baby," she said.

CHAPTER 14

Mr. Cataliades came in to tell us he'd been talking to Beth Osiecki by cell phone and that he had an appointment to meet her and review my situation. Diantha rode into town with him; I didn't ask what her part in this consultation was supposed to be, and she didn't volunteer. Barry decided to ride in with them, too, and see if there was another car to rent locally while he was in town. He'd called ahead to make sure Chessie Johnson would be at home and was willing to talk to him.

Barry was used to getting answers from people indirectly, by listening to their heads when they were in conversation with others. In other words, eavesdropping. Since he'd be the one asking the questions in this instance, he was a little anxious about the process. I briefed him as thoroughly as I could on the Johnsons and on Lisa and Coby. He had prepared a list of questions to which he needed answers: Whom had Arlene been planning to meet? Where had she been staying since she got released? Whom had she talked to? Who had paid for the new lawyer and her bail?

"If you can," I said quietly, "please find out what's going to happen to the kids. I feel bad for all they've been through." Barry could see what was in my head. He nodded, his face serious.

Bob got on the phone to a touch psychic, though since we didn't have possession of the scarf I couldn't see the point. Bob seemed sure we'd be able to lay hands on it. The touch psychic, a Baton Rouge woman named Delphine Oubre, would drive up to Bon Temps the next morning, he said.

"And do what?" I tried hard to sound grateful and appreciative, but I didn't think I managed. I had done the most accurate drawing of the scarf that I could, and I'd described the pattern and the colors to Diantha, since saying "teal green" and "peacock blue" to Mr. Cataliades had just resulted in a blank stare. Diantha had done a second version in color, and it had looked very like what I'd remembered.

"I wouldn't worry about that if I were you. Your demon buddies are pretty resourceful." Bob smiled mysteriously and glided out of the room. In some ways, Bob was still very catlike.

Amelia was researching spells to make Arlene's mysterious male friends talk, if we could find them. I had a moment of longing for Pam. She could make anybody talk, no spell involved, unless you considered vamp hypnosis a spell. Pam would rather beat it out of them, anyway. Maybe I'd give her a call. *No.* I told myself this firmly, and frequently. At this point, it was better if I simply let all connection with the vampires drop. Sure, Bill still lived next door, and it was inevitable that I'd see him from time to time. Sure, Eric had left a couple of things in the hidey-hole in my guest bedroom. Sure, Quinn reported that he'd smelled two vamps (almost surely Bill and Karin) in the woods. But I'd decided I was going to pretend there was a wall between me and every vampire in Area Five. Between me and every vampire in the world!

I checked my e-mail. I'd gotten one from Sam. Full of anticipation, I clicked on it. "Come to work this morning," was all it said. Quinn had e-mailed me, too. "Saw a couple of people I thought I recognized in the motel bar last night," I read. "I'm going to follow them today."

Who on earth could it be? But at the idea that things were moving along, I felt a rush of optimism. I went into my room to shower and dress with a smile on my face.

When I emerged from my room ready to go to work, I found Bob and Amelia in the backyard. They'd built a little fire in a circle of old bricks, and they were scattering some herbs on it and chanting. They didn't invite me to join them; and truthfully, magic smelled weird and made me really nervous, so I wasn't eager to ask any questions.

I went into Merlotte's to find it was exactly as usual. No one blinked an eye at my presence or expressed surprise that I'd turned up. As it happened, we were extremely busy. Sam was there, but every time our eyes met he looked away, as if he were ashamed of something. But I swear he was glad to see me.

Finally, I trapped him in his office. I was blocking the only exit, unless he wanted to duck into his tiny bathroom and lock the door, and he wasn't craven enough to do that.

"Okay, spill," I said.

He seemed almost relieved, as if he'd hoped I'd demand an explanation. He looked directly at me, and if I could have climbed inside his brain and looked at it, I would have. Damn shifters.

"I can't," he said. "I swore not to."

I narrowed my eyes while I considered. It was a serious thing, swearing, and I could hardly threaten to tickle him until he talked, or tell him I was going to hold my breath until he spilled. But I had to know what had changed. I'd thought we were getting back to normal, that Sam had started to rebuild himself after his death experience, that we were on solid ground.

"Sooner or later you're going to have to tell me what's wrong," I said reasonably. "If you can think of any way to give me a hint, that would be a good thing."

"I better not."

"I wish you could have come out last night," I said, changing tack. "We had a good supper, and the house was full last night."

"Did Quinn stay?" Sam asked stiffly.

"No, too crowded for that. He's got a motel room out on the interstate. I wish you'd be friendly to him. And all my guests."

"Why do you want me to be friendly with Quinn?"

Yeah, some jealousy there. Good Lord. "Because all my company came from miles away, and they all came to help clear my name."

Sam froze for a minute. "Are you hinting that I'm not helping you like they are? That they care more about you than I do?" He was obviously angry.

"No," I said. "I don't think that." Wow, he was *super*-touchy. I said hesitantly, "I did kind of wonder why you didn't come to the court hearing?"

"You think I want to see you in handcuffs, robbed of your dignity?"

"I'd like to think I always have my dignity, Sam, cuffs or not." We glared at each other for a second or two. Then I said, "But it was pretty humiliating," and to my embarrassment, my eyes filled with tears.

He held out his arms to me and I hugged him, though I could feel the uneasiness in him. The oath he'd sworn had something in it about physical contact, I concluded. When the hug naturally ended, he kind of held me away. I let it be. I could see he thought I was going to ask him more questions. But I thought better of it.

Instead, I invited him out to the house for dinner the next night. I'd looked at the work schedule, and I'd seen that Kennedy would be behind the bar. He agreed to come, but he looked wary, as if he suspected I had a secret motive. Not at all! I just thought the more I was in his company, the more chances I'd have to find out what was going on.

I'd been worried that people would shy away from me, since I'd been accused of killing Arlene. As I waited tables, I came to understand the shocking truth: People weren't worried much about Arlene's death. Her trial had taken her reputation away from her. It wasn't so much that people loved me; it was that people realized a mom shouldn't lure her friend to her death, and then get caught, because then her children were left in the lurch. I came to see that despite the fact that I'd dated vampires, I had a good reputation in many respects. I was reliable and cheerful and hardworking, and with the people of Bon Temps that counted an awful lot. I put flowers on my family's graves every holiday and on the anniversary of their deaths. Plus, through area gossip, it had become known that I was taking an active interest in my cousin Hadley's little boy, and there was a widespread, pleasant hope that I would marry Hadley's widower, Remy Savoy, because that would tie things up neatly.

Which would have been great . . . except Remy and I weren't interested in each other. Until real recently, I'd had Eric, and to the best of my knowledge, Remy was still dating the very cute Erin. I tried to imagine kissing Remy and simply wasn't inclined to go there.

All of these thoughts kept me engaged and busy both outside and inside, until it was time for me to go. Sam smiled and waved when I took off my apron and handed over my tables to India.

No one at all was at my house when I unlocked the back door. That was strange, since it had been such a beehive that morning. Moved by an impulse, I went into my bedroom and perched on the side of the bed, close to my bedside table. Thanks to my compulsory cleaning during my three days off, neatly located in the top drawer were all the things I might need at a moment's notice during the night: a flashlight, Kleenex, ChapStick, Tylenol, three condoms Quinn had left when we'd dated, a list of emergency phone numbers, a cell phone charger, an old tin box (full of pins, needles, buttons, and paper clips), some pens, a notepad . . . the usual mixture of handy items.

But the next drawer held memorabilia. There was the bullet I'd sucked out of Eric's flesh in Dallas. There was a rock that had hit Eric in the head in the living room of Sam's rental house in town. There were various sets of keys to Eric's house, Jason's house, Tara's house, all neatly labeled. There was a laminated copy of my gran's obituary and my parents', and another laminated newspaper story published the year the Lady Falcons had won their division at state, with a few nice lines about my performance. There was an ancient brooch in which Gran had placed a lock of my mom's hair and a lock of my dad's. There was the old pattern envelope containing a letter from Gran and the velvet bag that had contained the cluviel dor, and the cluviel dor itself, now dull and divested of all its magic. There was a note Quinn had written me during our dating period. There was the envelope in which Sam had given me a partnership agreement to the bar, though the actual partnership document was in a lockbox at my lawyer's. There were birthday cards and Christmas cards and a drawing made by Hunter.

It was dumb to keep the rock. It was too heavy for the drawer, anyway, and made it hard to open and close. I put it on top of my night table, planning to set it in the flower bed. I got out the keys to Eric's house, wrapped them in bubble wrap, and put them in a padded mailer to send to him. I wondered if he'd put the house up for sale, or what? Maybe the next sheriff would move into it. If Felipe de Castro appointed him or her, I realized that my grace period was very short. With any new vampire regime, it would be open season on me . . . or would they just forget about me? That would be almost too good to be true.

A knock at the back door was a welcome diversion. The packmaster himself had come to call, and he seemed more at ease than I'd ever seen him. Alcide Herveaux looked comfortable in his own skin and pleased with the world. He was wearing his usual jeans and boots — a surveyor couldn't tromp through ditches and woods in flip-flops. His short-sleeved shirt was well worn and tight across his wide shoulders. Alcide was a working man but not an uncomplicated one. His love life, up until now, had been nothing short of a disaster. First, Debbie Pelt, who had been a bitch on wheels until I'd killed her; then the very nice Maria-Star Cooper, who'd been murdered; then Annabelle Bannister, who'd been unfaithful to him. He'd had a thing for me until I'd persuaded him that would be a bad idea for both of us. Now he was seeing a werewolf named Kandace, who was new to the area. She would be up for membership in the pack later this month.

"I hear we need to try to find a trail of someone who stole that scarf," Alcide said.

"I hope you can pick up something," I said. "Wouldn't be court evidence, but we'd be able to track down him or her."

"You're a clean woman," he said, looking around the living room. "But I can tell there've been lots of people in here lately."

"Yeah," I said. "I got a houseful of company. So the best place to catch a scent would be in my room."

"That's where we'll start," he said, and smiled. He had white teeth in a tan face and lovely green eyes, and Alcide's smile was something else. Too bad he wasn't for me.

"You want a glass of water or some lemonade?" I said.

"Maybe after I get the job done," he said. He took off his clothes and folded them neatly on the couch. Wow. I struggled to keep my face neutral. Then he changed.

It always looked like it hurt, and the sounds were unpleasant, but Alcide seemed to recover quickly. The handsome wolf in front of me padded around my living room, his sensitive nose recording scent trails before he followed them into my bedroom.

I stayed out of his way. I sat at the little desk in the living room where the computer was plugged in, and I passed the time by deleting a lot of old e-mail. It was something to do while he searched. I banished all the spam and the department store ads before a big wolf head thrust its way into my lap, and there was Alcide, tail wagging.

I patted him automatically. That was what you did when a canine head presented itself. You scratched between its ears and under its chin, you rubbed its belly . . . well, maybe not a wolf's belly, especially a male wolf's.

Alcide grinned at me and changed back. He'd become the fastest changer I'd ever seen. I wondered if that ability came with the packmaster job.

"Any luck?" I asked, keeping my eyes modestly focused on my hands while he got dressed.

"At least you didn't clean the throw rug by your bed," he said. "I can tell you that one person who's been in your room, I don't know at all. But your friend Tara's been there, right by your bed. Your two fae buddies were in there, but then, they lived here."

"They were searching my house while I was gone every day," I said. "They were searching for the cluviel dor."

"That's sad, that your kin would do that," Alcide said, and he patted me on the shoulder. "Who else did I smell? Eric, of course. And you know who else? Arlene. She was carrying a charm of some kind, but definitely Arlene."

"I didn't remember you'd met Arlene." I grasped at an irrelevant issue because I was stunned silly.

"She served me once or twice when I came by Merlotte's."

I figured out her access after five seconds' more cogitation. "She knew where I hid my keys from when we were friends," I said, infuriated by my own carelessness. "I guess before, or even after, she came to Merlotte's, she let herself in here and got the scarf. But why?"

"Someone told her to, I expect," Alcide said, buckling his belt.

"Someone sent her here to get the scarf that would be used to kill her."

"Apparently, that's what happened. Ironic, huh?"

I couldn't think of any other explanation.

And it made me sick.

"Thanks so much, Alcide," I said, remembering my manners. I got him the glass of lemonade I'd promised him, and he drank it in one long gulp. "How's Kandace doing, integrating into the pack?" I asked.

He smiled broadly. "She's doing real well,"

he said. "Taking it slow. They're warming up to her." Kandace had been a rogue wolf, but because she'd turned in some worse rogues, she'd gotten a chance to join the pack while the bad ones had been banished. Kandace was quiet and tall, and though I didn't know her well, I knew she was the calmest person Alcide had ever been with. I had the sense that after a life on rough seas, Kandace was looking for inland waters.

"That's real good to hear," I said. "I wish her luck."

"Call me if you need me," Alcide said. "The pack stands ready to help you."

"You've already been a help," I said, and I meant it.

Two minutes after he left, Barry pulled up in a car he'd rented from a new place out by the interstate. He'd also brought Amelia and Bob. Amelia said, "I'm asleep on my feet," and headed for the bedroom to take a nap, Bob hard on her heels. Barry ran upstairs to plug his cell phone into his charger. I glanced at the clock and realized it was time to get busy. I began cooking supper for six. Country-fried steak took a while, so I got that in the oven first. Then I cut up crookneck squash and onions to sauté, and I chopped okra and breaded it to fry, and I put bakery rolls on a baking sheet to pop in

314

the oven right before I served supper. I'd start the rice soon.

Barry came into the kitchen, sniffing the air and smiling.

"Did you have a productive day?" I asked.

Barry nodded. He said, *I'll wait until everyone gets here so I'll only have to say it once.*

Okay, I said, and wiped the flour off the kitchen counter. Barry cleared the counter of dirty dishes in the best possible way, by washing and drying them. He was far more domesticated than I'd ever suspected, and I realized there was much more to know about him.

"I'm going outside to make some phone calls," he said. I knew he wanted to be out of my earshot and mindshot, if I can put it that way, but that didn't bother me in the least. While he was outside, Bob ambled through the kitchen and straight down the porch steps, carefully easing the porch door closed.

A few minutes later, Amelia came out into the kitchen sleepy-eyed. "Bob went for a walk in the woods," she muttered. "I'm going to splash some water on my face." Mr. Cataliades and Diantha came in the back door ten minutes later. Diantha looked exhausted, but Mr. C was positively bubbly.

"I am smitten with Beth Osiecki," he said,

beaming. "I'll tell you all about it over our meal. First, I must shower." He sniffed the air in the kitchen appreciatively and told me how much he looked forward to dinner before he and a silent Diantha went upstairs. Amelia came out of the bathroom; Mr. Cataliades went in. Bob returned from the woods, sweaty and scratched and with a bag full of various plants. He collapsed in a chair and begged for a big icy glass of tea. He drank it dry. Diantha had stopped at a roadside stand to buy a honeydew melon, and she cut into it. I could smell the sweetness as she cut out the fruit and diced it.

My cell phone buzzed. "Hello?" I said. The rice was boiling, so I turned it down and covered it. I glanced at the kitchen clock so I could turn it off in twenty minutes.

"It's Quinn," he said.

"Where are you? Who were you tracking down? We're about to eat. You coming?"

"The two men I saw were gone this morning," he said. "I think they caught a glimpse of me and checked out during the night. I've spent all day trying to find them, but they're in the wind."

"Who were they?"

"Do you remember . . . that lawyer?"

"Johan Glassport?"

316

"Yeah, how'd you know?"

"Barry saw him in New Orleans."

"He was here. With some guy who looked kind of familiar, though I couldn't put a name to him."

"So . . . what are your plans?" I glanced at the clock anxiously. It was hard to concentrate when I was trying to put a meal on the table. My gran had always made it look so easy.

"I'm sorry, Sookie. I have other news. I've been called away to take a job, and my employer says I'm the only one who can do it."

"Uh-huh." Then I realized I hadn't responded to his tone of voice, but his words. "You sound pretty serious."

"I have to stage a wedding ceremony. A vampire wedding ceremony."

I took a deep breath. "In Oklahoma, I take it?"

"Yes. In two weeks. If I don't do it, I'll lose my job."

And now that he was going to have a kid, he couldn't afford to do any such thing. "I get it," I said steadily. "Really, I understand. You showed up, and I love that you came here."

"I'm so sorry I couldn't catch up with Glassport. I know he's dangerous."

"We'll find out if he has anything to do with this, Quinn. Thanks for your help."

And we said good-bye a few more times, in different ways, until we had to hang up. By that time, I had to get busy with the gravy or supper would be ruined. I simply had to postpone thinking of Eric and Freyda's wedding until later.

After twenty minutes, I was calmer, the food was ready, and we were all seated around the kitchen table.

No one joined in my prayer but Bob, but that was okay. We'd said one. Getting everyone served was a ten-minute process. After that, the floor seemed open to discussion.

Barry said, "I visited Brock and Chessie, and I talked to the kids."

"How'd you get in?" Amelia asked. "I know you called 'em before you went."

"I said I'd known Arlene and I wanted to say how sorry I was. I didn't lie to them after that." He looked defensive. "But I did tell them I was a friend of Sookie's, and that I didn't think she had anything to do with Arlene's death."

"Did they believe that?" I said.

"They did," he said, with an air of surprise. "They don't believe you killed Arlene, strictly from a practical point of view. They

318

said you're smaller than Arlene and they didn't think you could have either gripped her neck hard enough *or* gotten her into the Dumpster. And the only person they could think of who would help you is Sam, and he wouldn't have put the body behind his own bar."

"I hope a lot of people have figured that out," I said.

"I said Arlene hadn't called me when she got out of prison. They told me that they hadn't had any warning, either, which was what I wanted to know. She'd just shown up on their doorstep three days before her death."

"What did they observe about her demeanor before her death?" Mr. Cataliades said. "Was she frightened? Secretive?"

"They thought Arlene looked kind of nervous when she came by to see the kids. She was excited to see them, but she was scared about something. She told Chessie she had to meet some people and she wasn't supposed to talk about it, that someone was going to help her pay her legal bills so she could get back on her feet and take care of her kids."

"That would have interested her, sure," I said. "Maybe applying for a job at Merlotte's wasn't her idea. Maybe these mysterious men put her up to it. Maybe she *did* know how unlikely it was that she'd be hired back."

"The Johnsons don't know anything more specific than that? They didn't see the people she was going to talk to?" Amelia was impatient. This didn't seem like much information to her.

"It confirms what I heard from Jane Bodehouse," I said. "Jane saw Arlene meeting with two men in back of Tray's old place the night before we found her body."

A shadow crossed Amelia's face at the mention of Tray Dawson. They'd been close, and she'd hoped they'd get closer, but Tray had died.

"Why there?" Bob said. "It would have been a lot easier to meet at an isolated place rather than out back of someone's house, especially someone who would definitely ask questions."

"That house is empty, and the garage next to it, too," I told him. "And I don't know if Arlene had a vehicle or not. Her old car was parked at the Johnsons' house, but it may or may not have been running. Plus, as the crow flies, Tray's place is not far from Merlotte's, and that's where they were going to take her. They didn't want her to have time to figure out what was going to happen."

There was a long pause while my friends worked this through.

"Possible," Bob said, and everyone nodded.

"How are Coby and Lisa?" I asked Barry.

"Stunned," Barry said shortly. "Confused." From his head, I could see the images of the kids' bewildered faces. I felt horrible every time I thought about those kids.

"Did their mom tell them anything?" Amelia asked quietly.

"Arlene told them she was going to take them away to live with her in a cute little house — that they'd be able to get nice food and clothes without her having to work such long hours. She told them she wanted to be with them all the time."

"How was she going to do that?" Amelia said. "Did she tell them?"

Barry shook his head. He was feeling a twinge of self-disgust, and I didn't blame him. Somehow it seemed ignoble to read the minds of children when they'd suffered such a string of misfortunes. But it wasn't like Barry had been giving them the third degree, I told myself.

"The bottom line is, Arlene planned on doing something for these two men, something that would pay off big," Barry concluded.

"When is your touch psychic coming?" Mr. Cataliades asked Bob.

"She's getting here tomorrow morning after she finishes feeding her animals or something." Bob reached out for another piece of country-fried steak. He narrowly missed getting stabbed in the hand by Mr. Cataliades, who was after the same piece.

"I got your scarf, Sookie," said Diantha, who was eating very slowly. Her voice and demeanor were pale shadows of her normal hypervitality. She was even speaking slowly enough to be understandable.

Silence fell around the table as we all regarded her with awe. Mr. Cataliades was looking at his niece fondly. "I knew she could do it," he told us, and I wondered if he'd actually had a foreseeing or if he just had a lot of faith in Diantha.

"How?" Amelia asked. (Amelia never hesitated when it came to asking a direct question.)

Diantha said, "I went in the police station after I saw the big woman cop."

Everyone else looked at her blankly.

"She turned herself into Kenya Jones," I explained. "Kenya's a patrolwoman who's been trained to do crime-scene processing."

"We waited at the police station a long time this morning, Sookie," Mr. Cataliades explained. "I had to interview Detective Bellefleur personally, and Detective Beck, too, since I am now co-counsel on your case, thanks to Ms. Osiecki. During our long, long wait we had time to find out all kinds of interesting information. Like where the evidence locker is and who can check out items from it. Diantha is so quick and devious!"

Diantha smiled faintly.

"How'd you manage it?" Amelia asked. She looked admiring.

"I had a scarf in my pocket in a plastic bag. It was pretty close to Sookie's description. We found it at Tara's Togs. I turned myself into Kenya. I went to the locker and storage area. I told the policeman there I needed to see the scarf. The old guy, he brought it to me in a plastic bag. I looked at it, and when he went to the bathroom, I swapped it for the scarf I'd brought. I handed it to him when he came back. I walked out." She reached for her glass of tea in a weary way.

"Thank you, Diantha," I said. I was both happy she'd done such a ballsy thing and sorry she'd done something illegal. My law-abiding half was kind of appalled that we were screwing around with real evidence in a real murder. But my self-preserving half was relieved that we might find out something, now that we had the real scarf . . . if the touch psychic lived up to her billing.

Diantha perked up after receiving a good helping of praise from all of us. Though she was still moving and speaking slowly, after she ate everything on the table that wasn't on someone's plate she seemed to have taken a big step toward restoring her strength. Obviously, the transformation she'd accomplished had burned up a tremendous amount of energy.

"It's much harder when she has to speak as the person, rather than just resemble them," Mr. Cataliades said quietly. He'd read my mind. He treated her with courtesy and respect, refilling her glass with tea and passing her the butter with great frequency. (I made a mental note to add butter to my store list.) Barry had bought a cake at the bakery. Though Gran would have thrown up her hands in horror at having a store-bought cake in her house, I was not so proud, since I hadn't had time to bake. Diantha was definitely on board for dessert, which I planned to dish up as soon as the kitchen was clean.

Amelia was such a clear broadcaster. She stared across the room at Diantha, lost in thought. While we were clearing the table, I had to listen to her reassessing Diantha's abilities and cleverness. She was really impressed with the part-demon girl. Amelia was thinking about Diantha's amazing elasticity. She wondered if Diantha was transforming her actual flesh or if she was casting an illusion. Diantha's success made Amelia feel she hadn't done her share of the detecting.

"Of course," Amelia said abruptly, "Bob and I couldn't cast the spell we wanted to cast, since we haven't found the two men yet. But after Barry came back to get us in his snazzy rental" — this was a joke; Barry had come back in a battered Ford Focus — "we did go to all the apartment and house rental places in Bon Temps, including answering the newspaper ads. We were ready to insist on seeing any unrented apartments or houses we'd seen an ad for, because we thought the owner would say, 'Oh, sorry, we just rented that place to two guys from wherever.' Then we could go check them out. But we didn't get a lead."

"Well, that's good information to have," I said. "They're too smart to stay locally." I could tell Amelia was steamed that she and Bob hadn't tracked down the two guys and handed them over to us.

"However," Bob said, "we did verify why

your flowers and tomatoes are growing so well."

"Ahhhhh . . . great. Why?"

"Fairy magic," he said. "Someone has charged all the Stackhouse land with fairy magic."

I didn't tell them I'd already figured that out, because I wanted them to feel good. I remembered my great-grandfather's good-bye embrace, when I'd felt a jolt of power. I'd thought it was the finality of his farewell . . . but he'd been, for want of a better term, blessing me and my house. "Awww," I said softly. "That's so sweet."

"He would have done better to put in a giant ring of protection," Amelia said darkly. She'd been outmagicked on several fronts, and while normally she was a practical person, she was also proud. "How did Arlene get past your old wards?"

"Alcide thought she had a charm," I offered. "I'm assuming someone gave her magic."

Amelia flushed. "If she did have a charm, another witch is involved in this, and I want to know who. I'll take care of that."

"Gran would have loved seeing the yard like this," I said, to change the subject. I smiled at the thought of the pleasure my grandmother would have felt. She'd loved her yard and worked in it tirelessly. The flowers would bloom and flourish, the bulbs would spread, the grass . . . well, it was growing like wildfire. I was going to have to mow it tomorrow, and frequently thereafter.

That was fairies for you. Always some blowback.

"Niall did more for you than that," Mr. Cataliades said, distracting me from my unwelcome thoughts.

"What are you talking about?" I said, and that didn't sound as civil as I meant it. "I'm sorry. You must know something I don't." I managed a more cordial tone.

"Yes," he said with a smile. "I do know many things you don't, and I'm about to tell you one of them. I would have come to Bon Temps without your being charged with murder, because I have business with you as your great-grandfather's lawyer."

"He's not dead," I said immediately.

"No, but he doesn't plan on returning here. And he wanted you to have something to remember him kindly."

"He's my family. I don't need anything else," I said. Which was crazy, I knew it the moment I said it, but I have a little pride, too.

"I would say you do need a few things, Miss Stackhouse," said Mr. Cataliades mildly. "Right now, you need a defense fund. Thanks to Niall, you have one. Not only will you be receiving a monthly income from the sale of Claudine's house, your great-grandfather deeded the club to you, the one called Hooligans, and I have sold it."

"What? But that belonged to Claude, Claudine, and Claudette, the triplets who were his fae grandchildren."

"Though I don't know the story, I understood from Niall that Claude did not buy the club, but was given it because he threatened the true owner."

"Yes," I said, after I thought about it a bit. "That's true. Claudette was dead by then."

"That's a story I'd like to hear another time. Be that as it may, when Claude plotted treason against Niall and became his prisoner, he forfeited all his possessions to his ruler. Niall gave me instructions to sell the properties and give the proceeds to you in the ways I've described."

"Who — ? To me? You already sold the business and the house?" And *Claude was a prisoner.* I hadn't missed that part of the speech. Though he richly deserved to be imprisoned after attempting a coup that would have ended with Niall dead, I would always have some sympathy for anyone in a

328

cell. If that was how they locked up people in Faery. Maybe they stowed them in giant pea pods.

"Yes, the properties have already been sold. The proceeds have been put in an annuity. You'll be getting a check every month. After we fill out the papers, it can be direct-deposited to your checking account. I'll bring them down after we dine, along with the check for the business. Though part of the proceeds from that went into your annuity."

"But Claudine already left me a huge chunk of money. There were some whistles blown on the estate bank, and everything froze. A week ago, the paper said the inspectors hadn't found anything." I should call my bank again.

"That was from Claudine's personal estate," the lawyer said. "She was a frugal fairy for many decades."

I couldn't comprehend my good fortune. "It's a huge relief to have the money to defend myself. But I still hope that someone will confess and spare me the trial," I murmured.

"We all hope that, Sookie," Barry said. "That's why we're here."

Amelia said, "After supper, while it's still light, Bob and I are going to cast a circle of aggressive protection around the house."

"I'm grateful," I said, taking care to make eye contact and parcel out some sincerity to both of them. It was lucky that Barry could read minds, but not Amelia. While I knew Amelia was anxious to do something to contribute, and I knew she was powerful, sometimes things went wrong when she cast important spells. But I couldn't see a way to turn down her offer that would sound polite. "I guess Niall was concentrating on making the land fertile, and that's a really wonderful thing. But some protection would be great."

"There's an elvish warding spell in place," Amelia admitted. "But since it's not human in origin, it may not be totally effective in protecting against human attackers or vampires."

That made sense, at least to me. Bellenos the elf had scoffed at Amelia's spells and added his own, and there wasn't anything human about Bellenos.

I felt guilty at doubting her. It was time for me to act happy. "Having defense money calls for some ice cream with that cake. How about it, you all? I've got Rocky Road and Dulce de Leche." I smiled all around the kitchen. While I was dishing up the ice cream (everyone wanted some), I was keeping my fingers crossed that Amelia and Bob would cast a good spell.

After dessert, as the two witches went outside to work and Barry covered the remains of the cake while I put away the ice cream, Diantha said she was going upstairs to sleep. She still looked exhausted. Mr. Cataliades went up with her and came down with the papers about the monthly payment and a check for the property sale. It was attached to the legal documents with a paper clip in the shape of a heart.

I rinsed my hands and dried them on a dish towel before I took the documents from him. I glanced down at the check, with no idea what to expect. The amount made my head swim, and the letter clipped to it said I would be getting three thousand dollars a month. "This year?" I asked, to be sure I understood. "Three thousand a month? Wow. That's amazing." A whole year of luxury!

"Not this year. For the rest of your life," Mr. Cataliades said.

I had to sit down very quickly.

"Sookie, you okay?" Barry asked, bending over. *Bad news or good news?* he asked.

I can pay for my legal defense, I told him. *And I can get the house sprayed for bugs.*

CHAPTER 15

At midnight the alarms went off.

I hadn't known there were alarms and I hadn't known it was midnight, but when the chiming started, I glanced at the clock. I'd been having the best sleep I'd had in days, and I experienced a moment of vicious disappointment before I launched myself out of bed.

From across the hall, Amelia shouted, "It *worked*!" I flung open my bedroom door and stumbled out. Amelia and Bob, in a nightgown and sleep shorts respectively, were hurrying through their doorway and heading to the back door. I heard Mr. Cataliades bellow something. Diantha shrieked back. They were pounding down the stairs completely dressed in their day clothes. Barry staggered down after them in LSU sleep pants and shirtless.

We all crowded onto the back porch, staring outside. There was one big security light in the back, but we could also see that a ring of blue light had sprung up around the yard and house. A body lay on the ground outside the ring. "Oh, no!" I said, and put my hand on the porch door.

"Sookie, don't go out!" Amelia said, grabbing my shoulder and yanking me backward. "That's someone who tried to sneak up on the house."

"But what if it's Bill and he was only coming to see if everything was okay?"

"Our defensive circle recognizes enmity," Bob said with simple pride.

"Diantha, do you have your cell phone?" Mr. Cataliades asked.

"SureIgotit," she said, and I spared a moment to be relieved that she was back to normal.

"Go take a picture of the person who is lying on the ground, but from well within the circle," he directed.

Before we could think to stop her or argue with the procedure, Diantha was out of the house and running across the backyard at an incredible speed. The phone was out in her hand, and as she reached the perimeter of the protective circle, she paused and took a picture. Then, before we could be more frightened for her, she was back.

Mr. Cataliades turned the little screen

toward me. "Do you recognize this vampire?" he asked.

I peered at it. "Yes, I do. That's Horst Friedman, Felipe de Castro's right-hand man."

"I thought as much. Amelia, Bob, I congratulate you on your power and your perspicacity."

I didn't know what "perspicacity" was, but Amelia did, and she beamed with delight. Even the dour Bob looked proud.

"Yes, thanks," I said with extra enthusiasm, hoping it wasn't too belated. "I don't know what he wanted, and I don't want to know, at least right now. Do you have to recharge the circle, or something like that?"

"We should retest it," Bob suggested, and Amelia nodded.

I saw Barry's gaze encompass the nightgown and Amelia in it, and he looked away resolutely. I *really* didn't want to hear his thoughts about my witch friend. I said *lalalalala* inside my head for a moment so the lust could abate.

"Sookie!" The call came from outside, from the dark woods.

"Who's there?" I called in reply.

"Bill," he said. "What has happened here?"

"I guess Horst tried to sneak up on the house, and Bob and Amelia's witch spell zapped him," I yelled. I opened the back door and took two steps down. I figured if I was still standing on the steps, I could jump back inside.

Bill emerged from the tree line. "I felt the magic from my house," he said. He looked down at Horst's limp body. I wondered if the vampire was finally dead, but his body seemed intact. "What shall I do with him?" Bill asked me.

"That's up to you," I called, wishing that I could walk out to the blue ring and lower my voice. I was afraid to, though. "You gotta keep the peace with the king, I guess." Otherwise, I might be tempted to ask Bill to use a little persuasion on Horst when the vampire woke up, so we could discover what Horst and his boss had had in mind for me.

"I'll take him to my place and call the king," Bill said, and he hoisted the unconscious vampire to his shoulder as if Horst weighed nothing. In a moment, Bill and his burden were out of sight.

"That was exciting," I said, trying to sound calm and casual. I stepped back onto the porch. "I guess I'll go back to bed. Thanks, you two, for putting that protection around. Diantha, I appreciate your help. You all okay? Anybody need anything?"

"We'll be right back in as soon as we test

the spell," Bob said, and turned to Amelia. "You up to it, babe?"

"We should check its strength now that it's reacted," she said, nodding, and they went down to the yard in their bare feet. Without any consultation, they each took the other's hands and began to chant. A strong scent wafted across the back porch, and I knew it was the scent of their magic. It was musky and heavy, like sandalwood.

It wasn't easy to get back to sleep after such a rude awakening, but somehow I managed it. For all I knew, the sudden drop into deep sleep was part of the spell my friends were casting in my yard. When I next opened my eyes, the room was full of light and I could hear my guests moving around the house.

Though I knew I was being a bad hostess, I checked my cell phone for messages before I went out to the kitchen. I had one, a voice message from Bill.

"I called Eric and told him I had the king's friend at my house," he said. "Eric asked what had happened, and I told him about the witches' circle. I told him that you had many friends staying with you and they were prepared to defend you. He asked if Sam Merlotte was among them, and when I said I hadn't seen him, he laughed. He told me he would tell the king where Horst was. Afterward, Felipe sent his woman, Angie, to collect Horst, who was only beginning to recover consciousness by the time she got here. Angie seemed quite angry at Horst, so I suspect he was on an unauthorized mission. Your witch friends did a good job." Then he hung up. Older vampires are not into phone etiquette.

It wasn't pretty, the picture of Eric laughing at Sam's absence. It made me think furiously.

"Sookie, do you have any more milk?" Barry called. Of course, he would know that I was up.

"I'm coming," I yelled back, and pulled on my clothes.

The needs of the world went on, no matter how many crises erupted. "All God's children got to eat," I said, and found another quart of milk at the back of the top shelf and handed it to Barry. Then I poured myself a bowl of cereal.

Bob said, "The psychic's going to be here any minute." He was not trying to sound like he was telling me to hurry up, but it was a timely reminder. I was horrified when I looked at the clock.

Everyone but me had already eaten, rinsed out the dishes, and stacked them by the sink. I should have felt embarrassed, but instead I was simply relieved.

Just after I brushed my teeth, an ancient pickup truck rumbled into my front parking area. Its motor cut with an ominous rattle. A short, stocky woman slid out of the high cab to land on the gravel. She was wearing a cowboy hat decorated with the tip portion of a peacock feather. Her dry brown hair brushed her shoulders and almost matched her skin, as tan and weathered as an old saddle. Delphine Oubre was nothing like I'd imagined. From her battered boots and jeans to her sleeveless blue blouse, she looked like she'd be more at home at a country and western bar like Stompin' Sally's than coming to the house of a telepath to practice her touch psychic-ness.

"Paranormal psychometry," Barry corrected.

I raised an eyebrow.

"It was just called psychometry originally," he said, "but in the past few years 'real scientists' " — he made the imaginary quote marks — "have started using that term to designate . . . well, measuring psychological traits."

That didn't sound much like a science to me.

"Me, either," he confessed. *But I read up*

338

on this online last night to get ready for her visit. In case Bob is mistaken about her talent.

Good move, I told him, watching Delphine Oubre come up the back steps.

"You don't need to tell her your names," Bob said hastily. "Just mine, that's all she needs."

Up close, Delphine seemed to be about forty years old. She wore no jewelry or makeup; her only decoration was the feather in her hat. Her cowboy boots were ancient and venerable. She looked like she could pound in nails with her bare hands.

Bob introduced himself to Delphine, and though (following his orders) I didn't tell her my name, I offered Delphine a drink (she wanted water from the tap, no ice). She pulled out a kitchen chair and took a seat. When I put the glass in front of her, she took a big swallow. "Well?" she said impatiently.

Diantha offered her the scarf, still in its plastic bag. I hadn't seen it, hadn't wanted to see it. The scarf had been cut off Arlene, so the knot was intact. It was twisted into a thin rope, and it was stained.

"Dead woman's scarf," Delphine said, though not as if that worried her.

"No, it's my scarf," I said. "But I want to know how come a dead woman was wearing it. Do you have a problem with holding something that killed someone?"

I wanted to be sure Ms. Oubre wouldn't start screaming when she touched the fabric. Though judging by what I'd seen of her so far, that didn't seem likely.

"It ain't the scarf that killed her, but the hands that tightened it," she said practically. "Show me your money and hand it over. I got cows to feed back home."

Money? Bob had called her. Since he'd done the arranging, I'd forgotten to ask him what the payment should be. Naturally, she wouldn't take a check.

"Four hundred," Bob murmured, and I could have slapped him for neglecting to tell me this. Of course, I should have asked. As I tried to remember what was in my purse, my heart sank. I'd have to pass Delphine's cowboy hat to come up with the cash on the spot.

Mr. Cataliades's hand appeared in front of Delphine with four hundred-dollar bills in it. She took the money without comment, stuffing it in her chest pocket. I nodded my thanks to my demon benefactor. He nodded back in a negligent way. "I'll add it to my bill," he murmured.

Now that that was settled, we all watched the touch psychic with anxious interest.

Without further ado, Delphine Oubre opened the plastic bag and extracted the scarf. The smell was pretty bad, and Amelia immediately went to a window and opened it.

If I'd thought twice, I'd have done this outside, no matter how hot it was.

The psychic's eyes were closed, and she held the scarf loosely at first. As it revealed things to her, her grip tightened, until she was clenching the material tightly. Her face turned slightly from side to side as if she sought a better view; the effect was indescribably eerie. And believe me, seeing inside her head was eerie, too.

"I've killed women," she said suddenly, in a voice that was not her own. I jumped, and I wasn't the only one. We all took a step back from Delphine Oubre.

"I've killed whores," she said gloatingly. "This one's close enough. She's so scared. That makes it sweeter."

We were frozen, like we'd drawn a collective breath and were holding it.

"My friend there," said Oubre, still in the slightly accented voice, "he's squeamish, just a bit. But it's his choice, you know?"

I almost recognized that voice. I associated it with . . . trouble. Disaster.

I turned to look at Barry, at the same moment he took my hand in his.

"Johan Glassport," I whispered.

My comfort level had just shot out of the uneasy area and into the blood-pressure-medication zone. Barry had mentioned seeing Glassport in New Orleans, and Quinn had seen him at an area motel; but I couldn't figure out why. Glassport had no reason to dislike me that I knew of, but I didn't believe that reasons were a big part of his operating system when he wasn't on the clock as a lawyer.

When I'd met Glassport, we'd been on an airplane flight to Rhodes, both hired by the then-queen of Louisiana, Sophie-Anne. I was supposed to listen in to human brains at the vampire summit, and Glassport's job was to defend her against charges brought by a contingent of Arkansas vamps.

I hadn't seen Glassport since the Pyramid of Gizeh had been blown up by human supremacists who wanted to make a statement about vampires — namely, that they all ought to die.

I'd thought about Glassport from time to time, always with distaste. I had happily assumed I'd never see him again in my life. But here he was, speaking through the mouth of a Louisiana rancher named Delphine Oubre.

"Whose choice?" Bob said, in a very quiet voice.

But Delphine didn't respond in the Glassport voice. Instead, her body changed subtly, and she swayed from side to side, as if she were riding an invisible roller coaster. It slowed down and then stopped. After a long minute, she opened her eyes.

"What I see is this," she said in her own voice. She spoke rapidly, as if trying to get it all told before she forgot. "I see a man, a white man, and he's bad most of the way through, but he keeps a good façade. He enjoys killing the helpless. He killed that woman, the red-headed one, on assignment. She not his usual style. She not some random pickup. She knew him. She knew the man with him. She couldn't believe they were killing her. She thought the other man was good. She was thinking, 'I done everything they ask me. Why they not killing Snookie?'"

We hadn't introduced ourselves. "Sookie," I corrected her absently. "She wanted to know why they were killing her instead of Sookie."

"That you?" Delphine asked.

Catching Bob's eyes on me and his warning shake of the head, I said, "No."

"You lucky if you're not Sookie. Whoever

343

she is, they'd sure like to kill her."

Damn.

Delphine stood up, shook herself a little, took another swallow of water, and walked out the door to get into her pickup to go home to feed her cows.

Everyone carefully avoided looking at me. I was the one with the big *X* on her forehead.

"I have to go to work," I said, when the silence had lasted long enough. I didn't give a damn about what Sam thought about it. I had to get out and do something.

Mr. Cataliades said, "Diantha will go with you."

"I would be extremely glad to have her with me," I said with absolute truth. "I'm just not sure how to explain her being there."

"Why do you have to?" Bob said.

"Well, I have to say *something,* don't I?"

"Why?" Barry asked. "Don't you own part of the bar?"

"Yes," I admitted.

"Then you don't have to explain diddly-squat," Amelia said, with such an air of magnificent indifference that we all laughed, even me.

So Diantha and I walked into Merlotte's, and I didn't explain her presence to anyone but Sam. The part-demon girl was wearing a relatively quiet outfit: yellow miniskirt, kingfisher blue tank top, and rainbow platform flip-flops. This month her hair was a platinum blond, but there were a lot of artificially platinum blondes around Bon Temps, though not many who looked like they were at most eighteen.

I don't know what Diantha thought about Merlotte's clientele, but Merlotte's clientele was wild about her. She was different, she was alert and bright-eyed, and she talked so fast that everyone thought she was speaking a foreign language. I discovered that since I could evidently understand that language, I had to translate for her. So off and on during the day, I was called on to tell Jane Bodehouse or Antoine the cook or Andy Bellefleur what my "little second cousin" was saying. I don't know where they got the idea that she was my second cousin, but after the first thirty minutes it became an established fact. I don't know where they thought she'd come from, since everyone in the bar knew my entire family history, but I guess since I'd introduced the fairy Dermot (a dead ringer for Jason) as my cousin from Florida, and I'd said Claude was from the wrong side of the blanket, my townspeople figured the Stackhouses were simply unpredictable.

We were real busy that day, though since I was teamed with An Norr, I didn't have to run as fast as I would've with some other waitresses. An was such a worker ant. And with Diantha and An both in the bar, not a single guy thought about my boobs, which were old news to the regulars anyway. I smiled down at my chest. "Girls, you're outdated," I said. Sam gave me a strange look, but he didn't come over to ask me why I was talking to my breasts.

I stayed away from him, too. I was tired of trying to break through his defenses. I felt like I had enough trouble without trying to coax him out of his funky cave.

I was surprised when he spoke to me as I was waiting for an order for Andy and Terry Bellefleur. (Yes, it was awkward to see Andy, since he'd put me in handcuffs. We were both trying to ignore that.)

"Since when do you have a demon for a cousin?" he asked.

"You haven't met Diantha before? I couldn't remember."

"I can't say that I have. And I definitely think I'd recall it."

"She and her uncle are at my house. They're part of Team Sookie," I said proudly. "They're helping clear my name.

So I don't have to go to trial."

I didn't expect my words to have such an effect on Sam. He looked almost simultaneously pleased and angry. "I wish I could be there," he said.

"Nothing's stopping you," I said. "Remember, you said you'd come to dinner." I'd passed beyond confusion at Sam's weirdness. I was somewhere in the "What the *hell*?" zone.

SOOKIE'S HOUSE

There was a sort of muted thump at the back door, as if someone were perhaps carrying in bags of groceries and therefore tried to open the door with a finger or foot.

Bob, just back from town with Amelia and Barry, opened the back door and stepped out on the screened-in porch to investigate. He wasn't really thinking about who might have arrived. Truth be told, he was worried about Amelia's pregnancy on many different levels. He was smart enough to know they couldn't take care of a baby on the meager money they brought in now, and he was also smart enough to know that accepting money from Copley Carmichael (besides the indirect revenue Amelia got from renting out the apartment on the top floor of the house her dad had given her) would

347

be a grave error.

So Bob was preoccupied, which was why he didn't react instantly when the man beyond the screen door pulled it open and lunged in. Bob thought, *Tyrese,* and then he remembered Tyrese worked for a man who'd sold his soul. Bob shoved Tyrese, hoping desperately to knock him down the back steps and out into the yard so Bob could retreat into the kitchen and lock the door.

But Tyrese was a man of action, and he was full of the fire of despair. He was quicker. He pushed the smaller man back into the house. The door shut behind them.

Amelia was coming out of the hall bathroom, impelled by a sense that something was wrong. When the two men staggered into the kitchen, she screamed. Barry, in the living room, dropped his e-reader and dashed for the kitchen. Bob landed on the floor, Amelia gathered her power, and Barry stopped dead behind her in the hall.

But a Glock trumped Amelia's attempts at a spell, since it was pointed at her chest and her man was on the floor and groaning. Barry was intent on Tyrese's thoughts, which were full of despair, with a curious deadness to them. Though Tyrese wasn't sending out any interesting or usable information, Barry was pretty good at interpreting body language.

"He's got nothing to lose, Amelia," he said, when she stopped screaming. "I don't know why, but he's given up hope."

"I got the HIV," Tyrese said simply.

"But . . ." Amelia intended to point out that treatment now was far better, that Tyrese could live a long and good life, that . . .

"No," Barry warned her. "Shut up."

"Good advice, Amelia," Tyrese said. "Shut up. My Gypsy killed herself; I just got the phone call from her sister. Gypsy, who gave me this disease, who loved me. She killed herself! Left a note saying she had murdered the man she loved and she couldn't live with the guilt. She dead. She hung herself. My beautiful woman!"

"I'm sorry," Amelia said, and it was the best thing she could have told him. But even the best thing wasn't going to save them.

Bob struggled to his feet, taking care to keep his hands visible and his movements slow. "Why are you here with a gun, Tyrese?" he said. "Don't you think Mr. Carmichael is going to be pretty unhappy about this?"

"I don't expect to live through this," Tyrese said simply.

"Oh, Jesus," Barry said, and closed his

eyes for a second. He realized he had no advantage at all. He simply could not hear Tyrese's thoughts clearly enough.

"Jesus ain't got nothing to do with it," Tyrese said. "The devil got everything to do with it."

"So, again, why are you here?" Bob moved so that he was standing between the gun and Amelia. *Maybe I can save Amelia and the baby,* he thought.

In the meantime, Amelia was struggling to gain control of her fear. She was thinking of spells she could use to temporarily neutralize her father's bodyguard. She was trying to remember if there were weapons around the house. Sookie had said something about a rifle in the coat closet by the front door, she remembered. Maybe it was still there. *BARRY!* she screamed in her head.

"Ow," he said. "What you got, Amelia?"

Rifle in the front closet, maybe.

"The stair closet?" he yelled. Amelia was smart to send thoughts to him, but she couldn't receive his.

No, the coat closet by the front door.

"Okay! Tyrese, listen to Amelia!" Barry began edging to his left, hoping Amelia would take his cue and distract Tyrese. He didn't think there was a chance in hell he

350

would get to the closet, find the rifle, understand how to use it, and shoot Tyrese Marley. But he had to try.

"Tyrese, please tell me what you're doing here," Amelia said steadily.

"I'm here," said Tyrese, "because I'm waiting for Sookie Stackhouse to come home. When she does, I'm going to kill her."

"Really!" Amelia said. "Why?"

"She's why your dad got mad," Tyrese said. "She took the thing he wanted so bad. So he said she had to die, and we came up here to do it. But we can't get her alone. We don't want to run her off the road; he wants a sure thing, he says. Shoot her, Tyrese, he says. She lost her vampire protection; no one will care."

"I care," Amelia said.

"Well, that's the other thing; he wanted that fairy thing because he wanted to control you. Course, he called it 'getting you back into his life,' but we know better, huh? Now he's so mad at Sookie, he doesn't care what you want," Tyrese said. The Glock was steady in his grip. It looked huge from where Amelia was standing, and she thought Bob standing between the gun and her was the bravest thing she'd ever seen.

"Where's my dad, Tyrese?" Amelia asked, trying to keep his interest so Barry could get the gun. She turned her eyes very slightly to read the clock on the wall. Sookie should have finished her shift by now. She'd be on her way any minute. This whole pile of shit was Amelia's father's doing, and Amelia had to try every strategy she could devise to prevent her friend from getting killed. She wondered if she could cast a stunning spell without any herbs or preparation. It wasn't like in the Harry Potter books, though she and every other witch of her acquaintance had often wished it were.

"He's in our hotel room, far as I know. I went outside when I got a call from Gypsy's sister on my cell phone. I walked around the corner so I could talk to her without Mr. Carmichael hearing me. He doesn't like it when I get personal phone calls when I'm with him."

"That's kind of crazy," Amelia said at random. She couldn't turn around to see where Barry was, so she was prepared to keep on talking forever if she had to.

"That's small stuff compared to his real crazy ideas," Tyrese said, and laughed. "You come sit in this chair, Amelia." He nodded at one of the kitchen chairs.

"Why?" she asked instantly.

"Doesn't make any difference why. Because I told you to," he said, giving her hard eyes. At that moment, Bob jumped Tyrese.

The boom of the Glock filled the room, and then there was blood. Amelia screamed until Barry clapped his hands over his ears, the horror in her thoughts beating at him. While he'd worked for the vampires in Texas, Barry had seen some bad shit, but Bob's body in a pool of blood on the kitchen floor was way up there with the worst of those memories.

"See what the devil made me do?" said Tyrese, smiling slightly. "Amelia, you shut up now."

Amelia clamped her mouth shut.

"You, whoever you are," Tyrese said. "Come here now."

Barry had run out of time and options. He went into the kitchen.

"Put Amelia in that chair."

Barry, despite the fact that he was shaking and felt scared down to the marrow of his bones, managed to help Amelia to the chair. Amelia had blood spray on her arms and chest, and in her hair. She was as pale as a vampire. Barry thought she might faint. But she sat straight in the chair and stared at Tyrese as if she could bore a hole in him with her eyes.

Tyrese had groped around on the back porch while Amelia sat, and now he tossed a roll of duct tape at Barry. "Secure her," he ordered.

Secure her, Barry thought. *Like we're in some kind of spy movie. Fuck him. I'll kill him if I get the chance.* Anything to avoid thinking about the bloody body at his feet.

Just as he was looking down at the thing he least wanted to see, he was sure Bob moved.

He wasn't dead.

But it would only be a matter of time, if they didn't get some help.

Barry realized appealing to Tyrese was a waste of breath. Tyrese was not in a merciful mood and might just kick Bob in the head or shoot him again. He hoped Amelia would have an idea, but her head was full of horror and regret and loss. Not a single idea in the place.

Barry had never secured anyone with duct tape before, but he bound Amelia's wrists together behind the chair, and that would have to do.

"Now," Tyrese said. "You sit on the floor and put your hand on that table leg."

That would put him closer to Bob, and there was nothing Barry could do to help the witch. He sank to the floor and gripped the table leg with his left hand.

"Now duct tape your hand to the table,"

354

Tyrese said.

With a lot of clumsy effort, Barry managed, ripping off the tape with his teeth.

"Scoot it across the floor to me," Tyrese said, and Barry did.

Then there was nothing left to do.

"Now we wait," said Tyrese.

"Tyrese," Amelia said, "you ought to shoot my dad, not Sookie."

She had everyone's attention.

"It's my dad who got you into this. It's my dad who sold your soul to the devil. It's my dad who doomed your girlfriend."

"Your dad done everything he could for me," Tyrese said stubbornly.

"My dad killed you," Amelia said. Barry admired her courage and straight speaking, but Tyrese did not. He smacked Amelia across the face, and then he taped her mouth shut.

Barry thought Amelia was absolutely right. And maybe if Tyrese had had a chance to absorb the worst of his grief, he would have seen that, too. But in his rush to do something, anything, in the wake of hearing about Gypsy's suicide, Tyrese had committed himself to this course of action, and he would not be dissuaded. He would never admit he'd done something so incredibly stupid.

You have to admit, Barry thought, *that Tyrese is loyal, in a weird way.*

Barry thought of Mr. Cataliades and hoped he'd be alerted to the fact that something was wrong in the house. He was tough. He could handle this situation. Or maybe when Sookie and Diantha pulled up, she'd hear Tyrese's thoughts, though where she parked it was doubtful she'd be able to get a reading. But if she counted heads in the house, she might think something was off — though she'd have no reason to suspect danger.

Barry's thoughts went around in circles as he tried to think of some way to extricate them all from this situation, some way that wouldn't get them killed. Get *him* killed. He wasn't much of a hero; he'd always known that about himself. He did good when it would not put him in peril; he believed that in this, he was like most people.

Suddenly Tyrese, who'd been leaning against the wall, straightened. Barry heard a car coming, and there was another sound, too. Was that a motorcycle? Sure sounded like one. Who could it be? Would the presence of other people be enough to stop Tyrese?

But there wasn't any going back for the

356

bodyguard, apparently.

As the car's motor died and the other motor, too, Tyrese grinned at Amelia. "Here goes," he said. "I'm going to make everything even. This woman is going to die."

But the person driving the car might not even be Sookie. What if it was Mr. Cataliades in his van? Tyrese didn't even look. He'd gotten the whole story set in his mind. This would be Sookie, and he would kill her, and then everything would somehow balance out.

Tyrese swung around to face the back door, the smile still on his lips. Barry started screaming at Sookie in his head, because that was all he could do, but he didn't think she'd hear him. He looked up at Amelia and saw the strain in her face. She was doing the same.

And then Tyrese took a step forward, and another. He was on the porch. He wasn't going to wait for Sookie to enter the house, which would have been a sure thing. He was going to meet her.

MERLOTTE'S
earlier
Sam's lips parted and I just knew he was finally going to explain. But then he looked past me and the moment passed. "Mus-

tapha Khan," he said, and he definitely wasn't happy to see Eric's daytime guy.

As far as I knew, Sam had nothing against the werewolf. Surely he couldn't blame Mustapha for beheading Jannalynn? After all, it had been a fair fight, and Sam, though a shapeshifter, was very familiar with Were rules. Or was it Mustapha's job as Eric's daytime guy that made Sam so grumpy?

I wondered, things being how they were, why Mustapha was coming to see me. Maybe something had been decided about who would take over Fangtasia, and Eric wanted me to know.

"Hello, Mustapha," I said, as calmly as I could. "What brings you here today? Can I get you a glass of water with lemon?" Mustapha didn't take stimulants of any kind: coffee, Coca-Cola, anything.

"Thank you. A glass of water would be refreshing," he allowed. As usual, Mustapha was wearing dark glasses. He'd removed his motorcycle helmet, and I saw he'd shaved a pattern in the stubble on his head. That was new. It gleamed under the lights of the bar. An Norr did a double take when she got a good look at the muscled magnificence that was Mustapha Khan. She wasn't the only one.

When I brought him an icy glass, he was

sitting on a bar stool having some kind of silent staring contest with Sam.

"How is Warren?" I asked. Warren, possibly the only person Mustapha cared for, had been awfully close to dead when we found him at Jannalynn's folks' empty garage apartment.

"He's better, thank you, Sookie. He ran half a mile today. He walked the rest, with some help. He's out there waiting, right now." Mustapha inclined his patterned head toward the front door. Warren was the shyest man I'd ever met.

I hadn't known Warren had been a runner before his ordeal, but I figured the fact that he'd resumed the exercise was pretty good news, and I told Mustapha to give the convalescent my good wishes. "I'd have sent him a get-well card if I knew his address," I added, and felt like a fool when Mustapha took off his dark glasses to give me an incredulous look. Well, I would have.

"I come here to tell you Eric is leaving tomorrow night," he said. "He thought you should know. Plus, he left some shit at your place. He wants it back."

I stood very still for a long moment, feeling the finality of it hit my heart. "Okay, then," I said. "I do have some stuff of his in my closet. I'll send it — where? Though I don't suppose they are things he'll miss." I tried to not add any layers of meaning to that.

"I'll come get them when you get off work," Mustapha said.

The clock was reading four thirty. "I should be through here in thirty minutes or so," I said, looking to Sam for confirmation. "If India gets here on time."

And here she came, through the front door, weaving her way between the tables. India had had her hair done, a process she'd described to me in fascinating detail, and the jeweled balls on her braids clicked together as she walked. She spotted my companion when she was a couple of yards away. She had a startled look, which she exaggerated for effect when she drew up to us.

"Brother, you are almost enough to make me wish I was straight!" she said, with her beautiful smile.

"Sister, right back at you," he said politely, which perhaps answered a question I'd had about Mustapha. Or perhaps not. He was the most secretive and closemouthed person I'd ever encountered, and I must admit I found that refreshing — occasionally. When you're used to knowing everything, including a lot of factoids you wish you had never learned, it can be mighty frustrating to wonder.

"Mustapha Khan, India Unger," I said, trying to keep up my end of the exchange. "India's here to take over my tables, Mustapha, so I guess you can come out to the house now."

"I'll see you there," he said, nodding good-bye to India before striding out the door. He was donning his dark glasses and helmet as he walked.

India shook her head as she watched him go, thinking about how fine his ass was. "It's the front half that doesn't appeal to me," she said, before going to the lockers to put on her apron.

Sam was still standing in the same spot, and he was giving me a big stare.

"Sookie, I'm sorry," he said. "I know this has to be tough. Call me if you need me." And then he had to turn away to make a mojito for Christy Aubert. His shoulders were stiff with tension.

He was a problem I couldn't solve.

Diantha followed me out to the car. "Sookieunclejustcalledheneedsme. You'llbeallrightwiththewolf?" I assured her I would.

"Okaythen," she said, and went back into Merlotte's, I guessed to wait for Mr. C to pick her up. I wondered what India would make of her.

When I pulled out from behind Merlotte's, Mustapha was waiting for me. Warren perched behind him on the Harley. Warren was like a bird compared to Mustapha — small, pale, narrow. But according to Mustapha, Warren was the best shot he'd ever seen. That was a compliment Mustapha would not give out lightly.

As I drove home down Hummingbird Road followed by the Harley, I found myself feeling relieved that Eric would be gone soon. In fact, I wished he were gone already.

I'd never imagined feeling this way, but I couldn't handle this emotional jerking around. I'd start to feel okay, then I'd get poked in the sore spot, like taking a scab off my knee when I was a kid. In books, the hero was gone after the big blowup. He didn't stick around in the vicinity doing mysterious shit, sending messages to the heroine by a third party. He hauled his ass into oblivion. And that was the way things should be, as far as I was concerned. Life should imitate romance literature far more often.

If the world operated according to romance principles, Mustapha Khan would tell me that Eric had always been unworthy of me and that Mustapha himself had harbored a deep love for me from the moment he'd met me. Did Harlequin have a line of books for guys-out-of-prison-get-redeemed romances?

I was just distracting myself, and I knew it. I noticed as I pulled to a stop that Barry's rental car was parked in my yard, but Mr. Cataliades and his van were in town, of course.

I got out of my car and turned around to tell Mustapha that I had company. "You and Warren come on in. I'll have Eric's stuff together in a jiffy," I said. I put my hand on my car door to close it, and Mustapha got off his bike. I raised a hand to Warren, and hearing the creak of the screen door, I turned my head slightly to see who was coming out the back door. I caught a glimpse of someone I hadn't seen in a long time. I couldn't recall his name . . .

And he had a gun. He called out my name in a terrible voice.

Mustapha, his eyes hidden behind his shades, was reaching toward me, quick as only a werewolf can be. When I saw that skinny blond Warren, still on the bike, had drawn the biggest handgun I'd ever seen in my life, I had a moment to be afraid. I had time to think, "Oh Jesus, that guy is going to kill me," when two things happened almost simultaneously. From behind me I heard a *crack!,* and my left shoulder burned as I staggered because Mustapha was flinging me face-first to the ground. Then a house landed on top of me. And I heard a voice screaming from inside the house, a voice that was not mine.

"Barry," I said. And a huge bee advised me that it had dug its stinger into my shoulder.

Life just sucked some days.

CHAPTER 16

At that point, it would have been nice if I could have fainted. But I didn't. I lay there and tried to gather my wits, tried to comprehend what had just occurred. My shoulder was warm and wet.

I'd been shot.

I slowly understood that Mustapha had tried to save me (and himself) by throwing us to the ground, while Warren had fired at the shooter. I wondered what had happened inside the house.

"You hurt?" Mustapha growled, and I could feel him sliding off me.

"Yes," I said. "I think I am." My shoulder hurt like the very effing hell.

Mustapha had gotten to his knees but pressed himself against my car, using the still-open door as cover. Warren moved past us, gun at the ready, looking like a different person from the wispy ex-con who normally seemed a mere shadow of his brawny friend.

Warren looked utterly deadly.

"A rattlesnake in a moth outfit," I said.

"Say what?"

"Warren. He looks like a movie shooter now."

Mustapha glanced after his buddy-and-maybe-more. "Yeah, he does. He's the best."

"Did he get the guy?" I said, and then I groaned between clenched teeth. "Wow, this hurts. We calling an ambulance?"

"He's dead," Warren called.

"Good to know," Mustapha called back. "I figured. Good shot."

"How's Sookie?" Warren's boots came into my constricting field of vision.

"Shoulder, not fatal, but she's bleeding like a stuck pig. You calling 911?"

"Sure thing." I heard the beeps and then the voice of the dispatcher.

"Need at least one ambulance, possibly two," Warren said. "The Stackhouse place on Hummingbird Road." I felt I'd missed part of the conversation.

"Sookie, I'm going to turn you over," Mustapha said.

"I'd rather you didn't," I said between clenched teeth. "Really. Don't."

I could endure the status quo, but I was afraid any movement at all would make things worse.

"Okay," he said. "Warren's going to hold this jacket against your shoulder to apply some pressure, slow down that bleeding."

Big boots were replaced by little boots. "Pressure" sounded painful. Sure enough, it was.

"Shepherd of Judea," I said through clenched teeth, though I wanted to say something much, much worse. "Wow, *dammit*. How are the people in the house?"

"Mustapha's checking on them now. I just glanced in to make sure they were all friendlies. One of 'em's on the floor."

"Who shot us?"

"Big guy, looks black but with a lot of white mixed in," Warren said. "His features are real fine. Well, they were. And his hair is almost red."

"Wearing . . . a uniform?"

"No," Warren said, puzzled by my question. But I remembered the face and the hair, and I associated it with a uniform of some kind. Not armed forces . . . if I could just stop hurting, I could remember.

Someone in the house started screaming, and this time it was a woman.

"Why is she screaming?" I asked Warren.

"I guess she's worried about . . ." Warren said.

I must have missed another second or two.

Well, the pressure on the shoulder, Warren was serious about maintaining it. Mustapha was back when I opened my eyes. "Warren's not supposed to be armed," he told me.

"Huh?" I said with a huge effort, because I actually was beginning to feel swimmy and weird. Finally. *Bring on the unconsciousness,* I thought; and for once, I got my wish.

I woke to chaos. The two paramedics who had come to get Tara when she went into labor were now bending over me. They looked intent on their work, which at that moment was wheeling my stretcher to the ambulance.

So here's the story, a voice was saying in my head. Thoughts don't have voices, of course, and I wasn't sure who was telling me this, since I was too tired to turn my head to look around the yard. *The gun is yours. Someone gave it to you. You asked Warren to take you target shooting because you wanted to be sure you knew how to use it. He cleaned it for you. That's the only reason he had it with him. Then that asshole came out of the house and fired at you, and naturally, Warren fired back, since he didn't want you to get killed. Nod if you understand.*

"That's what really almost happened," I said, moving my head up and down. The medics looked at me with concern. I had misspoken. "That's what happened, but not really." More accurate?

"Sookie, how are you feeling?" one of them asked. The taller one.

"Not too good," I said.

"We're getting you to Clarice. You'll be there in ten minutes," she said, a little optimistically.

"Who else is hurt?" I said.

"Just worry about yourself right now," she said. "The guy who shot you, they tell me he's dead."

"Good," I said, and they seemed surprised. Is it not okay to be glad that someone who tried to kill you is down on the ground? If I were a better person, a much better person, I would be sorry that anyone in the world ever got hurt, but I had to face the fact that I was never going to be that nice a person. Even my grandmother hadn't been that good.

We got to the hospital, and everything that happened after that was really unpleasant. Fortunately, I don't remember a lot of it. And I took a nap for a while after it was over.

I didn't hear the whole story until much later that evening. Andy Bellefleur was sitting in my room when I woke up. He was asleep, which I thought was almost funny.

When I giggled out loud, he stirred and looked at me.

"How you feeling?" he asked sternly.

"Okay," I said. "I must be taking some excellent painkillers." I was aware that my shoulder really hurt, but I didn't care very much.

"Dr. Tonnesen took care of you. We got to talk, now that you're awake."

While Andy took me through the story of what had happened that evening, all I could think about was how weird it was that he and Alcee had the same initials. I pointed out that fact to Andy, and he gave me a look of sheer incredulity. "Sook, I'm going to come back to talk to you tomorrow," he said. "You ain't making any sense."

"Did you tell Alcee to search his car? There's something bad in there," I said solemnly. "Now I've told you three times. He should do it. Do you think he'd let a friend of mine check it?"

Andy looked at me, and this time I could tell he was taking me seriously. "Could be," he said. "Could be I'd let someone do it if I was standing right there. Because Alcee ain't acting like himself, not at all."

"Okeydokey," I said. "I'll take care of that just as *soooooon* as I can."

"Doc's just keeping you for the night, she says."

"Good."

As soon as Andy left, Barry came in. He looked like he'd been rode hard and put up wet. There were actually circles under his eyes. He told me what had happened in my house.

"How's Bob doing?" I asked him out loud. I couldn't even think at him, I was so out of it.

"He's alive," Barry said. "He's stable. Of course, that's where Amelia is."

"Where's Mr. C and Diantha?" I asked.

"Don't you want to know who the dead man was?"

"Oh. Sure. Who?"

"Tyrese Marley," Barry said.

"I don't get it," I said. "Of course, I'm really on some drugs. Excellent drugs. Tyrese split some firewood for me the last time he was at the house. But why was Tyrese at my house, and why did he try to shoot me?"

"You should see the inside of your head, Sookie. It's like a rainbow in there. Tyrese drove Copley Carmichael's car, but he left it in the cemetery and walked through the woods to your house."

"So where is Copley? Did they really sell their souls?"

371

"No one knows where Copley is, but I'll tell you what Tyrese told us . . ."

Barry told me about Tyrese's Gypsy, about the HIV, about Copley's conviction that by using the cluviel dor (Barry had trouble explaining that part since he didn't know much of anything about the cluviel dor) I had robbed Copley of regaining possession of Amelia and her life.

I listened to all this with very little comprehension. "I don't get why Tyrese would set off to kill me when he learned that Gypsy was dead. Why wouldn't he shoot Amelia's dad? It was *his* fault."

"My point exactly!" Barry sounded triumphant. "But Tyrese was like a gun pointed in one direction, and her suicide pulled the trigger."

I shook my head very, very gently. "How'd he even get to the house? Amelia and Bob put wards on the house," I pointed out with great clarity.

"The difference between the vampire who got fried and Tyrese . . . Well, there are two big differences," Barry said. "Tyrese was a live human without a soul. The vampire was a dead person. The wards stopped him, not Tyrese. I don't know what to make of that, and when Amelia can spare time to think of it, maybe she can tell us. Maybe we can talk about it tomorrow, okay?" he said. "Meanwhile, there are some other people waiting to see you."

Sam came in silently. His hand found mine.

"You gonna tell me what's wrong?" I whispered. I was fading into sleep.

"I can't," he said. "But I couldn't stay away when I heard you got shot."

And then Eric was behind him.

My hand must have jerked, because Sam's tightened around it. I could tell from his face that he knew Eric was there.

"Heard you were going," I said, with an effort.

"Yes, very soon. How are you? Do you want me to heal you?" I couldn't interpret his voice or the fact that he was here. I was too exhausted to try.

"No, Eric," I said, and I only sounded flat. I just couldn't find nice words. "Good-bye. We need to let go of each other. I can't do this anymore."

Eric glared at Sam. "What are you doing here?" he asked.

"Sam came because I was shot, Eric. That's what friends do," I said. Each word was a labor to enunciate.

Sam didn't turn to Eric, didn't look him in the eye. I held on to his hand so I

373

wouldn't drift away.

Eric spoke once again. "I will not release you." I frowned. He seemed to be speaking to Sam. Then he walked out of the hospital room.

What the hell? "Release you from what?" I said, trying to will Sam to tell me what was going on.

"Don't worry," he said. "Don't worry, Sookie." And he kept my hand.

I fell asleep. When I woke up hours later, he was gone.

CHAPTER 17

Before I checked out of the hospital the next day about noon, Amelia came in. She looked exactly like someone who'd been held hostage by an armed gunman and watched her boyfriend get shot and sat up all night by a hospital bed. Which is a long way of saying she looked like hell.

"How are you?" She stood by the bed and looked down at me, swaying slightly on her feet.

"Better than you, I think." My head was a lot clearer today. I was going to defer the painkillers until I got home.

"Bob's going to be okay," she said.

"That's a huge relief. I'm so glad. You going to stay here?"

"No, he's being transferred to Shreveport. The best I can tell, once he's had a day there, they'll reevaluate. Maybe they'll be able to send him down to New Orleans, which would really be better for me, but maybe he'll have to stay in Shreveport if transporting him would be too hard on him."

A lot of uncertainty. "Any word from your father?"

"No, and none from Diantha and Mr. C, either."

There were ears all around at the hospital, and we didn't need to say any more to know we were both worried about that silence.

"I'm sorry," she said suddenly.

"About your dad? You didn't have anything to do with it. That's all on him. And I'm sorry about Bob."

"Totally not your fault. We okay?"

"We're okay. Please let me know how he progresses. And the baby." I could feel the presence of another mind — but not any thoughts, of course. This baby was going to be an exceptional witch; I'd never been able to detect a pregnancy this early.

"Yeah, I told the ER doctor, and she gave me a quick exam. Everything seems okay. She gave me the name of an ob-gyn in Shreveport, in case Bob stays there."

"Sounds good."

"Oh, and the wards. Sorry. I couldn't have known that a soulless person wouldn't be affected, so I think I can give myself a pass on that one. How often do you meet someone with no soul?"

"You've got a new piece of lore to tell your coven," I said, and Amelia brightened a bit, as I'd known she would. "Evidently Bill came by here last night while I was out of it, and he left me a note. I can see his handwriting. Would you mind handing it to me?" I pointed to the rolling table, which a nurse had shoved against the wall. Obligingly, Amelia handed me the envelope. I'd read it when she left.

"Sam came by to ask if I needed anything," Amelia told me.

"Not surprised. He's a good guy." And if I felt well enough, next time I saw him I was going to shake the hell out of him, because I wanted to know what was going on between him and Eric.

"One of the best. Well, I'm going back out to the house to take a shower and pack up our stuff," Amelia said. "I'm sorry our attempt to help you worked out so bad."

"So bad for you," I said. "It was pretty great for me. Thanks for coming to my rescue. It shouldn't have ended up with you all getting hurt."

"If I knew where my dad was, I'd kill him myself." She meant it.

"I understand," I said.

And then she left, after giving me a light

kiss on my forehead.

I was sure Bill had left me a flowery get-well note, but as I read the fine script, I realized it was anything but.

Sookie, I hope you are recovering. About the incident of two nights ago: I have just received a very reluctant apology from my king. He told me that he regretted that Horst had come into my home territory and caused me so much inconvenience by attacking my friend and neighbor.

Apparently, Horst thought it would please Felipe if he came to threaten you with something gruesome, thereby ensuring you didn't interfere in the arrangements Felipe had made with Freyda. Felipe asked me to apologize to you, too. He will allow Eric's measures to remain in place if Eric leaves for Oklahoma tonight. I have some interesting news to tell you, and I will see you as soon as I can.

I wasn't totally sure I understood Bill's note, but if he was coming to see me, I'd have to possess my soul in patience. Dr. Tonnesen released me, with a long list of restrictions and instructions, and I called Jason. On his lunch hour, he showed up to wheel me out of the hospital. He'd come to the hospital the night before to fill out my admission papers and to give them what insurance information I had, and he'd been out to the house after the police had finished with processing the shooting scene. I was sure giving Kevin and Kenya a workout for their newfound skills.

"Michele put a casserole in your refrigerator for tonight. I hope you don't mind, Sook, but Michele and An are out there scrubbing everything down," he said in a subdued way.

"Oh, that's wonderful," I said, with heartfelt relief. "God bless 'em. I owe them big-time."

He tried to smile. "Yeah, you do. Michele said she hasn't cleaned up so much blood since her cat brought in a rabbit that wasn't quite dead, and it got away in the house."

"I never made it inside the house." I was kind of glad about that. I didn't need to see my poor kitchen torn up again.

"Why'd that fucker shoot you? Why'd he shoot Bob?"

"I'm not sure," I said. "I don't remember too much of what Amelia told me."

"This guy was her dad's chauffeur? What was his issue? He ever have a thing with Amelia? Maybe he was jealous of Bob."

That sounded pretty good. "Maybe that's

it," I said. "Has Mr. Carmichael turned up?"

"Not that I heard of. Maybe this Tyrese guy bumped him off first."

I wouldn't feel easy until I knew where Copley was. I didn't think Tyrese had killed him. Soulless or not, Tyrese was a loyal employee. Did the two of them have something to do with Arlene's death? Were they working with Johan Glassport? That didn't make any sense. None of this made any sense. I leaned my head against the glass of Jason's pickup window, and I kept silent the rest of the drive home.

The first thing I noticed was my car, exactly where I'd left it yesterday when I'd climbed out of it and gotten shot. At least someone had shut the driver's door. My blood was still on the ground beside it. I tried not to look. Jason came around to open the truck door, and I slid out carefully. I could walk on my own, but I wasn't super-steady, and I appreciated the fact that he was there.

He walked me right through the kitchen and into my bedroom, only letting me pause long enough to thank An and Michele. After depositing me on my bed, he vanished to return to work. I promptly got off the bed and shuffled into my bathroom to clean up, an awkward process with my bandaged shoulder, which had to be kept dry. In the end, I was a bit cleaner than I had been, though I couldn't wash my hair. With some difficulty, I put on a clean nightgown. At that point, Michele came in to scold me and order me to get back on the bed. We compromised with the couch in the living room. She turned on the television, brought me the remote and a big glass of tea, and made me a sandwich for a belated lunch. I ate about half of it. I wasn't that hungry, though it had been a while since I had eaten a real meal. Maybe the painkillers were suppressing my appetite, maybe I was depressed that there was so much death around my house, or maybe I was worried about Bill's enigmatic note.

An and Michele finished about an hour after Jason left, and I insisted on getting up to admire the job they'd done. My kitchen shone like a showroom kitchen and smelled like pine-scented cleaner. That was a big improvement, An informed me. "My whole family hunts, and I know nothing smells up a place more than blood," she said.

"Thank you, An," I said. "And thanks, almost-sister-in-law. I sure appreciate you two doing this for me."

"No problem," An said.

"Just don't let it happen again. This is the

one and only time I'm scrubbing blood out of your kitchen," Michele said. She was smiling. But she meant it.

"Oh, I can promise it will be," I said. "I'll call someone else next time." They laughed, and I smiled back. Ha effing ha.

An gathered up her cleaning supplies in a big red bucket.

"I'll give you some Pine-Sol for your birthday, An," I said.

"You betcha. There's nothing like it." She looked around at the sparkling surfaces with some satisfaction. "My daddy the preacher always said, 'By your works shall they know thee.' "

"Then you're an industrious and generous woman," I said, and she beamed. I hugged them both in a lopsided way. Before they left, Michele asked me if I wanted her to put the casserole in the microwave ready for me to heat for supper. "It might be too much for you to handle," she said. She was determined to feed me.

"I'm sure I can do it later," I said, and she had to be content with that. The house felt pleasantly peaceful after they'd left, until I drifted out from under the painkillers long enough to wonder where Mr. C and Diantha were. I hoped they were okay. And since it seemed apparent that soulless people could come through the wards, I got out my critter rifle. The shotgun would have been more effective, but I simply couldn't handle it in my weakened state. If Copley Carmichael came around to finish what his minion had started, I had to be armed and ready. I locked the house up tight, closed the curtains in the living room so he couldn't tell where I was, and tried to read. Finally, I gave it up. I watched something totally brainless on TV. Sadly, that wasn't hard to find.

I kept my cell phone by me, and I got a call from Kennedy Keyes. She was as happy as I'd ever heard her. "Me and Danny are going to rent one of Sam's little houses," she said. "Across from the duplexes. He said you'd know where."

"Sure," I said. "When are you moving in?"

"Right now!" She laughed. "Danny and one of his buddies from the lumberyard are carrying in the bed right at this moment!"

"Kennedy, that's wonderful. I hope you'll be real happy."

She talked for a while, giddy with her new situation. I had no idea if their love for each other would last, but I was glad they were giving it a chance, despite the very obvious differences in their upbringings. Kennedy's family, as she'd described them to me, had been determined social climbers, wondering where their next step upward would take them. Danny's family had worried more about their next meal.

"Good luck to both of you, and I'll get you a housewarming present," I said, when Kennedy began to wind down.

About an hour later, I heard a car park in the gravel area by the front door. After the engine cut off, footsteps and a gentle knock told me my caller had decided to carry through with the visit, though I was detecting a lot of hesitation.

I picked up the rifle. It was going to be hell to get a good shot with my weak shoulder, and it was going to be painful. "Who is it?" I called.

"Halleigh."

"You alone?" I knew she was, but with undetectable people around, I had to check. Her thoughts would tell me if someone was forcing her to knock on the door.

"I am. I don't blame you if you don't want to open up," she said.

I opened the door. Halleigh Bellefleur was younger than me, a nice-looking brown-haired schoolteacher who was really, really pregnant. Tara had not fared as well when she was expecting the twins; Halleigh was truly blooming.

"Come in," I said. "Does Andy know you're here?"

"I don't keep secrets from my husband," she said, and she came up to me and hugged me very gently. "Andy's not too happy right now, but that's too bad. I don't believe you killed that woman. And I'm really sorry that man went crazy and shot you. I know your friend must feel horrible, the one whose dad is missing. This guy worked for her dad?"

So we sat for a moment and talked a little, and then Halleigh stood to go. I understood that she'd visited to make her point, both with Andy and with me. She stood by who she liked, no matter what.

"I know Andy's grandmother was a trial," I said, surprising even myself, "but you're so much like Miss Caroline in so many ways."

Halleigh looked startled and then pleased. "You know, I'll take that as a compliment," she said.

We parted better friends than we'd ever been.

It was twilight when she left, and I began to think of eating supper. I heated part of Michele's enchilada casserole in a bowl and dumped salsa on top. It was good, and I ate the bowlful.

The minute it was full dark, Bill was at

my back door. I was very tired by then, though I hadn't done a damn thing all day, and I shuffled slowly to the door toting the rifle with me, though I was sure from the — well, from the feeling of the hole a vampire's head left in my other sense — that this "hole" represented Bill.

"It's Bill," he called, to confirm his identity. I let him in, undoing the locks with one hand, and stood aside to let him pass. With this much traffic, I was going to need a schedule to keep up with all my callers. Bill stepped in and gave me a sharp once-over. "You're healing," he said. "Good."

I offered him a drink, but he looked at me and said, "I can get something myself, Sookie, if I need a drink. But I don't right now. Can I get you something?"

"Yeah, actually. If you wouldn't mind pouring me another glass of tea, I'd sure appreciate it." The pitcher was pretty heavy to deal with one-handed. Gripping anything with my left hand made the shoulder hurt in a most unpleasant way.

We sat in the living room, me curled up on the couch, Bill in the armchair opposite. He smiled at me.

"You're cheerful," I observed.

"I'm about to do something that gives me intense pleasure," he said.

Huh. "Okay, have at it," I said.

"Do you remember what Eric did to me in New Orleans?" he said, and nothing could have surprised me more.

"You mean, what Eric did to us? By telling me that instead of you being spontaneously smitten with me, you were ordered to seduce me?"

It had hurt then. It hurt now. Of course, not as badly.

"Yes, exactly," Bill said. "And I'm not ever going to explain again, since we've said all this out loud and in our heads so many times. Even though I can't read minds, like you can, I know that."

I nodded. "We'll take all that as done."

"That is why it gives me intense pleasure to tell you, now, what Eric has done to Sam."

All *right*! This was what I had waited to discover. I leaned forward. "Do tell," I said.

CHAPTER 18

When he had finished, he left, and I called Sam at the bar. "I need you to come out to the house," I said.

"Sookie?"

"You know it's me."

"Kennedy's not here, so I have to stay at the bar."

"No, you don't. You're not supposed to talk to me or come see me. But I'm telling you I want to talk to you now, and I expect someone to take care of the bar for you while you get yourself out here." I was very, very angry. And I did something so rude that Gran would have choked. I hung up.

In thirty minutes I heard Sam's truck. I was standing at the back porch door when he walked up. I could see the cloud of regret around him as clearly as if it had been a tangible thing.

"Don't you tell me how you're not supposed to be here and you can't come in," I said, though it took me a minute to stoke my fire back up after seeing his unhappiness. "We're going to talk." Sam hung back, and I reached out to take his hand the way he'd taken mine at the hospital. I pulled him closer, and he tried to stay away, he really did, but he couldn't bring himself to do anything rough. "Now, you come sit in the living room and you talk to me. And before you start making up a story, let me tell you . . . Bill came by and he had a very interesting tale to tell. So I know everything, though not all the details."

"I shouldn't. I promised not to."

"You don't have a choice, Sam. I'm not giving you one."

He took a deep breath. "None of us had enough money for your bail. I wasn't going to have you spend any more time in that place than you had to. I called the bank president at home to ask him about a loan on the bar, but I got turned down."

That, I hadn't known. I was horrified. "Oh, no, Sam . . ."

"So," he bulldozed over me, "I went to Eric the second it got dark. Of course, he'd heard you'd been arrested and he was totally pissed off. But he was mostly angry that I'd tried to bail you out on my own. That vampire, Freyda, she was sitting right by him." Remembering, Sam was so angry that his teeth were bared. "Finally, she told him he could go on and bail you out, but with conditions."

"With her conditions."

"Yeah. The first condition was that you never see Eric again. Or enter Oklahoma. On penalty of death. But Eric said no, he had a better idea. He was trying to let her think he was doing something bad to you, but he was really doing something bad to me. He agreed to the part about you not entering Oklahoma, and he agreed that he would never be alone with you again, but he tacked on another one she wouldn't have thought of. It was that I could never tell you I'd *asked* Eric to put up the bail. And I could never try to . . . court you."

"And you agreed." I was feeling about five different emotions at once.

"I agreed. It seemed to be the only way to get you out of that damn jail. I confess that I needed sleep bad and my thinking may not have been real clear."

"Okay. Let me tell you something right now. As of this morning, the assets of Claudine's bank are now unfrozen, and I can post my own bail. I don't exactly know how to do it, but we can go to the bondsman tomorrow, and tell him I want to give Eric's money back and put mine in its place. I'm not real sure how all that works, but I'll bet it can be done." Finally, I had a coherent picture. Eric had been angry at losing control of his own life. Further, Eric was convinced Sam was waiting in the wings to take his place in my bed. There were some implications that I'd store away to think about later.

"So, are you mad at me?" Sam asked. "Or do you think I'm wonderful for getting you out? Or a fool for making a deal with Eric? Or lucky that Bill told you the truth?" His head was full of optimism, pessimism, and apprehension. "I still don't know what to do about the promise I made Eric."

"I'm just relieved that you're okay now. You did the best you could when you thought of it, and your whole reason to agree to such a stupid thing was to get me out of a terrible situation. How can I not be grateful for that?"

"I don't want you grateful," he said. "I want you mine. Eric was right about that."

And my life turned upside down. Again. "Either there was just an earthquake in here, or you said . . . you wanted me to be yours?"

"Yeah. No earthquake."

"Okay. Well. I guess I have to ask, what

changed? I was the last person you wanted to see while you were . . ."

"Getting over being dead."

"Yeah. That."

"Maybe I felt then like you're feeling now. Maybe I felt like I'd come so close to forever-death that I'd better step back and take a look at my life. Maybe I didn't like a lot of what I'd done with it so far."

This was a side of Sam I'd never seen. "What didn't you like?" I knew he wanted to move on to the issue that sat between us like an elephant, but I had to have some answers.

"I didn't like my choices in women," he said unexpectedly. "I'd been picking women who were on the far side of acceptable. That didn't even occur to me until I knew I didn't want to take Jannalynn home to meet my mother. I didn't want her to meet my sister and my brother. I was scared for her to play with my niece and nephew. And that made me ask myself — why was I dating her?"

"She was better than the maenad," I said.

"Oh, Callisto . . ." He reddened. "She's a force of nature, you understand, Sookie? A maenad is impossible to resist. If you're a shifter or a wild thing of any sort, you have to answer her call. I don't know how sex is

392

with a vampire, I never did that, but you always seemed to think it was really great . . . and I guess Callisto would be sort of the shifter equivalent. She's wild herself, and dangerous."

There were things about his analogy I didn't like, but it wasn't the time to discuss details. "So, you've dated women you're not proud of dating, and you think you picked them because . . . ?" I really wanted to know where this was going.

"There was a part of me that recognized . . . Oh, this sounds like the worst self-serving bullshit. There was a part of me that kept insisting that I was a big bad supe and born to be a lone shifter, and the women I wanted had to be as wild and antisocial as that stupid picture I had of myself."

"And now you feel you are . . . ?"

"I feel I'm a man. A man who's a shifter, too," he said. "I think I'm ready to begin a relationship . . . a partnership . . . with someone I respect and admire."

"Rather than . . . ?"

"Rather than another sociopathic bitch who just offers excitement and wild sex." He looked at me hopefully.

"Okay, I think you kind of took a wrong turn there."

"Uh-oh." He thought about that. "Some-one I respect and admire whom I also suspect is capable of exciting and wild sex," he amended.

"Better."

He looked relieved.

"I'm not as surprised by this as I ought to be," I said. "I guess Eric read you better than I did. He knew if he let me go, you were standing first in line waiting. Not that I think there's a line!" I added hastily, when Sam looked startled. "I just mean . . . he saw more than I did. Or he could see it more clearly."

"I'm kind of ready for Eric to have no part of this conversation," Sam said.

"I can manage that."

"Do you still love him?" Sam promptly reintroduced the forbidden topic.

I thought before I answered. "I guess the cluviel dor magic changed you into someone who wants a different thing out of life than you wanted before. Well, using it changed me, too. Or maybe it just woke me up. I want to make sure. I don't want any more impulse relationships or relationships that could kill me. I don't want any secret agendas or misunderstandings on a massive scale. I've done enough of that. Call me chicken, if it seems I'm being cowardly. I want something different now."

"All right," he said. "We've listened to each other. Enough serious stuff for today, huh? I'm going to help you get to bed, because I think that's where you need to be."

"You're right," I said, stifling a groan as I got up from the couch. "And I'd appreciate your help. Would you bring me a pain pill and some water? They're on the kitchen counter." Sam vanished. I called after him, "I keep expecting Mr. Cataliades and Diantha to come in. Or Barry. I wish I knew where my houseguests are."

Sam was back with the pill and a glass of water in nothing flat. "I'm sorry, Sook. I got so — distracted — by our talk. I forgot to tell you Barry came into the bar early this evening to say that he and the two demons were looking for something. Or someone? He said to tell you not to worry, they'd be in touch. Oh, and he gave me this. If you hadn't called, I would have sent Jason out here with it."

That made me feel some better.

Sam pulled a folded yellow sheet of paper from his pocket. It was legal paper, and it smelled faintly as though it had come out of a garbage bag. With no regard for the lines, one side was covered by large writing in very strange penmanship. Whoever had done the writing had used a fading Sharpie. It said, "Your front door was open, so I stored something in your hiding place. See you later."

"Oh my God," I said. "They've put something in the vampire hidey-hole, the one in the guest bedroom." Bill had built it when I was dating him, so he could spend the day in my house if he had to. The floor of the closet in my guest room could be lifted up. Mustapha had come to get a few possessions of Eric's from it before Eric left. I wondered if he'd had the chance to complete that task the day Warren had shot Tyrese.

"Do you think there's a vampire in there?" Sam was startled, to put it mildly. He handed me the water and pill, and I swallowed and drank.

"If it were a vampire, he'd be up by now."

"I guess we better check," Sam said. "You don't want to spend the night wondering what might come out of that hole." He helped me up, and together we went to the guest bedroom. We opened the door and went into the room. Amelia had packed all her belongings and Bob's, too, but the bed was disheveled. I spied a sock under the night table as I got a flashlight out of the drawer and handed it to Sam.

He had the unenviable job of opening the hole.

The tension got worse and worse as he figured out how to lift the floor of the closet. Then he swung it up and looked inside the hidey-hole.

"Well, shit," Sam said. "Sookie, come see."

I slowly made my way over to the open closet door. I looked down over Sam's shoulder. Copley Carmichael was there, securely bound and gagged. He glared up at us.

"Close it up, please," I said, and walked out of the room slowly.

I'd imagined spending a day or two relaxing and recuperating, reading in bed with maybe a foray into the living room to watch television or to try to learn how to play computer games. There was plenty of food in the refrigerator since I'd so recently stocked up for my houseguests. I would not have anything more to worry about than getting well and who was working in my place at the bar.

"But *no*," I said out loud. "Unh-*uh*. Not gonna happen."

"Are you feeling sorry for yourself?" Sam asked. "Come on, Sook, if we're not pulling him out, let me help you climb into bed."

But I sat down in the chair in the corner of my room. "Yes, I'm feeling sorry for myself. And I may whine a little. What's it to you?"

"Oh, nothing," he said, with a suspicion of a smile. "I'm all for a good sulk every now and then."

"I'm just supposing that Mr. Cataliades or Diantha thought this would be a good after-birthday present for me, if they're responsible," I said. "I wonder what they're doing for their follow-up. Maybe they'll wash my car. I wish they'd call. I'm kind of worried about Barry." In case it wasn't obvious, the pain pill was beginning to work.

"Have you checked your cell phone or your answering machine?" Sam asked.

"Well, no, kind of busy getting shot and going to the hospital," I said, my self-pity deflated by Sam's practical suggestion. After a moment, I asked Sam if he'd bring me my purse from the kitchen.

I had all kinds of voice mail: Tara, India, Beth Osiecki, the bank, and, weirdly, Pam, who only said she needed to have a word with me. I subdued my curiosity and continued going down the list. Yes, here was a call from Mr. Cataliades.

"Sookie," he said in his rich voice. "When we returned and found you had been shot, we knew we had to search farther afield. Copley Carmichael has vanished, but we are on the trail of other game. I truly think you take the prize for having more people wanting to kill you than anyone I've ever known. I'm only trying to get to them first. But it's fun, in a way."

"Right," I muttered. "I arranged all this so you'd have a good time. Sounds like Mr. C and Diantha didn't know Copley was in my house all today."

"Text him and then move over," Sam said. "You're in the middle of the bed. Pick a side."

"What?"

"I need to take a nap. Move over."

I blinked. "Presuming? Much?"

"If someone comes to get him out of the hole, wouldn't you rather have me in here beside you?"

"I'd rather have you out on the porch with a rifle," I muttered, but I moved over a little.

"Doors are locked," Sam said. His eyes closed the second he lay down. And within two minutes, he was asleep. I could tell by his breathing and his brain waves.

Well, damn. I was in bed with Sam Merlotte, and we were both going to sleep.

When I woke up, it was daytime again. I heard someone moving around the house. I didn't open my eyes. Instead, I reached out with my other sense, the sense that Mr. Cataliades had given me. Tara was here, but I couldn't sense Amelia's dad, so I assumed his soullessness was really acting as a mask. Apparently, not having a soul nullified you as a person.

Tara came in, wearing her new shorts. "Hey, sleepyhead," she said. "I was just going to come wake you up. Sam had to go do some paperwork, so he asked me if I could come over to stay for a few minutes. He said you'd started tossing and turning." She tried very hard not to stare significantly at the dent in the pillow beside me.

"Hey, sleeping was all that went on," I told her.

"With the vamp gone, the door's wide open," she said innocently. "Nobody to say nothing about how you spend your time. You're a free woman."

"I'm just saying, that's premature." I gave her a no-nonsense look.

"All righty. If that's the way you want to play it."

I gritted my teeth. "I'm not playing it. That's the way it is. I'm still working through some stuff."

Tara looked at me blandly. "Sure, that's real smart. You need to get up and have some sausage-and-egg biscuits. My mother-in-law says it'll build your blood back up."

"Sounds good to me," I said. Suddenly, I was hungry.

While I ate, she showed me a few dozen pictures of the twins and talked about the babysitter she'd just hired, Quiana something. "She's like me, she's got a bad past," Tara said. "We're going to get along fine. Listen, I know Sam's handy, and since you and him are so tight, maybe you can help us? We're going to plan how to make the baby's room bigger. We sure can't afford to move."

"Sure, after my shoulder gets better. Just name the day," I said. It was nice to think about the future. A home-improvement project sounded both wholesome and normal.

Tara got restless after ten minutes, and I could tell she was thinking about getting back to the twins. There was a suspicious damp spot on the front of her blouse. I hurried her off with sincere thanks for the meal, and after she was gone, I got dressed, which took time and a surprising amount of energy. I also put my phone on its charger and began returning calls. I tried very hard to forget there was a bound man in my closet, and I tried not to imagine how many hours he'd been there without access to a bathroom. I had no sympathy for Copley Carmichael, and more practically, I couldn't even imagine how I could get him to a toilet without endangering myself.

Calling Andy Bellefleur flitted across my mind for maybe half a second. I could just see myself trying to explain that I really hadn't known my friend's dad was tied up and a prisoner in my home. Even I could hardly believe it, and I knew it was true. I would not go back to jail for anything. Anything.

So, for the time being, there Copley Carmichael would have to stay, even if he peed all over himself.

CHAPTER 19

A HOUSE IN A BON TEMPS SUBURB
the same day

"You're friends of Sookie Stackhouse's?" Alcee Beck stood in his doorway, eyeing his visitors with deep suspicion. He'd heard about the girl; everyone in Bon Temps who'd been in Merlotte's had talked about the girl. Platinum hair, bizarre ensemble, talked in a foreign language. Her companion was not as weird to the eyes, but something about him set off an alarm in Alcee Beck's head, and Alcee was never one to ignore such an alarm. It was how he'd stayed alive in the air force. It was how he'd stayed alive when he'd come home.

"We are," said Mr. Cataliades, his voice as smooth and rich as cream. "And we've brought a coworker of yours with us." He indicated the car parked by his van, and Andy Bellefleur emerged, looking horribly self-conscious but determined.

"What are you doing with these people, Bellefleur?" Alcee said, and the threat was clear in his voice. "You shouldn't bring anyone to my house. I should beat you senseless."

"Honey," said a quavering voice from behind him, "You know you like Andy. You got to listen to what he has to say."

"Shut up, Barbara," said Alcee, and a woman appeared behind him.

Alcee Beck had many faults, and they were well-known, but it was just as well-known that he loved his wife. He was openly proud of Barbara's college degree and her job as the only full-time librarian working in Bon Temps. He was rough with the rest of the world, but he minded his manners with Barbara Beck.

That made her appearance all the more shocking to Andy Bellefleur. Barbara, always well groomed and dressed, was wearing a bathrobe and no makeup. Her hair was a mess. And she was obviously terrified. If Alcee hadn't hit her yet, it was evidently something she had cause to fear. Andy had seen a lot of battered wives, and Barbara was as cowed as a woman who'd been hit more than once. And Alcee Beck had no notion he was behaving in a way contrary to his normal practice.

404

"Alcee, your wife is scared. Can she come out of the house?" Andy asked, in a neutral voice.

Alcee looked both startled and angry. "How dare you say such a thing?" he bellowed. He spun to face his wife "Tell them that isn't true." For the first time, he seemed to take in her demeanor. "Barbara?" he said uncertainly.

It was obvious to them all that she was afraid to speak.

"What do you want?" Beck asked his visitors, all the while looking at his wife with a troubled face and a troubled mind.

"We want you to let us search your car," Andy said. He'd gotten closer while Alcee was staring at his wife. "And just in case you think I'd plant something in your car, we'd like it if you'd let this young lady do the search."

"You think I'm taking drugs?" Alcee's head swung around like an angered bull's.

"Not for a second," Mr. Cataliades reassured him. "We think you have been . . . bewitched."

Alcee snorted. "Right."

"Something is wrong with you, and I think you know it," Mr. Cataliades said. "Why not let us check this simple thing, if only to rule it out?"

"Alcee, please," whispered Barbara.

Though he was obviously unconvinced there was anything in his car, Alcee agreed with a nod to the search. He withdrew his car key from his pocket and unlocked the car doors with the electronic key without moving from the front door. He gestured with the hand holding the key. "Knock yourself out," he told the girl. She gave him a bright smile and was in the car so fast she seemed to be a blur.

The three men moved closer to Alcee Beck's car.

"Her name's Diantha," Mr. Cataliades told Alcee Beck, though Alcee hadn't asked out loud.

"Another fucking telepath," Alcee said, with an ugly sneer. "Just like Sookie. Our town didn't need the one we got, much less another one."

"I'm the telepath. She's much more. Watch her work," said the part-demon proudly, and Alcee felt compelled to watch the white hands of the girl as she patted and probed every inch of his car, even leaning close to smell the seats. He was glad he kept his car clean. The girl — Diantha — slid bonelessly from the front seat to the back and then froze in place. If she'd been a dog, she'd have been on point.

Diantha opened the back door and emerged from the car with something clutched in her left hand. She held it up so they could all see it. It was black and stitched with red, and it was mounted on twigs. It had a vague resemblance to the omnipresent dream catchers sold in fake Indian stores, but it emanated something much darker than the desire to make a buck.

"What is that thing?" Alcee asked. "And why is it in my car?"

"Sookie saw it get thrown in, when you had your car parked in the shade at Merlotte's. Someone in the woods tossed it through your window." Andy tried not to sound relieved. He tried to sound as though he'd been confident all along that such an object would be found. "It's a charm, Alcee. Some kind of hex thing. It's made you do stuff you really don't want to do."

"Like what?" Alcee didn't sound disbelieving, just startled.

"Like persecute Sookie when the evidence is far from conclusive that she is guilty. She has a good alibi for the night of Arlene Fowler's murder," Mr. Cataliades said, reasonably. "And also, I believe you haven't been yourself at home since the murder." He looked at Barbara Beck for confirmation. She nodded violently.

"Is this true?" Alcee asked his wife. "I've been scaring you?"

"Yes," she said out loud, and took a step back, as though she feared he would sock her in retaliation for her honesty.

And with that clear evidence that Barbara feared him for the first time in their twenty years of marriage, Alcee had to admit that something was wrong with him. "I'm still mad, though," Alcee said, sounding more grumpy than enraged. "And I still hate Sookie, and I still think she's a murderess."

"Let's see how you feel once we destroy this thing," Mr. Cataliades said. "Detective Bellefleur, do you have a lighter?"

Andy, who smoked the occasional cigar, slid a Bic out of his pocket and handed it over. Diantha squatted to the ground and laid the charm on some dry grass blown out by the Beck lawn mower. She flicked the Bic, smiling happily, and the charm caught fire immediately. The blaze flared up much higher than Andy would have guessed, since the charm itself had been small.

Alcee Beck staggered back when the flame began to catch hold, and by the time the charm had burned away, he'd sunk to his knees in the doorway, clutching his head. Barbara called for help, but by the time Andy hustled over to him, Alcee was already trying to get to his feet.

"Oh, my Lord," he said. "Oh, my Lord. Help me to the bed, please." Andy and Barbara steered him back inside the house while Mr. Cataliades and Diantha waited outside.

"Good work," said Mr. Cataliades.

Diantha laughed. "Kid'swork," she said. "Iknewwhereitwasafterasecond. Ijustwant-edtomakeitlookgood."

Mr. Cataliades's pocket buzzed. "Oh, bother," he said quietly. "I've ignored it as long as I can." He took out his phone. "I've got a *text message,*" he told Diantha, in the same way another man might have said, "I've got herpes."

"Who from?"

"Sookie." He studied the screen. "She wants to know if we know who tied up Copley Carmichael and left him in her hidey-hole," he told Diantha.

"What'sahidey-hole?" she asked.

"I have no idea. You would have told me if you'd captured Carmichael?"

"Sure," she said, nodding vigorously. She added proudly, "InaNewYorkminute."

Her uncle ignored the expression. "My goodness. I wonder who put him there."

"Maybewe'dbettergosee," Diantha suggested.

Without further ado, the two part-demons got into their van and drove back to Hummingbird Road.

SOOKIE'S HOUSE
I was glad to see Diantha and Mr. C.

"We un-bewitched Alcee Beck," Diantha said slowly, by way of hello.

"There really was a voodoo doll in his car? Dang, it's good to be right."

Enunciating carefully, Diantha said, "Not a voodoo doll. A complex charm. I found it. I burned it. He's in bed. Okay tomorrow."

"Does he not hate me anymore?"

"I wouldn't go that far," said Mr. Cataliades. "But I'm sure he'll admit you couldn't have killed Arlene Fowler and that he was wrong to drive the investigation in a false direction. The district attorney is going to be embarrassed, too."

"As long as they know I couldn't and didn't kill Arlene, they can dance naked on the courthouse lawn and I'll show up to clap," I said, and Diantha laughed.

"To get back to your query via text message," Mr. Cataliades said. "We don't know who is responsible for capturing Amelia's father or for placing him in . . . whatever you've found him in."

"My vampire hole," I explained. "See? In

410

here." I led the way into the bedroom and opened the closet. I knelt with some difficulty and reached in for the hidden lever Eric had had installed. It hitched up the edge of the false floor. Then it was easy to work my fingers under the edge and hoist it up, especially when Mr. Cataliades knelt beside me to help. The lid came up easily and we swung it out of the closet. We looked down into Copley Carmichael's face. He wasn't as angry as before, but that might have been because he'd spent some more hours in there. The hole had been made for a night's shelter for a vampire, not for a permanent resting place. An adult could lie down in it in a fetal position, without curling up tightly. At least it was deep enough that he could sit up with his back against the wall.

"Luckily for him, he is not a tall man," said Mr. Cataliades.

"Small in stature, large in venom," I said. Mr. C chuckled.

"He'sasnakeallright," Diantha said. "He'sinprettybadshape."

"Shall we hoist him out?" Mr. Cataliades suggested.

I moved out of the way so Diantha could take my place. "I'm not much up to hoisting," I explained. "Shot."

411

"Yes, we heard," Mr. C said. "Glad you're better. We've been tracking various people."

"Okay, you'll have to fill me in," I said. For two creatures who'd come to help me, they were certainly matter-of-fact about my getting shot. And who'd they been tracking? Had they been successful? Where had they spent the night before?

And where was Barry?

With no apparent effort, the two pulled Copley Carmichael up out of the hole and propped him against the wall.

"Excuse me," I said to Mr. Cataliades, who was looking at Amelia's father with a speculative gleam in his eye. "Where is Barry Bellboy?"

"He detected a familiar brain signature," Mr. Cataliades said absently. He checked Copley's pulse with a large finger. Diantha squatted to peer into the captive's eyes curiously. "He told us he'd catch up with us later."

"How did he tell you this?"

"Via text messaging," Mr. Cataliades said distastefully. "While we were following a false trail for Glassport."

My teeth were on edge. "Should we be worried about him?"

"He's got his car and a cell phone," Diantha said slowly and carefully. "And he has our numbers. Uncle, did you check your other messages?"

Mr. Cataliades made a face. "No, Sookie's news startled me so much I gave up on doing so." He brought out his phone and began looking at it and pressing things on the screen. "This man is dehydrated and bruised, but he doesn't have internal injuries," he told me, nodding toward our captive.

"What am I supposed to do with him?"

"Whateveryouwant," Diantha said, with a certain amount of glee.

Copley Carmichael's eyes widened with fear.

"Of course, he did try to have me killed," I said thoughtfully. "And he didn't care who got caught up in his vendetta against me. Hey, Mr. Carmichael, you see this big bandage on my shoulder? That's courtesy of your man Tyrese. He almost got your daughter, too." The man's color wasn't good, but it got worse. "And you know what happened to Tyrese? He got shot dead," I said.

But this wasn't a pastime I could really call fun. Even though Carmichael deserved a lot of bad things, taunting him would not make me feel better about myself or anything else.

"I wonder if he's responsible for the

413

voodoo doll, or whatever it was, in Alcee's car," I said.

I watched his face carefully as I said this, and all I got was a blank stare. I did not believe Copley had put a hex or curse on the detective.

Mr. Cataliades said, "Yes, I do have a message from Barry. Voice mail." He held the phone to his ear.

I waited impatiently.

Finally, Mr. Cataliades lowered the phone. He looked serious. "Barry says he is following Johan Glassport," he said. "That is not a safe thing to do."

"Barry knows Glassport killed Arlene," I said. "He shouldn't take the chance."

"He wants to identify Glassport's companion."

"Where was he when he left the message?" I asked.

"He doesn't say. But he left the message at nine last night."

"That's bad," I said. "Really bad." The problem was, I couldn't think of anything to do about it, and I couldn't imagine what to do with Copley Carmichael.

A knock at my door startled us all. I was definitely distracted. I hadn't even heard a car come up the driveway. My neighbor from up the road, Lorinda Prescott, was at the front door with her fabulous supper dish that was supposed to be scooped up with tortilla chips. And she'd brought Tostitos, too. "I just wanted to thank you for the delicious tomatoes," she said. "I've never tasted any as good. What brand were they?"

"I just bought 'em at the lawn and garden center," I said. "Please come have a seat." Lorinda said she wouldn't stay long, but I had to introduce her to my company. While Lorinda was being charmed by Mr. Cataliades, I raised an eyebrow at Diantha, who slipped back down the hall to shut the door to the guest bedroom, where Copley Carmichael was still propped against the wall. After that, Diantha and Mr. Cataliades went upstairs, having said polite things to Lorinda, who seemed a bit stunned at Diantha's ensemble.

"I'm so glad you've got someone staying with you while you're getting better," she said. She paused, and her brow wrinkled. "My goodness, what's that noise?"

A dull thumping sound was issuing from the guest bedroom. Damn. "That's probably . . . gosh, I guess they shut their dog in that room!" I said. I called up the stairs, "Mr. C! The dog's acting up! Can you get Coco to calm down?"

"I do beg your pardon," Mr. Cataliades

said, gliding down the stairs. "I will make the animal keep silent."

"Thanks," I said, and tried not to notice that Lorinda was looking a little shocked to hear Mr. C call his dog "the animal." He went down the hall, and I heard the door to the guest room open and close. The thumping ceased abruptly.

Mr. Cataliades reappeared, bowing to Lorinda on his way through the living room to the stairs. "Good afternoon, Mrs. Prescott," he said, and vanished into one of the upstairs rooms.

"Gosh," said Lorinda. "He's mighty formal."

"Comes from an old New Orleans family," I explained. A couple of minutes later, Lorinda decided she needed to get home to start supper, and I bowed her out of the house with lots of pleasantries.

When she was gone, I breathed out a deep sigh of relief. I was hurrying to the guest bedroom . . . and the phone rang. It was Michele, checking up on me, which was a nice thing for her to do, but real bad timing.

"Hi, Michele!" I said, trying to sound perky and healthy.

"Hey, nearly-sister-in-law," she said. "How are you today?"

"So much better," I said. That was only half a lie. I was better.

"Can I come by and pick up your laundry? I'm doing mine tonight, so Jason and me can go line dancing tomorrow night."

"Oh, have a good time!" It had been ages since I'd been dancing. "I'm caught up on my laundry, thanks so much."

"Why don't you come to Stompin' Sally's with us, if you're feeling so much better?"

"If my shoulder isn't too sore, I'd love to," I said impulsively. "Can I let you know tomorrow afternoon?"

"Sure," she said. "Anytime before eight, that's when we're leaving."

I finally got to the guest bedroom. Copley was there, unconscious, still breathing. I hadn't been sure how Mr. C had silenced him, but at least it was not by snapping his neck. And I still didn't know what to do about him.

I called up the stairs to Mr. C and Diantha to tell them supper was ready. They came down the stairs lickety-split. Each of us had a heaping bowlful of the ground meat, beans, sauce, and chopped peppers, and I shared out the bag of tortilla chips to use in scooping up the mixture. I had some shredded cheese, too. And Tara had left a pie made by Mrs. du Rone, so we even had dessert. By tacit agreement, we didn't discuss the disposition of Copley Carmichael until we'd finished eating. The locusts were singing their evening chorale while we tried to reach a consensus.

Diantha's opinion was that we should kill him.

Mr. Cataliades wanted to lay some heavy magic on him and put him back in place in New Orleans. Like substituting a ringer for the real Copley Carmichael. Obviously, he had a plan for using the new version of Amelia's father.

I couldn't see letting him back into the world, a soulless, devil-tied creature with no impulse for good. But I didn't want to kill anyone else, either. My own soul was dark enough. While we debated and the long evening turned into darkness, there was *another* knock at the back door.

I couldn't believe I'd ever longed for a visitor.

This one was a vampire, and she didn't bring any food.

Pam glided in, followed closely by Karin. They looked like pale sisters. But Pam seemed energized, somehow. After I'd introduced the two vampires to the two part-demons, they took seats at the kitchen table and Pam said, "I feel that I've interrupted you when you were talking about something important."

"Yes," I said, "but I'm glad you're here. Maybe you can think of a good solution for this situation." After all, if anyone was good at disposing of humans or bodies, it was Pam. And perhaps Karin was even better, since she'd had longer to practice. A light-bulb lit up suddenly in my brain. "Ladies, I wondered if either of you happens to know how a man ended up in my bedroom closet?"

Karin raised her hand, as if she were in grade school. "I am responsible," she said. "He was skulking. You have many people watching you, Sookie. He came through the woods the night you were in the hospital, and he didn't know what had happened, that you weren't here. He meant you ill, if the gun and knife he had on him are any indicators, but your magic circle didn't stop him as Bill says it stopped Horst. I would have liked to see that. Instead, I had to stop him. I didn't kill him since I thought you might want to talk to him."

"He did mean me ill, and I thank you most sincerely for stopping him," I said. "I just don't know what to do with him now."

Pam said, "Kill him. He is your enemy, and he wants to kill you." This sounded pretty funny coming from someone who was wearing flowered crops and a teal T-shirt. Diantha nodded vigorously in wholehearted agreement.

"Pam, I just can't."

Pam shook her head at my weakness. Karin said, "Sister Pam, we could take him with us and . . . think about a solution."

Okay, I knew that was a euphemism for "get him out of sight and kill him."

"You can't wipe his memory?" I said hopefully.

"No," Karin said. "He has no soul."

It was news to me that you couldn't put the whammy on a soulless person, but then, it had never come up before. I hoped it would never come up again.

"I'm sure I can find a use for him," Pam said, and I straightened up. There was something expansive about the way my vampire buddy said that, something that made me pay attention.

Mr. Cataliades, who'd had more years than I to study language (both body and spoken), said, "Miss Pam, do we have reason to congratulate you?"

Pam closed her eyes in contentment, like a lovely blond cat. "You do," she said, and a tiny smile curved her lips. Karin smiled, too, more broadly.

It took a minute for me to get it. "You're the sheriff now, Pam?"

"I am," she said, opening her eyes, her smile growing. "Felipe saw reason. Plus, it was on Eric's wish list. But a wish list . . . Felipe didn't have to honor it."

"Eric left a wish list." I was trying not to feel sorry for Eric, going to a strange territory with a strange queen, without his trusty henchwoman at his side.

"I think Bill told you about a few of his conditions," Pam said, and her voice was neutral. "He had a few wishes he expressed to Freyda in return for signing a two-hundred-year marriage contract instead of the customary one hundred."

"I would be . . . interested . . . to hear what else was on it. The list."

"On the selfish side, he told Sam that he could not tell you that Sam had actually been the moving force behind bailing you out. On the less selfish side, he made it an absolute condition of his marrying Freyda that you never be harmed by any vampire. Not harassed, not tasted, not killed, not made a servant."

"That was thoughtful," I said. In fact, that changed my whole future. And it wiped out the bitterness I'd begun to feel toward a man I'd loved a lot. I opened my eyes to see

421

the pale faces staring at me with round blue eyes, eerily alike. "Okay, what else?"

"That Karin guard your house from your woods, every night for a year."

Eric had already saved my life again and he wasn't even here. "That was real thoughtful, too," I said, though with an effort.

"Sookie, take my advice," Pam said. "I'm going to give it to you for free. This was not 'nice' of Eric. This was Eric protecting what used to be his, to show Freyda that he is loyal and protects his own. This is not a sentimental gesture."

Karin said, "We will do anything for Eric. We love him. But we know him better than anyone, and this calculation is one of Eric's strengths."

"As a matter of fact," I said, "I agree." But I also knew that Eric liked to kill two birds with one stone. I thought the truth lay somewhere in between.

"Since we agree that Eric is so practical, how come Eric can do without you both?"

"Freyda's condition. She did not want him to bring his children with him; she wanted him to assimilate into her vampires without having a cadre of his own people."

That was real smart. I had a second of thinking how lonely Eric would be without anyone familiar around, and then I choked off that sadness at the throat.

"Thank you, Pam," I said. "Freyda banned me from Oklahoma, which is not important. But Felipe banned me from Fangtasia, so I won't be visiting you at work. However, I'd love to see you from time to time. If you're not too important now that you're sheriff!"

She inclined her head with an elaborately regal gesture, meant to amuse. "I'm sure we can meet somewhere in the middle," she said. "You're the only human friend I've ever had, and I would miss you a little if I never saw you again."

"Oh, keep up the warm and cuddly," I said. "Karin, thanks for stopping this man from killing me and for putting him in here. I'm guessing the house was unlocked?"

"Yes, wide open," she said. "Your brother, Jason, came to get some things he needed for your hospital stay, and forgot to lock it."

"Ah . . . and how do you know that?"

"I may have asked him a few questions. I had no idea what had happened at your house, and I could smell your blood."

She'd taken him under with her vampire wiles and interrogated him. I sighed. "Okay, bypassing that, I guess Copley came along later?"

"Yes, two hours later. He had a rental car. He parked it in the cemetery."

I could only laugh. The police had removed Copley's own car, driven there by Tyrese. Copley had repeated the pattern of his bodyguard, but hours later. But by now I'd resolved I wouldn't have Copley in my house any longer. "If he left his rental car so close, maybe you all should drive him away in it. I assume the keys are in his pockets."

Diantha obligingly went to look and returned with the keys. Searching for things was definitely her favorite occupation.

Mr. Cataliades and Diantha offered to move the prisoner outside. Mr. C carried Amelia's father over his shoulder, and Copley's head bounced limply against Mr. C's broad back. But I had to harden my heart about it. He couldn't be hypnotized, and he couldn't be set free, and I couldn't keep him prisoner forever. I tried not to think that it would have been better (by which I meant easier) if Karin had killed him immediately.

When Eric's children rose to leave, I got up, too. To my astonishment, they gave me a cold kiss apiece, Karin on the forehead and Pam on the lips.

Pam said, "Eric told me that you refused his healing blood. But if I may offer mine?"

424

My shoulder was aching and throbbing, and I figured this might be the last time in my life I could dodge physical pain. "Okay," I said, and took off the bandage.

Pam bit her own wrist and let her blood drip sluggishly onto the ugly wound on my shoulder. It was puffy and red, and scabby and sore, and altogether yucky. Even Karin made a moue of distaste. As the dark blood ran slowly over the damaged flesh, Karin's cool fingers gently massaged it into my skin. Within a minute, the pain subsided and the redness vanished. The skin itched with healing.

"Thanks, Pam. Karin, thanks for looking out for me." I looked at the two women who were so like me and yet so completely different. Hesitantly, I said, "I know Eric intended to turn . . ."

"Don't talk about it," Pam said. "We're as close to friends as we can be, human and vampire. We'll never be more, and I hope never less. You don't want us to think too much about how it would be if you became like us." I made a resolution then and there to never refer to Eric's intention of having the three of us as his children.

When Pam was sure I was not going to add to her statement, she said, "Knowing you, I'm sure you will worry about Karin being bored out in the woods. After the past few years of her life, that will be a good thing for Karin, to have a year of peace."

Karin nodded, and I knew I really didn't want to find out what she'd been up to the past few years. "I'll be well fed from the donor's bureau," she said. "I'll have a mission, and I will get to be outside all the time. Perhaps Bill will come over for a conversation every now and then."

"Thanks again to both of you," I said. "Long live Sheriff Pam!" Then they were gone out the back door, to drive Copley Carmichael away in his rental car.

"A neat solution," said Mr. Cataliades. He'd come into the kitchen while I was taking a pain pill, the last one I would need. My shoulder was healing but twingeing as it did so, and I had to go to bed. Frankly, I also figured taking a pain pill would squash staying awake to worry about Barry.

"Barry's got demon blood and he's a telepath. Why can I read his mind and not yours?" I asked him out of the blue.

"Because your power was a gift from me to Fintan's lineage. You're not my child as Pam and Karin are Eric's, but the result is somewhat the same. I'm not your maker; I'm more like your godfather or your teacher."

"Without ever actually teaching me anything," I said, and then winced when I heard how accusing that sounded.

He didn't seem to take offense. "It's true, perhaps I failed you in that respect," Desmond Cataliades said. "I tried to make up for it in other ways. For example, I'm here now, which is probably more effective than any attempt I might have made when you were a child to explain myself to your parents and tell them they had to trust me alone with you."

There was a pregnant silence.

"Good point," I said. "That would *not* have flown."

"Plus, I had my own children to raise, and pardon me if they took precedence over the human descendants of my friend Fintan."

"I get that, too," I said. "I am glad you're here now, and I'm glad you're helping." If I sounded a little stiff, it was because I was getting tired of the need to thank people for helping me out of trouble, because I was tired of getting *in* trouble.

"You are very welcome. It's been most entertaining for Diantha and myself," he said ponderously, and we went our separate ways.

CHAPTER 20

The demons departed the next morning before I got up. They left me a note on the kitchen table to the effect that they were going to comb Bon Temps to look for traces of Barry. It was kind of nice to have a morning to myself again and to prepare breakfast only for myself. It was Monday and Sam had called to say Holly was working in my place. I'd started to protest that I could work, but in the end I just said, "Thanks." I didn't want to answer questions about the shooting. Give the excitement a week to die down.

I knew exactly what I did want to do. I put on my black and white bikini, slathered myself with lotion, and went outside wearing dark glasses and carrying a book. Of course it was hot, really hot, and the blue sky was decorated with only a few random clouds. Insects hummed and buzzed, and the Stackhouse yard bloomed and bloomed with flowers and fruit and all sorts of vegetation. It was like living in a botanical garden, except without the gardeners to keep the yard mowed.

I relaxed on my old chaise and let the warmth soak into me. After five minutes, I flipped over.

In the way your brain will work hard to keep you from being 100 percent content, the notion suddenly popped into my head that it would be nice to listen to my iPod, a belated birthday gift from me to me, but I'd left it in my locker at Merlotte's. Instead of going inside to get my old radio, I lay there and let the lack of the iPod nag at me. I thought, *If I just jump in the car, I can be back here listening to music In twenty minutes, tops.* Finally, after saying "Dammit" a few times, I dashed in the house, pulled on a sleeveless gauze cover-up and buttoned it, slid into my flip-flops, and grabbed my keys. As often happened, I didn't meet a single car on my way to the bar. Sam's truck was parked at his trailer, but I figured he must need some rest and recuperation as much as I did, so I didn't stop. I unlocked the back door of the bar and trotted in to my locker. I didn't meet anyone along the way, and from the low buzz I could hear and the visual aid of very few cars in the parking lot, I could tell we were having a slow day. I was out in less than a minute.

I'd tossed the iPod through the open window of my car and was about to open the door when a voice said, "Sookie? What you doing?"

I looked around and spotted Sam. He was in his yard, and he'd just straightened up from raking twigs and leaves.

"Getting my iPod," I said. "What about you?"

"The rain knocked down some stuff, and this is the first chance I've had to get it cleaned up." He wasn't wearing a shirt, and the blond-red hairs on his chest shone in the bright light. Of course, he was sweating. He looked relaxed and peaceful.

"Your shoulder," he said, nodding at it. "How come it's looking so good?"

"Pam came by," I said. "She was celebrating being made sheriff."

"That's good news," he said, while he went over to his garbage can and dumped the armful of trash in. I glanced down at my shoulder. It still showed reddened dimples and it was tender, but it was maybe two weeks better than it should have been. "You and Pam have always gotten along good."

I went over to the hedge. "Yeah, some

430

good news for a change. Ummm . . . your hedge is looking nice and even."

"I just gave it a little trim," he said self-consciously. "I know people laugh about it."

"It looks great," I assured him. Sam had made a double-wide into a little slice of suburbia.

I stepped through the gate in the hedge, my flip-flops thwacking on the pavers Sam had laid to form a path. He propped his rake against the only tree in his yard, a small oak. I looked more closely at him. "You got stuff in your hair," I said, and he tilted his head down to me. His hair was always such a tangle, of course he wouldn't have even felt anything in there. I removed one twig with great care, then extricated a leaf. I had to get very close to do that. Gradually, as I worked, I became aware that Sam was standing absolutely still. The air was still, too. A mockingbird did his best to sing louder than all the other birds. A yellow butterfly drifted through the air and landed on the hedge.

Sam's hand came up to take mine the next time I reached up to his hair. He held it against his chest, and he looked at me. I came a few inches closer. He bent his head and kissed me. The air around us seemed to tremble in the heat.

After a long, long kiss, Sam came up for air. "All right?" he asked quietly.

I nodded. "All right," I whispered, and our lips touched again, this time with more fire. I was completely pressed up against him now, and with only a bikini and a gauze cover-up on me and shorts on him, we were sharing plenty of skin. Hot, oily, scented skin. Sam made a noise deep in his throat that sounded suspiciously like a growl.

"You mean it?" he asked.

"I do," I said, and the kiss deepened, though I hadn't thought that possible. This was so fireworks and Fourth of July and oh my God I wanted him so bad. I thought if we didn't get down to it soon I was going to explode, and not in the way I needed to.

"Please don't change your mind," he said, and began walking me back to the trailer. "I think I'd have to go out and shoot something."

"Not gonna happen," I said, working at the button on his shorts. He said, "Hold up your arms," and I did, and the gauze cover-up was history. We'd made it to the trailer door, and he reached behind me to turn the knob. We tumbled into the dark interior of the trailer, and though I paused by the couch, he said, "No, a real bed." He picked me up and turned sideways to get us through the narrow trailer hall, and then we were in his bedroom and there was indeed a bed, in fact a king-sized one.

"Yay," I said as he laid me on the bed and joined me, practically in one movement, and then I couldn't say another word, though I was thinking plenty of them, one-syllable words like *good please again dick long hard.* My bikini bra was history, and he was so happy with my breasts. "I knew they'd be even better than I remembered," he said. "I am so . . . wow." And while he was busy with those, he was working with the bikini bottom, which proved Sam could multitask. I was freeing him from the ancient cutoffs he'd been wearing, and they might have had a new hole or two by the time I finally skinned them down his legs and tossed them off the bed. "Can't wait," I said. "You ready?" He fumbled in his night table drawer.

"I've been ready for years," he told me, and he rolled on a condom and plunged in.

Oh my God, it was so good. The years of experience of my vampire lovers might have made them skillful, but there is so much to say for sheer heartfelt enthusiasm; and the heat of Sam, the warmth of him, it was like the sun was soaking into my body. The tanning lotion and the sweat meant we slid against each other like seals, and it was wonderful all the way to the shuddering, straining climax.

Would we have ended up making the best love ever if we both hadn't been altered by the magic of the cluviel dor, if Sam had never died and I had never brought him back?

I don't know and I don't care.

The air-conditioned cool of the trailer was heaven after the heat of our joining. I shivered with the cooling of my skin and the aftershocks of the explosion.

"Don't even think of asking if it was good for me," I said in a limp voice, and he laughed breathlessly.

"If I lie very still for about four hours, I might be ready to see if we could match the experience," he said.

"I can't even think about that right now," I said. "I feel like I just plowed the back forty with a team of mules."

"If that's a euphemism, I can't figure it out," he said. The best I could manage was a feeble giggle.

Sam rolled to his side to face me, and I mimicked his move. He put his arm around me. I could feel him get ready to say something at least three times, but every time he'd relax, as if he'd thought the better of it.

"What do you want to tell me that's taking you so long?" I asked.

"I keep thinking of things to say and deciding not to," Sam said. "Like, I hope we can do this again, and lots. Like, I hope this was something you wanted as much as I did. Like . . . I hope this is the beginning of something and not just . . . recreation. But you aren't casual about who you decide to go to bed with."

I thought carefully before I spoke. "I wanted to do this a lot," I said. "I've put you off forever, because I didn't want to lose the good thing I had in my job and your friendship. But I've always thought you're wonderful, a great man." I ran my thumbnail down his back, and he did a little shivering of his own. "Now I think you're even greater." I kissed his neck. "It's awful soon after the ending of my relationship with Eric. For that reason, if no other, I'd like to take the heart-to-hearts slow. As we said when we first talked about this."

I could feel him smiling against my forehead. "Are you saying you want us to have wild, insane sex and not talk about a relationship? Are you aware that's most guys' dream?"

"I'm real aware of that, believe me," I said. "Telepath, remember? But I know there's more to you than that, Sam. I'm giving you respect, and I'm giving myself some time to make sure I'm not rebounding."

"Speaking of rebounding . . ." Sam guided my hand down to his shaft, which was already well on its way to being up for activity. He didn't need four hours after all.

"I don't know," I said, considering. "This seems more like a ricochet."

"I'll ricochet *you,*" he said, grinning.

And he did.

Back in my own bathroom later that afternoon, I took my own sweet time soaking in a hot tub. My favorite bath oil scented the air pleasantly as I shaved my legs. Though I'd been tempted to linger in Sam's bed all day, I'd made myself get up and go home . . . to get ready for our date.

Sam had agreed to come line dancing with me tonight, which was a happy thing for many reasons. For one thing, I was excited about spending time with him now that we'd smashed down a huge barrier. For another thing, it would be nice not to be a third wheel with Jason and Michele. For a third thing, I hadn't heard a word from Mr. Cataliades or Diantha, so I was still in the dark about where Barry was and what he was doing, and I didn't want to sit at home thinking about what his absence might mean.

And here's my selfish confession: I was so happy, while I was soaking in the bathtub, that I almost resented having to worry about something, since I wanted to just roll in the pleasure of the moment.

I reminded myself in severe terms that my previous lover had barely left town and that it was absurd for a grown woman to plunge into something else so quickly. And I'd told Sam we were going to go slow about making promises and commitments to each other. I meant those things. But that didn't mean the physical release and the excitement of having great sex with Sam wasn't completely satisfying.

I shaved my legs and curled my hair and got my cowboy boots out of the closet. I'd had them for years, and since I wasn't an actual cowgirl, they were still in really good shape. Black and white with red roses and green vines: I was proud every time I looked at them. I could go fundamental cowgirl with tight jeans and a sleeveless shirt, or I could go flirty dance hall with a full short skirt and an off-the-shoulder blouse. Hmmm.

Yep, flirty dance hall it was. I made my

hair big and ripply, and put on my push-up bra to make my assets look outstanding and tan under the off-the-shoulder white eyelet blouse. The red-and-black-roses skirt swung with every step. I felt so good. I knew I would have to go back to my troubles and worries the next morning, but I was enjoying taking a little break from them tonight.

I'd called Michele, and we were meeting her and Jason at Stompin' Sally's, a big western bar out in the middle of the country twenty miles south of Bon Temps. I'd been to the bar/dance hall only twice in my life, once with JB du Rone and Tara back in our younger years, and once with some guy whose name I couldn't even recall.

Sam and I got there about ten minutes late because we'd been a little shy at meeting again after our amazing encounter, and he'd wanted to break the ice by making out a little. I'd had to remind him sternly that we were going out tonight, not staying in.

"You were the one who said no love talk," Sam said, his sharp teeth nipping my earlobe delightfully. "I'm willing to go there. Roses. Moonlight. Your lips."

"No, no," I said, pushing him away, but quite gently. "No, buster, we're going to go dancing. You start up this truck."

In an instant, we were going down the

driveway. Sam knew when I was serious. During the drive, he wanted an update on the overall picture, and I described the evening before, including Karin's yearlong mission and the fact that I'd turned over Copley Carmichael to the vampires.

"Good Lord," he said. I braced myself to receive his condemnation of my action. After a moment, he said, "Sookie, I didn't know that soulless people can't be glamoured. Huh!"

"Got anything else to say?" I asked nervously.

"You know, I never did like Eric. But I've got to say that if he was fool enough to leave you for a dead woman, he did try to make life a little easier for you. End of subject."

After a pause, I let out my breath, and I asked Sam if he could line dance.

"You just watch me," he said. "You notice I'm wearing my cowboy boots."

I made a derisive sound. "You wear cowboy boots about half the time," I said. "Big whoop."

"Hey, I'm from Texas," he protested, and the conversation got even more trivial from there.

Stompin' Sally's was out in the middle of a field, and it was a big place. It had its own brand of fame. The parking lot was huge. A lot of pickup trucks, a lot of SUVs. Big garbage cans set at strategic intervals. Some lights, not quite enough. I spotted Jason's truck two rows closer to the entrance, so we started in. Sam insisted on walking behind me to admire the way the skirt swayed, until I reached back with my hand and caught his, drawing him to my side. Xavier, Sally's bouncer, was western from head to toe, including a white hat. He gave us a smile and wave as Sam paid our cover charge.

In the dim, noisy cavern of the dance hall, we finally tracked down Jason and Michele. Michele had gone the tight-jeans-and-tube-top route, and she looked delicious. Jason, his blond hair carefully combed and styled, hadn't decided on the cowboy hat, but he was ready to dance. That's one ability both Jason and I inherited from our mom and dad. We sat down at the table, watching the dancing, for a while until we'd each had a drink. There are a hundred versions of "Cotton-Eyed Joe," and one of my favorites was playing. My feet began to itch to get out on the dance floor. Jason was getting that itch, too; I could tell by the way his knees were jiggling.

"Let's dance," I called to Sam. Though he was right next to me, a raised voice was necessary. Sam was looking a little worried as he eyed the dancers. "I'm not *that* good," he called back. "Why don't you and Jason take a turn while me and Michele admire you?" Michele, who was able to hear the gist of the exchange, smiled and pushed Jason, so my brother and I went out onto the dance floor. I saw Sam watching, smiling, and I felt truly happy. I knew it might be only for a moment, but I was willing to take it when I could get it.

Jason and I stomped and sashayed and moved smoothly through all the steps in good synchronization, beaming at each other. We started out side by side, me in the outer ring, Jason in the inner, and as we circled, we moved away from Sam and Michele's table at the back of the big room, and closer to the door. When the inner circle rotated a bit, I looked to my left to see my new partner — and recognized the Reverend Steve Newlin.

The shock almost knocked me down, and I lunged away from him with no plan except to put distance between us. But someone stopped me. An iron grip caught my arm and pulled me toward the door. Johan Glassport was much stronger than he looked, and before I knew it, I was on my way out into the parking lot. "Help!" I yelled to the big bouncer, and Xavier's eyes widened and he stepped forward, his hand extended to Glassport's shoulder. Without slowing down, Glassport shoved a knife into the poor man and yanked it out, and I filled my lungs with air and screamed like a banshee. I drew plenty of attention, but too late. From behind me, Newlin shoved me out the door, and Glassport dragged me to the van waiting there, engine idling.

He pulled the side door open and shoved me inside, launching himself in on top of me. From the flurry of knees and elbows, I could tell Glassport had jumped into the van, too. We took off. I could hear yelling behind us and even a gunshot.

I was gasping for air and sanity. I looked around me, trying to orient myself. I was in a large van with two small passenger and driver doors at the front, a larger side door. The back seats had been removed to create an empty, carpeted space. Only the driver's seat was occupied.

From my position sprawled on the floor, I tried to identify the driver. He half turned to look down at me. His face was like a nightmare, scarred and twisted. I could see his teeth, though he wasn't smiling, and I saw shiny red patches on his cheeks. Someone had burned this guy, recently and severely. Only his long black hair seemed familiar.

Then he started laughing.

Full of horror and pity, I said, "Shepherd of Judea! Claude, is that you?"

CHAPTER 21

My fairy cousin Claude was never supposed to see the human world again. Yet here he was, with two of my worst enemies, and he was kidnapping me. I lost it.

"How many enemies do I *have*?" I screamed.

"Lots and lots, Sookie," Claude said. His voice was smooth and silky, but not warm. The seductive voice combined with the nightmare of a face . . . oh, it was horrible. "It was very easy to hire Steve and Johan to help me track you."

Steve Newlin and Johan Glassport had sorted themselves out and were sitting against the walls, congratulating each other on a job well done. Steve was smiling the whole time. "I was glad to help," he said, as if he'd taken out the garbage for Claude. "After what happened to my poor wife."

"And I was glad to help," Johan Glassport said, "just because I hate you, Sookie."

"Why?" I really couldn't understand it.

"You nearly ruined everything for Sophie-Anne and me at Rhodes," he said. "And you didn't come to get us when you knew the building was going to collapse. You got your pretty boy Eric, instead."

"Sophie-Anne is dead, and it doesn't make any difference," I snapped. "I figured you were like a cockroach, you'd survive a nuclear blast!"

Okay, that maybe wasn't the smartest thing I'd ever said, but honestly! It was insane to think I'd run to help two people I didn't particularly like when I knew the hotel was going to explode any second. Of course I'd gotten the people I had the strongest feelings for.

"Actually, I just like to hurt women," Glassport said. "I don't really need a reason. I like dark women better, but you'll do. In a pinch." And saying that, he poked the flesh of my arm with the knife. And I shrieked.

"We practically fell over the other guys who were after you," Newlin said conversationally, as if I weren't bleeding on the van floor. He'd pulled himself against the driver's-side wall of the van. There was a strap there for him to hold on to, which he needed, because Claude was driving very fast, and he wasn't a good driver. "But apparently you've taken care of them. And with the vampire on guard duty in your woods, we couldn't watch you at night. So we knew God was being good to us when we saw our opportunity tonight."

"Claude, what about you," I said, hoping to put off Johan sticking me anymore. "Why do you hate me?"

"Niall was going to kill me, anyway, since I was trying to organize a coup against him. And that would have been a noble death. But after Dermot blabbed about me searching for the cluviel dor, my dear grandfather decided killing me was too quick. So he tortured me for quite some time."

"It hasn't been that long," I protested.

"You've been tortured," he said. "How long did that seem to you?"

Good point.

"Besides, we were in Faery, and time passes differently there. And the fae can take more punishment than humans."

"Though we intend to discover your limits," Glassport said.

"Where are we going?" I dreaded the answer.

"Oh, we've found a little place," Glassport said. "Just down the road a piece." He delivered the colloquialism mockingly.

Pam had wasted her blood healing me. I'd

just have more flesh to torture. I don't mind saying, I was at my wit's end and then some. I didn't know how fast Sam or Jason and Michele would be able to follow me, if they even had a clue which direction the van had taken. Maybe the furor over the abduction and the stabbing of the bouncer would impede them even getting out the door. And my guardian vampire, Karin, was back at my house, presumably making sure no coons came out of the woods to steal my tomatoes.

The first rule about kidnapping attempts is, *Don't get in the car.* Well, we were already past that, though I'd given it a try. Probably the next rule was, *Observe where you're going.* Oh, I knew that! We were going either north or south or east or west. I told myself not to be a Helpless Hilda, and I thought back. We'd turned to the right out of the parking lot, so we were going north. Okay. That should have been visible from Stompin' Sally's, because there weren't many trees to obscure the line of sight . . . if anyone had had the presence of mind to watch.

I didn't think Claude had made any turns since then, which even Claude would know was dumb, so we were going straight to whatever place they'd decided was secure,

447

and it must be very close. I assumed they planned on getting there and concealing the van pretty quickly, before pursuit could even start out.

I felt like giving up right then. I didn't think I'd ever felt so defeated. Johan Glassport was still looking at me with that sickly anticipation, and Steve Newlin was praying out loud, thanking the Lord for delivering his enemy into his hands. My heart sank as low as it could go.

I'd been tortured before, as Claude had so thoughtfully reminded me, and I still bore the scars on my body. I had the scars on my spirit, too, and I always would, no matter how well I'd recovered. Worst of all, I knew what was coming. I just wanted the whole thing to be over, even if I died . . . and I knew they intended to kill me. Death would be easier than going through that again. I was very clear on that. But I tried to rally. The only thing I could do was talk.

"I feel sorry for you, Claude," I said. "I'm sorry Niall did that to you." His face was an especially cruel target, since Claude had been outstandingly handsome and very proud. If he'd wanted women, he could have had them by the dozens, instead of sampling one now and then. As it happened, Claude liked men, men rough around the edges, and they'd responded to him with enthusiasm. Niall had found a perfectly devastating punishment for Claude's treachery.

"Don't feel sorry for me," Claude said. "Wait to see what we're going to do to you."

"Cutting me will make you well again?"

"That's not what I'm after."

"What are you after?"

"Vengeance," he said.

"What did I do to you, Claude?" I asked, genuinely curious. "I let you live in my house. I cooked for you. I let you sleep in my bed when you were lonely." Of course, all the time he was scouring my house looking for the cluviel dor, but I hadn't known that. I'd been genuinely glad to have him there. I also hadn't known anything about the plot against Niall, the rebellion Claude was fomenting among the other fae who hadn't made it into Faery when Niall closed the portals.

"You were the cause of Niall's wanting to close Faery off," Claude said, surprised at my even having to ask.

"Wasn't he going to do that, anyway?" Geez Louise.

Steve Newlin leaned forward to bitch-slap me. "Shut up, you godforsaken whore," he said.

"Don't hit her again unless I tell you to," Claude said. And he must have given them great cause to fear him earlier in their partnership, because Glassport put his knife away and Newlin settled back against the wall of the van. They hadn't tied me; I guessed that was the weak point of an impromptu kidnapping, nothing to bind the victim with.

"You think I am unfounded in hating you," Claude said, and we made a hard left turn. I rolled over on my side, and only when the van straightened out was I able to make some cautious moves to sit up myself. To avoid the two men, I had to stay in the middle, so any turn or bump in the road was going to knock me over. Well, great. Then I spied a grip on the back of the passenger seat, and I grabbed it.

"I do think so," I said. "There's no reason for you to hate me. I never hated you."

"You didn't want to sleep with me," Claude pointed out.

"Well, damn, Claude, you're gay! Why would I want to have sex with someone who's fantasizing about beard stubble?"

Neither Claude nor I considered what I'd said anything extraordinary, but you'd have thought I'd stuck a cattle prod where the sun didn't shine on the two humans.

"Is this true, Claude? You're a fairy who's a fairy?" Steve Newlin's voice had gone super-ugly, and Johan Glassport had pulled his knife out again.

"Uh-oh," I said, just to alert Claude — since, after all, he was *driving the vehicle* — that there was dissension in his ranks. "Claude, your buddies are homophobes."

"What does that mean?" he asked me.

"They hate men who like men."

Claude appeared perplexed, but I could see the distortion and hatred in the brains of the two men, and I knew that completely without intending to, I'd hit the perk button on their ethical coffeemaker.

Ordinarily, in the interest of making trouble in the ranks, I'd be glad they had such a huge issue with Claude's orientation. But then again, he was driving and I was the instantly available victim.

"He seemed like a tough man to me," Glassport said to Steve Newlin. "He would have killed that young man if the lawyer hadn't interfered."

I finally had a clue about what had happened to Barry. I hoped the "lawyer" reference meant Mr. Cataliades had rescued him.

Claude said in a puzzled way, "Johan, are you calling me less than a strong man

451

because I like other men in bed?"

Glassport winced, and his mouth compressed with disgust. "I am saying that I think less of you," he replied. "I do not like contact with you."

"And I think you're going straight to hell with the imps of Satan," Steve Newlin said. "You're an abomination."

There was more than one "abomination" in the van, but I wasn't going to point that out. Very cautiously, I wiggled a little closer to the spot where the back of the passenger seat was very close to the sliding side door. Glassport had his back against the door a little farther away from the front of the van.

If Glassport would move away from the door, just a little, I would open it and throw myself out. I could see that the door was unlocked. Of course, it would be nice if Claude slowed down first. I had no idea what was outside the van, since I couldn't see out the front windows; but I was assuming we were still in farmland, and there was a chance that with all the rain we'd had lately, I could make a relatively soft landing. Maybe. I would have to act with speed and no hesitation.

I defy you to throw yourself out of a moving vehicle without hesitating. Just the idea was giving me qualms.

"Then we have to have a serious discussion," Claude said, and his voice became sexy as hell. "A very serious discussion about how we all have the right to find someone who wants to have sex with us." The voice oozed over us like warm caramel.

It wasn't working nearly as much on me as it was affecting Newlin and Glassport, who were looking oddly shaken and horribly frightened.

"Yes, many men love to think about the curved hips and firm thighs of other men," Claude said.

Okay, he could stop anytime now. I was acutely uncomfortable.

"To think about their hard dicks and full balls," Claude said, spinning a spell with his voice. That popped the sexy bubble for me, but the two men were eyeing each other with obvious lust, and I couldn't bear to look at their crotches. Oh, yuck. Not these guys. Gross.

And then Claude made a huge mistake. He was so confident in his own sexuality, he was so sure of his audience, that he did the psychic equivalent of flipping them off. "See?" he said, and the spell dropped away. "There is nothing to it."

Steve Newlin went apeshit. He lunged at the driver's seat, grabbed Claude by the hair, and began punching him in the face. The van swerved all over the place. Johan Glassport was thrown across to the other side with a particularly violent lurch, while I half turned to clutch the grip on the back of the passenger seat with both hands.

Claude tried to defend himself, and since Glassport had his knife in his hand, I figured it was time to get the hell out of there. I got to my knees to see where we were going. The van crossed a lane of traffic, which was thank-God empty, and then we went down a shallow embankment and up again to end up in a field of corn. The headlights shone through the stalks in an eerie way, but eerie or not I was getting out of the van *now.*

I yanked the handle and the door opened, and I rolled out onto the ground. Johan yelled, but I scrambled to my feet and ran, ran, the corn making an ungodly noise at my passage. I was as obvious as a water buffalo, and I felt just as unwieldy and clumsy.

I thought the cowboy boots would come off, but they didn't, and I spared a sliver of a second to wish I'd taken the jeans option for the bar. No, I'd wanted to *look cute,* and here I was, running through a cornfield in danger of getting killed in a flirty skirt and a formerly white eyelet blouse. Plus, my arm was bleeding. Thank God there weren't any vamps after me.

I wanted away from the light. I wanted to find a place to hunker down. Or a house full of shotguns, that would be good. We'd swerved south into the field from a west-bound road. I began to push my way across the rows rather than running with them. If I went west, and then started north, I'd hit the road. But I had to find a dark patch of the field to obscure my movement, because God knew I was making enough noise.

But it just wouldn't get dark. Why not? Fields, night, one vehicle . . .

There was more than one vehicle.

There were ten vehicles streaming up the two-lane to the place the van had left the road.

I abandoned my plunge westward. I changed directions and ran toward them, thinking that at least one would stop.

They all stopped. They all angled so their lights were shining out into the field to illuminate the van. I heard lots of shouting and lots of advice, and I ran right toward them, because I knew all these people had followed the van out of the parking lot to rescue me. Or to avenge the bouncer. Or just because you don't disrupt a good bar or a line dance by grabbing a dancer. Their brains were full of righteous indignation. And I loved each and every one of them.

"Help!" I yelled, as I made my way through the corn. "Help!"

"Are you Sookie Stackhouse?" called a deep bass voice.

"I am!" I called. "I'm coming out now!"

"The lady's coming out," the bass voice boomed. "Don't shoot her!"

I broke out of the corn about ten yards to the west of where the van had gone in, and I ran down the edge of the field toward the line of saviors.

And the man with the bass voice yelled, "Duck, honey!"

I knew he meant me, and I dove into the ground like I was entering the ocean. His rifle took out Johan Glassport, who'd broken out of the corn behind me. In a second I was surrounded by people who were helping me up, exclaiming over my bleeding arm, or passing me by to stand in a silent knot around the body of the murderous lawyer.

One down.

A large posse headed out into the cornfield to see what had happened at the van, and Sam and Jason and Michele claimed me. There were fraught feelings bouncing around, there was self-blame, there were tears (okay, that was Michele), but what mattered was that I was safe and I was with the people who cared about me.

A heavy, silent man drew near and offered me his handkerchief to bind my arm. I accepted and thanked him sincerely. Michele did the binding, but my arm would need stitches. Of course.

There was another wave of exclamations. They were bringing Claude and Steve Newlin through the trail of wrecked stalks the van had made.

Claude was badly wounded. Glassport had gotten to use the knife on him at least once, and Steve Newlin had pummeled his face.

They'd made Newlin help him to the road, and he hated that worse than anything.

When they were close enough to hear me, I said, "Claude. Human jail."

His thoughts focused, though I couldn't read them. Then he understood. As if someone had given him a shot of vampire blood, he went nuts. Utterly reenergized, he spun on Steve Newlin, throwing him down with a terrible force, and then he leaped for the nearest Good Samaritan, a man wearing a Stompin' Sally's shirt, and the Good Samaritan shot him dead.

Two down.

To make things even simpler, Claude had thrown Steve Newlin down with enough force to fracture his skull, and I heard later that he died that night in the Monroe hospital, where they moved him after stabilizing him in Clarice. Before he did, he was moved to confess his part in Arlene's murder. Maybe the Lord forgave him. I didn't.

Three down.

After I talked to the law, Sam took me to the hospital. I asked after Xavier; he was in surgery. The ER doctor thought a butterfly bandage was enough for my arm, to my profound relief. I wanted to get back home. I'd spent enough time in hospitals, and I'd spent enough nights scared.

Now, everyone who wished me ill was dead. That is, everyone I knew of. I wasn't happy about that, but I wasn't grieving, either. Each of them would have been glad enough if I'd been the one on my way to the grave.

I was pretty shaken up by my abduction from Stompin' Sally's. A few days later, Sally herself called. She said she'd sent me a gift card for ten free drinks at her establishment, and she offered to buy me a new pair of cowboy boots, since mine would never be the same after my flight through the cornfield. I appreciated that — but right then, I wasn't sure about any future line dancing.

And I knew I'd never be able to watch *Signs* again.

There was no way to thank everyone who poured out of the bar and into their trucks to try to track down the van. At least five other vehicles had headed south, just in case Claude had doubled back that way. As the bartender told me, "We had your back, little lady."

This little lady was grateful. And also grateful that out of all the people who heard me remind Claude of what he'd be facing, only the Stompin' Sally's bartender who'd shot him found a moment while we were waiting for the police to ask me what I'd meant. I'd explained as simply and tersely as I could. "He wasn't human, and I knew he'd be in a human jail for a century or more. That would have been pretty awful for him." That was all I had to say.

"You know I had to shoot him 'cause you said that," the man said steadily.

"If I'd had a gun, I would have done it myself," was all I could offer. "And you know he was attacking you and would have kept on going until he was stopped." I could tell from the man's thoughts that he was a

459

veteran and he'd had to kill before. He'd hoped never to do it again. This would be another thing I'd have to live with. He would, too.

CHAPTER 22

I went to work the next day. I'd missed enough, I figured. I won't say it was an easy day to get through, since I had moments of sheer panic. That would have been the case if I'd stayed home, and at least at the bar I was able to hear that Xavier had made it out of surgery and would recover. Sam's presence behind the bar was reassuring. And his eyes followed me, as if he were constantly thinking of me, too.

I drove home while it was still light, and I was glad to get in the house and lock the door behind me. I was less glad to find Mr. Cataliades and Diantha already in the house, but I felt better about their presence when I saw they'd brought Barry. He was in bad shape, and I had a hard time persuading them that he could not heal himself the way demons could. In fact, I was pretty sure that Barry had broken a bone or two in his face and one of his hands. He was bruised and puffy all over and moved with excruciating care.

They'd put him on the bed in the guest room across the hall from mine, and I had an appalled realization that I hadn't changed the sheets since Amelia and Bob's stay. But after evaluating Barry's physical damage, I realized that worrying about used sheets was the furthest thing from his concerns. He was more worried about peeing without blood.

"I feel pretty rough," he said, between cracked lips. Diantha watched me give him some water, very carefully.

"You gotta go to a hospital," I said. "I guess you can tell them a car hit you while you were walking by the road or something. And you were unconscious."

I was aware, even as I said this, that it was utter bullshit. Not only would any competent doctor be able to tell that Barry had been beaten, not hit by any car, but I was sick of trying to explain away awful stuff like this.

"Isn't worth the trouble," Barry said. "I'll just tell 'em I got mugged. More or less the truth."

"So Newlin and Glassport grabbed you. What did they think they could beat out of you?"

He tried to smile, but the attempt was pretty ghastly. "They wanted me to tell them where Hunter was."

I sat down in a hurry. Mr. Cataliades stepped forward, his face grim. "You see why it is a good thing they are all dead," he said. "Newlin, Glassport, the fairy."

"He told them," I said, and it was almost funny how deeply hurt I was that Claude had betrayed a child.

"It wasn't the money he paid them," Mr. Cataliades said. "That was not what made them persist beyond all reason in trying to capture you. The two humans knew Claude wanted you, wanted to kill you, and they were very willing to go along with that. But they wanted the boy. To mold to their own purposes."

The enormity of it washed over me. I felt no guilt or regret about their deaths any longer, not even about the ex-soldier who'd had to shoot Claude.

"How did you find Barry?" I asked.

"I listened for him," Mr. Cataliades said simply. "And Diantha and I searched, following his mind like a beacon. He was alone when we found him, and we took him away. We didn't know they were coming after you."

"Wedidn'tknow," Diantha said sadly.

"You did great, you did the best thing ever," I said. "And I owe you one."

"Never," said Mr. Cataliades. "You owe me nothing."

I looked at Barry. He needed to get out of this area, and he needed a place to heal. His rental car was in downtown Bon Temps, and I'd have to drive it back to the rental place and turn it in; he wouldn't have wheels, but he was too battered to drive, obviously.

"Where can we take you afterward?" I asked Barry, trying to sound gentle. "You got a family to go to? I guess you could stay with me."

He shook his head feebly. "Got no family," he whispered. "And I couldn't stand being with another telepath all the time."

I looked through the open door at Mr. Cataliades, who was Barry's relative for sure. He was standing out in the hall, looking pained. He met my eyes and shook his head from side to side, to tell me that Barry couldn't come with him. He'd tracked Barry and saved his life, and that was all he could do. For whatever reason.

Barry really needed someone to convalesce with, someone who would let him be, let him heal, but be there to give him a hand. I had a sudden inspiration. I picked up my phone and found Bernadette Merlotte's number. "Bernadette," I said, when we'd done a polite greeting exchange, "you said you owed me a life. I don't want a life, but a friend of mine is hurt bad and he needs a hospital and a place to stay while he recovers. He's not a lot of trouble, I promise, and he's a good guy."

I told Barry five minutes later that he was going to Wright, Texas.

"Texas isn't safe for me," he protested.

"You're not going to a major urban center," I said. "You're going to Wright, and there's not a single vampire there. You're going to stay with Sam's mom, and she's nice, and you won't be able to read her mind clearly because she's a shapeshifter. Don't go out at night and you won't see any vampires. I told her your name was Rick."

"Okay," he said weakly.

Within an hour, Mr. Cataliades was driving Barry to the hospital in Shreveport. He told me solemnly that he would take Barry to Wright when he was discharged.

Barry e-mailed me three days later. He was safely ensconced in Wright in Sam's old room. He was getting better. He liked Bernie. He had no idea what he would do next. But he was alive and healing, and he was thinking of his future.

465

Slowly, I began to relax. I heard from Amelia about every third day. Bob had been transferred to New Orleans, finally. Her father was missing; his secretary had filed a missing-person report. Amelia didn't seem too concerned about his whereabouts. She was all about Bob and the baby. She'd seen Mr. C, she said. He was trying to find out what witch might have made the charm that had enabled Arlene to enter my house, but Amelia was of the opinion that Claude had made it. I was sure the part-demons would get to the bottom of that question.

Less than two weeks later, I walked down the "aisle," actually a narrow grass path through a happy crowd of people. The folding chairs were already set up at the tables scattered around the lawn, so the guests would stand for the short service. I went slowly, to keep time with the fiddlers playing "Simple Gifts." I was carrying a bouquet of sunflowers, wearing my beautiful yellow dress. Michele's minister was standing under a flowery archway in Jason's backyard (I'd been more than glad to supply the greenery), and Michele's parents were smiling as they stood waiting by the archway. There was no family to stand on our side, but at least Jason and I had each other. Michele looked beautiful as she walked up to meet Jason, and Hoyt didn't lose the ring.

After the wedding party — all four of us — had our pictures made together and separately, Michele and Jason took their places behind the meat table with aprons on over their wedding clothes, and they served ribs or sliced pork to the guests, who then descended on the tables full of vegetables and breads and desserts, all brought by the guests. The cake, contributed by a church friend of Michele's mom, stood in lonely splendor under a tent.

Everybody ate and drank and made lots of toasts.

Sam had saved me a seat by his, at the newlywed couples' table, marked off with a white ribbon. Jason and Michele would join us after they'd served the first wave of guests.

"You look real pretty," he said. "And the arm looks fine, too." I'd been able to leave the bandage off today.

"Thanks, Sam." We hadn't seen each other (except at work) since the night at Stompin' Sally's. He'd given me the slow time I'd asked for. We had signed on to help JB and Tara in their little home-improvement plan, and we'd decided to go to a movie in Shreveport in a week or two on a night we both had off.

I had my own ideas about how our relationship was going to progress, but I know that nothing is worse than assuming.

Late that evening, after we'd helped my brother and his bride fold up all the chairs and tables and load them on a trailer to take back to the church, Sam helped me into his truck. As we drove to my house, he said, "Little lady, I got a question." (He'd picked that up the night of the cornfield, and he wasn't letting it go.)

"Yes, what?" I said, with elaborate patience.

"How did Claude get out of Faery? You said it was sealed up. The portal in your woods was closed."

"You know what I found blooming in my yard yesterday?" I said.

"I don't know where you're going with this, but okay, I'll bite. What did you find growing in your yard?"

"A letter."

"Seriously?"

"Yeah. Seriously. A letter on a plant. It was one of the roses on my rosebush, you know the big red one by the garage?"

"And you spotted it?"

"It was white. The rosebush is red and green. I park right by it."

"Okay. Who was the letter from?"

"Niall, of course."

"And what did Niall have to say?"

"That he had purposely created the opportunity for someone to break Claude out of fairy jail, because he was sure he hadn't caught all the traitors yet. When his suspect made the attempt, Niall would nab the traitor, and Claude would have to languish — that was the word he used, 'languish' — in the lands of the humans forever, robbed of his beauty."

After a short silence, Sam growled, "I don't believe Niall thought about how unhappy Claude would be when he found himself back in the USA without a job, money, or looks. Or who he'd blame for all that."

"Putting himself in someone else's shoes is not the Niall way," I said. "Apparently, the traitor did break Claude out, and Claude decided vengeance was first on his list. Also, he must have had a bank account that Niall didn't know about. Claude contacted Johan Glassport, who'd acted as his lawyer before, because Glassport was the most ruthless human he knew. He bribed Glassport to take part in phase one of the 'get Sookie' project, which apparently was to ensure I went to jail for my whole life so I'd see just how Claude would have had to live. They needed someone else motivated by Sookie-hate to help them out, someone who would be tempted by the unusual bribe — money *and* a little telepath. Glassport tracked down Steve Newlin. Then they needed the perfect victim, so Glassport argued Arlene out of prison."

"That's pretty convoluted," Sam said.

"Tell me about it. I mean, when I thought about Claude in fairy jail, I kind of got where he was going with it, but still. He would have been much better off if he'd just stolen a gun and shot me."

"Sookie!" Sam was genuinely upset. We were parked at my back door. I glanced out the window and thought I saw a flash of white at the edge of the woods. Karin. Or Bill. She and Bill must be seeing a lot of each other during the night.

"I know, I don't like the mental image, either," I said. "But it's true. Going elaborate reduces your chance of success. So remember this for your future vengeance projects. Short, direct." We sat a moment in silence. "Seriously, Sam, I would have died if I'd been tortured again. I was ready to go."

"But you got them angry with each other. You started them fighting. And you lived. You never give up, Sook." He took my hand.

I would have disputed that if I'd cared to speak. I'd given up a lot, so much I couldn't even begin to evaluate it, but I knew what Sam meant. He meant I'd kept myself and my will to live intact. I didn't know what to say. And finally, that was exactly what I told Sam. "I'm left with nothing to say."

"No, never that." He came around to my side of the truck and helped me slide down in the high heels and snug dress. There might have been a bit more contact than strictly necessary. Even a lot more contact. "You have everything," Sam said. "Everything." His arms tightened around me. "I wish you'd reconsider, about me staying the night."

"I'm tempted," I confessed. "But this time, we're going to be slow and sure."

"I'm sure I want to get in bed with you." He rested his forehead against mine. Then he laughed, just a little. "You're right," he said. "This is the best way to do it. Hard to be patient, though, when we know how good it can be."

I enjoyed my arms around him, the sense of him next to me. And if you were to ask me, I would confess that I thought Sam and I would be together, maybe by Christmas, maybe for always. I couldn't imagine a future without him. But I also knew that if he turned away from me at this moment, somehow I would survive that, and I would find a way to flourish like the yard that still bloomed and grew around my family home.

I'm Sookie Stackhouse. I belong here.

ABOUT THE AUTHOR

New York Times bestselling author **Charlaine Harris** writes both fantasies and mysteries. She lives in a small town in southern Arkansas with her family.

The employees of Thorndike Press hope you have enjoyed this Large Print book. All our Thorndike, Wheeler, and Kennebec Large Print titles are designed for easy reading, and all our books are made to last. Other Thorndike Press Large Print books are available at your library, through selected bookstores, or directly from us.

For information about titles, please call:
  (800) 223-1244

or visit our Web site at:
  http://gale.cengage.com/thorndike

To share your comments, please write:
  Publisher
  Thorndike Press
  10 Water St., Suite 310
  Waterville, ME 04901